A

In Fall

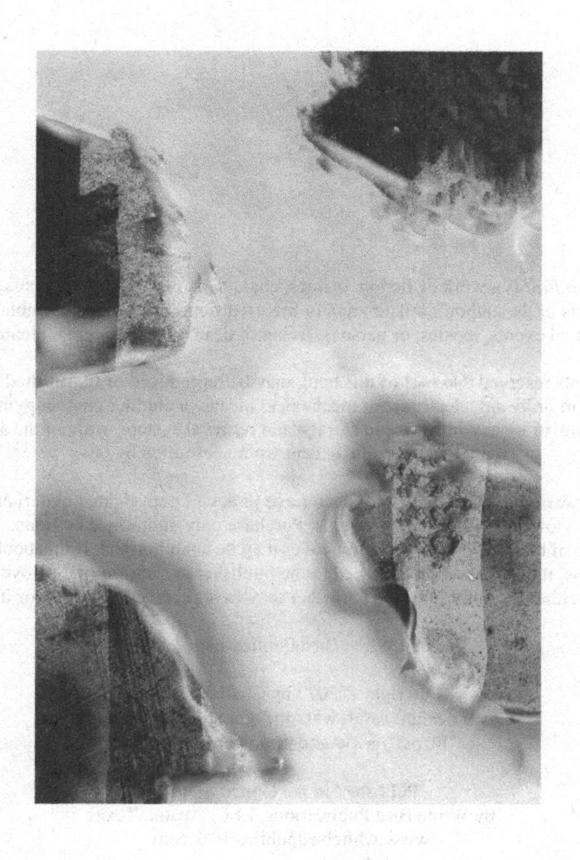

Charles Harned

2022 White Bird Publications, LLC

Cover design: sarah.watson@ghostbookwriters.org
https://www.ghostbookwriters.org/

Published in the United States
by White Bird Publications, LLC, Austin, Texas
www.whitebirdpublications.com

Paperback ISBN 978-1-63363-588-3
eBook ISBN 978-1-63363-589-0
Library of Congress Control Number: 2022934878

PRINTED IN THE UNITED STATES OF AMERICA

Acknowledgments

This book wouldn't have been possible without a handful of people. A special thank you to Erin for always being supportive and understanding when I was up late writing or had my head buried in a book. I have my family to thank, and my grandparents in particular, for inspiring a lifetime obsession with reading and a zeal for knowledge. I owe a debt to the writers before me who have impacted my life and influenced my work in ways I can't begin to describe: Carlos Ruiz Zafon, Daniel Silva, Sidney Sheldon, John Berendt, and Erik Larson to name a handful.

I would like to sincerely thank everyone at White Bird Publications, without whom my dream of becoming a published author would still be just that.

Finally, to all involved in the tireless fight against tyranny, corruption, and authoritarianism, *A Day in Fall* is for you. America as we know it wouldn't exist without unsung heroes that forge democracy's continued existence every single day and champion truth, knowledge, and justice over lies. I was fortunate while writing to have many amazing academic resources at my disposal, and would like to specifically mention Brighton Antifascists, The Guardian, and The Cable News Network for the journalistic work they have done to expose the growing threat of right-wing extremism. Too many others to name contributed material pertaining to history, locales, and geopolitics used in this book, but their assistance is no less appreciated.

A Day In Fall

White Bird Publications

PART ONE

Chapter One

The triangular strip of land where the Potomac converges with the Anacostia River and flows into the Chesapeake Bay was once nothing more than swamp. In many ways, especially in the devilish throes of mid-August, it still was. The controversial businessman turned even more controversial president had vowed behind podiums and atop stages to drain the swamp. Steadfast will and iron fists promised to agitate the snakes from hiding and jettison them into far-off wilderness. A tall order for even the most motivated.

Downtown Washington could have passed for much more than a scorching precursor to hell at the apex of summer's hottest month. Cherry blossoms had long since bloomed and wilted away. But the scientist leaving the IMA World Health building on M Street at precisely half-past three was not focused in the least on heat. His significant mental capacity was at that moment dedicated to pondering the president's strong-worded edict recited time and time again.

Could it be done? Rather, was it wise to attempt an upheaval of the very system that had delivered him into power? Lip service, the scientist reasoned, but that was a tactic of every successful politician. This president was new to politics, but he already understood its most critical stratagem: Say and do whatever necessary to get elected.

In a way, the political world had its business condensed to a laboratory experiment.

The scientist had a name, but he felt privy to remove a laminated tag oozing bureaucratic importance and sealed-door privilege as he left the impressive glass and steel structure and let it drop into the nearest of several waste bins dotting the street corner. His identity was easily discerned without a name card to those in his narrowed field, and to the rest he preferred to remain anonymous.

Blessed with a head of dark, unruly hair that had receded and gone dusty around the temples and a slight frame starting to round out with middle age, he was glad nonetheless not to glimpse his own Slavic features plastered on billboards and advertisements that mobbed downtown.

America's preeminent scientific authority on population control chose to move through the scorched, muggy streets of the nation's capital like any other person.

Downtown had become a maze of gyms, high-end retail stores, and glistening nonprofits. He took it all in with the most passive of glances whilst crossing the busy thoroughfare and passing a concrete and glass façade of yet another office building. He moved swiftly, not in the least because he understood that his life's work was quite contentious throughout the nation he had called home for thirty years.

"Everything has become controversial," he couldn't help but mutter aloud.

On sporadic occasions, usually in concert with a press circuit surrounding a newly published piece of research, he received malicious calls and death threats. The scientist had learned to ignore them long ago. He lived a private life in a stylish high rise with a doorman near Central Park. There was no reason to suspect any crazed individual would ever make good on one of the various intimidations.

As if by chance, Igor Stregor drew even with a rented Hyundai sedan parked along the curb.

Here he paused. Checking his watch, a scowl deepened the faint lines of his face. His flight back to New York City wasn't due to take off for several hours. It made no sense to return to the airport now and pass time in a crowded concourse. He glanced around and slipped behind the wheel. No, Igor had something much better in mind.

That Americans could agree on nothing seemed to be about the only reality with which they could successfully come to terms. Igor ruminated on this as he let Rhode Island Avenue ferry him out of Washington, in the opposite direction of both major airports. For the first time that day, he felt a twinge of pride for his native land. It was often breezed over by his employers that Igor wasn't a native of Washington, or anywhere else in the United States. In fact, he wasn't American at all.

Igor couldn't resist contemplating his past as traffic lessened and scenery shifted to sprawling suburbs. Born half a century ago into a small and forgotten Estonian village, his former community had been handed nothing to prosper save subsistence farming and a flawed communist system.

"We may not have had much, but we survived," he grumbled under his breath. Igor failed to voice how his father had smuggled him and the rest of his family out of Estonia and eventually into America on the shaky bona fides of a diplomatic passport.

Several minutes later, his destination swam into view at the end of a shaded residential vista.

The Franciscan Monastery of the Holy Land in America graces a hill in Brookland outside the capital called Mount Saint Sepulcher. Consecrated a century previous, its grounds contain gardens, several replicas of shrines recreated to remind visitors of the Holy Land, and the bones of Saint Benignus of Armagh, an Irish chieftain baptized into Christianity in the fifth century. The neo-Byzantine sanctuary itself, designed by famed Roman architect, Aristide Leonori, was built to resemble the Church of the Holy Sepulcher in Jerusalem.

That the monastery was a friary and retained the mislabel at the behest of reluctant Catholic church officials was of relative unimportance to visitors passing its limestone gates each day. Igor contemplated doing the same. He eased to a stop in a shaded parking lot across the street and unlatched the rental car's door when he instinctively froze.

A sleek Mercedes G-Wagon pulled into the parking lot a few seconds after him and stopped, engine idling. Its back faced a wrought iron railing separating asphalt from an adjacent park. Igor contemplated it with a shrewd gaze. Something about its arrival left him with a funny feeling that rooted around somewhere in the pit of his stomach. Due to his timing—mid-afternoon on a weekday—there were not many other cars in the parking lot.

He had a clear view of the black G-Wagon. The windshield's tinted glass made surveying its interior problematic. One thing was certain, however; the figure behind the wheel, intricacies of form shrouded by distance and the sun's glare, stared at him.

Igor opened his door. The G-Wagon's driver did the same. When he caught full sight of the figure, a heat wave could do nothing to unravel the icy chill that cloaked him.

Unlike most Americans, Igor had a knack for nationalities. The man was British, judging by his rigid demeanor and dress. He wore dark pants and a light tunic visible under an unseasonable Savile Row jacket. His slicked hair lent the air of a London street criminal. But it was his face that held Igor's eye and filled him with fear.

A pale mask of death.

Igor took one look and fled in the monastery's direction.

As he burst into the domed sanctuary, Igor took no notice of the chancel's elaborate gilding atop a raised dais and polished marble tiles that amplified his clattering steps. He ignored a stunningly lifelike representation of Jesus Christ being offered a wine-soaked sponge while suspended from a cross over the narthex, along with his Ascension to heaven at the nave's opposite end. The first wizened member of the Order of St. Francis to spot him looked as if he'd seen a madman. He crossed himself and mumbled a silent prayer.

It wasn't until reaching a second friar with a kind face and ample flesh that Igor dared to speak. Glancing over his shoulder, he returned his frantic gaze to the man of God and refrained from clinging to the front of his brown cassock with both trembling hands.

"I need to use a telephone!"

Worry creased the friar's features. He appraised the situation for several long moments that to Igor bordered eternity. Visitors around them had given the interaction a wide berth, casting lingering glances but refusing to let less than four rows of wooden pews come between them and the unconventional proceedings.

Igor stared into the friar's calculating eyes, fearing at any moment heavy doors behind him would open and the very embodiment of death would sweep into view.

At long last, the man of God nodded.

"This way."

He led the frightened scientist into a sparse office off the north transept. On a plain desk sat an outdated phone.

Before the rotund friar could react, Igor slammed the door in his face with a mumbled apology and wedged a heavy chair against the handle. Ignoring the holy man's cries of indignation, he lunged for the telephone.

As he dialed a number by heart, Igor realized that deep in his subconscious a latent fear of this day had always lingered. There was no telling who *they* were, but eventually they would come for him. Paranoia fostered during his years living behind the crumbling Iron Curtain had prolonged his survival, but that good fortune had come to an end.

Now he was down to his last hope. A man not unlike the figure depicted throughout this monastery when it came to his ability to work miracles within the secretive intelligence world. The only man who had a hope of ushering him unscathed from this disagreeable predicament.

What Igor Stregor got was something utterly and entirely different.

Chapter Two

The Franciscan Monastery of the Holy Land's brown-cassocked friars huddled in the choir near stairs leading to a recreation of Christ's tomb, their heads bowed low, mimicking silent prayer. Nothing could have been further from the truth.

Father Angelico, the initial friar to lay eyes on the deranged man, was first to speak. "We should call the police," he urged. A severe Florentine native with sallow features and a beaked nose that clashed with his plump figure, his colleagues frequently bent under his iron will.

Another, Father Pio, responded. "Who knows what he means to do here. Perhaps a bomb disposal squad…"

A jumble of unintelligible voices rose from the others. Father Angelico cut through the chaos. "That's preposterous. He showed no sign of violence, bomb-related or otherwise."

Another friar ruminated on the possibility of eavesdropping on the man's call. This was met with a chorus of general approval. He was desperate to get in touch with someone, Father Pio argued. Perhaps it had to do with some illegal or nefarious purpose.

They remained at a brief impasse until Father Leonard, who had unwittingly admitted the man into the now sealed office, spoke. "We will do nothing for the time being," he said with uncharacteristic edge to his soft voice. "We will not stoop to eavesdropping in the house of the Lord. I gazed into the man's soul, and what I observed was fear. We will monitor the situation and make a decision as things develop."

Begrudgingly, the other friars agreed. They would not have to wait long.

The receiver fell from Igor's hand and crashed atop the desk. Fresh waves of fear washed over him; the one person capable of saving him wasn't coming. For fifteen minutes, he didn't move, waiting for the telltale sounds of his assailant come to finish the job. He was surprised by a knock on the door.

Igor stood rooted to the spot. He was unsure how to proceed. Another knock, louder, jarred him into action.

An unfamiliar face filled the crack between heavy door and frame. Igor kept his weight against the leather-wrapped wood, ready to slam it shut if he sensed trouble. He need not have bothered. The newcomer was neither a friar nor the haunting figure he had encountered outside. Before Igor could blink, a man with Hispanic features wearing the black clerical vestments and Roman collar of a priest edged his way inside. At once, he forced the door shut and faced Igor with languid eyes that betrayed a mixture of concern and pity.

Igor took a step back.

"Who the hell are you?"

The newcomer ignored him. With one hand, he dragged

the Roman collar from his throat with a flourish while the other patted for something at the small of his back.

"Explain yourself!"

"That's no way to speak to a priest," the other man said. He swept around the cramped office, giving each wall a cursory glance before returning to the door.

Igor watched, his bewilderment intensifying. "I would consider heeding your advice if I were speaking to an *actual* man of God. But the fact of the matter is you are no priest. And you aren't who I requested."

The other man, despite his choice of clothing, possessed all the telltale markings of someone who took part in the secretive world of intelligence. The fierce expression he fixed Igor with was enough to drive the point home.

"*He* wasn't available," his counterpart said. "And if you wish to leave this monastery and return to New York City in one piece, then I suggest you follow my directives with extreme care."

His eyes alone added: *Is that something you're capable of doing?*

Igor weighed his options. Following the man in priest's garb meant taking a risk. The man didn't look as if he would be all that useful in a fight; perhaps he was better with a gun. But left to fend to his own devices, if what Igor had witnessed and felt in his gut were real, he was dead.

"Do I get to know your name?" he asked.

"No."

The mysterious newcomer eased the office door open and peered into the abandoned north transept. Over his shoulder, Igor caught a glimpse of friars looking on. Some were aghast while others did their best to obfuscate expressions of disdain.

They slipped into the transept. Igor followed the other man, who acted as though they were the only living souls inside the sanctuary.

"What is our plan of escape?" he asked as they crossed the patterned marble nave toward the main altar.

"We are heading down, Igor." The intelligence agent pointed toward a set of cleverly concealed stairs.

They made Igor's heart pound.

"In order to deliver you to salvation, we must descend into the pits of hell."

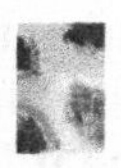

The man called Thatcher observed the professional and his charge duck around a waist-high postern and disappear into an opening in the church's flank from a position high in the shadowy gallery. He made no immediate move to follow. His part in the matter had been played to perfection. All that remained was for the trap to tighten around its prey.

Slipping inside the monastery in wake of the terrified scientist and taking up his post had proved an exercise in simplicity. Not a single cassocked friar or visitor—too alarmed by Stregor's fitful behavior—noticed the grotesque figure standing in their midst. Thatcher much preferred it that way.

He eyed the domed sanctuary. Constructed in the form of a Jerusalem cross, its many altars and replicas of Holy Land shrines paid homage to a religion Thatcher—and much of the world—considered obsolete. He had no problem spilling blood inside such a place. Thankfully for the friars now buzzing about, some migrating over to peer into the chasm where the two unwanted individuals had disappeared, it wouldn't be necessary.

Thatcher left the gallery and exited through the same heavy doors by which he'd entered. Heading toward the visitor parking lot across the street, he pondered what was to come.

Chapter Three

Underneath forty-two acres of northwest Washington D.C. is buried perhaps one of the capital's best-kept secrets. A facsimile of the ancient entombment sites deep below Rome, the Order of St. Francis had thought fit to construct a labyrinth of catacombs at the turn of the twentieth century.

Igor allowed himself to be led down a set of stone steps smoothed by time that sank into the earth. Neither man spoke as the monastery above gave way to a gloomy underworld of rough walls and low ceilings. A fetid realm where death was never far off. Igor let an anxious quiver escape his body. It was a mistake allowing the other man to talk him into venturing down here. Taking his chances with a potential madman suddenly sounded like a far better option than walking foolish and afraid into the dark wings of something resembling Dante's hell.

The other man seemed to notice his hesitation. He pointed at a bright light—a lone beacon in the surrounding darkness—at the chamber's far end.

"The shrine of the Annunciation." He beckoned Igor closer. A phrase in Latin had been carved into the stone. "*Verbum caro factum est*—The word was made flesh."

Igor followed him from the chamber through a dark tunnel. Gradually, his eyes adjusted. Faint light emanated from hanging fixtures. The tunnel was rounded and narrow, so much so that his shoulders brushed either wall as he walked.

"Are you religious, Igor?" the intelligence man asked. He paused to examine a niche in the wall and glanced at his charge.

"Not particularly. I never saw much use for it, if truth be told. I am a man of science, after all." He shrugged one shoulder.

"Catholic, born and raised." He gestured to the wall. "These tunnels are a recreation of the ancient Roman catacombs. Indentations in the wall represent closed graves."

"Is anyone buried down here?"

"Yes, Igor."

The narrow passage gave way to a chapel that was the first underground space Igor considered reasonably well-lit. Murals etched into black marble lined all four walls. A solemn altar draped in white stood at the center.

His pulse quickened. Something about this room wasn't right. His foreboding premonition was confirmed.

"This is the Purgatory chapel. Men have always had an interesting fixation on beating death." He pointed once again. "The bones of Saint Benignus lie in that small cavity off from the chapel. All of them except his skull."

Igor cracked. "What the hell are we doing here?"

The other man's expression turned bemused. "I promise what awaits you above is far more concerning than an old pile of bones lying under the earth. Be patient, Igor. I am shepherding you to safety."

The shepherd led him through several more tunnels and past a pair of shrines and another small chapel housing the bones of a child alleged to have been martyred alongside his family by Romans. An earthy, musty smell pervaded everything. After several more tense minutes that did nothing to help Igor's frayed nerves, the corridor widened, and they entered a large room fitted with hanging lamps and a hexagonal dais flanked by blood red curtains. Stairs that rose and curved out of sight swam into view. The scientist couldn't believe what he was seeing.

He eyed his counterpart. "Where do we go now?"

"Like Dante escaping the pits of hell, we ascend."

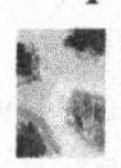

The bright hues of a Washington summer afternoon were painful after being trapped underground. Squinting, Igor did his best to match the other man's swift pace while checking over both shoulders to make sure they weren't being followed. Monastery gardens and a network of smaller aboveground chapels gave way to suburban streets outside high limestone gates. Igor was ushered into the passenger seat of an expensive-looking Jaguar.

The agent and his charge sped off in the direction of downtown.

"I must thank you," Igor mumbled. He remembered something. "My rental car—"

"Forget it. Someone will take care of the car for you."

"Are you sure?"

The other man's tone stiffened. "As far as you're concerned it's already done."

He reached over and dropped a set of keys into the scientist's palm. With the bored tone reminiscent of speaking to a child, the agent denoted the loaner vehicle's make, model, and color, and where to leave it—with keys locked inside—once he'd arrived at Dulles International Airport. Neither of them referenced the price point of the new vehicle, which was far higher than Igor was accustomed.

A parking garage attached to a glass office building eased into view.

"It's on the third level," the agent added. "Twentieth spot down if you're coming from the stairwell. Don't stop for any reason and speak to no one."

He pulled alongside the curb and waved two fingers in front of his eyes, signifying that he planned to stay and run surveillance. Igor opened his mouth to speak and thought better of it as he opened the passenger door and slid onto the sidewalk. With one last glance over his shoulder, he let the parking garage envelope him.

Igor entered the shadowy confines of a stairwell surrounded by the sound of his uncomfortable shoes on concrete. The third level was deserted. Posters slathering the cool walls in various stages of cleanliness were in consensus on the vogue issues of the day. If nothing else, Washington was an empowered city.

The monotony was broken by a new echo of uneven footsteps that were not his own as he traversed the aisle. Refusing to break stride, Igor quickened his pace. He glimpsed a vehicle that matched the description given by his rescuer. And then the source of the staccato footsteps stumbled around a corner into view.

Homeless were nothing new to Igor. Coming from the cramped confines of New York City, he was aware of them if not entirely comfortable with their presence. Strewn across doorways, dragging around mangy animals for companionship, drifting from one city landmark to the next like the aimless shifting of wind.

The distant figure's ambling walk gave Igor a swift impression of drunkenness. A brown-bagged bottle in his hand all but confirmed the theory.

Panic stabbed him. Even after all this time, the dangers of Eastern Europe during the Cold War were not forgotten. How any stranger could have a hidden motive, a concealed purpose. The garage's narrow aisle acted as a collision course. Reluctance giving way, Igor diverted his own path safely to the opposite row.

His unsavory counterpart appeared not to notice. The man's head was lowered, bobbing along after feet in careworn shoes as they jerked forward. To Igor, the vehicles on the third level were all painted shades of paranoia. He yearned to feel doors lock, to breathe a relieved sigh and free himself from the garage's musty darkness.

A white van caught his eye, a few rows ahead. Igor slowed, waiting for the beggar across the aisle to pass. He was upon the van when the two drew even.

He veered around the van's wide backside when the homeless man lurched, taking a drunken misstep toward him. For the second time that afternoon, Igor froze, his thin body tilting forward to keep his balance. The soles of his shoes clattered backward across the slippery cement. Igor locked onto the beggar's face, now staring at him without a trace of intoxication. His steady gaze rose to a spot over Igor's right shoulder.

In the commotion, Igor didn't hear the figure approach from behind. He hadn't been able to see around to the van's far side, hadn't known that the sliding door was propped open several inches.

He had one last fleeting glimpse of the peculiar vagrant and the waiting vehicle that he would never reach before experiencing immense pain. It began at the crown of his skull and flooded through his central nervous system, cascading to each limb in the fraction of a second it took him to crumple.

Igor's brain was fuzzy, his world rapidly going dark. He stared at the garage's textured ceiling until something broke the dull canvas. A face swam into view, hovering over him with distorted, oversized features. At the same time, something sharp stabbed into the fleshy area below his shoulder. Whatever it was sent a burning sensation flooding down his arm.

His brain was shutting down. Igor understood what happened to unfortunate souls in his situation, knew he was about to vanish without a trace. He made one last feeble attempt to capture the masked assailant in his memory before the light faded and his consciousness went blank.

Chapter Four

The first and only man to make the connection between white nationalist riots in Charlottesville, Virginia and a prominent demographist going missing in the nation's capital was not cloistered inside an office as the night hours threatened to be burned off by the coming dawn. Michael Larson had instead chosen to sequester himself in one of two penthouse suites at the Hotel Washington on Fifteenth Street, near the undefined border where America's lone *sui generis* district bled into the idyllic square blocks of Georgetown.

He stood bare before a floor-to-ceiling window that provided a magnificent view of Washington under a clear night sky. His thoughts strayed to the rooftop bar down the hall, still open but unwilling to accommodate him in his disrobed state. Getting dressed and going for a drink was tempting, but his feet stayed put, so he continued observing the city. A half-moon winked back at him.

To his own reflection, ghostly in the dark glass, he gave

a sidelong glance. He was in good shape considering he hadn't played an organized sport since his first year at Washington and Lee. Unlike many of his colleagues, Larson took physical training seriously and forced himself into the gym five days a week. Short-cropped hair that had managed to stay thick into his thirties gave way to a good-natured face and the shadowy hint of stubble around his jawline. He thanked Swedish immigrant great grandparents for skin that had so far avoided wrinkling and only bagged a touch under his eyes, more from lack of sleep than genetics. It was the serious face of a banker or businessman that had the uncanny ability to blend in no matter where he went.

"You'd be thrilled if the whole world saw you like that," came a sleepy voice from across the room. Larson turned and watched his partner stirring in bed. Tousled auburn hair spread across a small mountain of pillows as she sank into them and fixed him with an amused expression.

Miranda Cusimano had been a friend for several years, but this was the first time he had invited her to accompany him after late dinner at a crowded Ethiopian restaurant nearby. Their conversations skirted the edges of his work but, unlike some, she didn't ask probing questions. Having served as Director of Luther Sackler Art Gallery for years, Miranda was an invaluable acquaintance for her list of professional contacts alone. Larson had always found her intelligent and charming.

He pulled on an undershirt and a pair of shorts and sat in front of his laptop. The screen flashed to life. After logging into a secure VPN, several open tabs arrayed themselves in a neat row. Larson clicked through them one by one—an electronic Washington Post headline about the weekend's events, a map of the rioters' path noting critical junctures with bulbous, red dots, and several accounts from firsthand witnesses.

The last tab comprised a headline proclaiming a different kind of story. The reason he found himself unable to concentrate on the beautiful woman lying in his bed.

"Are you always this committed to your work?" she asked. "Most people prefer sleep."

"Yes, when it's something too stubborn to shake." Sleep would be futile regardless.

"Anything you want to talk about? You look concerned."

He refocused on the block of text below the headline. The world-renowned scientist and leading expert on population control had managed to slip off the face of the earth. Though no photograph accompanied the short piece, Larson visualized the man's appearance with ease.

"We live in a dangerous world," he said. "I fear it gets more dangerous by the day."

"Just what every woman wants to hear before she falls asleep."

"Don't worry. I'm here to protect you."

Miranda stirred for a few more minutes before her eyes drifted shut. Larson returned his considerable focus to the computer's backlit screen. He had known Igor Stregor, and while they were never close enough to be considered friends, he had provided Stregor a secure number to call if he ever ran into trouble.

"Where are you?" he murmured at the screen. Igor had called the number in desperation bordering on panic forty-five minutes before he disappeared.

There was one problem. Michael Larson, Echelon's rising star, had not been there to save him.

Chapter Five

The following morning Larson sped down the four-lane beltway that ran like a concrete artery between Washington and Georgetown. Truth be told, the dark Mercedes sedan was not his but appeared so in every conceivable realm of legality. With a tap on the brakes, he diverted onto a ramp for the Francis Scott Key Bridge that spanned the Potomac like an arrow poised for flight.

Despite the mid-morning hour, traffic was light. Larson had allowed himself one final tryst with Miranda before she departed for the gallery's leisurely ten o'clock open. He showered, dressed, and collected the Mercedes from the Hotel Washington's complimentary valet. He did not live there, but even so the valet and concierge both recognized him by a false name he'd given on numerous occasions.

The bridge gave way to several lesser veins that wrapped around Rosslyn—a small, urbanized district of Arlington that sat abreast the Potomac's western shore. The Pentagon's distinctive architecture stood three miles southeast. Arlington National Cemetery lay sandwiched in a regal shroud of green between the two.

Larson zipped through a green light and under an overpass and entered the close-cropped jungle of steel and reflective glass. Traffic thickened as he drove into its heart. He dissected his vehicle from the masses and directed it into the modest entrance of a parking garage under a steepled tower that was sure to give pilots fits as they descended out of the clouds for final approach on Reagan National Airport.

He appeared to reach a dead end. Larson stopped briefly before swinging toward a striped arm blocking his way forward. An unrecycled mix of choked air and exhaust fumes invaded the cabin as he rolled down the window. Flipping open his wallet, Larson flashed a badge that would have been foreign to the rest of the intelligence community save the raised ID number at its base and gazed into a fisheye lens that swung round to meet him.

The camera blinked for several long moments before allowing the arm to swing open. He accelerated around a corner and down a ramp, parked, and walked toward an elevator fixed with another cognizant eye. This checkpoint required a thumbprint scan along with an additional examination of his badge to coax the heavy doors open.

Larson counted as the elevator sped upward. There was no ding at the eighteenth floor, no cool, welcoming voice letting him know that he'd arrived. Instead, it came to a stop and slid open onto a plain lobby with a potted plant and a windowless door. It was impossible to access the eighteenth floor from the building's main elevators. Crossing the lobby, Larson stopped at the door and waited for a resonating click. Upon sounding, he turned the handle and stepped into the headquarters of the forgotten unit known only as Echelon.

There is a common belief in intelligence that information is only as secure as its weakest safeguard. Certain organizations, hell-bent on protecting their secrets and classified manifestos, hunker down in concrete fortresses without windows and guard the rabbit holes leading in and out of their burrows with enough men and firepower to stave off an apocalypse.

Echelon lived with no such fears. Small and agile, they had embraced technology and the burgeoning advances of software security in a way their lumbering predecessors had not. Larson strode into a hive of sunlit cubicles. Offices lined the perimeter walls and oblong conference rooms occupied each corner. That the eighteenth floor's outer windows and those above and below were made of glass strong enough to stop a fifty-caliber round, and that the trio of levels had its own internal support system, generators, and refined steel reinforcing was something scarce few knew and those who did thought little of.

A solitary figure waited in his darkened office. Larson slipped inside and seated himself behind the desk before glancing his way. The other man didn't say a word, waiting for him to break the silence as a pair of overhead lights stirred.

"You don't have to be afraid, Diego. I invited you, remember?"

The other agent's repentant expression shifted in the reflection of Larson's opened Lenovo notebook computer. On the surface, Diego Rivera seemed to be everything his counterpart wasn't. Rash and often headstrong, he had been recruited to Echelon as the prototypical functioning agent. Collaborating on several projects—as operations were known in team lexicon—he and Larson had grown as close as could be expected in the guarded world of intelligence. Composure bordering detachment under extreme pressure, silky charm, and an unheard-of gift for persuasion more than made up for his colleague's detrimental traits. Just not this time.

"Do you have the file?" Diego asked.

Larson didn't answer. He logged into a secure VPN available to Echelon personnel and within a few seconds had loaded an audio file whose diminutive icon hung in the middle of the otherwise blank screen. With a sharp glance at his colleague, he clicked play.

From start to finish, the conversation lasted seventy-nine seconds. An eternity when it came to gleaning a person's emotional state. In this case, the caller was audibly distressed, growing more so as the moments dragged on until an apex of sorts was reached. What followed seemed to be an apathetic accepting of fate. For all Larson knew, Igor Stregor never expected to survive even before he was disconnected from the professional voice on the line's other end.

"He wasn't willing to settle for anybody but you," Diego said.

Larson raised a finger. He reset the audio recording and played it through a second time.

"Igor's confidence in me, though flattering, was misplaced. Nothing I could have done would have made the slightest difference."

"You would have followed him inside the garage instead of running surveillance on the street. I should have—"

"I wouldn't be so sure, Diego. Whoever did this would have tailed Igor to the airport and abducted him there. The venue may have changed, but our man was getting taken one way or another."

He minimized the audio file and opened a separate folder labeled with a series of random numbers. The first frame of grainy surveillance footage labeled *August 12—Connecticut Avenue* jumped across the screen.

"Where did you get that?" Diego asked.

Larson leveled him a conspiratorial look. In truth, a field hand had approached the building's controller and requested a copy of the garage's interior footage a day after Igor went missing. Once obtained, it was picked apart by a group of Echelon analysts before being forwarded to Larson. His keen eye had spotted what they missed.

Hitting play, they watched a familiar short, middle-aged figure gripping a plain briefcase walk past a row of parked cars.

"How much do you know about him?" Larson asked.

"Only what was shared on my way over. Which is to say, his name and little else. I made a point to avoid the articles about his disappearance."

"Igor worked at the World Health Organization headquarters in New York City. He's considered the nation's foremost scientific authority on overpopulation and its effect on mankind's future."

"What's his take?"

Larson continued to watch the demographist's strides in slow motion. "Recently, he's become a vocal advocate for the notion that humans as a species are doing irreversible damage to the planet and our chances of survival. He, and other like-minded thinkers, don't believe we'll last another century."

Diego whistled. "That's morbid. What the hell was he even doing in Washington?"

"Delivering a speech at the IMA World Health headquarters on the dangers of overpopulation in developing nations."

He hit pause at the point where Igor crossed to the opposite row of motionless vehicles. Pointing at the unmarked van parked ten yards away, Larson said, "They knew he was coming. The exact location. I'm guessing whoever instigated this had been tracking him for some time."

"How is that possible?"

Larson pressed play. Subtle changes in shadow signified the van's far door, obscured from the surveillance camera's lens, sliding open. After a few more frames, another figure stumbled into view. He gestured at the newcomer.

"He's what made Igor cross to the opposite side of the garage and walk in front of the van. Only, that's not your common degenerate. I'd bet my life on it."

Diego's brow furrowed. "Did you run his face through

our databases?"

"I tried. But he was a professional, our man. He gave the analysts nothing to work with."

They observed the stumbling persona lunge toward Igor and watched him comically freeze. At that exact moment, a third party crept into view, face covered by a caricature mask, and delivered a blow that sent the scientist toppling to the ground. He stood over Igor. The syringe's hypodermic needle was impossible to make out, but Larson could tell that the masked man inserted it into the felled victim's upper arm with precision. An unconscious Igor was dragged over his shoulder and deposited in the van's middle compartment. The supposed homeless figure kept walking, oblivious to what was happening feet away.

"Notice how he's not stumbling drunk anymore?"

"You've got a point," Diego said.

The masked figure disappeared into the driver's seat, and the van reversed out of its parking space until it vanished from the surveillance camera's frame. Larson hit pause.

"Any tags on the van?"

"None. And they paid cash leaving the garage."

"How far did cameras track it?"

"The garage's surveillance lost it heading south on Connecticut Avenue. Traffic cameras dredged up a little more, but they went dark near Dupont Circle."

Diego rubbed the bridge of his nose as he played the footage over again. "Where do you think he went?"

This time, Larson had no firm answer.

"Top priority would have been leaving the capital. After that it's anyone's guess." He paused. "Apparently, Igor gave the doorman of his building special instructions to inform the WHO if he ever didn't show on a day he was expected."

"Almost as if he anticipated foul play."

"It could have just been precaution. He did grow up during the height of the Cold War. I'm sure living behind the Iron Curtain left an impact."

Diego changed tack. "Did anyone ever locate the van?"

Larson nodded. It had been found abandoned under an overpass in Tyson's Corner. The outside had been vandalized with all manner of lurid graffiti. Plenty of Igor's DNA remained inside, but there was no point in hiding that. One thing was certain; whoever carried out the abduction were trained professionals.

"The chief is going to want to know all of this," Diego said.

Eiran Katz, dubbed 'the chief', had served as Echelon's Director since its formation. Rumors circulated that it had been his idea alone to form a small coalition against the growing threat of domestic extremism. After being confronted with the data, several of his former superiors in the CIA and DIA had agreed.

Katz's appearance alluded more to a calculating Wall Street executive than one of the most progressive minds in the United States Intelligence Community. He wore tailored suits far too expensive for a government salary and a sharp haircut sewn with copious gray. Despite his most ardent wishes, it was beginning to bald at the pate. Narrow eyes and bony features lent him a hawk's predatory look.

Despite his meticulous sense of style, Katz was at ease in a world of anonymity. After an upbringing in Tel Aviv that included mandatory service in the Israeli army, he met his first wife while on vacation abroad and immigrated to America. From there, he had gained citizenship and experienced a swift rise through the enigmatic world of intelligence.

Unmentionable was the older brother he lost to a car bomb in Jerusalem. Equally so was the fact that the chief possessed the temperament of a man who had seen death and more than likely been responsible for some himself.

He would never get public credit for his brainchild. All but the most senior members of the FBI and CIA and the Director of National Intelligence were unaware of Echelon and the man in his late forties enthroned in the glassy tower across the Potomac River.

"The chief will find out everything soon enough," Larson replied.

He snapped his attention away from the surveillance footage filling his computer screen and stood. Whoever had abducted Stregor, and wherever they had taken him, constituted a serious problem. There was one way to get to the bottom of this. It started and ended at the source.

Chapter Six

Larson directed his Mercedes out of Rosslyn onto Key Bridge back to Washington. At the early afternoon hour, traffic had increased, but it was still easy to speed between slower moving packs as he crossed the Potomac and let the causeway spill him into Georgetown.

The day Larson first stumbled across mention of a nationalist radical movement he had never heard of Echelon and possessed only the most far-flung dreams of working in intelligence. It came in the form of a *Washington Post* article floated across his desk four years ago while he'd sipped his morning coffee. At first, he read with nothing more than mild interest. Fringe groups were a vital part of democracy like any other and had persisted like insects thriving under a rock throughout history.

Three months after reading the article he arrived at the Silver Spring headquarters of *FireWise*, a security tech startup he helped found on a morning that proved to be the last ordinary day of his life.

Larson fought M Street traffic until it bled into Pennsylvania Avenue. Georgetown didn't look all that different from any bustling metropolis in the southern half of the country; brick storefronts once considered quaint but in the modern era commandeered by fashionable shops and restaurants, the sort that had one-word names that gave little away. These were the only businesses that could afford rent. Shopping in the area ebbed and flowed on the whims of the upper class and turnover along the homogenous streets, with a few oddball gray or yellow facades thrown in at random, was frequent.

He crossed into the District and his surroundings became more professional and the traffic, if possible, worse. Weaving between cars and accelerating hard at a yellow light, he thought back to that day.

His assistant, Mallory, had buzzed after ten with an odd message. A man had phoned, and suggested Larson take a meeting. Despite the wording, it was not posed as a request.

At half past eleven, he left the office and walked in the opposite direction from a café down the block where he normally grabbed a quick bite to eat. His assistant had provided the requisite instructions. He waited in front of a bright, art deco building on Spring Street, scanning the crowds. When a man with a hat pulled low and a tan overcoat hurried past, Larson let him disappear and instead continued to a small park a block away.

The park was guarded by tall spruce trees. Pangs of uncertainty overtook Larson as he stepped away from the comforting sounds of urban bustle. More trees separated the towers and glass fortresses of downtown Silver Spring from suburban sprawl that claimed the surrounding territory. It struck him in that moment that if he were kidnapped nobody would ever find him. The labyrinth of residential streets lay complete minus a stalking minotaur.

Those thoughts heightened at the crackle of twigs underfoot. An unimposing man with the shrewd eyes of a predatory bird disentangled himself from a clump of shrubbery. Larson recalled how the man had leveled his piercing gaze before proffering a name that was false and leading him deeper into the hollow.

"We've been keeping tabs on you for some time," Eiran Katz admitted. "I've been anxious to arrange this meeting."

"My assistant insinuated you became adamant."

Katz nodded. "What we're dealing with is beyond serious, even if the public and the puppets on Capitol Hill don't know it yet."

Larson waited for him to explain. He acquiesced as they reached a deserted tract of mammoth firs at the park's rear that erased all noise.

"I work in American intelligence heading a small and overlooked unit that I helped form three years ago. We aren't the CIA, and we don't track religious terrorists or spy on foreigners. My team is focused on a growing threat much closer to home."

He was nonplussed. "What does that mean?"

"Are you familiar with the alt-right movement?"

Something clicked and Larson recalled the *Washington Post* article he'd glossed over. The one that had overturned the rock hiding a new sect of extreme right wingers that were unhappy with their party's trajectory and wanted to stymie globalism in favor of cultural segregation.

Katz didn't wait for an answer, changing tack and saying, "It's an impressive thing you've built with *FireWise*. Cyber security is playing a heavy role in how my team and the rest of United States intelligence combat outside threats."

Larson turned defensive. "What do you know about my company?"

The other man chanced a tepid smile. He didn't look like a spy; that was certain. But there was an air of secrecy about him, an all-knowing, all-seeing sense that put Larson on guard.

"I know that its software uses advanced analytics to identify threats and adapt to stopping them better than just about every other competing firm. You don't have funding to hang with the big players yet, but you're onto something. And I also know that you designed a security application fresh out of college that was bought and utilized by several government agencies. It made you wealthy, but even so, you've been pouring your time and expertise into this new startup and failing to claim a salary. Unlike your founding partners, I might add."

"How do you know all this?"

Katz gave him a coddling look. "It's my job to know. I told you, my team is very interested in what you have to offer. I don't take meetings without air conditioning and a comfortable chair often."

"This isn't a meeting. You demanded to see me and scared my assistant half to death."

"Maybe that was the only way you'd show up."

"And if I hadn't?"

Katz shrugged. "A new batch of prodigies graduates every few months. The intelligence community isn't lacking qualified candidates."

Larson called his bluff. Smiling, he replied, "Then you don't need me," and turned to walk away. He expected the unusual man to give in, ask him to wait, maybe even place a firm hand on his shoulder. Larson didn't look back until the elevator doors closed behind him inside *FireWise's* building.

The next morning, he left his apartment on Seventeenth Street and found Katz eyeing the block cagily next to an expensive German sedan. Saying nothing, Larson crossed the road. The two fell into step. He didn't bother to ask how the older man had found out where he lived.

"You're bored," Katz muttered at his feet. "You aren't driven by money, unlike most people. You'll stick with *FireWise* for another year, maybe two, before leaving for a different startup, or perhaps a nonprofit. And you'll exist that way, hopping from one big idea to the next. The excitement of a business venture in its infancy is the only thing keeping you going."

"What if it isn't?"

"It is," Katz said without looking up. "Some people yearn for a higher purpose. You think you're close to it now, on the precipice, but you'll never reach it."

"You said yourself that *FireWise* is an impressive venture."

"I'm not denying that. But your heart's not in it."

"And it would be if I worked for you?"

They rounded the corner onto S Street and the other man met his eyes.

"I'm offering you the chance at something more, something greater. To be part of a team whose work is critical to America's safety. And I'm offering you the opportunity to help us outwit a skilled and manipulative adversary."

His last sentence gave Larson pause. Katz's words were like a spark, setting aflame the competitive nature that helped him thrive.

"The alternative right is this adversary?" he asked.

"They're one head of the beast."

He drew to a halt before a turreted colonial. "What branch of intelligence does your team fall under?"

"It's actually a very long-winded and—"

"Tell me."

"The Department of Homeland Security Office of Intelligence and Analysis. But if you ask all but the most senior bureaucrats, we don't exist."

Larson nodded. "At the most fundamental level, what would I be working against?"

Katz threw him a long, calculating look. As if he were measuring Larson with his eyes, deciding if a suit stitched with a mantle of such importance could be tailored to his athletic shoulders. Finally, he answered.

"Domestic extremism. And all the dangers it's spawned."

Larson navigated onto the moderate residential quiet of L Street and followed a flatbed truck into the heart of downtown. Trees shrank away and buildings rose taller, hemming in lines of vehicles that flowed like ants scurrying through aboveground asphalt tunnels.

He turned on Eighteenth Street and after a few blocks found what he was looking for, the entrance to a parking garage hidden behind a twinkling glass façade. Ignoring cars leaving early to enjoy one of the last pleasant summer weekends, Larson slipped into shadow and parked at the first available space on the ground floor.

He got out and made for the stairwell, feeling as though he had entered a tomb.

Chapter Seven

The stairs were more claustrophobic than the rest of the garage. Larson climbed to the third level, listening to his own footsteps echo in the manmade silo.

They would have heard him coming. Whoever had been waiting to abduct Igor would have received plenty forewarning of his approach. These men were professionals—the surveillance footage was all the proof he'd needed on that account. Most likely, someone had tailed the scientist long before he ever entered the garage.

Larson reached the third level and strode forward, mirroring the path Igor had taken, imagining a white van among rows of temporarily abandoned cars. He doubted the van would've given Igor much pause. He would have been intent on picking out the unfamiliar loaner vehicle Diego had described. Once spotted, he wouldn't have been aware of anything else.

Until he realized he wasn't alone. Larson imagined uneven footsteps reverberating off the ramp that led to the upper levels as an unfamiliar figure wobbled around the corner. Posing as homeless, the man had been disheveled and holding a bottle. He meandered within three feet of the row of cars on his left, forcing Igor to cross to the aisle's other side.

Larson studied his performance while watching the surveillance tape. He caught one critical detail the analysts missed. Even though the vagrant appeared drunk and stumbled repeatedly, he never varied his spacing from the parked cars. That struck Larson as odd. He pictured an uncouth figure nearing him and crossed the aisle as Igor had done.

The van's sliding door was already propped open. Covered by uneven footfalls, it would have been easy for an assailant to lower himself onto the stained concrete without Igor hearing. Any shadow would have been hidden by the vehicle's flank; by that time, Igor was too close to see under the van's chassis. Adjacent cars negated that ability regardless, making his attacker invisible until he slipped around to the near side.

Using the vagrant as a distraction had been a clever cover, Larson conceded. He very much doubted whether he had been genuine. More likely, he was part of the snatch operation from the start. Larson was willing to bet a sum worth several nights at the Washington Hotel's penthouse suite that the bottle held by the fictitious vagrant contained a substance no more potent than water.

Lunging at Igor had been the ace in the hole. The whole operation would have hung in the balance for that split second, its outcome hinging on how the guarded scientist reacted. Again, Larson acknowledged a stroke of operational brilliance. Igor's captors had done their research. Instead of fleeing, or worse, lashing out in anger, Igor had frozen, giving the assailant behind him a clear window to deliver a powerful blow to the back of his head.

Larson, standing in the spot where Igor was felled, paused now. He pictured the vagrant dart across the aisle and lunge. Surveillance footage indicated that just before he'd made his move the masked assailant had edged around the van's nose. Igor's body would have flooded with adrenaline, his senses overloaded by what was happening in front of him. There was no way he could sense anyone approaching from behind until it was too late.

Despite being unable to recover a usable face for Echelon's sophisticated recognition software, surveillance cameras had proven successful tracking the vagrant as he left the garage. They followed him up the block until he entered a sandwich shop on the ground floor of an office building. No one fitting the same physical description ever emerged.

A noise interrupted his thoughts. To be precise, it was a lack of noise, which often created the same effect. No distant roar of a car making a quick exit a level below, no carrying conversational voices in the stairwell. He went still, listening hard. It struck him that Igor's captors might have continued reconnaissance on the location, waiting to see if any interested party turned up.

A bolt of panic tore through him as faint footfalls careened off the nearest down ramp hidden from view. Larson went still, concentrating on the sound. These weren't the uneven, drunken steps precluding Igor's abduction. The crisp tapping of a hurried gait emanated throughout the third level. He glanced around to make sure no one was approaching behind him. Then his gaze darted back to where the echo was loudest.

A long-legged woman in high heels appeared and walked directly toward him. Despite his distinct confusion, Larson couldn't help admitting that she was stunning. A sheet of dark hair bounced off her shoulders with each step, and a pencil skirt clung to her slender hips.

She held a bag that looked like it had been foisted from one of Georgetown's copious designer shops. When she stopped before Larson, he wasn't sure if she meant to hit him with it or offer it to him as a gift.

The silence was far-reaching.

"Who are you?" he asked.

Her Slavic complexion and hooded eyes only added to her beauty. When she spoke, there was a hint of an Eastern European accent, pruned with care but still resonating beneath the surface.

Tilting her head and narrowing her brows, she replied, "My name is Elena Stregor."

A hundred questions flooded into Larson's head all at once. She seemed to surmise this from his expression. Glancing around, she motioned toward the stairwell.

"We can't talk here, it isn't safe."

"What do you mean?"

She refused to stop walking. Over her shoulder she said, "The men who took my brother might come back."

Chapter Eight

"Your brother?"

Larson and Elena Stregor sat at a table for two on the patio of a trendy Italian restaurant. Fiola Mare possessed an unmatched view of the Potomac as it carved its way around Theodore Roosevelt Island. His companion nodded.

"Igor was my brother. I'm afraid he is no more."

"Why do you say that?"

Elena hesitated, then raised her napkin to dab at her eyes. When she removed the cloth, they were red. It did nothing to diminish her appearance.

"Mine are a fatalistic people, Michael. We trust in many things that Westerners find illogical. I believe that I would be able to feel my brother's presence if he were alive on this earth. I search for it, even now. But I cannot."

Larson swilled a gin martini delivered by a waiter dressed in black uniform. "I knew your brother. Why did he never mention you?"

He seemed to have struck a chord. Elena bowed her

head low and took several deep breaths. Composing herself, she raised her eyes to Larson's.

"He and I underwent a falling out and haven't spoken in several years. He disagreed with a few decisions I made. Igor could be very stubborn. Despite what happened, I still loved him dearly. I'm not sure he loved me anymore."

Changing the subject, Larson asked, "What would be the sense in abducting Igor just to kill him? They could have killed him in the garage."

"Are you familiar with my brother's work?" Her voice was in danger of floating off in the riverfront breeze.

"He was employed by the World Health Organization, although he contracted out his remarkable research to medical journals and private companies. He was considered the foremost authority and mouthpiece for the overpopulation crisis."

"Then you know why he wasn't shot or stabbed to death in a parking garage. His death will have served some higher purpose."

"Don't," Larson admonished. He didn't enjoy contemplating a dead man. "I intend to search for your brother and find proof before jumping to conclusions."

"I cherished Igor," Elena said. "He was my older sibling, my protector. I never would have survived in a strange new country, where I could hardly speak the language, without him. You can't imagine what arriving in America was like after having known only hardship and oppression. Shock alone was almost too much to overcome."

She shook her head, taking a sip of white wine and waving the waiter off with an imperious gesture as he crossed the terrace.

"You've done your research. Can you think of any motives for his…kidnapping?"

She spoke the last word in strained tones, as though it was a struggle to quell the expression she wished to utter. There was something about her eyes egging Larson on, luring him nearer the truth.

He leaned forward in his chair and took the bait.

"Igor's research—and the topic of population control—is quite controversial. The human population explosion is a classic example of an exponential curve, but findings have been met with resistance. There are always reactionary sects suspicious of scientific discovery, believing them self-serving. Others don't want to admit that the problem is real and serious."

"Human nature is reactionary," Elena scoffed. "Why is a growing population seen as a problem?"

"Because, as your brother contested, an overpopulated earth is the cause of every major crisis. Climate change, food shortages, and water scarcity—all mere byproducts of a deeper issue. And, given the numbers, humankind will be unlikely to survive another century with current technologies."

"He was very blunt when it came to that prophetic conclusion. Not that he cared about the hysteria such a revelation could cause." She shook her head. "That's a scientist's way."

"Certain people didn't like his revelation."

"Correct. One political ideology denies everything you said as contrived research aiding a sinister hidden agenda. And the leader of that party just assumed the presidency a few short months ago."

"He wouldn't have cause to take your brother out of the picture."

For the first time she said nothing.

Larson paid, and they exited Fiola Mare's white cloth terrace, walking east along the waterfront. By now, it was evening, and the sun dipped lower. A slight breeze tracked in off the placid water to dilute the summer heat. Despite this, pedestrians spilled onto the walkway and congregated at blue umbrella tables adjacent the terrace. Throngs in search of an evening cool Larson doubted would materialize, or else eager to wallow in sticky misery with their fellow Washingtonians under the artificial blow of the restaurant's fans.

He led Elena onto a strip of wooden planks that bordered the Potomac. The crowd here was thinner. They skirted a couple taking over-romanticized pictures on the boardwalk. Larson ignored them, looking across the water to the green foliage of an islet with the setting sun flaming the background. A welcome reprieve from Washington's warren of concrete and steel. He explored the island once, several months ago, pacing along wooded trails in thoughtful silence and taking in a grandiose monument dedicated to the nation's cavaliering twenty-sixth president.

They neared the boardwalk's end. Larson could make out the infamous Watergate Hotel looming ahead. Elena spoke as they passed a lamppost covered in blooming flowers and topped with a tapering American flag.

"The men who took my brother are no doubt watching you."

"Do I know them?"

"Indirectly, perhaps."

"You know who they are?"

Her silence was all the answer he needed.

"Why won't you tell me?"

She fixed him with a piercing gaze. Her answer took him aback. "Mr. Larson, do you understand the concept of key man risk?"

He tilted his head a fraction and let his chin sink in the affirmative.

"A key man possesses critical information. The type that would cause an enterprise to crumble if he were liquidated or removed. It's common in the business world. The key man is indispensable."

"I'm familiar with how businesses operate. What's your point?"

She hesitated, casting a sideways glance at a passing group in matching T-shirts before responding. "I don't wish to reveal everything to you right away. If I did you wouldn't place such importance on keeping me alive."

Her expression turned dark, her eyes going dead as if the light behind her pupils had been switched off. Larson pictured the idyllic waterfront around her vanishing, her thoughts returning to life as a young girl, oppressed by Stalin's warped successors.

"I'm sure they'll come for me too."

He was baffled. "Why do you say that?"

The ominous look intensified. "I haven't told you what I do for a living."

Chapter Nine

The three-story townhouse on N Street snugged between two redbrick colonials with gaslight spilling over the front steps had a balcony with an excellent view of the backyard garden and Thirty-third Street. Two blocks from Wisconsin Avenue, it stood close enough to catch pleasant byproduct sounds of music echoing from Georgetown's bars and clubs and pick up on the palpable energy of pedestrians making their way toward the excitement.

Larson had stepped foot in the neighborhood and fallen in love with its maze of residences and cramped, tree-lined streets. Georgetown was a haven for the nouveau riche and old money alike, an easy place for someone to blend in and be forgotten. His gray-brick domicile rarely became the subject of unwanted attention, other than a singular request to be included in a home and garden shoot that Larson had politely declined. By and large, Georgetown was a peaceful exculpation from life in the capital.

The cork made a hearty thunk as it escaped the wine bottle. Larson poured two glasses of Merlot and carried them through an open sliding door to the balcony. He handed one to Elena. They drank, looking over the iron lace railing at the darkened street and listening to faint hum of music. Larson marveled at Georgetown's beauty. Just as he marveled at the woman standing next to him. The woman he had just discovered, as they slipped inside his cool foyer, was in much graver danger than he could have realized.

"You and Igor came a long way from your family's humble roots."

Her gaze was fixed on the railing. Moonlight could have been deceiving, but he caught her smirk.

"Our parents were adamant that our lives be better than theirs. Stanford undergrad. A doctorate at Johns Hopkins and intermittent furloughs to guest teach at Oxford. It was more a lifestyle requirement than a choice." She let out a long breath. "Not that I'm complaining."

His eyebrows arched. Not so much at Elena's schooling, though it was impressive, but at the fact she'd done all that and looked no older than thirty.

"I'm thirty-five," she said, reading his mind again.

"And you might not live to see forty at the rate things are going."

She laughed at his dark humor. "Igor never spoke out directly against the president and look what happened to him. I may not last through the end of the month."

Larson stepped inside and refilled her empty glass. As he performed the task, he thought about what she had confessed to him.

Her hand had flitted over his. "I've spent my adult life becoming an expert in cognitive psychology. Over time, my position has lent me a respected platform among psychologists. That platform has begun to reach beyond the confines of the scientific community. And since the current president was elected, I've used my newfound pseudo-celebrity—"

"To become vocal about his neural shortcomings," he said.

"I don't feel remorse for demonizing him. Every word of it is grounded in psychological truth. Only those who have been silenced can understand the need to speak out at all costs, Mr. Larson. It's something ingrained in our nature."

"Speaking out could cost you your life, and it could have cost your brother his."

Elena had shot him a terrifying look. "Igor had his own reasons for drawing their attention. As for me…" Her expression softened. "I accept whatever fate I've brought upon myself. Someone must be heard."

Larson returned to the balcony and handed Elena her glass.

"People like my brother and I don't matter to the current regime because we're immigrants," she said. "Even though immigrants built this country."

"The president's wife is an immigrant." The comment roused another half-hidden smirk.

"I wouldn't envy being in her shoes. I suspect she's little more than a prisoner in her own home."

"At least it's a big one."

He was beginning to tire. Larson could tell from the look on her face that Elena was too. She glanced around and focused grimly on him.

"You should look into hiring some private security."

"I can handle myself."

She shook her head. "I'm afraid I've put you in significant peril. I'm all but certain they'll come after me, it's just a question of when. Now that they've seen us together."

"Do you think they're watching?"

"It's possible. There's no telling the ends to which the current regime will go. They know no limits. That gun you're carrying will be of little help."

"How did you—?"

"You forget my childhood. I'm used to spotting when a man is carrying a weapon."

Larson emptied his glass still in disbelief. Then inspiration came over him, as if the ruby liquid had fortified his insides. A swelling of courage.

"I'm going to find your brother, Elena. And I'm going to make sure nothing happens to you. The agency I work for will be able to help with that."

"Unless they're in on the plot."

He brushed her comment aside. The night grew comfortable as he followed Elena inside and bolted the glass door behind them. The digital clock in the upstairs sitting room showed it was nearing midnight.

"You're welcome to stay the night," he said. Elena seemed to know what he was getting at.

"Thank you. I should be getting home." She started down the stairs to the second floor.

"You have someone waiting for you?"

She paused on the landing. "No, I live alone."

She waited until Larson was two feet from her before placing a foot on the top step.

"It's late. I don't want you riding alone in a taxi. It'll be much safer for you to stay here."

She appeared torn.

"I have plenty of extra space." He edged toward his master bedroom at the far end of the hall.

"You're sure you don't mind?"

"I insist."

Elena followed him down the hallway. She pushed a door open with her heel. "What's in here?"

"A guest bedroom. It never gets used."

It was true; he rarely invited friends over. His parents, retired in Arizona, hadn't come to visit in close to a year.

Elena slipped inside and pulled the door shut, letting her thin face fill the dark crack.

"Goodnight, Michael."

With a smile, she closed the door, leaving him standing dumbstruck in the hallway.

"Goodnight, Elena Stregor."

Chapter Ten

Larson woke and rose from bed as though he were still caught in the hazy trappings of a dream. He pulled on a shirt and slipped into the hallway. Judging by the color of what little light filtered through the windows overlooking N Street dawn was not far off. He crept toward the stairs. The door to the guest room Elena commandeered was still shut tight.

Reality didn't set in until he reached the ground floor and cool tile met his bare feet. Feeling the lingering effects of the previous night's wine, he crossed the kitchen to the coffee maker without surveying the rest of his surroundings. The invigorating smell combined with a glass of cold water was enough to spur him into action.

Returning upstairs with mug in hand, Larson showered and dressed. He slipped a scrawled note explaining where he was going under Elena's door before leaving the townhouse and easing behind the wheel of his Mercedes parked along the quiet street.

Without traffic, Rosslyn was less than a ten-minute

drive from Georgetown. Larson managed to get halfway across the Potomac River when his iPhone in the center console lit up. He slowed at a red light on the far side of Key Bridge and inspected the device.

A single message had been delivered from an unknown sender. Pausing, he considered deleting the new arrival and thought better of it. Getting an unsolicited message to appear on his government-issued iPhone was no easy feat.

The first pang of worry churned in Larson's gut as he tapped the highlighted icon. A lone photograph was all it contained. He examined the image with a keen eye. It showed a wooded path lined with trees and underbrush. From the dappled quality, it had been taken in daylight. There was nothing whatsoever in the foreground to identify the source; it could have come from one of the many parks within Washington's boundaries or any number of forested areas beyond.

Perplexed, Larson followed the short line of cars into Rosslyn. The small, urbanized hamlet of Arlington was starting to come alive as the sky continued to lighten.

At the next traffic light, he checked his inbound messages again. Another image file appeared from the same unidentified number. Larson expanded the photograph to fill the screen and froze.

This time, a rock-strewn trail carved a neat path, pausing where a bridge rose like a hump across a dried creek bed. Further ahead the trail forked, spiriting hikers in two separate directions that both led into denser foliage judging by the way the light seemed to melt away. Larson stared at the image. Now there was no mistaking it. He was intimately familiar with the place.

A third chilling photograph made sense of everything. He hadn't taken his foot off the brakes when it flashed to life on the screen, pulling his focus away from the towers coalescing ahead. Larson stomped on the gas pedal, swerving around a stopped car and cutting through oncoming traffic. Narrowly avoiding a serious collision, he turned left onto a bisecting road. His iPhone's screen went dark, but it didn't matter. The final image was seared into his mind.

One more left turn with no regard for traffic and he hurtled back the way he'd come. In seconds, Larson crossed Key Bridge once again with Georgetown in his sights. As the river disappeared in his rearview mirror, he dialed a familiar number.

The voice that answered sounded sluggish. Diego was much more alert by the time Larson finished speaking. He explained where he was headed and why and severed the connection after the other agent assured him he was on his way. Larson tossed his iPhone onto the passenger seat and pressed the gas pedal as far as it would go.

The entrance to Dumbarton Oaks Park was situated on R Street north of Georgetown. Never letting off the gas, Larson sped past a historic Tudor mansion that had yet to open its doors to the day's assortment of tourists and turned right onto R Street. He veered off the road in favor of a sleepy one-way lane leading into the secluded park.

A rusted iron bar blocking his path forced him to stop a short distance down the lane. Irate, Larson pulled over and abandoned the Mercedes, hurrying on foot through a narrow wicket lined with trees.

He neared a full sprint by the time he reached the familiar trail. Dumbarton Oaks was a place of quiet seclusion. Larson made a point to drive up at least once a week and jog a few miles on its winding, uninhabited paths. Fitting that whoever abducted Igor would lure him here of all places.

Rounding a corner and feeling his lungs seize with exertion, Larson considered the possibilities. The last image made it clear that Igor's condition was dire. His captors could be using the scientist as bait. Or perhaps they were toying with Larson. The lone scenario racing through his mind that lay outside the realm of possibility was that they intended to return Igor alive and unharmed.

Early morning light managed to filter through the thick canopy overhead, but what little reached the trail failed to disperse the prevailing darkness. Ten minutes later, his surroundings had lightened a few paltry degrees. Hardly enough to see a body, let alone deduce whether armed assailants lay in wait. The hollow echo of his feet thundering across a short bridge was accompanied by a growing sense of anxiety. He neared the familiar place he had seen minutes before on the screen. Peering into the distance, he tried to pick out a body hidden among murky shapes of tree roots and underbrush.

A snapping twig made him freeze. Larson swung his gaze in a full circle, trying to spot the offender. Apart from his own heavy breathing and a few chirping birds in the distance he was besieged by absolute silence. He moved forward once more, cautious. One final turn and the path's fork swam into view. Here he paused once again.

As if on cue, his phone vibrated. Larson pulled it from his pocket and hit the green answer button.

He didn't bother speaking. The other voice sounded formal and abnormally stiff. There was hint of a British accent. It made Larson's blood run cold.

"Keep walking forward."

Larson hesitated before obeying the command. He peered into the dense surrounding woods, trying to glimpse the caller. It didn't matter. Spotting the bodiless voice's source would do little good. He lamented the fact that he was unarmed. Doubtless his hidden adversary had not been so shortsighted.

"Walk slow. No sudden movements."

"Is he alive?"

It took a moment to comprehend the staccato sound that followed. Then Larson recognized laughter.

"I'd hate to ruin the surprise. You'll know soon

enough."

Larson swerved toward a movement in the underbrush. A piercing crack rang out through the trees to his left and something whizzed over his head.

Audible agitation met his ear. "That was your warning. The next round will find its mark in your spine. Do not deviate from my instructions."

Larson did as he was told.

The clearing came into greater focus. Larson made out a small copse with a shadowy mound of earth at its back and a wire fence running along each divergent path. But a dark form huddled at the base of the largest tree drew his gaze.

Even breathing on the other end of the line filled his ear.

"Tell me your name."

The voice sounded amused. "You're a professional, Mr. Larson. Names are something of a faux pas in this line of work."

He neared the copse, unable to tear his eyes away from the huddled mass as it grew larger.

"Tell me anyway. When I hunt you down and kill you, I want to know your name."

The voice seemed to be on the verge of responding and then paused.

Defying orders, Larson sped up and was enveloped by tight-knit trees. What little light that seeped into the park seemed to escape his field of view. It took everything to make out the dense patch mere feet away. A prone body curled into a ball in a perverse cradle of roots.

Praying Igor was alive, Larson knelt forward and reached out a hand.

"Thatcher," the voice spoke.

Larson ignored him. It was impossible to tell if Igor was still breathing. Larson pressed on what he hoped was the embattled man's chest and felt—

He sprang to his feet. The hand gripping the phone to his ear threatened to shatter the device into pieces. His voice filled with rage.

"Where is he?"

Whether it was a trick of the light or his imagination, what moments ago had been a body was now plain to see. Larson kicked the dark mass, scattering a pile of bloody clothes. Igor Stregor was nowhere to be found.

"Where is he?" Larson demanded again.

"I wasn't lying to you. The scientist is close."

"Where?"

"Turn around."

The line went dead.

Chapter Eleven

Larson spun in time to glimpse a figure stagger into the clearing. He seemed to materialize from nothing in the early morning gloom. Larson caught the diminutive man, barefoot and clad all in white, in his arms.

Igor fell to his knees as though all strength had been sapped from his body. Larson dropped his phone and lowered the other man to the leaf-strewn ground. Igor frantically tried to form speech. Larson leaned closer, fighting to understand what was happening.

What he saw made him reel back in horror. The scientist's plump features were sunken and waxy. His skin had a translucent, unhealthy pallor. As if much of his blood had been siphoned away. But that wasn't what caused Larson's shock.

A steel rod, pronged at either end, ran the length of Igor's neck. Droplets of blood leaked from where it pressed into his larynx and the base of his throat. That explained why he couldn't speak, could do no more than gesture as the spark in his eyes appeared to evaporate.

"Igor, I'm right here. Everything's going to be okay."

Larson spoke the words even though he knew they weren't true. He cradled the scientist's head in his hands and ignored the surrounding forest swaying with silent laughter. Blood trickled onto a blanket of dead leaves beneath them.

"Stay with me. Help is coming."

Igor's pulse faded. His breathing became shallower with each passing moment. He gave one last shuddering heave and went still. Larson glanced at his still lit phone screen lying nearby. It was three minutes past seven.

He rocked backward and let himself collapse with the fresh numbness of shock washing over him. He was afraid to take his eyes off the body, worried it would somehow disappear.

For several minutes that could have spanned hours, he sat unmoving. The sky overhead continued to lighten, blissfully unaware. Distant sirens coincided with another figure materializing in the abating gloom.

Larson dragged himself to his feet as Diego came into sharper relief. The other man took one look at the body and averted his eyes. He fixed them on Larson.

"What now?"

The sirens grew louder.

"Get me away from here," he said.

"You need a ride home?"

Larson shook his head. "Not home. There's work to be done."

Diego nodded. Turning, he led the way out of the clearing.

Echelon's headquarters contained four soundproof conference rooms, categorized based on importance. Larson spent the rest of the morning barricaded behind a heavy door labeled 'A'. Besides a long table lost under a chaotic spread of files and a projector screen the room offered a panoramic backdrop of Rosslyn and Washington across the Potomac. To Larson, the view may as well not have existed. His concentration was lost to everything save the sea of documents spread before him. Like the Biblical story of Exodus, one way or another they would part and reveal who was responsible for Igor's death.

A determined knock on the conference room door roused him from his work. Rising, he stepped around the long table and permitted Diego to enter his frenetic workspace. He added a thin folder to the heap of documents and accepted Larson's begrudging invitation to sit.

"What do you have for me?" he asked.

To Diego's credit, he didn't try to lighten the dour mood with humor.

Without flipping open the folder, he said, "We received word that Stregor's body reached the morgue. It's looking like we managed to make it out of Dumbarton Oaks without falling victim to any witnesses. But the conclusion of foul play is inevitable. Due to his high-profile nature, the FBI is likely to get involved."

"Have the local authorities found anything?"

"At this point it's too soon to know. But national news outlets are preparing to break the story. The original abduction may not have made much of a splash because it coincided with Charlottesville, but this is going to be big. The WHO has already been informed—they're going to release a statement after the story breaks."

"Anything else?"

Diego paused. "That thing strapped around Stregor's neck is called a Heretic's Fork. They were used to torture victims during the Spanish Inquisition. If he'd been wearing it long enough, it's possible Stregor could have died from the effects of sleep deprivation."

Feeling a pang of fury course through him, Larson stood. As he neared the door, he remembered that it was Saturday. It wasn't unusual for most of Echelon's members to visit the office over the weekend. These were men and women dedicated to their work, many without families or clinging onto relationships that were tenuous at best. Echelon itself was like a spouse of sorts, ever-present and nagging.

It struck him that Elena would find out about her brother's demise by way of every major news network if he didn't get to her first.

Larson posed a final question off-handedly. "Is Katz in?"

Diego's face split into a grin. "Naturally."

"Great. Don't tell him I was here."

Without thanking his colleague, Larson strode out of the conference room.

He got no further than a row of cubicles near the hall leading to the elevators before an office door swung open and Eiran Katz, Echelon's Director, reared his head. His eyes latched onto Larson like an angler fish trolling the inky depths. One finger beckoned.

"My office. Now."

Larson had no choice but to follow. The chief led him inside and shut the door. All extraneous noise was cut off. Larson accepted his usual seat in front of the formidable rosewood desk. Katz remained standing. He paced the outskirts of the office like a hyena prowling for a carcass.

"When did cozying up to a woman like Elena Stregor become part of this organization's mission?"

"You know who she is?"

"Of course, I do. She's been more critical of the new administration than perhaps anybody, and that's saying something."

"She lost her brother—"

"I'm quite aware. I also know you fled Dumbarton Oaks Park minutes before Igor Stregor's body was discovered. Now, I want to know what a dead scientist has to do with the alternative right, and why you're being spotted with Elena Stregor."

"She came to me," Larson admitted. He had learned long ago to never deceive Eiran Katz. There were times when it might be permissible to skirt the truth's edges, but never outright lies. "Elena believes that she's in danger as well. I think she's correct. What's more, I think there's a link between Igor Stregor's death and the riots in Charlottesville. They happened minutes apart."

Katz listened impassively until he fell silent. Then he frowned. "Your theory is nonsense. We're here to analyze extremist threats, not to solve the murder of dead scientists and play bodyguard to their bereaved sisters. Leave that to the FBI."

Larson scrambled to his feet.

"Where are you going?"

"I have to find her."

He thought Katz might rush him, keep him from leaving, but he remained rooted to the spot, his face turning beet red with anger. His voice spat venom. Larson was at the door, prying it open.

"You're not a spy, Larson. Drop any grand illusions of cracking the case, and leave Elena Stregor alone. She has nothing to do with our goal."

"And what is that goal?"

"To discover what the alt-right are planning next."

Larson's lips stretched into a hollow smile that made Katz's face riot with anger. "Then she is crucial to our mission."

He left the chief fuming and minutes later exited the elevator and seated himself behind the wheel of his Mercedes. Fifteen minutes elapsed before he pulled to a stop in front of the familiar townhouse in Georgetown. But when he entered through the garden gate, as was his custom, it was to find the guest bed made and all three levels deserted.

Elena was gone.

It struck Larson that he had no means of reaching her.

Chapter Twelve

Rain cascaded over the capital on Sunday. The kind of late summer downpour that Washington was famous for. Washing away countless sins—endless torrents flooded downspouts and made the facades along N Street appear to weep. Larson left home once, to pick up takeout from a nearby Chinese restaurant and nearly drown in the process. He flung his sodden raincoat in a laundry basket and watched the news as he ate alone, managing a few bites before losing his appetite.

Forgetting the diversion of lunch, he placed the paper cartons in the fridge and poured a lowball glass of scotch while the sky outside the kitchen windows darkened by intervals. Washington men were expected to drink scotch. He had been introduced to the faction of whiskey after college and developed a bona fide taste for it. It reminded him of happier times.

Larson sipped in silence broken by the crackling of ice in his glass, flicking his eyes now and then toward the muted television. As the porch's gaslights sputtered to life, there was a knock on the front door. He opened it to find her standing there, soaked to the bone. The considerable moisture on her face did little to hide the fact that she was crying. He pulled her inside without a word.

He switched on the living room fireplace while Elena changed into dry clothes upstairs. When she reappeared, she'd composed her face into the universal look of bereavement. There were no tears. Her eyes were rimmed red, the skin along her dimpled cheekbones sallow and drawn.

She collapsed into a leather recliner, curling her knees to her chest. Larson didn't have to ask if she'd seen the news.

"Would you like something to eat?"

Elena ignored him. "The WHO is arranging everything," she said in a brittle voice. "For the funeral."

He wanted to go to her, to hold her tight in his arms. Instead, he padded to the kitchen and poured her a scotch. Handing it over and sinking onto a beige sofa, he waited for her to speak again.

"I'm sorry to intrude like this. I didn't know where else to turn."

Larson didn't speak, instead raising his glass in salute and taking a long drink. Elena did the same. The steady patter of rain battering the townhouse was calming, peaceful. Thunder grumbled every few minutes as they sat in silence.

"Are you tired?" Larson asked after he refilled her glass. Elena shrugged.

"I have the guest bedroom ready for you again."

"Not the guest bedroom," she said, pulling herself unsteadily to her feet. "It's lonely. I don't want to be lonely tonight."

Larson helped Elena, who moved like a woman much older, up the stairs toward the bedroom at the hall's end.

"I won't leave your side," he murmured.

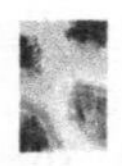

Afterward, they lay unclothed beneath satin sheets, embracing in the darkness as the storm wore itself out.

Larson glanced at the clock on his bedside table. Glowing numerals reported it was five after eight.

"You must be hungry," he whispered.

After a moment, he felt Elena nod into his chest. Suddenly he was starving. He propped himself up and kissed her on the forehead.

"I know just the place."

It would have been impossible to get a last-minute reservation at the upscale bistro across from the cult famous Exorcist Steps, but Larson knew who to speak to and which names to offer. At nine sharp, he and Elena stepped out of a drizzle that still henpecked the damp street and through a set of gilded front doors.

Taking its name from the year the United States Constitution was recognized, 1789 Restaurant had spent decades as one of the capital's most notable fine dining establishments. It also garnered significance from the year the country's first archbishop bought the property on which it sat. Originally a federal period townhouse, it was converted into a restaurant in 1960 by an enterprising Georgetown graduate. The building had changed hands once, undergoing extensive remodeling, but had clung to the history preserved in each of its six dining rooms.

"I thought this might take your mind off things," Larson murmured as the doors swung shut behind them.

He straightened his tie and shifted his shoulders beneath a blazer as they were led to a small table near the glowing fireplace in the John Carroll Room. He had left his collection of dark suits hanging in his closet, judging them too somber for the occasion.

Larson had never developed a strong affinity for formal attire. As he watched Elena float ahead of him, he thought it worthwhile in this instance.

The dress sweeping down her back was shimmering gray silk to match sleek heels that drew her eyes level with his. Elena wore borrowed sweatpants and a T-shirt back at his townhouse. Her eyes had widened, but she said nothing when he opened a small closet off the master bathroom and offered her the gown.

They sat and allowed the maître d' to slip menus under their noses while Larson ordered two martinis.

"They have good Russian vodka," he murmured over the steady rhythm of rain on glass. "Foreign diplomats often dine here. They expect a quality better than what's typically carried in the states."

"If there's one thing my original corner of the world knows well, it's vodka." Elena nodded and looked down at herself, as if she couldn't believe her eyes.

"You're stunning," he said.

She glanced up.

"This dress..."

Larson flashed a guilty grin that he tried unsuccessfully to hide behind his glass. "I find it comes in handy to keep a small selection of women's clothing on hand…for instances such as this."

"Where does your money come from if you don't mind my asking? You don't seem the type to suckle at the teat of family wealth."

"My family is comfortable but not the sort you're referring to. My mother was a teacher and my father worked in Baltimore for a firm that consults for various government branches. They're both retired." He cleared his throat. "I helped design a small security software application. With some good fortune and assistance, it garnered interest. Through a former professor, I was put in contact with an entrepreneur abroad who purchased the application. Its sale allowed me to experience wealth that most at such a young age aren't accustomed to."

"It hasn't seemed to go to your head."

"There's more to life than money. That notion is what attracted me to the agency I work for."

"What is the name of your agency?"

He met her inquiry with an opaque silence that intoned, *some questions can't be answered.*

Several minutes passed before Elena raised the subject Larson knew she would be unable to resist. He had been bracing himself. As her lips parsed, he made a promise in his head not to lie.

"My brother—"

"I'm sorry I was unable to save him, Elena."

She batted away his apology. "There was no hope. Sometimes you can feel these things. Seeing his face plastered all over the news—"

"I'm sorry."

She brushed away a forlorn tear and smiled.

"I will grieve for Igor and carry on living my life. Our parents are dead. I am the only one left now. But I will not know peace until I discover who was responsible for his murder."

Larson took a sip of the red wine that accompanied dinner—plates of beef tenderloin and Norwegian salmon—and dabbed the corners of his mouth.

"I'm going to do everything I can to bring those responsible to justice."

Elena nodded, satisfied.

"Did Igor have any specific enemies? Anyone he ever mentioned that made him feel uneasy or overtly cautious."

She appeared to think hard.

"It is easy to attract rivals in the scientific community. The competitive nature of our work makes it impossible to avoid. But Igor was revered in his field. There was no one, except what I mentioned previously. The new regime was at odds with my brother's findings, going so far as to issue statements calling him a fool and a spreader of doomsday prophecies. Science does not allow such farcical instruments to come within its sacred walls, Michael. It is concerned only with facts, with discovering truths. Any good scientist bases his work upon these covenants. Igor was a good scientist."

She fell silent as the waiter arrived to clear their table.

"There is a radical sect on the reactionary side of our political spectrum." Larson lowered his voice. "A growing faction has taken this ideology to a whole new level. These men—they are almost all men—range in background but all follow similar ideological tenets. They depend on homogeneity, they detest the foreign and unfamiliar, and their paramount goal is to preserve their own tribe and culture. They abhor globalism. Their kind would have America expel all immigrants and close its doors to the outside world. And they're becoming dangerous."

"What are you saying? That the alternative right could have had something to do with Igor's murder?"

Larson hid his surprise. "I'm saying it's possible. He was taken within hours of riots staged by the alt-right. The timing seems to lend itself to something more than coincidence."

On the wet sidewalk outside the restaurant, Elena clutched his arm. They walked along Prospect Street, parallel with the river.

"In addition to studying the president, I happen to know a great deal about the alt-right," Elena said.

He shot her a surprised glance. "Why didn't you say—?"

"I was curious to see what conclusion you would draw on your own without my interference."

She clutched his arm tighter as they skirted a glistening puddle.

"The alt-right are far from unintelligent. In fact, it's their intelligence that makes them so dangerous. They know how to attract followers from the disgruntled corners of conservatism and understand how to rouse empathy for their cause. I'm afraid they most certainly could have played a hand in Igor's death."

"Until now the alt-right hasn't shown any proclivity toward physical violence."

"Intelligence and patience." Elena tapped her temple. "Their leaders possess a masterful sense of strategy that most criminal enterprises lack. It was important for them to build a following and sense of legitimacy. With all that in place, they've decided the moment is ripe to push their boundaries, test the waters."

"The riots in Virginia—"

"I study people for a living, Michael. Those riots served a plain operational purpose; assess what the alt-right could get away with."

"There were no consequences doled out in the aftermath."

"The first prod of the pitchfork proved nobody will react. The president will never censure the alt-right; they're some of his most fervent supporters. No one else's voice is loud enough to matter."

Rage simmered under his skin, the same molten anger that had gripped him when he held Igor's lifeless body. Elena stopped unexpectedly, staring at him with a puzzling expression. Assessing him. Then she continued walking with a new zeal in her step. They rounded the corner onto Thirty-third Street when she spoke.

"I have a friend that is perhaps unlike any other person on this planet."

"Just a friend?" he raised his eyebrows.

Elena ignored his remark, strength building in her words.

"I consider myself lucky to know him. I think it is time the two of you meet."

Chapter Thirteen

Some men were born different. Reggie Thompkins had always found this to be the case as he watched the man and woman exit a fashionable Georgetown restaurant arm in arm. He knew their names, let them dance through his thoughts like synchronized performers atop a blinding stage.

Some men were born different. It had been that way growing up, an average boy in Columbus who hadn't lacked life's essentials but still failed to receive everything his childish heart desired. A mother and father who insisted spoiled children grew into rotten adults weren't outside the norm in those days, but it stung all the same, forced to witness friends playing with the latest GI Joe and Lego sets while he was stuck with a derelict medley of tin castoffs from some dinosaur era. It had stung more when his father, a white-collar worker in the burgeoning information age, was sent to jail for tax fraud.

Money wasn't the worst of it. As he got older, he'd noticed things—startling things.

They say children don't see color; maybe that's true. Or maybe children see what's in front of them and the cognitive parts of their brains aren't yet developed enough to appreciate what it means. But as he grew older, he began to understand. The city was filled with people different than him, and he didn't like it. Different colored skin, different languages, different food, and different ways of living. And everyone—schoolteachers and shop proprietors and even his neighbors—seemed intent on pushing those differences on him. Shoving them in his face like they were something to be celebrated. Like they weren't the same as being exposed to a sticky form of plague that came from overseas and refused to slither away and die.

Reggie Thompkins was still average in appearance, but there the holdovers from his past ended. He was a ghost.

The cold, hard truth of the gun clenched in his jacket pocket was the only thing warding off clammy uncertainty inspired by a world of differences.

He glanced at the man but paid closer attention to the woman as they passed the Black Box Theater. Even from his vantage point atop the Exorcist Steps, there was no denying she was attractive. He could tell that even though she clutched the man beside her she walked with purpose, a steadfast determination that refused to be snuffed out.

He stole forward and rounded a corner before his quarries could move out of sight. He knew where they were heading; he had made several passes by the townhouse on the corner of Thirty-third and N Street earlier that evening. The back gate's latch gave way noiselessly. A rear door could be forced.

Thompkins continued walking, the gun a tugging reminder with every step. Pooling water on the sidewalk made his footsteps resonate, but even on a Sunday evening there was enough traffic on nearby M Street to turn him into a soundless predator among brickwork and iron lace.

One sweaty palm closed around the gun's grip as the man and woman reached the intersection of Prospect and

Thirty-fifth. And then he did something peculiar. Pausing, he pulled a phone from his pocket and dialed a number from memory. A gruff voice answered on the second ring. Expectant silence was filled by a ten-digit numerical password recited in dull tones. Then static. When it cleared, a new voice greeted him, its breathing shallow and agitated.

The ghost spoke three words. "He's with her."

A grunt of understanding followed. Then the connection was severed.

Doubling back, he crossed the street and headed toward Georgetown University. The gun felt heavier. Itching for use. He rounded a corner. His heart pounded with an anticipation he refused to let overcome his even gait. No quickening stride as he passed the Georgetown Art and History façade that bled over into the township.

Beyond a subsequent trio of bleak structures stood a rustic edifice teeming with light. It was toward this light he let his feet carry him, unaware of everything save the gun's heaviness and dry warmth pouring from the grocery store's windows. The relenting rain had brought out an onslaught of people eager to complete some last-minute shopping before the coming week. A chime tinkled, from some distant universe, as the door swung open and shut.

Thompkins stopped across the street and waited. Smells from the deli wafted toward him each time the door opened, mixing with rain-scented air and hanging there. He steeled himself by squeezing the gun's hard grip the way a child squeezed his mother's hand.

When it was time, he marched forward.

Chapter Fourteen

Larson overtook a pedestrian-laden street near Capitol Hill and his cell phone stirred in his pocket. He redirected from the plaza onto a side avenue near the American Indian museum before pausing to read the message.

It was from Elena. A brief line of text instructed him to be at Ronald Reagan National Airport on Wednesday at two thirty. Two days to prepare.

It had taken her a fortnight to arrange the meeting with her unusual friend. Extraordinary, she had called him as they ambled through the sleepy Georgetown streets. That had only made Larson slightly jealous.

He left the museum's wake and crossed National Mall, skirting tourists and refusing a request to stop and take pictures of a family of four that hailed from a sleepy Midwest town if the slogan on their matching shirts was any indication. Giving the National Gallery of Art a wide berth, he continued into downtown and didn't slow until he passed the Federal Trade Commission and pivoted east along

Pennsylvania Avenue.

The Federal Trade Commission building, like many bureaucratic headquarters that dotted the capital, was plain, with nothing to identify its purpose. A tan monolith of federal infrastructure with a few Ionic columns and tapered levels that ran to a beveled tile roof invisible from ground level. The kind of building designed to blend in, so that the average American could pass and not realize they were witnessing a small cog in the massive, turning wheel.

It all served to lessen the threat of attack. A low profile meant less notice and interest, which equaled safety. Intelligence agencies hadn't gotten the memo. Sometimes the itching desire to boast outweighed security risks. Overconfidence in their own protective capabilities often played a role. The CIA refused to operate in an unassuming concrete rectangle on the corner of Pennsylvania and Seventh Street. The Pentagon wouldn't have proven any less vulnerable with four sides instead of five.

Larson was brought out of his reverie, not by the bustle of traffic on Pennsylvania Avenue, but by a familiar face appearing in a crowd maneuvering the sidewalk. It disappeared in an instant. He made a habit of studying faces, even while his mind wandered. His synapses pulsed with recognition.

He didn't turn back, instead cutting across the thoroughfare onto Sixth Street and rounding downtown's southern edge. It was another warm day, although the first vestiges of autumn were beginning to take hold. In a month, summer would be forgotten. In two, it would be remembered fondly.

The watcher hadn't faded from his mind when Larson noticed a much more thought-provoking figure idling near a glass explosion of a museum that loomed over the intersection. It attempted to blend in, that much was obvious, peering at several maps detailing color-coded metro routes while streams of pedestrians passed. His charcoal suit was slightly out of place in an area more saturated with tourists than lunchtime business crowds.

The man stared at the maps with the studied intensity of a novice but shot off sideways glances that set off alarms in Larson's head.

He didn't slow or do anything to intimate that he'd spotted Diego. But the game was finished. Dodging a concrete potter ripe with floral intrigue, Larson traversed the last bit of sidewalk like an inmate resigned for death row. He entered a trendy restaurant that had taken roost on the ground floor of an adjacent building.

The Source was glass like the nearby museum and catered to patrons who preferred a taste for the finer things in life. It was owned by a famous and absentee chef known for a unique brand of fine dining. This outpost paid homage to what a placard near the door termed 'Asian fusion'. As if Asian food was an unheard-of delicacy in Washington.

Larson brushed off the smiling host with a nod and navigated the dining room with the practiced step of a frequent guest. It was crowded for lunch. Distant chatter echoed from diners upstairs, tinkling of stemware and tumblers escaping a lounge in the restaurant's rear. Scanning the tables, he spotted the familiar receding pate of a man seated alone with his back to the door and a napkin draped across his right knee.

Sliding into the booth across from Katz, Larson grimaced as the chief's gaze found him and nodded appreciatively.

"Good of you to catch my drift," he muttered. "What gave it away?"

"You ought not to position your men so haphazardly if they're to go unnoticed," Larson said. The left side of Katz's mouth curled into a smile.

"Rivera was a bit too obvious."

Larson shook his head. "The first watcher should have known better than to make eye contact. I recognized him at once."

The chief winced. "McBride's still a little green, I'm

afraid. I thought using a newer recruit might fool you. Then again, you're one of the best when it comes to surveillance."

"I'm one of the few who take it seriously."

Katz conceded the point. "I suppose I could've called and told you to meet me."

"You doubted I'd come. And I wouldn't have if I'd known you'd chosen this out of all the establishment's seating arrangements."

"Pickings were slim. And I like sitting near a window."

Their table offered an excellent view of Sixth Street through tempered glass. A fact that deepened Larson's scowl. "People get killed sitting near windows. Especially in a catastrophe of a place like this."

"Where do you propose we sit?"

He nodded toward the back of the restaurant by the cocktail lounge.

"I feel trapped back there."

"There's always the kitchen."

Katz ordered two glasses of Syrah that arrived without pomp or circumstance. When the waitress departed, he inquired, "What are you thinking in the way of appetizers? I hear The Source has excellent ceviche."

"I want to know why I've been summoned."

Katz closed his menu with a snap that made little dent in the layer of noise around them. Larson could tell he was enjoying himself.

"Cheer up, Michael. I've come to deliver some very intriguing news."

He insisted on ordering first. And enjoying several mouthfuls of Syrah. When plates of ceviche and a Taiwanese beef noodle soup arrived, Katz allowed himself a tentative nibble before leaning forward and composing his sharp features in a way that meant business.

"It's time I shared with you a piece of information about which I haven't been entirely forthcoming."

Larson opened his mouth, but Katz stopped him with an upturned hand.

"*Nobody* knows, Michael. It wasn't just you. But you're the only one I'm telling." He eyed his charge with a grave importance that for a moment showed his age. "We have an informant."

Several thoughts rifled through Larson's head at once. He remained silent.

"A mole buried deep within the alt-right movement. I won't say his name here, but you'll learn it in due time."

"Why didn't you tell me?"

"It's paramount to play this close to the vest. As far as Echelon is concerned this is like a KGB general defecting at the height of the Cold War. Let too many people in on it and one day he's back in Russia slaving away at some Siberian gulag, or far worse. Our man's people might not have killed him if word got out, but our well of information would have dried up."

"How did you get him?"

"He came to us," Katz paused, "with some persuading. Analysis found him on an online message board called 8chan and used his IP to link him to several other white nationalist message boards. We discovered he lived right here in Washington. I ordered surveillance. Risky, I know, and on top of that, I instructed them to be anything but discrete. Let them go through his garbage in plain daylight. Scared him senseless. By the time I showed up on his doorstep he was already ours."

Larson couldn't help but tip his hat. He nibbled at an egg noodle and asked off-handedly, "How long?"

Katz had looked pleased with himself, but at the question his smile wilted.

"A year."

Larson's face remained unchanged. He took a final sip of his wine and made to stand. "I really do need to be going."

"You're not going to want to do that just yet."

Larson let out an upheaval of breath. "Get on with whatever it is you brought me here to explain." He remained seated.

"Our mole is rather important in the alt-right movement. Works for the same white nationalist think tank that's been around since the beginning. He doesn't report often, once every few weeks, but at our last rendezvous he mentioned rumor of someone dangerous they've got imbedded high in the federal government. Someone with a connection to the president."

"How dangerous?"

"According to him, the rumor tied this person to the alt-right. Not the ones bemoaning establishment conservatism from the safety of their keyboards. The kind of neo-Nazis that dream about jettisoning foreigners and upheaving society with justice dispensed down the barrel of a gun."

"And it's possible he's got the ear of some powerful people?"

The chief nodded, his eyes darkening. "We have a serious problem on our hands."

"How do I play into all this?"

"I've been considering your theory with the scientist and recent events. I think you should be present next time we debrief him."

Chapter Fifteen

As the Gulfstream left the runway a fortnight later and pointed its nose skyward, Larson leaned back into the headrest and closed his eyes. He didn't open them until the plane reached cruising altitude, signaled by a faint ding that broke the meditative quiet within the narrow fuselage.

Quiet was a relative term. Twin jet engines churned out a mind-numbing hum that he did his best to ignore.

The seatbelt signs glowed orange half an hour later. A display on the seatback announced that they were crossing into Canadian airspace. Elena had refused to tell him the plane's destination, or why she couldn't come with him, insisting that everything would be fine. The man he was meeting, she said, relied on discretion.

When pressed, she had relented, informing him it was a location to the north. The secretive destination sent a pang of unease through him that he tried to quell as the Gulfstream descended.

They landed in an unnamed city that turned out to be

Montreal twenty minutes later. The jet taxied toward the long arm of a terminal, and after several minutes of restless engine groaning, he escaped onto the tarmac. A solemn man who had sat at the plane's rear during the flight and looked suspiciously like private security followed.

"You're not taking me somewhere quiet to have me killed?" Larson asked. The man met him with grim silence. Together, they climbed a flight of stairs into the terminal and breezed through customs. Larson suspected the dark-suited figure at his side expedited the process; lines seemed to melt away and Canadian officials greeted them with a rushed cheeriness he had never experienced.

His minder approached a black sedan with opaque windows at the head of a long line idling on the curb outside the modern terminal. Bending his neck forward in a jerky fashion, he said, "Welcome to Canada, Mr. Larson." He opened the rear door. His minder closed it with a satisfying thud before situating himself in the passenger seat. Their driver wore wraparound sunglasses that covered much of his face and said nothing.

Montreal-Trudeau International Airport disappeared as they sped along Autoroute 20. Late afternoon traffic was heavy, the air thick with a rush-hour soundtrack, forcing their driver to honk and swerve around slower vehicles to maintain speed.

Larson paid sharp attention as the highway banked along a canal and trappings of industry gave way to the compact urbanization of inner city. Large towers overtook the skyline, and they were forced to brake as traffic thickened.

At an interchange, they exited the highway and zipped onto a lower road that crossed the canal and ran parallel before cutting back into Montreal's heart. He kept track of the turns—right, left, then right again—while his companions remained stoic in the front seat. They veered left once more, this time toward a massive, forested hill that loomed out of the cityscape.

"Impressive, huh?" his minder grunted over his shoulder.

"Mind telling me who I'm here to meet?" he asked.

Elena had remained mute on the subject. She was due to board a flight bound for New York City after Larson took off.

"You'll know soon enough."

They turned parallel to the massive hillock and drove onto a narrow forking lane that climbed in the shadow of a cylindrical tower. Larson scarcely had time to register what was happening before the sedan navigated a hairpin turn. Still climbing, low, cobbled walls and houses emerged out of forest growth. Not the kind of dwellings littering suburban America. Not even the kind lining Georgetown's avenues. A graceful ridge of stone fortresses overlooked the city.

The driver continued at breakneck pace, looping around and squealing to a stop in the driveway of a flagstone mansion. It looked capable of both holding off a barbarian assault and playing host to elegant assemblies of Montreal's most noteworthy and influential.

His door opened before Larson could properly take in the castle on the hill. He was escorted down a short path and through a side entrance and asked to pause in a high-ceilinged sitting room while he was searched.

The search produced nothing noteworthy; he had not thought to bring a gun. Echelon agents were issued weapons, but they weren't carried except for the most drastic of circumstances.

His next destination was an airy den sunk a step from the main level and adjoined by a spacious kitchen and bar. Bay windows held downtown Montreal in magnificent view and a giant unlit fireplace stood before him. The décor appeared handpicked by someone with expensive taste. A lack of clutter and an unused air led Larson to believe that whoever owned the house didn't spend much time there.

He glanced out the nearest window at an autumn sun

setting over distant towers and considered pouring himself a drink. The thought died when the hollow tap of designer shoes echoed across the floor behind him.

Samit Bathari was a man he would have instantly recognized, had he ever laid eyes on him. It was not his average height nor rounded cheeks and soft chin covered in dark stubble, nor curling hair that swept back off his high forehead. It was his eyes, molten and observant, sifting past the immaterial and mundane straight into the bared soul while one eyebrow cocked askew. Tinged faintest yellow and showing off the miniscule branch work of capillaries present in those who worked too hard or slept too little. He kept his mouth pressed tight and conveyed what he was thinking with ocular subtleties alone.

Or a sliver of what he was thinking. Larson doubted the moment he laid eyes on the man that his thoughts were ever anything less than weighty and teeming.

He stepped into the den and Larson noted that his clothes did not match his academic air. A tweed jacket with elbow pads and chalk residue from a recent lecture would have been appropriate. But taking him in, he doubted whether tweed was in Samit Bathari's wardrobe. The man wore the bottom half of a custom suit and a purple silk shirt rolled past his thin forearms. His shoes were Italian. The Swiss watch on his left wrist cost a small fortune.

Coming face to face with his counterpart, Bathari paused, collecting himself and letting out a deep breath.

"It's nice to meet you, Michael Larson. Elena has told me so much about you."

"Not too much, I hope."

Bathari laughed as the two grasped hands. "Would you like a drink?"

He was already striding out of the den as Larson answered in the affirmative. He eased open a glass cover and shifted bottles.

"I have to admit—I have a distaste for the spirits they imbibe in this part of the world," he spoke over his shoulder.

"Whisky doesn't suit me."

Bathari reached for an unfamiliar bottle and held it toward him.

"Dealer's choice," Larson said.

Bathari poured two amber measures before rejoining him.

"I'm partial to a few Indian liqueurs. This is a recreation of a recipe brewed by the royal families of Rajasthan before India gained its independence."

Larson raised his glass and tasted. A bitter flavor met his lips, nuanced with dates and a spice he couldn't put his finger on. Bathari motioned for him to sit across from the fireplace. His host sat as well, eyeing him with interest.

"I was sorry when I heard about Igor Stregor's passing. A dear friend and good man. Elena tells me you are looking into his disappearance."

"You knew him?"

Bathari clasped his hands together and let his mouth form a serene smile.

"Of course, I did. It was through him that I met Elena. Men like the late Dr. Stregor are important to know in my line of work. Men who seek the truth, even truths the public may not be quite ready to hear."

"What is your line of work?"

Bathari pursed his lips. "You'll learn everything you need to know about me in short order."

Larson switched tack and glanced around. "Certainly a nice place."

"I don't own this house if you were wondering. It was lent to me by a friend. A supporter, I should say. He's prominent in the American music industry, although he's managed to make his true fortune out of view of the public eye. A wise man."

"He has great taste."

Bathari spared the furnishings a sweeping glance. "His wife did most of the decorating. But the city was his choice. I've always loved Montreal. Even in winter. I find it necessary to avoid the United States at present. Montreal was the perfect landing spot."

The pace of conversation was accelerating, the room's energy heightening. Larson opened his mouth to inquire, but Bathari changed the subject.

"I trust Elena told you close to nothing about me. On my own wishes. I find it makes things simpler. I, however, did some background research on you, Mr. Larson. In less than a decade, you've managed to mold a more fulfilling career than many will in their lifetimes. I followed *FireWise* from afar during its infancy. Your work is impressive."

"How d'you—?"

Bathari cut him off.

"I have the pleasure of being acquainted with one of your old professors. I'm quite certain he mentioned you at a banquet we both attended several years back."

He'd heard enough. Leaning forward and bringing the polite discourse to a crashing halt, Larson stared at the man opposite and said, "Who are you?"

Samit Bathari smiled for a long moment. His knowing eyes glittered in the dying light.

"You're about to find out."

Chapter Sixteen

His story was long and winding, and in places hard to follow. But Larson listened. And what his ears imbibed his brain couldn't help being amazed.

Bathari had been born to poor parents in an overlooked village on the Kaveri River's northern bank in the Indian state of Tamil Nadu. His father rose before dawn each morning and took three buses across the river where he toiled in one of the nearby town's numerous factories. His mother scraped together enough change to buy scraps of cloth for fashioning clothes to sell at the village market. They struggled to provide a sound roof and food to eat, but they also labored for another purpose—a future. In that future mother and father left India for good and sailed for a land where achieving their dreams was possible. Pieced together one rupee at a time, that dream couldn't be allowed to die.

"I had an older brother, Ishaan," Bathari said. "For many years he was a hero in my eyes. As we aged, the relationship changed. Ishaan was tall and handsome, excellent at cricket, and could run further and faster than anyone in our village. As his popularity mounted, he surrounded himself with a legion of followers that ambled in his wake. Due to my incompetence at athletic endeavors and affinity for reading, I became their chief target."

He explained how Ishaan turned a blind eye to the bullying. In the following months, a strange name floated around the village. *Temple Hoppers*.

"The parents and elders would have put a fierce stop to such a thing if they had known. Temples served as a constant reminder of the divide between old and new. In those days, India was an amalgam. A land with vastly different cultures meeting headlong like two rivers crashing against one another. Like the rivers, different fragments were melding together, neither willing to give ground but also unable to stem the flow of change that blurred their edges and fused the two into something entirely foreign. New and old. Past and future. Fusion.

"Impoverished villages sat in the lap of cities teeming with concrete and buildings tall enough to blot out the sun. Women in traditional dress carried jugs to the river for water each day and were separated by a thin tree line from churning, mammoth hands of industry. The civilized world relied on India, and yet, India could not rely on itself."

Young Samit Bathari had been forbidden from leaving his village. He disobeyed. Following a dirt trail, he hugged where the forest bulged until he had no choice but to duck his small head and dive in. The trees were not so thick here, warm sunlight enveloping him in sheets, and there was little threat of an escaped tiger from the preserve fifty kilometers away stalking among the bamboo shoots. He had woven deeper until he reached a clearing marked by a pair of giant, fallen stones.

A temple sat half-eaten by vines and succumbing to the forest's slow reclamation as all things eventually were. Minute detailing and painted deities stood tall against time.

He returned the next afternoon and every day following. Using sheets of parchment and a charcoal sliver pilfered from his father's study, he sat against a tree and sketched the temple until he was satisfied with the rendering.

"It happened one day in June," Bathari said. His brother's band of delinquents hadn't gotten him in the schoolyard. They waited until he was in the no man's land between school and the family's cramped dwelling before closing in.

The first stinging blow came out of nowhere, knocking him sideways, and sending his glasses careening into the gutter. In his blindness, another paw crashed his books out of his hands. A balled-up fist connected with his chest and dropped him to his knees. Heaving for breath, he tensed for the next impact.

"I believed in that moment they meant to kill me. There are two paths in such a situation; you can accept your fate, or you can fight back. As my brother approached, for the first time in my life I did the latter. I think it took them all by surprise. Swinging my weak fists, I connected with humid air and another blow landed in the small of my back. Then the dust cleared, and my attackers were gone. Ishaan stood in their place. Saying nothing, he collected my books off the ground and handed them to me. And then he walked away."

But from that point, there was something different about Ishaan. He began to treat his younger sibling better, with something bordering respect. Samit was no longer the bookish prey of every village bully. He discovered he could walk home or read in the schoolyard without being bothered. Even the Temple Hoppers didn't glance twice at him.

Things had changed so much that by late August he had come to a decision. He found Ishaan lounging in the shade under the large *Arjun* tree in their yard. Buds that would turn to bulbs and with time become fruit were already visible on its branches.

Bathari said, "I confided in my older brother about my

secret temple in the forest. I can still remember the shadow of a smile on his lips. He was sure I was lying, insisted he had seen and climbed every temple from our village to Panjappur."

"But he went with you?" Larson asked.

"It must have been a peculiar sight, Ishaan following me along the dirt road that wound around the forest and into a dense thicket. When the forgotten temple came into view, he apologized for not believing me. And then he insisted on climbing. I stayed behind, watching him use a tree as a foothold and fling himself onto the faded masonry. He clutched a pillar and heaved himself skyward.

"He was perched high above the clearing when it happened. Ishaan's delighted cries were drowned by the tumultuous sound of large stones grinding against one another. I remember his glee turning to fear. He screamed as the stones he clutched gave way. The entire temple flank crumbled. And then he was falling."

Chapter Seventeen

"What happened?"

"He died." His face never wavered from its neutral expression.

Larson said nothing, waiting for his counterpart to continue. He rose and drifted toward a window streaked with the last weak light preceding dusk.

"I was devastated, but not so much as my village. Despite his oft-wicked ways, Ishaan had been beloved. The day we buried him, I saw how both my parents looked at me and knew they blamed me for his death. If only that had been the extent of it."

A shadow crossed Bathari's face for the briefest moment.

"It was ten days after my brother's funeral. Long enough for me to sink back into something resembling normality, but more than likely it had taken that long to come up with the plan. I was walking along the dirt path to school when four of my brother's old gang seized me. They didn't bother hiding their faces. I was bound by my hands and feet and carried off. Not in the direction of school, but south, toward the river.

"The Kaveri River hadn't overflowed its banks at that time, but it was still formidable. They marched me four kilometers, away from my parents, away from the only village I'd ever known. They didn't bother untying me before throwing me in."

Larson observed the slight man in awe. "How did you manage to survive?"

"At first, I was certain I would not. The water was muddy and the current strong. Before the jeering boys became a memory, I struggled to keep my head afloat. By some miracle, they hadn't managed to tie my hands tight enough, and I wriggled them free. I undid the bonds around my feet and at least kept from drowning. But it was terrifying, thrashing all alone in the middle of a wide river. I tried to swim to shore and found it more pointless than piling sand before an onslaught of waves on a beach. I was exhausted and close to giving up when two men aboard a skiff pulled me out of the water.

"They weren't nice men, but they served a purpose. I believe everyone and everything in this world has a purpose. I was treated cruelly, but they gave me morsels of food and kept me alive. They didn't have to, but they did. And while I thanked them, as soon as we reached the Bay of Bengal the two climbed the coast to Pondicherry and sold me aboard a cargo vessel headed north for the Ganges River."

"Did you go?" Larson hadn't moved from his seat, eyeing the other man over his drink while he recounted his tale.

Bathari nodded.

"I had no choice. Life was not so bad as a deck hand. The work was hard, but I became accustomed to it. And nothing compared with my astonishment at seeing the world for the first time. I sometimes think that if Ishaan hadn't been killed perhaps I would have never left our little village.

That notion, missing out on all I've experienced, saddens me more than any other.

"The Ganges, longest and holiest river in India, was fascinating. But while it captured my senses, it was not what I'd expected. The river was dirty and dangerous. I abhorred the squelching ranks of poverty, unknown even to my own conditioning in a meager southern village, that festered, squalid and desperate, along its banks. By the time my barge neared its destination, a port not far from Delhi, I longed to escape. I had spent weeks aboard the vessel. In India's capital that escape was granted."

He tilted his chin and bade Larson follow him outside. The wealthy neighborhood was deserted. Bathari led the way around Mont Royal bathed in fading light to a grassy park strewn with a handful of people enjoying the last vestiges of a pleasant Canadian autumn. They walked, trailed by a bodyguard twenty yards back. Near an impressive obelisk at the Mont's base, Bathari spoke.

"I once held aspirations of being an artist. Unfortunately, this world's reality withered the bristles of my brush and delivered me to a higher calling. I have built something of a reputation over the years. A following might be a better way of putting it. It has taken much time, and it has not proven easy, but I'm fortunate. People seem receptive to the ideas I have brought into existence."

"And those are?"

Bathari cocked his head and fixed him with a calculating expression. "Chiefly, that humans cannot continue living this way. The system is not sustainable, and there is no infrastructure allowing it to be repaired from within. Mankind must adapt to ensure its survival. It goes against human nature, but the lone solution is sweeping change."

Bathari's large eyes were on him, but he continued to stare ahead.

"A radical idea."

A quiver passed through the man on his left. Like he

had been shocked with a bolt of energy from a nonexistent cloud.

"For many years my focus has been on America, but no longer. We have become a global community, and any lasting change must be affected on a global scale. I don't think in terms of political party. Parties, alliances, are a way of pitting society against one another, and this crucial juncture requires unity and streamlined decision making. Americans are perpetually divided and have allowed themselves to be split into factions for decades, failing to grasp the bigger picture."

"Political parties act as a vessel through which citizens support what they believe."

"In another era that was acceptable. But the populace is so busy squabbling over guns and religion that they're putting themselves at dire risk."

"Do you think guns should be outlawed?" Larson asked.

Bathari shrugged. "It doesn't matter. In the next century or two, we will be fighting for our very survival. Humanity's path ends abruptly."

"What do you mean?"

"Igor did his best to popularize this research, but it's a polarizing topic. No politician will touch it because it's career suicide. That's what politicians are, not a voice through which their unified constituents may speak, but people like you and me whose livelihoods depend on being elected. Most won't champion anything of true importance, even if it's the right thing to do, because it's a risk to their livelihood. Politicians have become a farce, and the American political system is churning to a bureaucratic standstill."

The paths cutting through Jeanne-Mance Park became doused in shadow as the sun slipped further behind Mont Royal. A giant crucifix burned at its peak, caught in the last dying embers.

Larson's mind churned, snippets of Bathari's words

bubbling to the surface so that he was unable to focus on any one thing.

"Is this what you propose—overthrow the American government?"

"I realize I am speaking to a man employed by the federal government of the United States." He shook his head. "I am trying to give you a thorough introduction to my doctrine. I realize how it must seem to you. I am a logical man. Prioritizing issues and devoting energies toward solving those of greatest necessity is my chief concern. Every problem on this planet over which we have a modicum of control is caused by a growing human population. Our numbers once hovered around one billion. Two centuries after the Industrial Revolution, we've reached eight. By the turn of the next century, we are projected to have surpassed eleven billion. I see a real problem that no government on earth is willing to do anything about."

"Even if they wanted to act, what could they do? America has no control over any other nation."

Bathari's expression clouded. "For now, America is still viewed as leader of the global community. Change would be most prolific and powerful if it were to stem from the White House. But therein lies the problem. Your leaders have become no better than the masses. They show an identical lack of wisdom and foresight. That revelation will be humanity's downfall."

They reached a quiet street lined with brownstones. Among a thick cover of elms, streetlamps and porchlights flickered to life. Bathari's minder followed, one hand resting in the pocket of his jacket wrapped around a handgun.

"You're wondering how I can be of value in your investigation into Igor's death," Bathari spoke as they passed a townhouse with parapets and granite that mimicked a castle. "I'm afraid I don't have specifics, but I can offer some advice that may prove valuable."

"Anything would be welcome."

He smiled in the waning light. "I began as a scholar

who grew into a leader of the educated and enlightened. I care about survival. Amendments should be changed if they aren't suited to present conditions. A government should be altered if it is not operating how it was envisioned. I believe the current model will doom us. Vocalizing this sentiment has made me unpopular with the regime in Washington. I see them for what they are—a sensationalist group preying on the masses by offering a string of trivialities that keep public attention occupied."

"What do they have to do with Stregor?"

"Think about Igor; a man who understood and spread the truth. Or even his sister, Elena, who has aided in forming the psychological rationale behind my doctrines. Who would have wanted to eliminate a man like Igor, who purported scientific discovery over diffusion of rumors and nonsense? Once you decide who had a motive, think about who performed the deed. The two are not necessarily the same, but they are almost certainly linked."

Larson said, "I can't speak candidly about my work, but it involves the growing threat of extremism. Much of what we do centers around right wing groups that have formed and thrived in the past decade."

"Most of which are purely academic, but some, in their innermost coiled rings, have become desperate and violent," Bathari said. "The demented are beginning to infiltrate aspects of normalized life. Skinheads realized they can achieve their goals by growing hair and covering their tattoos."

"So to speak."

Bathari gave him a knowing look. "Think about who controls those factions, and how all these circumstances tie into the plight of our unfortunate friend."

Larson could feel his counterpart growing distant, as if the interview was ending. He had one final question. It was posed as they passed the imposing Mont and gazed into Montreal's distant heart.

"How do you propose to change the American

government?"

There was a brief twinkle in Bathari's eyes before they clouded with such an extreme exhaustion that Larson was taken aback.

"I have pondered that question for thousands of hours. No matter how hard I try evoking different paths of thought, I always land on the same conclusion. Any large entity is lethargic and ineffective not because it chooses to be, but because each faction is so concerned with defeating the others, they forget the greater goal. I have weighed risks and benefits and arrived at the best solution. A small nucleus of wise, forward-thinking leaders that will act in humanity's best interest."

"In the name of serving humanity you would replace a regime nudging against authoritarianism with an outright dictatorship. How ironic."

"Not a dictatorship; a streamlined version of government that acts for the greater good. I understand that is a remarkably similar statement to the credo of every tyrant the world has ever known. In this instance, I consider the significance of the ends to be worthy of the means."

"Does human nature allow for the success of such a group?"

"I have my doubts. But Mr. Larson, you must put yourself in my position and ask—is it better to risk change or wait for an inevitable fate?"

Chapter Eighteen

October neared with a sense of urgency infiltrating the eighteenth floor of a gleaming office building in Rosslyn, Virginia. The sentiment, like a darkening storm cloud, grew as members of the secretive team dubbed Echelon surveyed the nation's capital across the Potomac or watched their leader pace back and forth through his open office door. A collective breath was held, an unspoken question churning inside each mind.

The burden of answers fell predominately on Eiran Katz's shoulders, but he had siphoned off some of the weight and laid it across the back of one shining pupil. Larson no longer slept well. He stayed late at the office and drove home in a delirious daze, only to rouse himself at the crack of dawn and travel back across the river well before the mob of morning commuters.

Despite this obsession with the alt-right's plans, Larson found it impossible to put aside his meeting with Samit Bathari. After returning home, he had taken a reprieve from the monotonous barrage of work to have dinner with Elena.

"He's either a genius or a madman," he had uttered.

She let a confident smile play across her lips. "The former, I assure you."

"You know he wants to uproot the entire federal government? But that's neither here nor there. I've been thinking about what he said—the only rational explanation."

She watched him work the pieces together in his mind.

"There has to be a connection between your brother, the alt-right, and someone within the government."

"But who is that missing piece?" she asked. "And how do we prove these connections."

Dessert had arrived with Larson still at a loss.

Larson sat in his office on the final Monday of September. A small tremor rather than a knock disturbed his work as Katz bulldozed inside and pulled short before his spartan yet modern desk. Larson looked up, bemused, and chose not to speak after catching a glimpse of Katz's expression.

"He made contact."

Larson didn't have to ask who. "Any information?"

The fact that the chief was turning pale before his eyes answered in the affirmative. "He wants a meeting. Day after next."

"Where will you—"

Katz cut him off. "Not me. You."

Larson was caught off guard. The mole, their hope for heading off another riotous display by the alt-right, had requested a meeting with—

"I guess I'll need to learn his name."

Katz's unease intensified as he paced back and forth.

"You'll get his name. And plenty more. Are you sure you're ready for all this, Larson?"

He didn't bother answering. In any case, he didn't have a choice.

The chief wasn't quite finished. Larson raised a questioning eyebrow.

"There's something else. Something we've all been dreading. When our mole made contact, he didn't say much, but he made one thing clear. Another attack is coming. And our odds for stopping it aren't good."

Chapter Nineteen

American intelligence is home to the most expansive team of hackers and data miners on earth. Although small and secretive in nature, Echelon was no exception to the rule.

That explained why Larson was unsurprised to receive a secure message on his mobile phone Wednesday while he sped across the Fourteenth Street Bridge.

The analysts had unearthed something. Two words. A code tag by the looks of it. Larson glanced at it before replacing the iPhone, but by then it was burned into his field of vision.

DESERT OASIS

He came no closer to uncovering its meaning as he navigated Washington, emerging near Lower Senate Park as the sun dipped toward Georgetown. Continuing north, he passed Union Station and slowed when traffic became ensconced in shadow by the looming headquarters of an oft-listened radio broadcast network. Larson parked along the curb and stepped onto the sidewalk.

His destination was not the radio building but a nearby tower dwarfing the same street. A sign touted the name UNETSO in green letters from its square apex. Larson didn't bother admiring the building's lobby before boarding an elevator. Closing doors blotted out a smiling receptionist and an aesthetically pleasing fountain, and he shut his eyes while the elevator ascended.

He was not surprised to find the reception area on the top floor deserted save another smiling drone with blond hair and a skirt showing off her ample legs. He flashed his Echelon identification not to her but to an armed man with a crew cut who appeared the moment he disembarked the elevator.

Satisfied, the guard led him around the corner and down a corridor of private offices. A conference room at the hall's end stood ajar. He was ushered inside and told to sit. The man disappeared, shutting the door behind him.

He counted the minutes in silence. The walls were glass and had an impeccable view of the surrounding area. This office space had been rented under the guise of a fictitious company, Katz had informed him, to serve as a secure meeting place. Significant money and effort expended for a man whose name and lot in life sounded so insignificant.

The door opened and Larson's mind flashed to a setup, a burst of gunfire, before the mole strode inside unaccompanied and sat.

Reginald Thompkins painted an uninspiring character from looks alone. Not tall but skinny in all the wrong places, middle-aged with a receding hairline and heavy-framed glasses that magnified beady eyes. He wore an off-putting mustache. He exuded laziness like an odor through his chino slacks and oxford cloth shirt. Both, Larson noted, appeared custom tailored.

As he studied the mole, Thompkins surveyed him with an impartial expression. There was a stark familiarity to the man. Then it all fell into place.

"You've been following me."

Thompkins eyed him and gave a sly jerk of the head that surmised a nod.

"Why?"

"Casual observance."

The mole's voice barely resonated over the air conditioning's hum. Still, getting usable information from him was going to prove difficult. Larson changed tack.

"You requested this meeting." It was not a question.

"I wanted a fresh set of ears. Katz is hard to get a hold of. He doesn't always seem to take my information seriously…Doesn't understand the danger I'm putting myself in."

"I can assure you that everything you pass along is considered of vital import—"

Thompkins cut him off. His voice raised an octave. "I've been watching you, observing how you work. Katz is a bureaucrat, but you're a true operative. That's a dying breed these days."

Larson rose and drifted toward the nearest wall of glass. "Why did you decide to betray the alt-right?"

He watched Thompkins carefully. The man didn't flinch. His pallid face remained grounded in neutrality. But when he spoke, his tone carried a hint of excitement.

"That answer should be forestalled by some background," Thompkins said. "Politics brought me to Washington. At first, it was everything I'd imagined. But after years toiling on campaigns for next to nothing and running enough coffee through the doors of Capitol Hill to jolt awake a small nation, I became disenfranchised. The system was a sham, our supposed leaders accomplishing little. Rather than continue to watch democracy inch forward at a snail's pace, I got out."

"Where did you go?"

"This was before the turn of the decade. I possessed plenty of political experience, even if occupying a seat in the Senate was no longer in my future. Luck would have it that

I was able to secure a job with a think tank called the National Policy Institute, run by a man named—"

"Robert Spencer."

Thompkins nodded. "Knowing your line of work, I'm sure the name is familiar. Without my employer, your team might not even exist. Spencer coined the term 'alternative right'. I've worked for him ever since, rising through the ranks and hoarding trust."

Larson shook his head. "But you came to us." Thompkins appeared to gather his thoughts.

"Eventually it all went too far. The alt-right launched as a faction who wanted to preserve western culture. A noble ideal, in a vacuum. But the ideology grew and spread. Radicals and racists latched on. It turned into a marked group spewing hatred and isolationism, preaching violence. With the recent election, everything spilled over the top. Something had to be done. It was my duty to act."

"So, you found Echelon."

"Your group is difficult to contact, but I've acquired many connections over the years. I put out feelers and one managed to reach the ears of Eiran Katz. Almost like a Cold War defection, you might say."

"Plenty of those defectors were killed for what they did," Larson said.

Thompkins nodded in earnest. "That's why I'm here. A lot of people are going to die if you don't listen to what I have to say."

Larson placed both hands on the sturdy table running the room's length and leaned forward.

"What can you tell me about the phrase 'Desert Oasis'?"

Thompkins expression went blank. "I've never heard it—either in the course of my work with the think tank or the alt-right."

"Where will the next show of unrest take place?"

"I haven't been told. The men who head that part of the movement are very careful. Officially, they have nothing to do with the institute. Information is disseminated at the last possible minute."

"Give me something."

Thompkins swallowed hard.

"The extremist minority within the alt-right is gaining momentum. Several of them were interspersed in the masses that pervaded Charlottesville. Their leaders become more outspoken by the day in favor of a show of violent dominance."

Larson slammed his palm on the table.

"Something is coming," Thompkins squeaked. "And you were right, by the way. The timing of the scientist's capture and the first riot was not a coincidence."

"That's not enough to help us."

He sensed the man across the table wavering. And with a final prolonged stare, he broke.

"I caught wind of a date."

"When?"

"October First."

Larson turned without a word and was already retreating from the conference room before the alt-right mole could react.

Two days.

He had to reach Elena.

PART TWO

Chapter Twenty

A president couldn't be all-powerful. Not by himself. A complex network needed to be established. Layers of bedrock supporting the monument. A nucleus of aides surrounding him like moons orbiting a planet, serving as an information barrier, and delivering on myriad fundamental duties that were critical to success. How much of the public would balk if they found out a collection of ambitious twenty-somethings ran the show? How many would protest the system if they understood what went on behind closed doors?

A president was not all-powerful, even if he thought he was. And sometimes he wasn't even the brains of the operation.

Dillon Drollsworth was much more than an aide. For starters, he was older than all his fellow underlings. Much older. Then came the fact that, until ten months ago, he had never met the current president. But here he was.

He stepped through a discrete back door of the White

House complex, if any door in the pillared vicinity could be termed discrete, and into a waiting Chevy Suburban. Blacked out windows and rugged body armor—standard for all presidential vehicles.

The Suburban took off toward the property's heavily guarded perimeter. He had come from a heated Cabinet meeting. Drollsworth was no closer to being appointed a member of Cabinet than he was to playing guitar for Lynyrd Skynyrd, but he attended every meeting all the same. Special advisory capacity to the president, his haughty look said, steel eyes wide and baiting and one eyebrow cocked, when the Chief of Staff or Secretary of Defense shot him a scathing glance. He would smirk before turning away.

The scenery of Lafayette Square formed on his right. He let it roll by without seeing. His eyes were the stuff of a horror movie villain, dead and gleaming. Drollsworth had used them to scare opponents and pawns alike over the years. Wrinkles bunched at their corners and his waxy, pointed face gave as good an estimate as any to the number of years in question.

His windswept not quite blond haircut and a fictitious glow of sun on his skin would fool only the most gullible observers. Drollsworth failed to hide another malicious smirk as the motorcade turned onto New York Avenue and entered the area Washingtonians referred to as NoMa. A hoarse chuckle set his white teeth ablaze in the reflection. It fell flat on the cabin's dead air.

Appearance and a novice relationship with politics were all that tethered Drollsworth and the president. Unlike the latter, he was never drawn to the business world. Growing up on a family estate in the Louisiana heartland, his father saw to it that the young Dillon Drollsworth never wanted for anything. He was sent away to attend a prestigious private school on the east coast, and later spurned acceptance to several Ivy League colleges to return home and attend the state university.

A transformation into manhood hadn't happened all at

once. Snippets of the alteration overwhelmed his thoughts. Boarding a ship off New Orleans' muddy banks. Sitting cross-legged and sweaty on a crowded skiff humming down a river thousands of miles away, whose color and shape were that of a coiled anaconda. Standing in a tent full of smoke and feeling its effects coalesce in his veins, turning his steely rat's eyes into weapons that could pierce the forest. Coming to in a prop plane flying dangerously low over a ravine bisecting dense jungles in Southeast Asia, weightless as a gnat preparing to be swatted out of the humid air by God's thumb. Sensing the steel of pointed guns below.

Each flash of memory served a purpose. They had all led him toward one specific moment in time, although he wasn't aware of that transcendent bit of truth in those days. One figure would occupy that singular moment. Not his father, who he had followed like an obedient foot soldier. This person was different, infinitely more awe-inspiring. Meeting him had set Drollsworth's life in motion.

Destiny had arrived as promised. He turned to focus on the woman sitting to his left. Her attention fixed on the bright iPad screen in her lap. Fingers ending in painted talons blazed over its surface. Feeling his gaze, the hands paused, and she looked up.

Her complexion was pale and her features bordering Slavic, but no one had ever suspected that Hannah Harper was not a natural born American. Not when she came from a red-blooded family like the Harper clan, New York royalty, and owned a notable vacation home in the Hamptons that had made several appearances in both film and television.

But Drollsworth knew the truth. The youngest and least recognizable Harper had absconded a Belorussian orphanage before her tenth birthday and suffered everything down to the very essence of the motherland being teased out of her by the stern and unwavering hand of her new family.

Two decades later and she was startlingly pretty. Thick, arching eyebrows and pursed red lips complimented her face's ivory palette. Bone structure women everywhere would kill for. Her long hair was pulled back in a severe ponytail that had become her staple. The only thing ruining the effect was the monstrous pair of wraparound sunglasses she wore at all hours, as though she insisted on shielding as much as possible from view. Heat from her sizzling gaze behind the lenses hit him, each more impervious than the backseat window.

Some had taken to calling the young White House Communications Director 'Ground Control'. The temperamental presidential rocket couldn't fire into orbit without her permission. Hardly a word left his mouth without passing her screening process if she could help it.

Hannah Harper also served another purpose, one her slender acrobat's fingers were tending to on the tablet sitting atop a stack of folders in her lap.

"I *really* don't like when you look at me like that," she said before returning her furrowed gaze to the screen.

"I was hoping for a smile," he said with devilish intonation. She didn't take the bait.

"I'm busy, if you hadn't noticed."

Drollsworth sighed, pivoting away from her to glance out the armored window. They had left downtown behind and were spiriting through sprawling landscape between inner city and suburbs. A bus depot and a strip mall flashed by. Drollsworth disliked such areas. He abhorred anything that lacked concrete purpose.

As the Suburban exited a roundabout onto Montana Avenue, he tried again.

"Is there anything new to report on Elena Stregor?"

This time, she forgot the look of concealed disgust.

"She's in New York City, but our man was certain the two have communicated. Turns out he's correct. An hour ago, she booked a flight back that's due to take off at eight tonight."

"Larson summoned her?"

"It's possible."

"Does that mean he knows?"

She said nothing, but her expression indicated that that, too, was possible.

"You wanted Larson to find out."

"Yes. But I must admit that a significant part of me doubted whether he would. Perhaps I underestimated him. Has he booked a flight?"

Harper shook her head.

"Then maybe he hasn't discovered quite as much as we thought. Let me know if that changes. And our man on the ground?"

"Has made contact and received the package. Everything seems to be in order."

She was young, but clever. Ambitious. She would make a good politician one day, if she lasted that long. The lull in questioning started her back on the incessant typing.

He felt a sudden urge to take in some fresh air as they neared their destination. Something besides the fact that the rear window regulators had been disabled for security reasons made him resist.

Ever since coming to Washington, he had developed an affinity for the National Arboretum. Now they stopped in front of the R Street entrance, which was cordoned off by a sign alerting patrons to an unexpected closure. The Suburban banked left, nearly toppling the sign in its wide arc of rubber and fortified steel. An explanation still eluded him by the time they were rerouted along three narrow streets and arrived at the Arboretum's main entrance. This time, the gates were open. Drollsworth found the closure out of the ordinary but said nothing.

They drove deep into a maze of fields and forest that grew alongside the Anacostia River. Drollsworth waited for a particular moment, a familiar sight amid green patchwork.

A rectangular pattern of fading Greek columns sprang to life in a field where the trees gave way. Drollsworth didn't have to say a word. Their transport eased to a stop, and Harper handed him a mobile phone without looking up.

He emerged and exhaust dusted his lower legs when the Suburban pulled away. Drollsworth dialed a number from memory.

The conversation was quick, finished by the time his ride looped around to collect him. For discretionary reasons it was not allowed to take place in a vehicle operated by the President of the United States. Harper's iPad was technically her own personal property and never seen or referenced by the president or any member of his Cabinet.

Drollsworth slid back inside and handed off the burner with a feigned grimace. Harper slipped it inside a bag at her feet, understanding his expression without the need to question.

Their man in the city was in position. The package had already been received.

The contractor on the other end of the call had uttered one sentence. It sounded alien and clipped through a voice scrambler, but it carried all the information Drollsworth needed. Every detail was falling into place. He was about to board a plane.

Chapter Twenty-One

A lone sheep broke from the pack and shuffled courageously forward. The others watched it go until it was over a ridge and out of sight. When it didn't reappear after several moments, they seemed content to return to their grazing.

The hillside was bathed in swatches of green gasping for life amid mixing hues of bracken. It sloped down to the crescent harbor's steep cliffs, where land met frigid blue waters.

A singular red cottage broke the monotonous run of earth tones and patchy foliage. The aluminum roof could expect to be covered with snow in the coming weeks as the year's final months gave way.

Alongside the cottage, which had an outstanding view of the sound, a few outbuildings and a tight grove of resilient shrubbery were all that dotted the pastureland. From the air, it appeared that specks of snow were already beginning to congregate on the ground. Until they moved, that was, or one fluffy pinprick lifted its head with a baleful look and a mouthful of wilting vegetation. The flock was due for shearing.

The sound had been choppy that day and the wind was starting to strengthen. A bank of clouds gathered to the northwest, amassing over a neighboring island. There were none nearby, but squawking colonies of penguins to the south and a platoon of barking seals could be imagined as the storm rolled closer. Dark clouds brought along a nervous energy that animals could sense.

The cottage's owner could sense it too, although it had little to do with nature and more the voice that had spoken curt instructions via a tenuous cellular connection. He turned away from the cliffs, lit a cigarette, and ambled toward the cottage.

Thatcher had not always been his name. The original had died, like everything else concerning Elijah Brookmore, somewhere between Britain and the Falkland Islands. Before he'd known what it was like to stand on the cliffs of Port San Carlos, numb in the face from biting wind and a cigarette held in gloved fingers. If he had known, he would have cast aside the trappings of that old life much sooner.

Voluntary service in Her Majesty's royal army had been the triggering occurrence. The Falkland Islands, three hundred miles off Argentina's southern coast, were a foreign territory occupied by Britain. The military base at Mount Pleasant, thirty-three miles south of the archipelago's capital, was mountainous and secluded.

Thatcher had braved the base for a month, living in barracks and watching aircraft come and go. It had been noted by his superiors that he excelled in the tenets of combat, particularly marksmanship. In the eyes of the Queen's military, Thatcher stood out from the other grunts cohabiting the base. He stood out far more when they awoke one morning to find that he had vanished into thin air.

It was discovered after the fact that a military vehicle had been stolen and driven off base the previous night. Perimeter guards had remained nonplussed when interviewed. The driver—charming smile but eyes that never thawed in the meager Falkland summer—had proper documentation. How he managed to obtain it remained a mystery.

The vehicle resurfaced in nearby Fitzroy, where it was discovered by bewildered British officials submerged in a shallow harbor. Shortly thereafter, a small boat was reported stolen by a local fisherman. That boat, *Beautiful Nelly*, the distraught fisherman insisted it was named, was never seen again.

Thatcher glanced back for a moment at the inky spot where the derelict scraps of the john boat had vanished. Even near shore the water was deep, unlike the opposite side of East Falkland. Technically still a Brit, he'd considered himself a naturalized islander for the past decade.

After his disappearance, the army had searched for a month. Thatcher followed their efforts in the Falkland's newspaper as he moved from settlement to settlement, even spending some time in Stanley, the islands' lone reasonably sized township. He understood that if he remained careful, they would grow tired of searching. A soldier gone AWOL on a remote bit of rock in the South Atlantic could tie up tax funds for only so long. There was one resounding truth on the Falklands—a person could be left alone.

Except...

Thatcher's thoughts flitted again to the conversation. Less tête-à-tête, more specifics of an arrangement being laid forth. Nervous energy transformed into a twinging of excitement. There would be more to come as the time grew closer.

He slipped inside, changed out of ragged chinos into an expensive pinstripe suit, and packed a few sets of clothes into an Italian leather bag. Glancing down, he noted his physique under the suit. Trim and muscular. Two lethal appendages, still pink with cold, protruded from the hand-stitched cuffs.

He kept no mirrors in the cottage for good reason. Victim of a bomb placed by an anarchist group in the London metro, he had been badly burned as a child. Even after countless surgeries, his ruined face still resembled a pale death mask. It had been years since he last laid eyes on his grotesque features.

A Glock 18, his weapon of choice, was the last item he packed, tucking it into the bag along with a pair of silencers and a sleeve of ammunition.

A gaucho who lived in one of the refurbished outbuildings would take care of the sheep while he was gone. Thatcher left the cottage and a few moments later sat behind the wheel of a 1955 Austin-Healey Roadster.

Despite the cold, he drove fast along the two-lane road that was little more than a dirt tract through hilly pastureland bisecting the archipelago's second largest island. Mountains ridged along its center like a dragon's back. The first dark clouds tumbled over their rocky peaks as he zipped east. A storm was imminent.

Port Stanley Airport was little more than a runway and a tiny terminal facing two decrepit hangars that resembled oversized garden sheds. Thatcher threw a tarp over the vintage Roadster and left it parked near the terminal as he had dozens of other times. Clutching his solitary bag, he boarded a jet with *Aerolíneas Argentinas* painted on the side in blue letters.

The smiling stewardess waiting atop the stairs was unfamiliar. Her expression sank into a frown as she set her eyes on him. He worried she might speak, raise a warning palm to stop him, or even scream at his deformed facial features.

A man in a pilot's uniform happened to be passing on his way toward the cockpit. He took one glance at Thatcher and laid a hand on her shoulder. They communicated for a split second with their eyes. Smiling again, the flight attendant led him to a window seat in row three. Thatcher elected to keep his bag tucked at his feet. As the sound of the jet turbines coming to life drowned everything, he let his surroundings sink away.

Consciousness returned when the *Aerolíneas*

Argentinas jet landed in Buenos Aires three hours later. He walked through the concourse with the leather bag in his left hand, studying each traveler that passed. Pale faces and European features; packs of university-age girls gabbing to one another in Spanish or families herding their young like the sheep he'd left behind.

The setting sun poured into the concourse like molten gold coming through the many windows and glass porticos in the ceiling. Thatcher examined it all with muted disinterest until he reached the next gate and boarded a much bigger plane bound for Los Angeles.

He pulled out of the Avis rental lot at LAX in a black Jaguar F-Type on Saturday at mid-morning. His bag was stashed on the passenger seat and the gun secured in the waist of his pants. It felt at home, cold metal pressing against the skin of his lower back—ready for use.

Thatcher hardly noticed desert scenery flitting past as he drove. A sand-strewn, khaki wasteland in stark contrast to the last time he had visited the states. Desolate vegetation clung to life along the roadside. His considerable conscious was busy resurrecting the plan and poring over each detail. As if he could see into the future, he watched it all come to life, piece by piece.

When he caught sight of a city in the distant haze that had been named for meadows spread across a once empty desert valley, excitement swelled again. The skyline bloomed like lilies unfolding out of dust. A stir of elation. He had completed the drive in just over three hours. The first piece was falling into place.

Thatcher considered ordering a hooker as he checked in at a gaudy hotel where his lodgings had been pre-arranged. Anything to kill the time while he waited.

He remembered what the man on the line's other end had said and tensed as a smiling concierge activated his room key. The warning echoed until he slipped into his thoughts and shut it off.

She was coming, but she wouldn't be alone.

Chapter Twenty-Two

The last inbound flight from Dulles to McCarran International Airport landed three minutes after six in the evening. A solitary passerby, a tall gentleman loitering in the concourse and nursing a week's worth of hangovers while waiting for his flight, noted that a husband and wife were first to emerge from the jet way.

On second thought, perhaps the relationship was more platonic, or even familial, given the way they seemed to quarrel like siblings. The attractive woman he had taken for the man's wife appeared determined to keep pace, all the while whispering unintelligible waspish remarks at her partner's back. The man, for his part, was doing his best to ignore her.

The gentleman shrugged and turned away from the curious paring. By the time his flight was called over the intercom, he had already forgotten them.

Larson led the way through the concourse, glancing around to make sure they hadn't attracted undue attention. Elena was hot on his heels.

"What are we doing here?" she hissed.

She brushed his arm, but he continued walking.

"I agreed to board the plane with you, but now I require answers."

He had never seen her furious in the short time he'd known her. Still, he forged ahead in silence, putting distance between the gate and lagging passengers that receded with each heated step. When Elena squeezed his forearm with more force than expected, Larson shook her free and whipped around.

"I'll explain when it's safe. Not here, where we might be overheard."

"Like you explained on the plane?"

"It wasn't secure."

"Or back in Washington?"

"There wasn't time. You have to trust me, Elena. Soon you'll understand everything, including how dire the situation we're facing is."

She didn't respond. Larson took that as a resentful acquiescence. The desert sun was favoring distant California by the time they rented a car and mounted an outbound stretch of asphalt. Tourists flocked the base of the iconic signage on Las Vegas Boulevard. He was focused elsewhere. Namely, on what they were supposed to do next.

Elena huffed behind him and danced her weight from one foot to the other while he checked into a room at the Tropicana hotel. Dated in comparison to its behemoth neighbors, nevertheless the resort's interior appeared clean and modern. Larson ignored celebratory vibrations of gamblers in the nearby casino as he was handed two room keys.

When they reached the room, Elena brushed past him and flung herself onto the bed in a seated position. Fire danced in her eyes.

"Explain."

Larson's thoughts blurred together, caught in a whirlwind inside his head. He crossed to the curtained window and surveyed the outer fringes of the Strip before responding.

"Desert Oasis," he said.

Elena cocked her head and pursed her lips.

"Desert Oasis. The only clue we received as to what's coming. I couldn't fathom what it was supposed to mean, and then it clicked. Las Vegas. A figurative oasis smack in the middle of a desert. It makes perfect sense."

Elena's eyes widened. She let her rigid posture relax and unfolded her arms.

"And the timing—"

"The date was always firm. October first. I've been following local news—I don't think anything's happened yet. But something is coming."

She joined him at the window. Fear mixed with stubbornness amid the usual trappings of her beauty.

"How do we stop it?" she asked.

Silence filled the room.

"We'll find a way."

They left the Tropicana and crossed a pedestrian bridge over the busy thoroughfare. Crowds were beginning to swell as evening approached. Sin City's nocturnal visitors re-emerged into the last baking rays of light as the sun disappeared behind the opposite side of the Strip.

Larson bought dinner and they ate on the still-smoldering terrace. Up and down the Strip, signage flashed on hotel walls and electronic billboards for the finale performance of a music festival, a well-known country artist, taking place that night in Las Vegas Village.

He eyed the cowboy hat and expensive boots, and led Elena away with no destination in mind, searching his mind for a spark that would appear and prove to be their solution to everything.

No such spark flamed into existence as they entered a

mall in front of the ARIA Resort. Larson kept his eyes peeled, while Elena adopted the posture and gait of a model approaching a runway's end. Nevertheless, her eyes couldn't help fixating on the luxury stores lining the concourse.

"You have expensive taste," he murmured out of the corner of his mouth, watching her ogle a window display featuring a famous Italian designer.

"With what I've been through, I think life should concede me that much," Elena said. She squared her shoulders away from the panorama.

"You're nervous."

"Only that we won't find a way to stop this madness in time. I don't think I can stand more blood on my hands."

"We will."

They rounded a bend and passed another row of boutiques.

"And your hands are clean. That blood stained the men who killed your brother."

They walked for another half hour. Larson never stopped surveying their surroundings. They ascended to the second floor and slipped into a crowded shoe store. Elena pretended to browse, Larson humming as he stalked the tall aisles behind her. After several minutes, they left hand in hand.

Larson refused to glance over his shoulder. Instead, he leaned toward Elena and whispered in her ear, "I think you were wrong to worry."

"Why?"

He hesitated, familiar pangs of operational anxiety twisting his insides.

"We're being followed."

She went rigid but thankfully, he noted, had the good sense not to spin around. They returned to the ground floor; her sweaty palm still intertwined in his.

"How did they know where to find us?" Elena whispered.

He adjusted his sleeve and tipped her a knowing look. "I doubt we were discovered in a shopping mall. Odds are we've been marked since our plane touched down."

"What do we do?"

"Continue walking."

They exited amid model-clad wall ads and a giant black monolith promoting an adjacent resort. Larson directed his partner to a flight of windswept stairs ensconced in glass.

Hordes of happy pedestrians crossing the breezeway above mixed with the cacophony of traffic below.

They reached level ground and fought across a teeming walkway spanning the eight-lane street below. At the bridge's end, he guided Elena under a giant obelisk advertising a popular musical act and into the Cosmopolitan hotel.

The resort consisted of two towers set atop a massive platform several stories thick. Its base, plated with chrome and glass and brimming with pastimes of the desert town known as Sin City, was the perfect place to lose their tail.

Or, at least, glimpse his face.

Passing restaurants, they hurried through a windowless hall filled with slot machines and blackjack tables. Next to a strand of shops, they disappeared in a crowd of spiky haired gentlemen. When the crowd dispersed, Larson still sensed the third, trailing presence.

Rounding a bend, he chanced a glance at their adversary. It was quick, enough time to detect a sloping forehead and a pair of expressionless, cold eyes.

He led Elena outside at a more hurried pace. Another elevated walkway crossed Las Vegas Boulevard. Ducking around throngs of people, they entered a second gambling concourse. Their adversary quickened his pace.

This casino was less crowded; columns of light and a soft pink glow illuminated an Art Deco interior. He tugged Elena's arm, hurrying her past a row of floor to ceiling chandeliers that undulated like coiling jellyfish in the purple-hued foyer and up a flattened escalator.

An oblivious couple reached the bottom of the escalator and vanished from sight as the man with cold eyes arrived at its base. One weathered hand floated to his waist as he stared up at them.

"When we reach the top, be ready to run," Larson murmured.

Elena trembled against him.

Moving pathway yielded to glossy marble and they ran.

Heavy footfalls on a hollow surface informed Larson their assailant had done the same. He had time to see the concierge's jaw drop before he pulled Elena around a corner and through a softly lit lounge. Scattered guests stared at the man and woman sprinting across their vision. A bartender gave a halfhearted shout that was lost in the commotion.

Larson tore down a carpeted hallway with Elena on his heels. Breathing hard, his mind numb with shock, he plumbed its depths for their next move. It came in the form of a heavy door. He shouldered it open and pulled Elena inside the stairwell.

After three flights, the echo of their frantic footsteps was joined by sounds of another. Heavier and unhurried, like the drumbeat accompanying a death march. He slowed, panting, motioning to an exit on their right.

"Through here."

He turned the handle and heaved. His heart sank. The heavy door wouldn't budge.

An electronic pad designed to be activated by an issued room key flanked their escape. Elena let out a muffled cry of despair.

"Now what do we do?"

The cold-eyed man was getting closer. A true hunter, Larson thought. They were the prey he'd been hired to exterminate.

He was on the verge of telling Elena to continue climbing, that he would hold the attacker off, when he glimpsed the face crest around the corner. Not American. There was something in the way his thinning hair was coifed, or how his hideous, deformed features were arranged. And he was holding a gun.

Without thinking, Larson stepped sideways and shoved Elena out of harm's way. He crouched low as the gun's arc climbed higher, preparing to lunge at the assailant from his elevated position, when the heavy door to his right burst open.

In the moments that followed, Larson could do nothing more than throw himself to the ground and brace for impact. There was the ringing of gunfire. Two shots and a burst of smoke, then silence.

Larson straightened, keeping Elena pinned to the ground with one shaking hand. The would-be assassin lay on the concrete landing and rolled in agony. A modest figure three yards to their right stood with his head ducked and eyes half open. A gun was still raised in his trembling hand.

As Larson watched, it dropped to the ground, and he vomited violently.

"I've never shot a man before," Reggie Thompkins spoke in a quavering voice, straightening.

"You may have to do it again," Larson said. "He isn't dead."

"I-I can't."

He retrieved the forfeited gun and descended. The assassin clutched above his clavicle at the base of his neck. Blood spilled onto stained concrete like a park fountain gone awry. The other hand groped wildly for his own weapon.

Larson spotted it lying a couple feet away and kicked it out of reach. He leaned over, examining the dying man. Definitely not American.

"Who sent you?"

The assassin stared at him, eyes ablaze, and spat into the air.

He raised the gun in his left hand and pulled the trigger.

Chapter Twenty-Three

Thompkins was forced at gunpoint into a desk chair inside a plain room at the Tropicana hotel. His hands were bound by a roll of duct tape.

Dusk had arrived while Larson dragged the dead body to the stairwell's base and stuffed it in a dark corner. It would be found eventually, hopefully long after they had vacated the city.

Now he turned to Thompkins' tearstained face silhouetted by Las Vegas coming to life in the first throes of night and grimaced.

"Tell me everything you know." Larson held the gun, albeit dangling at his side with the safety in place. Still, he had few qualms about putting it to use if the man who had just saved their lives didn't start talking.

"What I know?" Thompkins blubbered. "I-I don't know anything."

He raised the gun and aimed between the prisoner's eyes while Elena watched from the bed over a steaming cup of tea. She appeared unfazed by the interrogation.

"You knew we would be here. How?"

Thompkins' eyes darted around the hotel room. After several moments, his incomprehensible stammers became silence.

Larson took an ominous step forward. "I met with you in Washington. Debriefed you. You told me something was coming. You didn't give specifics, said you hadn't been filled in on the details, but you had a date—October first."

He landed a crashing blow on Thompkins' trembling jaw with his right hand. The slight man cried out in pain.

"I need answers."

Thompkins leaned back as far as his rigid bonds would allow. Involuntary tears pooled in the corners of his eyes. His mouth sagged like a deflated circus tent.

"I-I found out you were coming here from your office. Something is going to happen today, but that's a-all I know. I swear!"

Larson's voice rose, nearing a crescendo. "Who was the man following us?"

"He was nobody. Contracted. I've heard others mention him but never even learned his name!"

They were getting nowhere. He had a feeling time was running out. A sharp look from Elena conveyed her agreement.

He yanked the captive forward and buried the gun's nose in the flesh of his paunchy cheek. Winding the front of his shirt into a ball with his fist, Larson breathed.

"It takes one trigger pull to put you out of business. And I'm willing to do it if you don't start talking."

There were more effective means of getting a confession, but there wasn't time. In hindsight, it needn't have mattered. The cold steel of the gun broke all resolve that remained in Thompkins' reservoir. He let out a gasping sob and closed his eyes.

"Talk!"

"Alright, I'll tell you everything. Please don't shoot!"

He didn't remove the gun until his captor's jaw ground haltingly into motion. When he did, as the words flowed, it was with much reluctance.

"I-I was told a date and nothing more. I passed it along to you. Yesterday, long after your analysts discovered the code phrase, *Desert Oasis*, someone with high standing at the National Policy Institute let slip the second attack's location. By the time I contacted my handler, you had already discovered the same and were on your way here.

"Rivera was the one who informed me where you'd gone. He overheard from an irate Director Katz. I saw no choice but to follow. Inadvertently, I was told other things. Things you could have no way of knowing."

"What kind of things?"

"She's wanted." Thompkins jerked his head in Elena's direction.

"I am well aware of this," she said with a scoff.

Larson hadn't taken his eyes off the bound man.

"You're wanted as well." He stared into the face of his captor.

"By whom?"

"The men I am betraying by speaking to you."

"The alt-right hired an assassin to come to Vegas and kill Elena?"

"And you," Thompkins said.

He caught Elena's eye. She stood and set her mug down hard.

"D-Don't you see?" Thompkins said. "It was a trap to lure the two of you here. Feed you little bits of information at a time. Tantalizing bits. And when you arrived, a very dangerous man would be waiting."

Larson moved behind the captive, in between him and the window awash with neon lights. His hand tightened on the pistol's grip.

"You do realize that the man who fed us those bits of information…was you."

"And I saved your life. I've been watching the pair of

you, on their orders, even back in Washington. But I never allowed you to come into harm."

Larson raised the gun, setting its nose into the crook at the base of Thompkins' skull. A whimper escaped him.

"So, there is no imminent alt-right attack?"

He let out an involuntary shudder. "No, the attack is real. It's due to start any moment. They must have seen it as a convenient ploy to lure the two of you into the desert and be finished with you. Now, I'm not sure you'll have time to save the day."

"What's going to happen?"

"I wasn't privy to every detail."

Elena strode forward and smacked Thompkins hard across the face. Larson kept the gun ground into his neck, index finger extended beside the trigger. She smacked him again with the other hand.

"Where?"

Reggie Thompkins had played his part. He didn't hesitate. He told her everything.

The taxi screeched to a halt on the corner of Las Vegas Boulevard. Elena flung a wad of cash at the driver and flooded out behind Larson. They sprinted toward a tri-sided tower glinting strips of gold that illuminated the entire block.

They navigated a walkway guarded by ornate winged dragons and decorative palm trees, then under a gazebo and along a jagged path crested by waterfalls and shimmering ponds.

She was panting behind him near the resort's covered entrance when gunfire erupted. At first a few pops, firecrackers bursting in the night. Then a barrage of hellfire that drowned out all sounds of the concert across the street.

Larson pulled her to safety as the rain of gunfire intensified. Round after round, pouring from a window high on the tower's eastern face. Its destination was confirmed after several moments when the echoing guitar and drums ceased and were replaced by screams that split the night apart and curdled her blood.

Larson clutched her near the elaborate entrance to Mandalay Bay and waited for the familiar flashes of color and sirens to pierce the evening.

Tears dripped down her face when the first responders arrived. Ignoring them, they rushed into the hotel with guns drawn. Many more had streamed in by the time the gunfire stopped.

For a moment, in between a swell of sirens and ambulances and screams of the wounded, the night was quiet.

Chapter Twenty-Four

October Third, 6:40 A.M.

I am so proud of our Great Country. God Bless America!

The text jumped off the screen. Posted to a popular social media platform in the immediate wake of the Las Vegas tragedy while most would still be enjoying their morning coffee. Sender—the President of the United States.

Larson reread the words as he turned onto a two-lane street and pulled to a stop along a brick sidewalk lined with lampposts and restored buildings. The makings of a historic town coming to life unfurled around him. After a third read, he darkened the iPhone screen. Grabbing a folded newspaper and a steaming thermos of coffee, he exited his Mercedes and walked.

Like most of the Washingtonian elite, Echelon's Director owned a summer residence outside the city. Easton was a Maryland town home to sixteen thousand people and situated ninety minutes from the capital on the Delmarva Peninsula. Known for its affinity for arts and culture, its colonial roots culminated in positioning ten miles from the locally renowned Battle of St. Michaels that took place during the War of 1812.

It didn't take long for Larson to reach his destination. He sat on a bench across from an impressive brick inn and eyed his surroundings. Shops and restaurants around the quaint intersection were still closed. A few cars and dispirited joggers passed. Nobody paid him any mind as he unfolded the newspaper and read.

The Vegas massacre was the headline, as it had been the previous morning. That an agent of the clandestine intelligence assemblage called Echelon and the sister of a notable murdered scientist had been close enough to touch the hotel when the shooting began was neither reported nor speculated.

Murky facts surrounding the shooting were largely identical, only this morning the death totals had been augmented. Fifty-eight killed. Eight hundred and fifty-one injured. The Route 91 Harvest music festival had been brought to an abrupt halt when a sixty-four-year-old man from a small town in Nevada opened fire from the thirty-second floor of the Mandalay Bay resort. Eleven hundred rounds were dispersed in a ten-minute span shortly after ten.

Disgusted, Larson unfolded the front page and delved deeper into the story. Many details had yet to come together. The killer's motive remained a mystery to the public. As did how he had smuggled so much heavy weaponry into his hotel room. Chief of all lingered a singular question: why had it taken law enforcement over an hour to breach the suspect's room?

Hoping to purport even more havoc, the shooter had fired at a jet fuel storage pod on the property of McCarron International Airport. Luckily, jet fuel contained kerosene and didn't ignite when struck by gunfire.

When police finally entered the room, it was to find the shooter dead of a self-inflicted gunshot wound in front of a shattered window that overlooked what amounted to a parking lot blighted by a sea of dead and wounded.

Larson glanced at the article's author beneath the bold heading before refolding the paper and setting it aside. It rang familiar, but in a way he couldn't quite put his finger on.

There was nothing left to do but drink his coffee and ponder until a familiar suited figure materialized on the sidewalk. Without a word he sat next to Larson, keeping his gaze focused straight ahead. For several placid moments neither man spoke.

Larson broke the silence. "You were summoned as well?"

"Yes, but not for the same reason as you," Diego said. "Katz thought you could use someone keeping an eye on you after what happened."

"He doesn't think I can look after myself?"

"I believe he mentioned something along those lines. He's not happy about your foray across the country."

"And does he realize that what happened in Las Vegas was the alt-right striking again?" Larson seethed. "I was the only one who tried to do anything about it."

Diego raised a noncommittal shoulder. "He didn't say."

Realizing he wouldn't get anywhere with this line of questioning he changed the subject. "Are you familiar with the name Karen Sanders?"

Diego looked bewildered. "Yes, aren't you?"

He shook his head.

"Obviously, or else you wouldn't have asked. You read her Vegas piece on the front page of the Post?"

"Yes, but I swear I've seen the name before."

"I don't see how you couldn't have. She's been crafting a persona as the most fearless woman in journalism for years. Karen Sanders isn't just willing to ask the hard questions, she goes where it's happening. She rode in a tank when American forces stormed Baghdad. There is some far-fetched speculation that she was even held hostage for a time while covering a rebellion in Venezuela."

Larson knitted his eyebrows. His colleague wasn't finished.

"These days she's best known for her stance against the new president's regime. With the way things are going, it's only a matter of time before they shut her up."

Just then, the person Larson least wanted to see appeared in a doorway across the street. His glare, visible despite the distance, was the inaugural sign that the coming interaction would not be pleasant. Without speaking, the chief raised one finger and beckoned. Heart sinking and catching a look of condolence from Diego as he stood, Larson dutifully obeyed.

Katz continued his vow of silence as they walked alongside a white picket fence, letting the tension build like a pressure cooker bound to explode. He siphoned off some steam in a seething sentence.

"You had no authority to do what you did."

He said nothing to abate the furious storm that was coming.

"Leaving Washington, going to Las Vegas. It's outside our jurisdiction!"

"We don't have a jurisdiction. We don't exist."

"Everyone has a jurisdiction. And from now on, yours doesn't extend beyond your desk. What would you have done if you'd encountered the shooter?"

"I would have tried to take him down."

"It took a trained SWAT team over an hour to get inside that room. Word has it that he had at least ten high-powered rifles, enough munitions to sink a ship. Again, what were you thinking?"

"I wasn't thinking." Larson spoke with a grimace. "I was doing my job. These attacks are continuing and growing worse, and we're no closer to stopping them. When are we going to act?"

His superior let out a huff as they crossed the street and bypassed a row of sleepy antique shops. His own Easton residence, a restored colonial relic inherited from his second wife's family, stood with the other grand manses dotting the shoreline. After this morning's events, Larson doubted an invite would be forthcoming.

Katz's anger gave way like a deflating bag. "Larson, the American government is large and multi-faceted. It's a bureaucracy. And bureaucracies move slowly. Everything it does, every decision made by this breathing behemoth, trickles down just as slowly. Echelon has been afforded unheard of clearances, but those clearances don't allow for vigilante behavior."

"But—"

Katz cut him off. "From now on you will do nothing in the field without my consent, or you will sit at a desk as an analyst until you turn fifty-nine and you're forced to retire."

He ignored the threat. "Something is going on. There's a bigger plot at work here—"

The chief's voice rose. It contained a note of finality. "Return to Washington and do your damn job."

Without another word he pivoted and strode away.

Half an hour later as Larson drove north up the Delmarva Peninsula with an autumn breeze whipping his hair, he carried a tantalizing idea in his brain. It might prove difficult, but he could think of no other way forward.

It was time to arrange a meeting.

Chapter Twenty-Five

Getting in touch with the renowned reporter proved more than difficult. Plans were laid over the next week. Larson was careful to keep them well hidden from Katz's prying eye.

It might have proved impossible had he not been gripped with a sudden stroke of inspiration to pick up the phone and call a woman he'd forgotten about.

Her voice was smooth and harbored no resentment. "Calling to arrange another late night at The Jefferson?"

Larson couldn't help smiling as he ambled along the Potomac. Cool wind blew across the river. Crisp leaves and a coming bout of weather wetted the air. "It was the Hotel Washington if I'm not mistaken. And perhaps another time. I have a favor to ask, Miranda."

After all, Miranda Cusimano, Director of Luther Sackler Art Gallery, was well connected. She was indeed acquainted with Karen Sanders, as Larson suspected she might be. Not well enough to snag an invite to a weekend in the Hamptons or skiing in the south of France, but enough to arrange a meeting.

From the waterside trail, it was possible to forget about Georgetown and the capital. Stretches of trees shielded downtown Arlington across the water.

He mounted a flight of wooden steps, crossed a thoroughfare busy with afternoon traffic, and walked until he was standing outside a trendy café with tables and chairs arranged along a brick sidewalk. A woman could be glimpsed sitting alone at the farthest table, reading a newspaper. She folded it away and smiled as he sat across from her.

"You're out of breath."

"It's a decent hike from the river's edge to Prospect. Lots of stairs."

Elena's face twisted into a look of lingering disapproval. "You should exercise more."

He grimaced. "Not everyone has time to conduct groundbreaking research and run five miles a day."

"I wouldn't consider anything I've done truly groundbreaking."

"It was relevant enough to make you a target for assassination."

She rolled her eyes.

He ordered coffee that came with a thick layer of cream swirled into the shape of a pumpkin. Elena drank tea. When the waiter disappeared, she contemplated him with a searching expression. Larson saved her the trouble of articulating a question.

"I was thinking. Getting away from the bustle of the neighborhood helps me focus."

"You weren't thinking of chartering a boat and sailing away?"

He shot her a dark look over his coffee. "Judging by the size of everything that hadn't been rented, I don't suspect I would get far. Besides, my job isn't finished yet."

"It may never be," she said.

"A similar thought crossed my mind."

It was nearing Halloween and many of Georgetown's storefronts were decorated with holiday trappings. A witch glared from a townhouse's lower window across the street. He sipped his coffee and changed the subject.

"We got the meeting. Miranda called back before I arrived. A week from today."

Elena showed a hint of trepidation. Possibly a shade of jealousy. "You're sure you need to talk to her?"

He nodded. "I feel as though a web of many interconnected points is beginning to come together. With any luck, Sanders will be able to knot some loose ends."

"You have a theory?"

"It's taking shape."

"Why can't she meet sooner?"

Larson gave her a knowing look. "Karen Sanders is a very busy person."

Aside from writing columns for several prominent newspapers, including the Washington Post, Karen Sanders made frequent television appearances to divulge her opinions on the most pressing political topics of the day, and acted as an overseas correspondent. Larson found it no great mystery that the controversial journalist was single and never married deep into her forties, although a glimpse of her house in the esteemed Barnaby Woods neighborhood could have alluded to a family of significant breadth.

It certainly alluded to wealth. That much was apparent by the modernist structure with a looping driveway that stood out among an array of colonial McMansions guarded by sycamores and oaks. The community had no fences or guard houses. None were needed; crime was at an all-time low.

Larson took an observational turn around the block before pulling into the empty driveway. He stepped from the car, glancing over his shoulder into the opaque night beyond the drive. Elena had chosen to join him. A lamp on the garage's stucco wall flared to life. Before Larson could reach for a knocker, a young woman in a pantsuit pulled open the front door.

Without more than a syllable of greeting, she ushered them inside and closed the door. The interior walls were white; framed artwork hung at intervals, and vases and exotic plants occupied niches behind decorative pillars. The hardwood floor had perhaps divested Brazil of all its remaining rosewood.

"I'm Jody. Karen is upstairs in her study," the young woman said. She pointed to an angular staircase truncating the view of an eclectic living room. "Third door on the left."

The study door was easy to spot—ebony in a sea of white. Larson knocked, and a full-bodied voice called from within to enter.

Karen Sanders was an angular woman. Much like her house, every part of her appearance seemed geared toward making a statement. High cheekbones traveled down to a sharp jaw and complimented hooded, astute eyes. Her highlighted blonde hair had been chopped above shoulder length and ran at a slight diagonal from left to right. She had removed the jacket of her Armani pantsuit—it hung near a massive desk covered by two open laptops and a wobbling stack of files.

She strode forward with a bejeweled hand outstretched. "You found the house okay? And you met my assistant, Jody, downstairs?"

Larson nodded.

Sanders turned to Elena. "I'm so sorry for the loss of your brother. Pain like that can never truly abate."

Elena bowed her head while Sanders' dangling earrings tremored. She gestured for them to sit, returning to a seat framed by white curtained windows opposite her desk.

The journalist's attention focused on Larson. "I appreciate you being willing to pay a house call so late. But if I may be blunt, who are you?"

He raised a quizzical eyebrow.

"Miranda said you work for the federal government and can be trusted. Other than that, I don't know a damned thing about you."

It was crucial that Sanders feel comfortable with him. He leaned forward. "Thank you for trusting Miranda and agreeing to this. She has only a modest inkling of what I do."

"What *do* you do?"

"I work for a small, classified government task unit that you've never heard of."

"I've heard of all of them." The air crackled with her words. "You know who I am, or you wouldn't be here."

"Not this one. We gather intelligence on a special kind of threat—political extremism within the United States."

"That's the FBI's job."

He let a soft grin escape. "We are much smaller and much more specialized. Are you familiar with the alternative right?"

She grasped a pen and let it hover poised in the air before setting it down again. Then she closed both laptops with a flourish. "That's what this is about. I don't like them watching me." She gestured to the laptops. "My webcams are all but certainly hacked."

"So, you're familiar?"

She didn't answer, instead pressing a red call button on her desk. "Jody, dear, bring me a scotch." She returned her attention to Larson. "Tell me more about this unit you work for."

He narrowed his eyes and remained stoic. "You ask questions for a living. And you understand better than anyone that there's not much more I can reveal."

"Who is your director? Who do you answer to?"

Silence.

"Then why are you here?"

She uttered the last question in frustration.

Larson leaned forward again and laced his hands. "The

reason I sought you out is tied to my employ in the intelligence community but officially off the record."

"Nothing is off the record."

Her voice made him cringe as if he had been stroked by the fire crackling across the room. The walls were covered with shelves of spotless leather-bound volumes and odes to her many journalistic accomplishments. A gilt mirror hung over the mantle, casting their tense assembly into oblong, circus house configuration.

"For the sake of national security, this will be."

Sanders pushed back in her chair and stood. "To hell with national security! The man sitting in the White House doesn't give a damn about national security, why should the cogs of his new government be any different?"

She paced, pausing when Larson spoke.

"His new government is what I'd like to discuss."

Elena shot him a sideways glance.

"In what capacity?"

"How it could be tied to the alternative right."

Sanders dropped back into her chair. "You're talking about Hannah Harper."

Larson's brow wrinkled. The name sounded vaguely familiar.

"Who?"

"Hannah Harper. The White House Communications Director. She's the one the president uses to contact Pyotr Volkov."

Larson and Elena stared at her.

Chapter Twenty-Six

"Pyotr Volkov?"

Karen Sanders wasn't listening. She thumbed the red button on her desk again. Crackling audio feedback broke the tension.

"Please dear, I need that scotch. The bottle on the top shelf collecting dust."

Once more, there was no reply until the static was deadened by releasing the intercom. She straightened and began pulling open drawers at random.

"Look at this."

It was a photograph the size of a sheet of paper. Its image was grainy, taken from a long distance and digitally enhanced. But there was no mistake. A silvery-haired politician holding a cellphone to his ear and identifiable as the vice president could be seen with his eyes trained on a hulking man whose sloping face resembled an Easter Island head.

It could have been a casual glance in real time. Caught

on the pixelated surface, the encounter was riddled with guilt.

"You'd wind up in jail if they discovered you laid eyes on that." She snatched back the photo and returned it to the drawer.

"Why is that?"

Sanders' mouth formed a thin line.

"Mr. Volkov is a Russian, although he's lived most of his life in Albania. That's what Russians prefer, to adore the Mother country from afar while spending as little time there as possible. Still, Albania isn't what I'd call an ideal alternative. Bleak place…That's not the point. Volkov is on watch lists ranging from Interpol to CIA, but he's very influential back home. If he ever stepped foot in Western Europe or America, he'd be picked up on the spot."

"What for?"

"Arms trafficking. Think of Zeus flinging lightning bolts into every unstable, developing country. But he's doling them out to both sides."

"A true capitalist."

"If you prefer your dividend in the form of innocent lives."

She went to the window and pulled the satin curtains closed.

"It's kept quiet as much as possible, but Hannah Harper is much more than the White House Communications Director. She's used to initiate contact with various figures that the United States government can't be on record communicating with. She sends emails, makes calls—her interactions are never part of any official transcript."

"Is she tied to the alt-right?" Larson asked.

Sanders shrugged. "Could be. Nobody can know for sure."

"How did you learn about Volkov?"

She tapped her powdered nose. "I have my ways. Digging is one. You don't last long in journalism without a few tricks. But the real trick is collecting proof on any of this. Which is what you'd need."

"And if you wanted to spin a bona fide connection between Volkov and the president to the press?"

"Forget about it. Half the country still refuses to believe that Russia meddled in the election. Or they simply don't care."

Elena changed the subject.

"Suppose Hannah Harper wasn't just contacting Volkov. What if she was in touch with members of the alt-right as well?"

"So, what if she is? When the term alt-right is used, I picture middle-aged men who've been spoon fed their whole lives and cling to their isolationist ideals because they're worried someone else might get a bite for a change. The average alt-righter works a white-collar job and never stirs the pot except behind a computer screen."

"The men who marched on Charlottesville weren't hiding behind keyboards," Larson said. "Neither was the one who opened fire in Vegas."

"What does he have to do with the alt-right?"

"At the moment I'm not sure I can say."

Sanders paced in front of the fireplace once again.

"Here's a theory of my own. Hannah Harper grew up modeling but may have worked for the National Policy Institute after sparking a desire to get into politics. She's important, but not the key player. That chess piece resides somewhere close to the president. Cabinet level if I had to guess."

Larson studied her features. Beneath Sanders' taut skin, she appeared frazzled. The color had sunk from her high cheekbones and her eyes darted around like a cornered wild animal. Every few seconds they locked onto the curtained window or flitted to the study door.

"What does a Cabinet member have to do with the alt-right and Russia?"

She locked onto his gaze and went still. Her voice trembled. "Potentially everything."

Then Sanders was back in motion, pivoting and heading for the door. "I can't wait on Jody any longer. Would anybody else care for a drink?"

They replied in the negative as she disappeared down the dark hall. He turned to Elena.

"Do you think she's telling the truth?"

Elena glanced toward the hallway. "It's hard to tell, but I believe so. I think you might have broken her down when you refused to talk. She's used to subjects caving to her stardom."

Larson let his ears search the periphery behind them, wary of the journalist returning. Nothing but silence.

"Hannah Harper seems like our best bet. But how do we get to her?"

"It's not her we need to get to, it's the Russian—Pyotr Volkov. There was a First Directorate general named Volkov during the height of the Cold War. I wouldn't be surprised if the surname's present embodiment was a relation."

"There's one option," Larson remarked. "Reach him through the White House Communications Director."

"But how? Volkov is untouchable outside the states."

Larson smiled. "We'll have to lure the snake out of his den and onto our home turf."

Elena was on the cusp of responding when she was cut off by a shrill blast. Larson launched to his feet. The alarm continued for several seconds, drowning out everything down to the minutest thought. Then it ceased.

In seconds, he was halfway across the long hall, crouched, and moving silently. Elena followed.

"Kare—"

Larson turned and threw her a furious look, pressing a finger to his lips. He had become statuesque on the staircase landing before she caught him. Without a word, he crept to the base, eyes sweeping the living room and deserted foyer.

A gust of cold wind greeted them.

"Where is she?"

Larson finished his descent. The front door had been left hanging ajar, allowing the advance troops of a frigid winter to bypass the house's defenses. His hands glowed pale in the porchlight's beam.

There was no sign of her assistant, but one thing was painfully clear. Karen Sanders, outspoken journalist and political talking head, was gone.

Chapter Twenty-Seven

Washington National Cathedral, all but invisible from Wisconsin Avenue behind a curtain of trees clinging to their mottled foliage amid the late stages of autumn, served as the city's Episcopal Diocese. It also happened to be the world's sixth largest cathedral.

Dual gothic towers and a buttressed nave showcased an iconic look that rivaled or even surpassed many of its European counterparts. Its limestone edifice was juxtaposed against the blended trees and parkland from which it rose.

As he neared the gleaming steps, Larson could focus on nothing save the man standing rigidly composed at their base. His gaze was fixed straight ahead.

The disappearance of Karen Sanders had taken Washington by storm. Few knew, however, that an Echelon agent and a woman in his company had been the last to see her. One of those who did was now rooted godlike in front of Washington's most imposing cathedral as though he had been delivered from on high by Emmanuel himself.

He reached the top step and bowed his head. Bypassing the rendezvous and slipping around the transept and returning to Georgetown on foot sounded tempting.

It wasn't Sunday, but pedestrians dressed in casual attire filed into the cathedral. Some glanced at the two stoic men with unease, as though apprehensive they might offer a word of greeting and a tri-folded church bulletin.

Eiran Katz spoke first. "I forbade you from making contact with her." He led his pupil away from the crowded steps along a path that unfurled before the cathedral's face. "What could have tempted you to defy my orders and do so anyway?"

"She was important," Larson said, "I had no choice."

"Your choice could have very well cost that woman her life."

Larson stopped beneath a gnarled sycamore. The concept of armistice rapidly evaporated between the two men still well within earshot of whirring cameras emanating from the cathedral steps.

"You and Elena Stregor were the last two who laid eyes on her."

"How could you possibly know that?"

Katz made no reply.

"I put my trust in you from the start," he said. "Are you having me followed?"

The chief fell into step once more and Larson followed. The older man's expression lightened as it broke in and out of shadow, turning from angry and combative to contemplative.

"American intelligence is like a many-headed monster. A labyrinth of offices, protocols, and clearances. You want answers that can't be given. Sometimes there are factors at play… Bigger fish enter the stream that prove untouchable."

Larson tried to make sense of what he was hearing.

"You knew I made contact with Karen Sanders?"

"Yes."

"And you knew she was abducted?"

"Long before the press got wind of it."

"Was that information shared with the FBI? Was anything done to find her?"

Katz's expression turned solemn. "The police have been working an ongoing investigation. But no, we did not feel it prudent to pass along any information gathered on Echelon's behalf."

Larson was incensed. "These events are all connected, how long will it take you to see that? Stregor's murder, the protests and mass shootings—a journalist with proof goes missing and you still refuse to accept the truth."

"And yet, she is gone, and you still have no evidence." Katz retorted. "The events may be linked, as you have insisted since August, but you forget—we do not exist. We are ghosts, buried deep in the vast network that is the Department of Homeland Security. We do not draw attention, lest our whole purpose be void."

"But to learn the truth. To save an innocent woman's life?"

They reached the path's end, where a thicket yielded to asphalt and noisy traffic. Katz didn't stop, but instead kept walking forward until he was in danger of stumbling headlong into traffic.

His escape route became clear a moment before the black Town Car with diplomat plates pulled to a halt along the shoulder, cutting off traffic. He pulled the door open and turned back.

"There was no saving Karen Sanders. She will resurface when her captors see fit, or else she will remain lost forever." He slid one gray pant leg into the interior, lowered his balding head.

"As for learning the truth; when you have done so, I may be willing to listen. Until then—"

Katz vanished and the door swung shut. The Town Car merged back into traffic and disappeared.

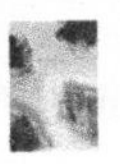

Larson had parked a few blocks north of the cathedral. He headed that way for a moment before changing his mind, instead turning southward and walking at a fast clip.

He slid into a taxi at the intersection of Wisconsin and Massachusetts with a feeling of grim satisfaction. Confronting the chief had been good for one thing. He had all but confirmed what a part of Larson suspected—the car issued to him by Echelon was bugged.

The taxi crossed into the capital, expertly navigating Dupont Circle and depositing him alongside the Eisenhower building near the western perimeter of the White House grounds.

Katz knew more than he was letting on, Larson was sure of it. As he walked, one fundamental collection of thoughts revolved in his head: the alternative right, Igor Stregor, Russia, and the United States government. Something, or someone, tied them all together.

He failed to notice that he'd spanned the National Mall and reached the Lincoln Memorial reflecting pool until he glanced down, and his own perplexed reflection rippled back. Thick clouds were coagulating overhead, and a strong breeze lifted currents in the pool and sent a gaggle of nearby sightseers scurrying for shelter.

Larson stared at the water's surface, letting his mind take over. He was aware of the presence next to him for several seconds before reacting. A rippling face materialized beside his own, features he had seen once before and known he would never be able to forget.

Neither pair of eyes—one brown, one blue—broke contact until Larson looked up and came face to face with Samit Bathari.

"Have you been well?"

Bathari nodded. "Any day is good when I can step foot in the United States of America."

They started walking.

"Customs didn't mind you coming?"

"It may be unwise saying this to a member of American

intelligence, but I used an alias." He nodded his head in Larson's direction and winked. "In certain matters of great importance, a bit of deceit is necessary. Don't you agree?"

"The American intelligence community has been in agreement with that statement since its inception."

They continued down the embankment toward the Washington Monument, as the sky grew darker.

"Has your predicament unraveled itself?" Bathari asked.

Larson shook his head. "It grows more complex by the day."

"I saw news reports about the journalist's disappearance. They said she lived here in the district. I take it you believe her to be involved?"

"Yes. She was taken moments before she would have been able to fill me in on several intricacies of my investigation."

"You're working with more than a hunch, I suppose?"

Larson's expression, dark like the gathering clouds, confirmed his statement. They exchanged a glance, and each gazed into the water. Bathari's mouth barely moved as he spoke.

"Ironic how of all places, Washington is one of the safest for me. I blend in with its visitors. No one can keep track of who is welcome and who isn't. But it was important that I speak with you."

"I have a phone, you know."

"In person."

Bathari's reflection grew tense, his eyes brooding.

"You are close to seeing the bigger picture. I'm confident that there is no one more capable than you in following to its conclusion. But I fear where that conclusion may lead." He paused. "Are you familiar with a term known as destabilization?"

"You're talking about tactics used to sow misinformation and distrust?"

Bathari nodded. "Often, it's much more effective to

leave things vague, to cast a veil of uncertainty so that everyone becomes a suspect. Destabilization as a tactic has been used for decades. One country still employs its surprising power quite often. That nation is said to have played a role in the current president's election."

"You believe Russia is attempting to undermine the United States?"

"Speculation is all it takes to give them the upper hand. Suspicion is a powerful thing. It has borne the brunt of many injustices throughout history."

"And your theory dictates that history will eventually repeat itself?"

Bathari shifted his gaze to the roiling cloud mass shrinking the airspace over their heads.

"History repeats itself all the time. But this plot goes deeper than striking uncertainty into the American public. What if the Russians are in league with your president? What if there is some bigger goal that serves both parties?"

That goal could be the key to everything. Bathari seemed to hear his thoughts. He gave his companion a searching look but said nothing. The two were bathed in shadow and the cool, energized breeze preceding a storm.

"It pains me to watch America falter. But at the same time, it fills me with hope. Despite many flaws, we have gotten so much right. America has long been a beacon of hope and a model of prosperity for the world."

"Yet you wish to change it?"

"It must adapt if it wishes to persist. The system, as it stands, dictates that the nation stay locked in contention until we pass the point of no return. Some push for isolationism, other globalism. Some champion free markets, others are more enticed by the idea of a planned state. It must stop."

"You would abolish capitalism?"

Bathari shook his head. "You misunderstand me. I have developed unique views on the efficacy of government, but I am a free market proponent. My detractors, many of them in this city, like to spread falsehoods that I'm another crazed collectivist with an oversized ego. This isn't true. There is nothing purer, nothing more Darwinian, than the free market. It mirrors nature—those who are able, prosper, those who are not, perish. Success is earned, and it is dictated by the consumer. No outside factor can provide an advantage."

"You don't see the rich as having a significant economic advantage over the poor?"

Bathari shrugged. "Capitalism will need to be amended, steered in the right direction as important outside factors are considered. Interference springs inefficiency, but there is no alternative."

"What do you mean?"

"A free market," Bathari replied, "cares nothing for the environment, or the survival of a species. It is guided by supply, demand, and paths of least resistance. In a vacuum, this would be ideal, but we live in a world growing increasingly muddied. The end goal is a global society where everyone can prosper, and any economic system must be tailored to support that endeavor."

They neared the Washington Monument. The first rolls of distant thunder sent the few lingering pedestrians hurrying for cover.

"How do you expect the collective world to ever be on the same page? Many would say it's impossible for even a solitary country to unite in thinking."

They both observed the Washington Monument, staring at the point where its obelisk tip pierced a bulwark of cloud.

"One country at a time," Bathari said. "Triumph in the United States is nothing but an indicator of more success to follow."

Larson had one more question. He spoke as the first frigid drop of November rain dotted his brow. "Are you familiar with a man named Pyotr Volkov?"

Bathari's expression darkened. "You're referring to the arms dealer, I take it?"

"He's a person of interest. What do you know about him?"

Heat seemed to rise off Bathari's skin from somewhere within. "I know that he has close ties to the Kremlin. When they instruct him to flood weapons into a specific region of the world, he does so, no questions asked."

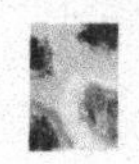

Larson was hailing another taxi by the time the rain started falling in droves. As he slid into the dry back seat, his thoughts were not fixed on the man who spread death and violence for a corrupt government, or on sheets of precipitation pummeling the windshield, but on bursts of fire raining over the Las Vegas strip.

Chapter Twenty-Eight

Eiran Katz lived in the coveted Palisades on the outskirts of Washington. His ambitious second wife held an important title with a favorably ranked investment bank. Their son spent most of the year at a boarding school in New Hampshire.

Larson, expecting Katz's wife to answer the door, found himself face to face with a liveried man sporting tufts of white hair around his ears after the third knock.

"May I help you, sir?"

He was spared an answer by the chief materializing over the wizened man's shoulder.

"Larson? What are you doing here at this hour?"

The butler retreated, sinking away from the open door as Katz strode forward.

He adopted an urgent tone. "I have to speak to you, sir."

Katz glared at him.

"It's about my meeting with Karen Sanders. You told me to come to you when I had information."

Larson took a step back and spread his arms wide. The chief's sardonic expression lightened a shade.

"I suppose you'd better come inside."

The meeting, or rather, locking of horns, between beleaguered mentor and obstinate student lasted until dawn paled the sky outside the curtained windows. By that time, as neighbors walking their dogs or going for a morning jog noticed a faint ray of warmth thawing the morning chill, argument gave way in favor of haughty silence.

The hours previous had been filled by pitching salvoes of heightened tones, so much so that the residence's live-in butler had disappeared into his quarters after setting out tea and a plate of jam cookies that went untouched. Raised voices became the melody of the evening and lasted well into the night, fluttering to a pinnacle around two in the morning and tailing off after a short epitaph sometime later.

At the end, much was still left on the table, but one matter was resolved. Capitulation was concise. An olive branch came in the form of a spoken address, a date, and a time. Larson didn't bother writing any of them down. They were seared into his mind. As was the embattled look on the chief's face, and minute beads of sweat curdling along his manicured brow.

Katz was showing his age. And on what was possibly the first occasion, he had been bested.

It had taken a night of convincing, but Katz had agreed to help. His first collaborative act, right there in the living room amid clouds of acrid smoke and cleared glass on a mahogany coffee table, was the concocting of a project. Rough and rudimentary. Crazy though it seemed, it was gutsy enough to work.

Larson arrived on a quiet block of P Street in Georgetown

as morning hung on the cusp of a cloudy and miserable afternoon. Fortunately, the weather was not dictated by his mood. He rang the doorbell of a brick townhouse and waited. After nine seconds, footsteps echoed off the hardwood within. A pause for four more, and the front door opened.

The waiting visage was not that of a butler, bodyguard, or assistant, but one that had been plastered ad nauseam over every major news network for the past week. It was careworn, though not unjustifiably so.

Rahim Gilbert's exodus from the White House's hallowed halls and ousting from his position as Chief of Staff had been made very public.

Dismissal for insubordination, in the vitriol-fueled eyes of the conservative media. Moderate outlets had a much more lenient take, not surprising given the fact that the man had worked for the previous president in a past life and was rumored not to see eye to eye with the current regime. How he had managed to wriggle into the role in the first place was noted by experts as one of the finest examples of political maneuvering in recent memory.

Larson was led inside and offered a firm chair in the study across from the former Chief of Staff. All the while, he pondered which side was closer to the truth. He didn't have to wonder long.

"Katz was kind enough to put us in touch with one another," the man said with a wry smile.

One truth was omnipresent: Rahim Gilbert did no wriggling. He had the statuesque build of an ex-linebacker who had lost neither his muscle definition nor his full head of hair. Despite the brutish physique, his face carried a soft quality—kohl-rimmed eyes and an expressive mouth that lilted toward a sturdy chin discolored by a day's shadowy growth. A dark complexion hinted at non-European descent. His suit hung off his frame, as though he had shed weight during the current media barrage.

Gilbert rose and poured coffee from a stainless carafe

atop a sideboard amid a collection of sandwiches on china platters. He indicated for Larson to do the same before swiping a sandwich and returning to his seat.

"Please, help yourself."

Larson refused while his counterpart took a bite and an audible sip, leading instead with a question.

"Is this your home?"

"No."

Larson shot an inquisitive look.

"It belongs to the White House. I was granted accommodation here for six months as part of my severance. Don't worry," he added, "my personal security contingent has already swept the place floor to ceiling for listening devices."

"You continue to use it after what happened?"

Gilbert glanced around with a shrugging gesture that implied clear meaning. "Wouldn't you?"

Larson relaxed. "I'm sorry about your dismissal."

"Don't be," Gilbert said off-handedly. "Talking heads around the country are making it sound as if I was moments from being led to a firing squad. In reality, I tendered a resignation before the president let me go. It seemed fitting that he drag my name through the mud anyway."

"Why did you do it? Resign."

Gilbert polished off his sandwich and stood for another. "I'd made a pledge to myself to act as custodian of this great country. That's why I took the job. America needs sane leaders who prioritize her best interests. If I could have succeeded in doing my part… Eventually the idealist in me fell back to earth. I was witnessing government devolve into a children's shouting match, seeing firsthand how the public became absorbed in trivial nonsense purveyed by an egotistical despot. I had no choice but to speak out in protest—it was my duty to this country."

"Could you have done anything to influence the president? Sway his thinking?"

Gilbert shook his head and spoke through another

mouthful. "Despite my position, I was never close to the president. He detested me from the moment I arrived at the White House. Both of my parents have Iranian blood. He took one look and pegged me as the enemy."

"Why did he appoint you in the first place?"

"Many influential friends provided strong recommendations and were careful not to draw attention to my past political alliances. They believed, as did I, that I could do some good for this country."

"But why not dismiss you at the first sign of trouble?"

Gilbert's dry expression betrayed the hint of a grin.

"The president, afflicted though he may seem, doesn't operate like that. He longed for an excuse to be rid of me but refused a dismissal without cause because that would prove that a mistake had been made in my initial selection. Our begrudging partnership persisted, until I gifted him the reason he'd been searching for."

Larson changed the subject.

"Katz said you would be able to help me."

His counterpart remained rigid and composed in the upright chair. He set plate and mug aside and clasped his hands together, signaling the time to talk business had arrived.

"Eiran Katz is an old friend. He's been keeping me under wraps this past week while I've been holed up here, as if I'm his secret prize. He promised me Broadway tickets when all this is over."

"I consider myself lucky to be sitting across from you."

Gilbert grinned. "That's a good answer. He was reluctant to have you meet with me. But I think it's time. He's already briefed me on everything."

Larson rose and poured a cup of coffee while Gilbert contemplated the reason for their meeting over steepled fingers.

"You don't think it's crazy," Larson asked, "that a staffer in the White House administration could have been hired to contact a Russian arms dealer?"

"Crazy?" Gilbert shook his head, eyes alight. "I think it's brilliant! Nefarious and lacking in integrity, but brilliant. Even more so given I never caught wind of it. It gives the president total control and him and everyone else plausible deniability. As far as they're concerned, she's an underpaid, overworked rogue with an iPad." He slid to the edge of his seat. "I wouldn't put anything past this regime; they're clever and willing to scale boundaries and protocols erected by decent people. I tried to stand in their way—you see what that accomplished."

"How do we out Hannah Harper to the public?"

"You don't, at least not until you're ready to out the entire scheme," Gilbert said. "You need proof. We'll have to catch her first."

"How?"

"You already know how. I'm confident your plan can work if the right people are involved."

"There are several Echelon agents who are more than capable."

The former Chief of Staff cut him off. "I had someone else in mind."

Behind him, down a short hallway a pair of French doors leading to the patio rippled with a human form and swung inward. Larson didn't blink as they snapped shut and the newcomer strode forward.

Elena, like usual, appeared as if she had been pulled from the display window of Saks. Gilbert eyed his reaction carefully, looking pleased.

He said, "I know the pair of you have already been acquainted but let me reintroduce you to the lead in our coming production."

Chapter Twenty-Nine

Larson sat taken aback as Elena perched on another straight-back chair and fixed him with a warm smile. Gilbert, failing to notice, was already speaking again. His tone coaxed the urgent professionalism of a Situation Room briefing.

"I can corroborate some of what you were told by Sanders. While it never amounted to anything, there were vague rumors regarding a line of communication with Russia. Every reporter in the country wants to break the story of how this regime used the Russians to rig the election, and it hasn't happened. That means that if there *was* any foul play, it's being kept under wraps. Hannah Harper, or using someone like her, fits that theory. Volkov may be supplying weapons, but he could also serve as go-between for the White House and the Kremlin."

Larson glanced at Elena. He could tell she was committing everything Gilbert said to memory.

"On the topic of the aide Sanders mentioned, I can provide more concrete facts. His name is Dillon

Drollsworth. During my time in the White House, I never confirmed if he had ties to the alt-right, but there's no denying he's close to the president. Unusually close. I, and the rest of the Cabinet, was disgruntled, to say the least, at Drollsworth's incessant presence. Much of the time it felt like he was the lone person who had the leader of the free world's ear."

"Do you think he's involved?" Larson asked.

"It's possible. But we start by focusing on Harper and the Russian."

"What about Karen Sanders?"

The other man shook his head. "A dead end."

Elena spoke. "Volkov is tucked away somewhere in Eastern Europe where he's untouchable. How do we get him to make an appearance on home soil?"

At that, the corners of Gilbert's mouth tilted and his businesslike tone vanished. "Elena, are you ready to put your integrity aside and your career on hold to publish a piece of research the alt-right can sink their teeth into?"

A moment's hesitation passed and the air in the sitting room grew heavy between them. She nodded.

From then on, the meeting was spent discussing what was to come. Framing Hannah Harper would not be easy. Luring the Russian out of hiding wouldn't be either.

When he left, the first call Larson placed was to a waiting Katz. Afterward, he dialed again.

His next call reached perhaps the most potent player in the United States intelligence arsenal, the behemoth juggernaut of cyberspace.

National Security Agency analysts were already setting to work by the time he entered his own townhouse on N Street. Elena had not accompanied him, citing the need to return to New York. Larson understood; she suddenly had much to accomplish in a short span of time.

He needn't have worried. A fortnight passed before Diego approached him one morning at Echelon headquarters in Rosslyn.

"This came for you." He pressed a large, bracketed manila envelope with **CLASSIFIED** stamped in bold letters into Larson's hands. By now, a small team within Echelon had been assembled. Diego was among them. With a knowing look, he watched Larson return to his office and close the door.

It had taken analysts at the National Security Agency one day to corroborate his theory. Despite scrambling and myriad other evasion tactics, an unearthed Washington IP address was discovered making repeated contact with another address roaming parts unknown deep within Eastern Europe. NSA analysts quickly verified Pyotr Volkov as its owner. The correspondent closer to home, the NSA confirmed after three more days' tireless effort, was none other than White House Communications Director, Hannah Harper.

Larson opened the envelope and pulled free a sheaf of unbound pages. Leafing through them, he skimmed long passages blocked around various supporting charts and diagrams. This concluded with a list of sources and relevant research and studies. But it was the title page that leapt out, succinct and electrifying:

Globalism Means Global Peril

Far different than her usual work, Larson noted. From the title alone, he could identify the hovering hand of Rahim Gilbert. Guiding, just as he had guided every facet of the project up to that point.

The first half dozen pages were enough to discern the paper's gist. So much so that he had no doubt certain ideological spheres would be salivating over its contents in the coming days. Elena's phrasing presented no moral qualms or indecision. The point was clear, and the apparent evidence damning.

She had deviated from the realm of cognitive psychology. Larson read with his brows ascending toward his hairline, all the while finding himself incapable of not being slightly impressed. Words were spun with venom, sentences laced with vitriol. And at the heart of it all, underlaid in every paragraph, one focal point—the scientific findings championed by brother to the author and now deceased Igor Stregor had been a complete farce.

He soaked it all in while Diego milled about in the hallway, trying to catch any snippet of reaction.

Overpopulation was fabricated, according to Elena. Earth did not have a people problem, rather, the opposite. The realization was dawning that the population was deteriorating so rapidly in many major areas that quite soon there wouldn't be enough bodies to keep them afloat.

Europe was declining, an unmatched stall that constituted an emergency. China had been too harsh with its birth control measures and was seeing adverse effects on its economy. America's growth had peaked, and it too was beginning to fade.

Her figures were backed by studies conducted around the globe as well as the testimony of various supposed experts who all substantiated the message in clear terms. A familiar graph jumped out to Larson. Igor's exponential curve representing global population had been co-opted and covered one full page. Only now it had been extrapolated another century; the steep slope rounded out at the year 2050 and plummeted.

The paper's greater purpose carefully came to light. Globalism had been championed by Igor, and many like-minded academics, as the solution to overcoming economic and logistical problems brought on by overpopulation. Only a worldwide community, he had preached, would possess the means to disperse resources in a way that would prevent massive loss of human life.

Elena disagreed. Isolationism, not globalism, was the

true psychological prerogative, she argued. Predetermined by centuries of cultivating unique cultures and ways of life. All of that, over time, created many inimitable peoples with vastly different ways of thinking. To cast aside those differences, in her words, would induce uncontrolled chaos. Better each culture go its separate way and stick to the status quo since that's what each had been programmed to do since the dawn of humanity.

It was all very persuading; Larson had to admit. Impossible to tell that it had been written by someone who believed quite the opposite. He hoped that it was good enough to go unquestioned by the men for whom it was intended.

The paper's introduction to the world at large was met with little fanfare, and indeed, almost no notice at all. But in a few circles, the cutting words of psychologist Elena Stregor took restaurant tables and dinner parties by storm.

The journal that published Elena's research, funnily enough, was not one of academic report or greater scientific purpose. Eight days after Larson slid the damning pages from their classified envelope, they appeared in *American Renaissance*, an oft-denoted mouthpiece for the alt-right, a short turn past the front page. That a reputable scientist entrenched with the opposition had experienced a change of heart and defected to their cause, it seemed, was no basis for concern.

On the contrary, it evoked a spouting of high praise for Elena, all the way to Robert Spencer himself. So much so, that the self-appointed brains of the alt-right decided that an award was in order.

It was sent in the form of an invitation—crème envelope embossed with sparkling gold print. It reached its destination in early December. The recipient, however, was not Elena Stregor.

Pyotr Volkov eyed the envelope with a feeling of curiosity that bled into satisfied, gloating pride as he slit it open and read. Between two sausage digits, he held the expensive card stock, glinting with the same gilded embellishment, informing him in glowing terms that he had been invited to the National Policy Institute's annual gala. He raised an expensive cigar to his lips and puffed.

The event was voraciously attended by leaders of the think tank as well as many influential figures littering the alt-right's ranks. Reliant on his attendance, Volkov would receive the group's most prestigious award, to be presented by none other than a converted advocate of all the movement stood for.

The award's justification was printed near the bottom of the invitation:

Albanian Alliance

Supposedly a nonprofit working to propagate self-sustainable growth and foster skilled labor within the impoverished country, it received a lion's share of its funding in secret from the arms dealer.

In reality, the Alliance was little more than a terrorist group using every despicable tactic it could imagine to drive outsiders away from Albania and the Balkans as a whole. Arson and extreme violence were daily occurrences. Murder as a scare tactic was not unheard of.

Volkov crushed the Cuban cigar in an ashtray on his desk and waited for the acrid haze to clear from around his temples. Along with the invitation, a copy of *American Renaissance* containing Ms. Stregor's article had been included. Volkov leafed through it, stopping at her photo underneath the title.

It was about time he was recognized for his extensive relationship with the alt-right, but she was the true prize. Her appearance aroused something primal within him that only ever emerged when a deal was about to close. An instinctual feeling urged him to leap up and overturn his desk. His hands were paws poised to choke the life out of any prey.

Instead, they slipped a razor-thin cellphone from the breast pocket of his tailored jacket.

Chapter Thirty

A steel sky hinted at snow when night came. The first heavy flakes fell from its bloated folds as Larson stood next to his partner, looking out a floor-length window over an icy balcony railing. Two spotlights across the street cast the wintry drift ablaze in concentrated halos that extended heavenward.

The subject of their surveillance was the iconic Meridian House across the serpentine asphalt folds of Crescent Place Northwest. On downtown Washington's northern outskirts, it had served as chief venue for events of any and all notoriety during its heyday decades previous. Restored to its former glory, it stood as a beige collection of stone cut edifices, parapets, and terraced balustrades amid a sea of burgeoning oaks and condominiums that rounded out the neighborhood. A limestone wall discouraged all viewing at street level.

Tonight, the cobbled drive and steps leading to Meridian House's wide entrance had been draped in red velvet. Every minute, like clockwork, a limousine or dark SUV pulled to a stop at the open gates and guests emerged.

Diego coughed and lowered his infrared binoculars. "No sign of them yet."

Larson wasn't worried. It was a quarter past eight and, as was custom, nobody of true merit bothered arriving to such a social function prior to eight thirty. Speeches and the awards presentation were not due to start until ten.

"Be patient, they're coming," he murmured under his breath. The glass inches from his nose transmitted the frosty chill outside. Stark contrast to the darkened living room where they watched; intruders standing on an area rug bisected by leather divan and ebony coffee table. A mounted flat screen offered an accusatory stare.

The M-shaped brick building offered an acceptable view of Meridian House. This unit's owners had been kind enough to turn off all the lights around dinnertime and vacate for several hours. They had placed a key to the front door in an envelope and, upon leaving, slid it under the doormat.

None of the neighbors seemed to find it odd when two men dressed in tuxedos and wearing nondescript backpacks appeared out of thin air a short time later. One glanced surreptitiously down the hall while the smaller of the two produced the key. When the door was unlocked, they disappeared.

Two security men wearing Meridian House credentials scrupulously checked the invitation of all arriving parties. What the guests were unaware of, however, was that both men were actually employed by Echelon. And that each, via earpiece, had a direct line of communication with Rahim Gilbert and Eiran Katz, who were closeted in a small room on the house's top floor that remained roped off and locked.

Minutes passed and Larson's watch ticked closer to the bottom of the hour. When it came and went, his partner shot him a look.

"What now?"

"Be patient."

A steady line of idling vehicles formed. Puffs of exhaust congealed in the night air and ascended in a collective haze. Larson caught the sidelong flash of a face or the swish of an overcoat pulled tight before the next SUV pulled forward to take the previous car's place. As fashion trended toward dark colors for formal events, the same could be said for the vehicles that bore patrons toward the red-carpeted entrance.

Larson's phone pulsed. Three quick vibrations. The NSA analysts were able to send him messages instantaneously via a secure connection. Judging by the unique pattern, one such message had just arrived.

"It's time."

Diego nodded.

There was no need to glance at the text. The staccato of crisp vibrations could only mean one thing. Their target was on the move.

The heavy Land Rover lurched to a halt, making Pyotr Volkov's vodka sway dangerously in its glass. The reinforced chassis rocked forward, causing some of the icy substance to dribble down his chin. Nothing was visible outside tinted windows shielding the cocoon where he sat.

He had downed his fifth vodka during the short drive from the Ritz-Carlton. The bottle sitting half empty in a bucket of ice on the leather console nearly cost more than the car. His bloated face was already turning ruddy in the cheeks, and pleasant heat spiraled off them. Always in stark contrast to the vodka, which he would accept only if it was at a temperature capable of eradicating survivors from sunken ocean liners and smooth enough to be mistaken for water. Volkov abhorred all things American, particularly the spirits that proliferated their bars and lounges. What passed for quality in a country built on consumerism, he marveled, was an utter disgrace.

He slicked his oiled hair back and braved a barrage of cold. The door was pulled open by his head of security, a short pit bull of a man named Boris Arkady, who preferred his receding hair shaved close to the scalp and had a nasty penchant for pain and suffering.

Volkov belched and emerged onto the sidewalk, steadying himself and passing through the gates to the shielded driveway. Two men he likened to Rottweilers appeared at his sides while Boris led the way.

He pulled his coat tight around him, enough fur that it might've easily taken several black bears to cover his astonishing breadth. Snow was falling, but the cold was not so bad. By the middle of December, Moscow would be reduced to a murderous sea of white that refused to relent until the following April. After that, it would be rainy and miserable until the brief reprieve of a meager, mosquito-filled summer. Nowhere else in the motherland was worth stepping foot.

Pivoting on the red carpet, Volkov glanced back at a second figure emerging from the Land Rover's spacious backseat. Hannah Harper had declined his vodka on the drive over and instead sipped nimbly from a glass of white wine, daring Volkov to forget about her. He had. She would have been pretty if he cared; a black dress that clung to her figure underneath an ermine coat he had presented her during his last innocuous travel to the states.

She'd treated him on this visit with an icy indifference; he couldn't help noticing. Volkov didn't offer to take her arm as the door slammed and the Land Rover sped away. Instead, he turned and allowed Boris and the others to hustle him inside, leaving Hannah Harper to follow alone.

The gala had managed to keep an unusually low profile this year, Hannah thought. She crossed Meridian House's impressive marble and limestone foyer and followed a flock of guests up the grand staircase. The National Policy Institute was not known for being discrete, but perhaps times were changing. She had lost contact with nearly everyone from her days at the think tank. She reached the venue's second level and doubted whether she'd recognize many of them.

The Institute was the alt-right's legitimate foray into the world of mainstream politics. It was for that reason alone that Hannah, as White House Communications Director and proud owner of an office in the prestigious West Wing, suspected she'd been invited.

But upon reaching the vast ballroom where most invitees were congregated, she became irritated when her arrival went unnoticed by nearly everyone in the vicinity. One aging man—shapeless, forgettable face and rumpled tuxedo—approached her. When he complimented her dress and the cluster of diamonds that hung at the hollow of her throat, she extricated herself and made for the bar.

A glass of quality chardonnay appeased Hannah's mood. She took a closer look at the crowd now and for the first time caught the subtle tinkling of music from a grand piano across the room.

A white-haired duo with quivering jowls were holding court over a group of ten, all men except a woman in a pantsuit with short-cropped hair. Her invigorated expression couldn't help but remind Hannah remarkably of the president's opponent from the previous fall. This woman was younger, no doubt, based on her dark hair and a waxen face devoid of wrinkles. Yet, something about her roused a stirring resemblance.

Hannah had still possessed ambitions of modeling back then. Even so, she'd had a feeling politics would be her true calling.

She eyed the two geriatric figures holding the group's collective attention hostage. Nothing they were saying could be made out, not that it would have interested her. Hannah drained her glass. The man on the left was speaking more forcibly than his colleague, enough so that the lower half of his face and ample midsection trembled with each syllable.

He was interesting. But why?

Yes, now she remembered. His face and his mannerisms were familiar from her days at the Institute. Hannah's certainty grew as she continued to observe. He had accosted her in a hallway once, inviting her to dine with him in an all too uncomfortable manner and being slow to accept her refusal.

Retribution had been won, she recalled, a few weeks later when he'd become violently ill after she slipped a few eyedrops into his drink during a cocktail reception.

The think tank was still something of an anomaly within Washington political circles. Unlike Brookings or RAND, it had never been accepted or acknowledged as a viable player. Still, only the blindest or most stubborn could deny that the National Policy Institute had become an influencer.

Failing to spot the Institute's progenitor while she skirted the gathering and accepted another glass of wine, she instead glimpsed the detestable Russian. Having drank himself into a near stupor on the drive over, Hannah watched Volkov elbow his way to the front of a line for hors d'oeuvres. He grappled for a plate while a pair of bodyguards skulked in the background and glowered at anyone who drew close. Volkov stumbled away, his plate piled high with caviar and calamari while those nearby fled from the onslaught.

It was amusing, in a way. It was clear the Russian fashioned himself a new age king. While disgusted, Hannah also couldn't help but be aroused by his brutish and barbaric manner. Something primitive that drowned her better senses.

Mostly it was the money and power. Hannah had always struggled to resist the pull of either—paired they were unstoppable. She would sleep with him, if she must, but it would take several more glasses of wine.

Hannah floated toward a spiral staircase that led to the top floor when a hand brushed her own. She turned and found herself locked on a pair of soulful eyes. They belonged to a distinctly Latin face with flowing dark hair, reminiscent of a man who recited poetry and walked along the *calles* of some distant land.

At once, Volkov disappeared from her mind. The stranger smiled and offered his name.

"Always so stuffy, these things," he said, craning his neck around the ballroom.

Hannah agreed. A waiter with a tray held high was passing. Her new partner leaned out and plucked a full glass from its surface. He handed over the wine and set her old glass on a windowsill.

"What kind of name is Rafael Burrow?"

"My parents were fond of old master paintings," he responded.

"Do you work for the Institute?"

Rafael gave her a quizzical look and ignored the question. "I was going to take a look upstairs," he said. "Would you care to join me?"

Meridian House's top floor had burgundy walls and a sloped ceiling that lent a claustrophobic air compared to the spacious rooms below. Molding around the floors and ceiling indicated craftsmanship from an age long since passed. Hannah did not know who had painted the oil portraits lining the walls, but she could tell at once that they were valuable.

Curtained windows overlooked a balustrade above the courtyard and adjacent street. Beyond trees and a row of brick apartment buildings, clustered lights from the capital were visible.

"It's beautiful up here," she murmured.

Her new companion led her down a hallway lined with oriental rugs and stopped at a pair of French doors. With a slight push, they opened, giving way to a half moon balcony.

Intersecting gravel paths and gardens created a fairytale grotto at the house's rear. Hannah spotted several gala invitees strolling between rows of vegetation that did their best to cling to life despite the bitter cold.

"They have no idea we're here, looking down on them," she whispered. He moved close beside her, grazing the waistline of her dress.

"I find it difficult to believe that anyone could fail to notice your presence."

She was used to flattery. It rendered itself an occupational hazard in the White House. "If you aren't with the Institute, what do you do?"

"I work for a firm that assesses the political climate in various regions around the globe. We compile data and conduct analytics for a list of clients. I'm afraid it's a job that involves frequent travel. At the moment, for instance, we have a team collecting data in the lower third of Africa on behest of several customers. One of those is the National Policy Institute."

"Where are you from?"

"I grew up in a rough neighborhood called Castilla in the heart of Medellin."

"How terrible."

"It taught me how to take care of myself. Outsiders are always surprised, but Medellin has some of the most mesmerizing landscapes and charming people in the world. Colombia isn't the country it was in the nineties. Times have changed."

"And your family?"

"My parents accomplished what I suspect was their one true goal in life. When the drug violence reached its peak, they were able to escape with my brother and I and come here to America. Life never materialized into quite the American dream they were expecting, and they missed home greatly, but all that was preferable to an existence marred by bloodshed and famine."

A faint buzzing triggered inside her skull. She swayed

as the wine took further effect. Overcome by momentary confusion, she asked, "What was it you said you did again?"

The handsome man called Rafael steadied her by the forearm. He stared into her eyes. "What I do isn't important. It's what you do that I find so interesting. I'll admit—I consider all aspects of your life fascinating."

"You just met me."

He retrained his gaze on the gardens below and spoke robotically.

"Your name is Hannah Harper. You work as Director of Communications in the White House. You were not a popular choice for the job. In fact, many posture to this day how you became so lucky. Too young, completely inexperienced in the field."

"How do you—?"

"I also know that, before your current foray into politics, you once worked for this think tank after concluding a lackluster career as a model."

Despite the wine, Hannah's wits returned. "Very good." She nodded. "Any of that could have been discovered via a quick internet search."

"What I have is much better than the internet. Can Google explain your relationship with the ill-mannered Russian stuffing his face downstairs?"

She balked.

"Would it paint a picture of how the two of you arrived together? Or how he purchased that ermine coat you're wearing the last time he came to town?"

Hannah's body went rigid. She tried not to betray the fear coursing through her nervous system. Her gaze remained rooted on the scenery below without seeing. Despite the December chill, it was suddenly hot.

Fixing in place a hollow smile that failed to thaw the glacial coldness of her eyes, she asked, "Really, who are you?"

Several incoherent thoughts rushed through her mind. That this charming newcomer would smuggle her out of the building. Or that he would simply push her over the balustrade or produce a gun and shoot her.

He did none of those things. Several heavy moments passed.

"My name is not Rafael Burrow. It is Diego Rivera. I'm not sure if you're aware of this, but we don't have much time. Tonight's gala culminates with an awards ceremony. Your Russian friend is to be honored. We'll have to have concluded our business before he takes the stage."

"What does that have to do with me?"

"I'm employed by a small group within United States Intelligence. I trust you don't have your iPad on you tonight?"

Hannah understood. As it all clicked into place, she moved toward the door.

She found her way to freedom blocked by a sturdy hand pressing against the frame. As she pulled back, Hannah cast a scathing look in his direction. "You're an undercover agent?"

"Something like that." He wore a roguish smile as if he were thoroughly enjoying the secretive nature of his role. "Before you can go there's someone else who needs to speak with you."

"Who?"

"She's waiting for you now."

Hannah allowed herself to be led off the veranda back through the portrait-lined hallway. Her captor ignored three doors before settling on a niche set back from the hall. The wooden door was ajar.

Diego Rivera, if that was his name, led her inside with a confident air as if he had run of the place. A study lined with bookshelves sagging under the weight of leather-bound volumes and lit by a crackling fire greeted them. Apart from two faded reading chairs and a standing lamp in the far corner, the only other furniture appeared to be a long couch sitting atop a magnificent Oriental rug.

In plain view, patiently waiting, sat a woman. A woman

who had been dubbed a guest of honor at tonight's gala. There was no need to compare her face to the one printed with glossy clarity alongside her headline in *American Renaissance*.

Hannah recognized her instantly.

Chapter Thirty-One

At the opposite end of Meridian House's top floor was situated another kind of room. The sort where brandy was sipped, and hatched plans were coaxed into being. Like the study, this room had a fire burning, albeit in a much smaller grate surrounded by tapestried walls.

Two men sharing a patched loveseat stared into the fire's depths and strained to hear what was happening across the hall. Both were well aware that even without the occasional tumbling of charred logs it would have been to no avail.

Gilbert and Katz had transfigured the den into their war room, but now all there was left to do was wait. Wait, and observe a monitor affixed to crumbling brick beyond the fire's tendrils. The live feed had no sound but showed a panoramic view of the study.

For several minutes, since she had moved into place, there had been one female form visible. Now, there were three figures in total.

"She's made contact," Gilbert said, more to himself than his counterpart.

Katz grimaced. "You're sure she knows how to play the game?"

The brunette figure of Elena Stregor rose to her feet. Together, she and Rivera ushered the target deeper inside.

"She's golden. Honestly, you Echelon boys are lucky to have her."

Katz said, "As far as I'm concerned, she's partially responsible for getting us into this mess."

Gilbert shook his head without letting his eyes leave the monitor but said nothing.

"How long do we have until Elena's due to deliver the award?"

He glanced at his expensive watch. "Just under thirty minutes."

Katz nodded curtly. "Right on schedule."

"I read your latest research," Hannah said, noticing for the first time that she was slurring her words.

"That's a shame."

Diego motioned for Hannah to sit and handed her a small glass of wine before lowering himself beside her. The tall woman with beautiful Slavic features remained standing.

"Are you not proud of your work?"

"I would be, if I even remotely considered any of it to be true."

"You're with them!" Hannah cried in a startled voice that echoed. "An undercover agent just like him." She tried to flail away from the man seated next to her.

"Please keep your voice down," Elena said. "There's still a party going on downstairs. I'm not an agent; I'm a scientist aiding the greater good. Everything published in that journal was meant to serve a larger purpose. The same one you're being called upon to assist."

"Drink your wine," Diego said gently.

"There's a man downstairs who wishes to speak with you. Before we take you to him, I would like you to answer a few questions. Start by telling us everything you know about the Russian you arrived with."

"And if I refuse?"

"You can't protect him," Diego murmured.

Elena nodded. "We need you to tell us everything. The intercepted messages between you and the Russian aren't enough. Volkov is due to receive an award in a few short minutes. Time is paramount."

Hannah swallowed another mouthful and pinged her eyes from one face to the other. The attractive man sitting next to her wore a kind expression. The woman was more severe. Her grimness juxtaposed with the satin open-back gown she wore was unsettling.

The choice was clear.

"There is nothing to tell. I don't know anything whatsoever about the Russian. We rode together tonight as mere coincidence."

"You can't protect him," Diego murmured once again.

"She's not," Elena said. "She's protecting herself. Poorly, I might add."

"I have nothing to tell you."

"Come now, everyone in this room knows that isn't true."

Hannah remained resolute. "I won't talk. You have a better chance of getting my clothes off."

Elena cocked a penciled eyebrow. "I have a feeling that isn't all that difficult. Even before the wine."

"Do you have any idea who I am?" Hannah's notion of rising to her feet was quelled by a hand on her shoulder. "The president will protect me."

"No," Elena said. She leaned forward. "The president will never get involved. One look at the transcripts we've managed to acquire, and your name will be taboo before they can clear your desk. You will no longer exist in the

White House, except to take the fall and be labeled a crazed outlier. Nobody is infallible, especially a young woman with few allies and no leverage. You were practically Heaven sent. When this information goes public no one will touch you."

She straightened, letting the words sink in. Hannah sat rigid for one long moment. Then she burst into tears.

"Stop crying, Hannah. There isn't much time."

She ran a hand across her eyes. The tall woman, Elena, was blurred, as was the surrounding room. Her life may as well have been fading to darkness.

The president would not come to her aid. Despite the wine, her head was clear enough to understand that to be true. The word 'scapegoat' repeated with singsong clarity, dancing out of reach where she was powerless to squash it. Neither would Drollsworth. There was a chance he had already been preparing for this exact instance.

As for Volkov—she didn't give one damn about Volkov. They could have that chauvinist pig. From the sound of things, they already did, and her along with him, trapped in the same net.

"What do I have to do?"

"We need to know where Volkov is staying. And when he plans to leave the country."

Hannah's first act of compliance was achieved with the mundane simplicity of discussing Washington's changing seasons.

"He has a suite at the Ritz-Carlton. As for the duration of his stay—he and his security team are flying out tonight."

"What airport?"

"Dulles. He has a private charter waiting, I believe."

"And what is the charter's destination?"

Hannah shrugged. "He didn't say. Pyotr Volkov isn't the chatty type, and I loathe him too much to ask many questions."

"He's a weapons dealer. Has he done any business since he's been on American soil?"

"How should I know? I wasn't tailing the man."

Elena made no response. She glanced at her watch. "Hannah, this is very important. You will need to follow the instructions I'm about to give you to perfection. That is, if you don't want to be locked away for a long time. Do you understand?"

Hannah looked to the man seated next to her. Gently, he unwound her fingers one by one from the wine glass and pulled it away. She nodded.

Six minutes later the study door eased open. Hannah was the lone figure to exit, walking with a purposeful, even gait. The transmitted instructions cycled round and round in her head. She clung to each echoing minutia as if her life depended on it.

Boris Arkady watched the young White House Communications Director materialize on the stairs. She kept her head aloft, rejecting eye contact as she descended into the gala.

He stood against the wall between two specimens of Impressionism and Cubism. The frames were exquisite, but had no one in Washington heard of an Old Master?

It didn't matter. Tonight, he was focused on priorities much more important than artwork, save the masterpiece in the tight black dress that had absorbed his attention.

Boris could observe her and still be well informed of his client's whereabouts, that much was certain. Even now, despite the clamor that had crept higher over the past hour, he heard familiar dulcet tones flaring.

Volkov was berating a cocktail waitress loudly enough to attract a small crowd of startled onlookers. From what Boris could surmise, the unfortunate woman had spilt a bit of martini on his client's fur coat. That Volkov had not shed the thing at the door was in poor taste, but money gave one the power to make such misguided decisions, he reasoned.

Hannah Harper was noticing Volkov's tantrum. He watched her head turn, glimpsed her eyes narrow and pouty lips curve down as she eyed the Russian. Boris was mildly surprised when she turned, hitching a vacant expression back into place and cresting the bottom of the stairs.

His surprise grew when she failed to direct herself toward the open bar. Hannah Harper strode forward as if the party didn't exist.

Boris was perplexed. As an important-looking man in a tuxedo approached the stage and the lights overhead dimmed, there went Hannah Harper, abandoning the proceedings. She crossed the ballroom and made for a door that led to the gardens behind the house.

He had always been a man who followed his instincts. Training had been rigorous and beneficial—first in the Russian army and Spetsnaz, and later for a brief time in the FSB. But in the most paramount situations, he had always fallen back on his instincts.

As the stage became awash in a spotlight's halo, Boris made his decision. Motioning the two bodyguards to stay close to Volkov, he slipped across the ballroom and reached the rear door as Hannah Harper disappeared.

He was now faced with two options: follow her or return to the party. A hasty glance back at his client, still shouting but flanked by Oded and Avner, made his decision for him. He followed in the woman's wake.

A cobbled footpath articulated a rectangle of withered lawn. It turned to gravel where the trees began. The light was much dimmer out here—stars and some unintended carryover from the city's heart—so that it took his eyes several moments to adjust.

He caught the hem of a black dress whipping around a bend. There was a reason Hannah Harper had picked this moment to slip away. His instincts told him as much.

But another instinct was beginning to materialize. He rounded a sharp turn and gnawing dread ballooned like a monstrosity in his gut. Something was horribly wrong.

With each step, the urge to turn back intensified. Something wouldn't let him. Boris hurried on, feeling his prey materialize and rounding another corner to find her shadowy form already flitting out of sight. Each infuriating escape pushed him, challenged him. Russian nature decreed a certain stubbornness.

Was that the same blonde hair? Same familiar black dress?

Boris careened headlong into the garden's heart and found himself face to face with a woman he didn't recognize. The path gave way to a clearing. She was seated on the rim of a playful fountain, still splashing despite the temperature. Dark hair and a satin gown that was gorgeous, but not black.

It all clicked.

Elena Stregor was smiling. "Not who you expected?"

Boris didn't hear her, hadn't seen her lips form words. He turned, and by the time her triumphant expression died, was sprinting as fast as his willpower and stubborn muscles would allow back toward Meridian House.

A rectangle of light grew as Boris ran, gaining perspective as the venue's limestone walls came into greater focus. He rounded the last bend and left the garden. Gravel turned to flagstones, and he was dashing up the stairs, urging his overweight body to move like it hadn't moved in years.

Boris launched himself through the door and was instantly rebuffed. It might have looked comical from afar, for in that instant he was certain laws of nature had made a mistake. Regaining his momentum, he flung all his mass forward once again.

This time there was no accident. His progress was curtailed by a wall of flesh; two immense chests side by side. No punches were thrown, no weapons drawn. Light pouring from the doorway had been diminished to pinpricks where two sets of hands dangled, club-like.

"Let me through."

The security men stood in stoic silence.

"I said let me through!"

The nearest boulder spoke in a rumbling voice. "This is a private event. You best be on your way."

The other patted his right hip in a way that made their intentions clear.

Furious, Boris stormed down the stairs. He was already reaching for his cell phone. When there was no answer, he tried calling a second time.

By then he was running again. His worst fears were coming true.

Chapter Thirty-Two

Meridian House has a veranda overlooking the narrow curvature of Belmont Street and a neighboring row of brick buildings. Hannah didn't walk into the gardens. Her gaze was focused on a fit man near the weathered balustrade, half in shadow. He eyed her patiently as she crossed the veranda.

"Who are you?"

"My name is Michael Larson. I'm an agent within American intelligence. And it's very important that I speak with you."

"What agency?"

"You've never heard of my team. We reside within the Department of Homeland Security."

"Try me."

He spoke the name. She returned his honesty with a quizzical look.

"Even with your position in the White House, I wouldn't expect you recognize us. Few are privileged to know that we exist. Fewer still understand what we do."

"What *do* you do?"

"Investigate growing extremist threats on United States soil. Namely, aggravations perpetrated by American citizens with limited outside influence."

"Then why are you interested in Volkov?"

"We both know why. It would be helpful if you'd cooperate, Ms. Harper. Time is of the essence."

"What is your theory?"

Larson took a step closer. "Pyotr Volkov has masterminded a supply chain that funnels weapons into the hands of American far right groups that would be either impossible or highly problematic to acquire domestically. While not operating from Russia, he does this with full knowledge and consent of his superiors in Moscow. With no true allegiances, they can deny any responsibility should things go awry. Am I right so far?"

She gave a halting nod. "Obviously there are details, much more that I've never been privy to, but that's the general idea."

"And it was your job to communicate with him?"

"I used avenues that couldn't be connected to anyone of importance. He was even charming at first, Volkov. You wouldn't believe it now—"

"On whose orders?"

Hannah hesitated.

"The president? Vice president?"

She shook her head.

"Who?"

"The man you are looking for is named Drollsworth. Officially, he's just an aide. But it goes beyond that. He's been given incredible latitudes while others have their every move monitored. He's constantly in the president's ear."

"And he's the one who suggested you contact Pyotr Volkov?"

"Drollsworth insisted. If I recall, he said it would be the most important task I performed during my employ inside the White House."

"Did you ever speak to anyone else about your new assignment?"

She closed her eyes. "Not once. Everything went through Drollsworth. He said I was never to breathe a word to another living soul. To him, that iPad he forced on me after drinks one evening was more important than my life."

"And you never tried to resist?"

"How could I? I'd been awarded a position beyond my wildest dreams. I was at the heart of everything, surrounded by powerful men running the country and ushering us into the future. The word 'no' is foreign to them.

"At first, I didn't know what I was getting into. Drollsworth conveyed an email address that I committed to memory. He instructed me on how to send and receive messages through a special program. He said the encryption was powerful enough to make them impervious to attack. Obviously, that wasn't the case."

"Drollsworth should have done some research on the capabilities of NSA hackers."

"I think he always believed," she said with a small shrug, "that the threat would come from somewhere outside our government. A probe by United States intelligence was the last thing on anyone's mind. Drollsworth and others believe that because they control the White House, they oversee every arm of the political machine."

"Luckily, the federal government still has employees that take the country's protection seriously." Larson pressed the conversation forward. "You understood what you had been tasked with?"

Hannah nodded. "Drollsworth taught me a code for communicating with Volkov. I was placing orders. They referred to weapons as different types of agricultural exports. Drollsworth would pass along specifications and amounts, and I would forward them across the Atlantic."

"How did you know the Russian was dealing weapons?"

"It became obvious after a few weeks. And the first

time I saw Pyotr Volkov in person whatever doubts I might have still harbored vanished."

She leaned her shoulders over the balustrade, inspecting the deserted street and a park that sank away in the distance. The man who called himself Michael Larson watched her carefully. Sizing her up, or maybe he was simply attracted to her.

"Where do we go from here?"

"That is entirely up to you."

She furrowed her brow before turning back to face the street. "Is that your way of inviting me to join your group…whatever you called it?"

In her periphery, she glimpsed him shake his head. Then he was at her side, taking in the cars that glinted in the light of streetlamps.

"I have no intention of tearing you away from the White House."

"How will I be allowed to return when they find out what I've done? I'll be lucky not to be thrown in prison on some fabricated charge."

"You assume too much. We don't plan on letting the White House in on what transpired tonight."

Hannah opened her mouth and shut it, dumbfounded. Next to her, the man spoke calmly without breaking cadence or deviating his gaze from a silver Audi parked across the street.

"Hannah Harper, White House Communications Director, will continue to exist in name only. From now on, you will be Hannah Harper, White House Communications Director and key asset of Echelon. You will not share this information with anybody in the regime or your personal life. You will be monitored—we'll arrange avenues for communication and will expect reports on certain figures. All of this will be performed indefinitely."

"And if I refuse?"

"I believe the possibility of being thrown in a cell with no key was mentioned."

"By sending me back to spy on them, you'll be signing my death warrant."

The agent turned to look at her. "You're in position to provide us with critical information. There are few promises in this line of work. If you agree to do this, your safety is one thing I'm willing to assure. These men are overconfident, and they trust you. At the first sign of danger, we'll order an extraction."

"What will Drollsworth think when the one outsider I'm connected to goes missing? Or are you intending to let Volkov go free as well?"

She spun around in time to see Larson already striding away. He was nearly across the veranda when he paused. "We'll be in touch. Leave Pyotr Volkov to me."

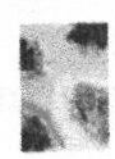

Oded was beginning to grow uncomfortable, a sensation that sparked agitated pangs. Like he was itching to release the compact pistol on his hip and aim it at someone's forehead. Instead, he clenched a glass of ice water that was in danger of shattering under his grip and paid careful attention to his quarry.

Volkov was attempting to tip back a fresh tumbler of vodka. Much of it failed to reach his mouth. Vodka dampened his silk dress shirt and beaded down his expensive tie like raindrops on a bird's feathers.

It seemed overindulgence had subdued him for a brief spell. But Oded could tell Volkov was growing impatient. A balding man on stage droned on in a manner that was impossible to tune out. Oded did his best to ignore the endless diatribe and focus on Volkov instead of the smatterings of approval that followed every pause.

The Russian should have been invited to the stage by now. Oded understood that much. He glanced at his watch and saw it was half past ten. The fact that he had yet to be mentioned, that the attractive woman scheduled to present his award was nowhere to be found, could only be classified as deeply troubling.

Oded glanced at his partner. Avner's gaze was not trained on Volkov but instead darted around the ballroom. It was a system; one focused on the client, the other searched for incoming threats.

Something wasn't right. Avner's eyes narrowed and locked onto a squat man with a shock of white hair who seemed to edge closer to Volkov. In the back of his head, Oded calculated the minutes, suspicions growing when Boris still hadn't returned.

He'd been gone far too long.

He took a step forward and was jostled by a passerby. He stumbled, knocked sideways by the impact of the collision, and lost sight of Volkov for the briefest moment.

A shrill blast issued from the stage. Instinctively, Oded spun toward the sound and raised his fists in a defensive posture. The droning man grappled with the microphone, its stand wobbling in slow motion and falling.

Realizing his mistake, Oded pivoted and was struck again by a sturdy torso that made him lose his balance. He and Avner had scrutinized every soul at the gala. There was no one in attendance capable of delivering that kind of force. Something was horribly wrong.

One directive flashed through Oded's head—get Volkov to safety. His heart plummeted. Their client was nowhere to be found.

Where Volkov had been standing was now a mass of flesh. At least twenty people, all dressed in tuxedos and fashionable gowns, crowded in like ants clinging together amid a flood.

Oded dove forward as more guests arrived, thronging around him so that he was lost in a sea of soft limbs and middle-aged visages.

He pulled his gun free. The crowd took no notice. Oded spotted Avner, waving his own pistol and pushing past guests. Panic overtook Oded and he flung patrons out of the way, burrowing between two portly men who were laughing boisterously and a group of gray-haired women that he cut through like butter.

Avner was making comparable progress. They crossed the sea of humanity to where Volkov must be, where he had to be.

Oded lunged past a man with horn-rimmed glasses and spun around. There was nowhere left to go. Avner reached him while the horde undulated like the beating heart of one living organism. The man on stage regained his microphone and continued as if nothing were amiss.

There was one problem.

Pyotr Volkov, furs and all, was nowhere to be found.

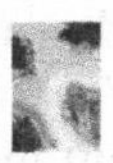

Boris clung to every stinging breath by the time he rounded Meridian House's wide berth and sprinted toward a line of idling cars outside the limestone walls. His frantic search for a black armored Land Rover was cut short by a throaty growl and bright flash of headlights as another car raced forward. Boris dove for cover as it screamed past. Despite a heavy tint on the windows, with sickening dread he could make out familiar features silhouetted in the sedan's rear seat.

He was already screaming at his driver as he heaved himself into the armored SUV. "Follow that car!"

The man wasn't shifting gears fast enough.

"Floor it, you imbecile!" Boris yelled.

They eased out of line and coasted forward when Boris was blinded by a flood of light in his face. Something scraped against metal. The Land Rover jerked to a halt.

When the light cleared, their vehicle was surrounded. The driver's door was being wrenched open. Several guns were drawn. An official-looking, unmistakable badge pressed against his window.

Boris let out a scream of fury and pounded his mallet fists on the dashboard in frustration. He didn't stop until the passenger door was thrust open and he was ushered into the cold.

Moments later, he found himself in the rear seat of a much different car. The men in dark suits dispersed, a fresh bout of falling snow absorbing his screams.

PART THREE

Chapter Thirty-Three

Residents lament that there are two seasons in Scotland: June and Winter. It was deep in the throes of the latter as Larson raced along the Scottish countryside under a swollen grey sky that once again threatened snow. Rolling hillocks gave way to beech firs and sycamores wound with bracken. Glimpses of an idyllic town or swath of loch intersected the wild growth at uneven intervals.

A Tesla had awaited him at the rental car hub as he emerged from Glasgow airport. It had been programmed with an address. No other clue to indicate what he was doing in Scotland.

He pressed the accelerator and nodded appreciatively. Whoever had arranged the rental seemed to be in agreement—the Scottish countryside was best taken in at high speeds.

A fug of mist settled over the road as it sloped upward. Larson passed a grumbling truck emitting a cloud of chicken feathers in its wake and coasted downhill. A hotel made with spires denoting centuries of existence gave way to another placid loch. He watched it flash by, rounding a bend and ascending the next hillock.

His thoughts were far removed from brazen Scottish scenery. Images of the past forty-eight hours remained vivid in his mind's eye.

Dislodging Volkov from his dogged bodyguards had been their only hope for a successful extraction. For that, they'd needed the woman who arrived with him, the woman who spent most of her waking hours feet from the most powerful man on earth.

Every guest at the gala had been on Echelon payroll or a stand-in supplied by the Department of Homeland Security. Additional Echelon agents had waited in a staging area across the street. It had been those agents who impeded Volkov's head security man as he tried to chase after the powerful client he had failed to protect.

The armored Land Rover was impounded, and its driver sent back to the Ritz-Carlton by way of taxi. Boris Arkady was detained along with both of his comrades when they, noticing their cause turning dire, made to slip off the premises. Officially, the men were held for questioning relating to the matter of an unrelated robbery several blocks away. In reality, all three underwent heavy interrogation ending in a forceful edict barring them from ever entering the United States again before being put on a plane bound for Russia.

Larson pulled himself back as he sped around a steep bend and drew alongside a wall of jagged black rock made slick with moss. A desolate park and ride littered with a few hatchbacks flashed by in a blur. His destination was still several kilometers west, along Scotland's longest loch that ran its cold fingers all the way out to the Firth of Clyde. He was thankful for the English translation beneath the Gaelic road signs and the helpful voice of the car's GPS system.

The sterile tone changed seamlessly to another, that of a large man with a heavy Russian accent. Volkov's drunken stammering mixed with angry screams from the head of his security detail as he was foisted from his armored carriage and led away.

Despite Boris Arkady's misconceptions, his quarry had never left Meridian House. Sedated mostly by his own doing and with help of a small needle plunged into his thigh, Volkov waited bound in a basement room until his bodyguards and all the guests had been ushered from the venue. Then he'd been escorted off the property under cover of darkness and taken somewhere much different.

Larson had arrived at this new location feeling that the night was on the cusp of success. But instead of trophies or medals, he was gifted a large Russian stripped to his trousers and bound to a metal chair in an otherwise empty room save a fire roaring in the grate. Several pokers and skewers rested white-hot at its flickering base. He had no intention of using them, but the desired effect had been achieved.

Waking Volkov proved on par with rousing a bear from hibernation. At first, he stared straight ahead bleary-eyed and unfocused. A forceful slap across his left cheek had jarred his senses and made him eager to return the favor. The Russian let out a roar when the tape over his mouth was ripped away and shook the chair as if it were made of crumpled tin foil. Another blow, this time a fist, steadied him into sullen silence.

The basement's stone walls boded well for the tiny microphones that had been wired throughout, allowing those sitting above to hear perfectly. A video feed showed with clarity the Russian's expression turn defiant as accented words issued from his mouth.

"You are making a grave mistake. Let me go."

Larson eyed the captive and shook his head.

"I've done nothing wrong."

"I'm afraid American intelligence feels differently."

The two men stared at each other, locked in a stalemate that commenced so many interrogations. Whoever made the first move would decide the routine's outcome.

"I have powerful friends in your country," Volkov said. "They will grant my release. Who knows what will happen to you?"

"I'm aware of your friends," Larson said. "As of this moment, they are regrettably oblivious to your predicament, but I promise no one will be clamoring to come to your aid."

The Russian's face turned menacing. Still, Larson noted him glance every few seconds at the medieval instruments positioned in the fire. He continued. "A man fitting your nationality and description was detained a few blocks from Meridian House for armed robbery. That man and his associates are being held without bail."

"And I assume you will make sure that man never sees the light of day."

Larson paced. "Not necessarily. I might be inclined to put him and his comrades on a plane and, assuming the plane doesn't malfunction mid-flight, send them east. Provided some questions are answered."

"What kind of questions?"

"The kind that have to do with weapons being supplied illegally inside the United States."

Volkov leered up at him. Firelight from across the room danced over his face.

"You have no idea what you're getting yourself into. I do not sell weapons. I sell a network. The people who request my services are situated in the highest alcoves of your country's leadership. It wasn't about money. I wasn't allowed to refuse. These people, if they knew what was happening at this moment, would have you stripped of your title and thrown in jail—"

Volkov fell silent as another fist connected with his jaw. Larson stepped back, wincing. "Please, continue," he urged his captive.

"There is something else to consider," Volkov said after a long pause. "The Russian president will demand my release. He is a man you don't want to cross, much more powerful and far richer than anyone in the American government. Your leader sits in the palm of his hand."

"That's enough," Larson said. "I don't care about elections or presidents. Tell me about the weapons, or this basement might be the last place you ever see."

The Russian breathed a deep sigh and relented. "I was approached one day in Albania by a man I trusted. He had worked with Albanian Alliance for many years. This man said he had a friend, an American, who was interested in our work. I would not contact this man directly, but instead communicate through a woman who was close to him."

His resolve to cooperate seemed to seep away. Larson said, "Remember our deal. There's a plane bound for Moscow leaving Dulles tonight."

Volkov sighed and nodded. "It did not take me long to realize that this man had no interest in Albania. He wanted weapons—the kind that cannot be obtained legally by American civilians. I wasn't familiar with the group he represented, but as months passed their name appeared more and more in your press."

He let his face reveal nothing. Inside, however, his mind was churning. There was one question he still needed answered.

"What was the name of the man who contacted you?"

Volkov leered one final time, the eyes under his heavy brow full of understanding. He uttered a name.

The basement and its bound captive dissolved, and Larson's gaze refocused on the Scottish countryside. The road ran parallel to a pebbly beach and the loch beyond, its unbroken surface a mirror of distant hills. He watched the loch widen and waited for a fabled monster to lift its head and shatter its placid glass.

Turning Hannah Harper had been the evening's true pièce de résistance. A masterful exhibition of fieldwork from an outside perspective. Larson harbored misgivings about such lofty merits. It was a delicate seduction, but a part of him, a large and confident part, had a feeling the White House Communications Director had been waiting for a moment like the one she was presented that evening. He wondered whether the strain of her role and the secrets she was being asked to keep were taking their toll.

The silhouette of a small town was growing clearer in the distance. Instability was not an option, Larson mused. He'd begun forming a plan the moment he finished interrogating the Russian.

His mind flashed back to Volkov, bound to a chair and gleaming triumphant. The syllables pounded his eardrums, inducing a ringing that refused to abate.

"He works for your president. Dillon Drollsworth."

Chapter Thirty-Four

Larson shifted the car into park and stepped into wan sunlight. Snow had held off, although judging by the accumulated mountains of gray slush along the roadside it would not do so for long.

He walked, following the cryptic directions he had been given. Trees surrounded what he took to be pastureland, although the only wildlife to be seen consisted of a few sheep congregating under a mottled oak tree decrepit without its foliage. The path was strewn with leaves and sludge from the most recent snow. A low hedge ran parallel.

He was starting to wonder what he was doing here when he spotted a familiar figure seated on a bench ahead. As Larson approached, the man rose, falling into step beside him.

Even deep within the Scottish Highlands, Bathari had not lost the look of an over-dressed academic. His jacket was sleek, but his hair was rumpled as though he had run his hand through it several times while pondering some arduous moral dilemma. Heavy bags under his eyes were further proof of a strain on the conscience.

Walking next to him, Larson at once felt at home on the narrow path, surrounded by fields that seemed to stretch on forever.

"Do you listen to music?" Bathari asked.

Larson nodded.

"It was during a meditative stay on an island off the coast of Africa that I came to love music. I've always believed genre is irrelevant. Powerful songs come in all forms, like a certain type of extraordinary person can originate from any background. Like songs, they're a rare breed, diamonds scattered among a mountain of coal. It took me many years to become my most purified self, someone who was fit to enact change and lead others. To vocalize it, that special thing inside me, was the greatest challenge. But it was in me all along. A special potential.

"Imagine a pendulum at the height of its arc, right when it's hanging and still. Filled with energy. You must let the potential out, let it manifest into something real. Most people never do, for whatever reason. Usually fear or a lack of necessary energy. It stays in their head where they can see it, keep it barely alive, and know they could've been great, but they never act. That gives them some small comfort. Ultimately it's comfort in failure."

They continued to walk, Bathari gazing forward with his hands clasped behind his back.

"I compare acting on one's potential to becoming enlightened—in the spiritual sense. You must start small in your everyday life. It took me years, but I figured that out and made it my reality. Big dreamers, visionaries, have a duty to let the world see what they're concocting, to not keep it locked away in their heads until it's too late."

A gust of wind blew past, rippling over the countryside. Larson pulled his jacket tighter, hoping they were headed somewhere indoors with heat or a warm fire. Lost in his musings, Bathari seemed not to notice.

"Humans are naturally reactionary. Therein lies the problem. So many, including those in power, will oppose progress by any means to keep their reality safe, to remain in their flawed bubble. The world's leaders aren't incentivized to be forward thinking or prevent catastrophe, they wish things to remain as they are. Only when they can be denied no longer will they scramble to solve our problems, after it's far too late. Science and reason are screaming in our faces. We must act."

"How do we act?" Larson asked.

For the first time Bathari turned, fixing him with a contemplative look.

"You've done more than your fair share on that front. Much more than I have, although I have been busy in the time we've spent apart. Have you put everything together?"

Larson nodded slowly. "Volkov proved forthcoming. He filled in most of the blanks. We can deduce the rest."

"The verdict?"

He took a deep breath. The air was icy in his throat and smelled like heather. Spires and crenellated battlements of a massive castle emerged between the trees.

"The White House has been funneling illegal weapons to the alt-right, who in turn use them to enact chaos and massacre American citizens. It is meant as a distraction. While the public work into a terrified frenzy, the president quietly seizes more and more power."

He trudged his feet to a halt, staring at the grand manor, still several hundred yards away.

"Removal via Congress is not realistic. Too many powerful people are already on his side. Outing the scheme to the media will be viewed as another ploy to sully the president's name. One option remains."

He could feel Bathari's eyes on him, watching intently. When Larson spoke, his world shifted.

"We need to remove the president."

Bathari's face remained a mask of neutrality. He could have been lost in thought, but then he nodded toward the castle and flashed a grin that made his eyes twinkle.

"I know a man that I believe can help us. You might remember him."

Chapter Thirty-Five

Larson and Bathari waited in an airy sitting room with a tea service on the coffee table before them. Neither touched their saucer. Both gazed at the open doors leading to a spacious hall framed by stone pillars dappled with sunlight.

The new arrival was tall and strapping, that much was obvious as he approached. He wore khaki trousers and a navy cardigan and seemed to glide down the long hall one moment and stand before them the next, posing where he would be framed by golden afternoon light.

Larson leapt to his feet, disturbing the delicate china.

"Be careful, that set once belonged to the Queen of England," Ian McInroe said, although he appeared hardly bothered.

"What are you doing here?"

"I live here," McInroe replied, waving a wrinkled hand for his counterpart to sit.

Larson sat, confused, while the other man graced a leather chair opposite and reached across the tea service to pour a steaming cup.

In a past life, Larson had known Ian McInroe quite well. Without the aging man who had a hint of Scottish fierceness about his features, it was safe to assume his life would have turned out quite different.

McInroe was born and raised in Scotland before moving to the United States in his adolescence for all the requisite schooling of the elite. After college, he set about building his empire.

Its modest beginnings started in real estate. With the help of a family fortune across the Atlantic, McInroe invested in the skylines of many American cities. Along the way, he developed countless important connections and befriended many of the country's power brokers.

By the time he and Larson were introduced, his empire had grown too large to fathom, but it centered around one thing—technology. And that was why he had found the young man with a bright idea so appealing.

Bathari leaned over the coffee table and spoke in a convivial whisper. "Where are all the tourists? The way the place looks one would think you didn't want any visitors."

"I don't." McInroe huffed.

He was in his late sixties; gray hair retreated around the temples and deep wrinkles creased his forehead.

"Had to drive them all away. It was weeks of dismantling signage and giving weepy tour guides the sack. It filled me with great joy."

"And your other little stunt," Bathari said. "It made the worldwide news, you know?"

"I only placed the bloody beast there to scare them all off. Now I'm being charged with disturbing the peace and setting a wild lion on the public. No mention that it was fake. There's a garden and hundreds of rooms, but apparently privacy isn't one of the amenities included within these grounds."

"How did you acquire them?" Bathari asked. "If I'm not mistaken, this house and the surrounding land have belonged to Clan Campbell for centuries."

"Three, to be precise. Bought it off the family, old sods. From what I was told, the Duke of Argyll ran into financial hard times. Don't ask what I had to pay. I've begged to have the signs in the village removed as well, all to no avail. Tourists still manage to dodge security and show up at my door, as if I'll be hospitable enough to give them a personal runabout. The audacity of it. You're lucky my security didn't try to drive the two of you away."

He set his cup down with enough force to make the tea service rattle.

"One of these days I'll become infuriated enough to go pluck the signs out of the ground myself. Then maybe everyone will forget that this place exists. I've made inquiries into buying the whole blasted town and constructing a high fence, but so far I'm being met with stubborn resistance."

He fell silent and studied his visitors.

"I don't know why you're here," he said at last, "But I have good reason to think it must be important."

Bathari nodded. "In the time you've been apart, Mr. Larson has made a considerably large change in profession—"

"You're in intelligence." McInroe uttered with the air of an overworked magician pulling a card from his hat. "Forgive me, I've been around intelligence men, and it's obvious. You hide it better than most. Some strut like they want the world to know they're spies, as if we'll think they're James Bond."

Bathari continued as though he hadn't been interrupted.

"The world owes him a huge debt. He and a handful of others have uncovered a disturbing plot. One that opens our eyes to an alarming set of circumstances. We come to you today, hat in hand, asking for your help."

"Fine. Let's hear it."

Bathari stayed quiet through the entirety of Larson's explanation. At the conclusion he added, "Volkov flooded weapons into whatever corner of the world the Kremlin desired. What we didn't know was that they were finding their way to American soil. And now we have proof that it was ordered directly by the White House."

"You don't have proof," McInroe said. "You have one criminal's testimony. Under duress, I might add."

"Volkov's account combined with corroboration from Harper is as good as proof," Larson said.

"Well, I don't like it," their host said, a bit of Scottish accent bubbling forth. "I get a horrible feeling whenever Russians are involved. They have a history of twisting things to deceive the public. Do you think they have truly infiltrated your government?"

Larson eyed the Scot. "Should we?"

McInroe tilted his head to the side and shrugged one broad shoulder. "I know quite a lot about Russians. They've been running disinformation campaigns since the days of Lenin and the Russian Revolution, most with the chief objective of undermining governments they view as threats. The Soviets supported European terrorist organizations in the seventies. They financed right wing parties in several countries—the ones they understood could be most influenced by fear and would propagate mass hysteria."

Bathari seemed to be contemplating. Larson leaned forward.

"What was the end game?" Larson asked.

"Russia has always operated under a doctrine that the greater the dissension in a country, the weaker it will be. The weaker an opposing country, by contrast, the more secure Russia. An important caveat to this strategy is that it's paramount for the masses to remain uncertain about who is being influenced and who isn't. Mystery and secrecy breed mistrust, which is its own victory. But I don't have to tell you that."

"Our president has been tied to Russia since before the election," Larson said.

McInroe scratched his chin absently. "They're using

him to destabilize America. It's very effective. And there's no proof. That's the genius of it. A steady flow of allegations that get swept into a swirling cloud of mistrust. Although you've uncovered what I think could actually prove useful."

The Scot stood and paced before an ornate mantle lined with delicate figurines. Beyond the sitting room, a maid traipsed down the long hallway.

"I follow current events pertaining to your country closely," McInroe said. "America was my home for many years, and the source of my affluence. I'm beginning to see many similarities between the current regime and tried and true Russian tactics. Fearmongering and deceit. These devices must only be used as an adjunct to real power. As a substitute, they always lead to failure. Russia is living proof. Their leaders were always more interested in manipulation plots than running the country. KGB men that were thrust into power became comfortable with strategies they were already employing. In the end, nothing can compensate for true military and economic might."

Larson followed his pacing. "Everything the alt-right does is reported by the media, which our leaders denounce as fake news meant to slander the regime. Nationalism is at an all-time high, yet the man breeding much of the hate pretends it doesn't exist."

"Chalking everything up to chaos," Bathari said. "Any negative report about this administration is condemned. By calling the media's veracity into question, he's created incredible tension. Nobody knows who to believe."

"It's a foolproof destabilization ploy," McInroe said. "By sowing distrust throughout America, your president makes himself untouchable. I'm not sure there's anything I can do to help, I'm afraid."

"You can," Bathari said. "There's something we need. One way the listing ship can be righted."

"What's that?"

It was Larson who answered.

"It's time for America to open her arms to new

leadership."

"Who will take the current president's place? It can't be his second in command. Most believe he's twice the bumbling fool."

McInroe stared at Larson, waiting for him to answer. With a slightly defiant air, he hesitated before nodding to his left, to the man seated a few feet away. Bathari appeared lost in a reverie that had little to do with either of them.

A light of recognition flamed the Scot's eyes. His mouth fell agape. When McInroe spoke, it was a solitary terse sentence.

"I think we should take a walk."

Chapter Thirty-Six

The three men found themselves hiking a gravel path, the entirety of the manor's southern façade save the pointed turrets fading behind sentinel evergreens. An inlet that fed the loch rose fast to meet them on their left across a frozen field. The grounds of Inveraray Castle held one inarguable advantage; it was possible to traverse endless acres without being overheard.

McInroe's Scottish deerhound, Augustin, padded obediently at his side and expelled saliva with every enthusiastic breath. The dog was meant to hunt deer, McInroe informed them, although deer had all but disappeared from the surrounding acreage. Instead, he had flown her on an expedition to Australia to hunt kangaroos.

The ground was hard with frost. As Larson acclimatized to the stiff winter air, he heeded the verbal sparring amassing like the impending snowstorm overhead.

"What makes you fit to lead?"

McInroe's tone, if anything, was harsher than the

weather. Bathari remained calm, almost disinterested.

"I have grappled with that question for months. Consistently, I arrive at the conclusion that I'm unsure whether I, or anyone, can undertake this task. It might prove more than can be asked of one man. But we must try. Things cannot be allowed to remain the way they are."

"Why not?" McInroe scoffed. "The world has never seen a greater age of peace and prosperity, even with all the bloody terrorism. It's tenuous footing, but it's more than we've ever been able to hope for."

Bathari's eyes beamed with eagerness.

"But we lack one crucial element—time. Time is running out. The political machine moves too slowly and backtracks with every paradigm shift. We'll never be able to make up lost ground. And this new regime is far too dangerous."

"What you're proposing sounds equally disastrous. You would end democracy, slow as it is, for what? A dictatorship? Have you not studied history?"

Bathari shook his head. "Not a dictatorship. Something more streamlined. It is a risk, I'm not denying that, and I've contended with the possibilities. But what the world needs is a group of leaders capable of focusing our collective energies to attack that which truly matters. If we don't, one day soon we'll wish we had."

To Larson's surprise, McInroe chuckled. "I suppose you do have a point. For every dictator that threatened to rip the fabric of society to bits there was a monarch that allowed his people to flourish. And for every tainted monarch there's a corrupted senator or member of parliament. The only difference is that in your version you risk one person running the whole train off the rails, whereas in a democracy a bad egg can't sour the system."

"That's a risk we have no choice but to take."

"You may very well be right. I had some dealings with your president in the past and I confess to categorizing him as a bad egg. And I reckon it won't be long before the

Russians find a way to ruin everything for good."

Augustin barked and bobbed his head in agreement near the waist of his master.

"Do you own all of this?" Larson asked, gesturing to the sloping field and fir trees that stretched in every direction. Again, his deerhound answered with wagging grace.

"All the way to that bridge. The tributary marks the property's eastern border. I wanted to purchase the entire loch, if truth be told, but the government blokes running the show refused. Loch is the old Gaelic word for lake, but all these inlets connect with the sea. I keep a collection of seafaring craft a couple miles from here in case I'm ever forced to make a quick getaway and find the helicopter unavailable."

"There's a helicopter?"

"Of course, lad. Did you not catch a glimpse before you were brought inside the manor? It's around back, funnily enough, where the visitor parking lot used to sit."

He turned back to their grouping's third. "Rumors about you have reached us across the pond. Amassing a following. I've heard more than a few of your supposed ideologies."

The tension rose, as though the crisp air had become taut and hard to breathe.

"Free markets and a global community," McInroe said. "It will never work. Even if you did the extraordinary and found a way for the current global climate to allow for it, you wouldn't get the initiative off the ground before sabotage ensued."

Bathari answered, "Our lone chance of survival is to find a way to cooperate as one people. Borders and regional strife must become a thing of the past. Squabbles over land and religious dogmas waste precious time. This is our task. It may prove impossible, but it is humanity's only hope."

"Don't you see what you're doing? You want to oust the man in power and fill the White House with something even worse. Next, you would come across the ocean and do the same with the British Queen. What then? Would you exile every prime minister and legislature until you control them all? The whole world in Mr. Bathari's palm. It's despicable. What happened to the people at large steering the government, deciding their own fate?"

"What happened is that the people were manipulated to serve a purpose that didn't align with the greater good. You spoke of Russian tactics for spreading fear and panic. They are being applied all over the world, leaving collective masses to run in circles while the privileged few line their pockets. It is time that a select nucleus took control to work toward first salvaging mankind, and then delivering upon it an enlightened age."

"Maybe I was mistaken. But your vision of a global market is now sounding dangerously close to neoliberalism."

"Neoliberalism has never been my aim," Bathari said. "You are not the first to suggest otherwise. Indeed, I understand how believing in the benefits of a capitalist system can be twisted into supporting something far more nefarious. What I'm focused on, at the heart of it, is coming together as one global people and working toward the greater good—sustainability."

"And what if you're wrong? What if our world is not ending, the planet remains perfectly healthy, and its people don't end up crawling over one another for a drink of water. What then?"

"We will have done a tremendous amount of good and avoided what could have been a species-altering disaster."

McInroe's long face split into something resembling a grin. "Spoken like a politician. But you aren't a politician, are you? No, you, Samit Bathari, are something very different."

The taller man fell silent. Augustin, the deerhound, bounded off when the brisk shoreline neared.

Larson fixed his gaze on a bridge spanning the

tributary, each rounded hump mirroring the steel sky. As if the heavens could stand their weight no longer, the first tumultuous flakes of snow lilted toward earth and clung to lichen before disappearing.

Finally, McInroe spoke as they breached a copse of trees overlooking the loch. "What the two of you are suggesting is radical, to say the least. I don't think any of it will work in the slightest, yet my people have never seen eye to eye with Americans and we watched them surpass us well over a century ago."

He stared at the manor house. "I don't necessarily believe in what you're doing, but I'm willing to help. To be perfectly honest, I have more money than I know what to do with. Wresting this property away from a noble family that held it longer than your country has existed was not enough to subdue me."

The Scot's voice neared a crescendo as he consulted Bathari.

"I've never been the type to ignore or doubt science. We may disagree over means, but it stands to reason that the American president and current trends are the greater evil. When push comes to shove, I'd rather be prepared and working to avert a crisis that may or may not be coming, and by all accounts is, than be caught with my pants down when it arrives."

They walked in the direction of the manor house.

"That leaves one final question. What do you require from me?"

"We need Ian McInroe," Bathari answered. "What you have to offer is much more substantial than simple currency or manpower."

"You have others already involved in this endeavor, I take it?"

Bathari nodded.

"Good. You will require powerful partners. I will lend any assistance I can. I have several connections in American media off the top of my head that we might get on board.

They can help improve your image, craft your message. And I know some methods for rapidly growing your following."

McInroe lowered his voice to conspiratorial tones. Larson got the sense that he had relished grilling the other man and was now enjoying their plotting.

"We will have to remove opposition when the time comes. Cutting off the beast's head and quickly replacing it will be paramount. That will take careful preparation."

He left them with a final epithet as they reached grand front doors.

"Bloodshed always follows a power struggle. It has been this way throughout all of history."

It was dark by the time Larson pulled on his coat and strode across the voluminous foyer. His rental car waited outside. Around him, the castle lay quiet, dormant.

Bathari had left in a rush two hours previous. A waiting Escalade had spirited him away to a private airstrip operated by the eccentric Scot.

A member of the hired help materialized and opened the front door like a medieval guard retracting the castle gate. A hand found Larson's shoulder, stopping him.

McInroe leaned forward, pressing something into the flesh of his palm. As McInroe pulled away, he whispered an aircraft tail number and a destination in his ear. And then he was gone.

A twinge of good fortune permeated as the Tesla wound its way around Loch Fyne, lost in a darkened countryside softened by a fresh coat of snow. Larson's next assignment, at least, would be much warmer.

Chapter Thirty-Seven

Fiumicino International Airport was a thirty-minute drive from Rome's ancient city center. Larson arrived in early afternoon by way of the A91, running parallel to the sacred Tiber River. This time, he wasn't seated behind the sleek wheel of a Tesla but piloted a small, boxy Fiat that pulled to the right when accelerating north of forty kilometers per hour.

Along the Via Merulana, the Fiat grumbled in an aggressive queue that ignored red lights and traffic directions and passed blocks of beige brick and stone buildings in a blur. It was common knowledge that Italian drivers paid little attention to rules of the road. At the Basilica di Santa Prassede, Larson turned left, delving into the old city's heart.

Ten minutes later, he skirted a cobbled side street and walked past a porter into the Grand Hotel de la Minerve, an ode to the ancient Roman goddess of the arts. A concierge at the front desk who spoke passable English saw him checked in and situated in room 415, a spacious suite on the hotel's top floor that overlooked the cobbled square.

Larson dropped off his belongings and vacated the suite for the much better vantage point of the hotel's terraced rooftop. Drink in hand, he perched near a cluster of abandoned divans and canvas umbrellas and gazed toward the Pantheon's faded stone walls. The weather was not cold despite it being the middle of December, and generous Roman sunlight spilled onto the red-brick terrace.

He searched beyond the Pantheon and visualized tourist crowds, even now, swelling en masse along the Via dei Condotti, flocking fashionable stores and departing with bags stuffed full of luxury items. It was somewhat humorous how one of the world's oldest cities could coexist with modern society. Churches that had braved existence for centuries stood across from stores peddling the height of Italian fashion.

A familiar face materialized at his side. She held a glass of Italian red wine to her lips. A thin, uncovered arm brushed against Larson's jacket sleeve.

"I didn't know they would send you."

"I asked to come," Elena said. "Katz saw no reason to object."

"He knows what I'm doing here?"

"Samit filled him in. The two of them, along with Gilbert, have been in constant contact. And your Scot, Ian McInroe, has already begun offering assistance. I'm afraid Katz and Gilbert aren't too fond of him. They're used to getting their way. At times, McInroe seems desirous of nothing more than inducing chaos."

"I think he believes in Bathari, deep down. Even if he questions humanity."

"And what about you? Do you believe in him?"

Larson said nothing for several long moments. "I believe that something has to change. Right now, he is our best hope. In retrospect, he won my loyalty that first day I met him in Montreal."

"This won't be easy, you know. It will be very dangerous."

"I knew danger would be involved when I agreed to join Echelon. And it's not just about saving the world. I promised we would deliver justice for your brother, Elena."

Stories below, tables were being arranged in the cobbled courtyard, white cloths and umbrellas unfolded for the upcoming dinner service. Restaurants and cafes were coming to life, aromatic scents wafting from open doors that reached their perch high above. A trickle of pedestrians, thickening as they watched, filled in empty spaces, loitering near the massive columned entrance, or listening to delicate music soak the air around them.

"It's beautiful, isn't it?" Elena whispered. "The Eternal City. I always dreamed of living here. That is, once I was privy to learn that anything outside the Soviet bloc even existed. It seemed so charming in my head, surreal."

"The reality doesn't exactly disappoint," Larson murmured, drawing a smile from her lips.

"Yes, but I would be hard-pressed leaving New York. For now, America is my home."

They retired downstairs to the suite. When Larson emerged, the sky was dark and some of the afternoon's warmth had been siphoned away. He wore a pair of crème trousers and a thick linen shirt hidden under a charcoal sweater. His shoes were Italian leather—expensive, but not so flashy as to draw unwanted attention.

It was a twenty-minute walk to the Colosseum. Although guides had long since left for the night, many tourists still lingered near Rome's most identifiable landmark. Larson sidestepped the crowds and slipped underground into the gaping bowels of the city metro. Making sure he wasn't followed, he rode the blue train to the Termini station.

He switched trains and rode to the Flaminio station. Near the Piazza del Popolo, Larson ascended back into the Roman evening.

The steps leading to the Villa Borghese, unnoticed by pedestrians teeming the piazza, had the uneven and careworn feel of masonry brought to life many centuries ago. As Larson climbed, they gave way to a winding path. Its scenery grew wild, receding from walls bedecked with fashion advertisements into a landscape bursting with trees and undergrowth.

The largest public garden in central Rome sat atop the ancient Pincian Hill. Dotted with umbrella pine and busts of several dozen notable Italians, its grounds were home to perhaps the most breathtaking city views.

Larson thought of neither Titian nor Caravaggio as he reached level ground and a gravel-strewn promenade overlooking the piazza below. An elderly Italian couple huddled together and gazing at the glowing Basilica in the distance hardly noticed him pass. He approached the only other figure in sight.

"You weren't followed," Diego said as he reached the concrete balustrade.

He nodded, gazing down at the radiant piazza with its obelisk that rose even with the terrace. "Rome was seven hills with a wall around them once," he mused. "Look at how it's exploded over the millennia." He turned to face his fellow Echelon agent. "Were you aware that Elena was coming?"

Diego was taken aback. "I like to think that I know everything, but on that account, I was in the dark." He shifted his feet over dusty concrete. "It's nothing to worry about," he said. "Elena can take care of herself."

"Easy for you to say," Larson said. He thought back to the attempt on their lives in Las Vegas.

"You need to be worried about what you have to do in a few minutes. Tonight is crucial if you want your plan to succeed. Difficulties may arise."

"Then I suppose I'll have to get creative. But let's hope it doesn't come to that."

Rome was alive around them. Diego, who had been

raised Catholic, gazed across the Tiber at the bulbous dome of St. Peter's Basilica.

"Do you think we're doing the right thing?" Larson asked.

His colleague didn't answer right away, spellbound by Christianity's epicenter.

"We can take a bold risk, or we can do nothing and surely fail." Diego pointed a finger at the Basilica. "Even the current Pope is realizing that change is long overdue. We live in a different world. Adapt, or it passes you by. Complacency will only see traditional powers wiped out."

He was at a loss for words. Diego glanced at him and grinned.

"Could you live with yourself knowing that you never jumped?"

"You know," Larson said, "that might be the most prophetic thing I've ever heard you say."

"What are you waiting for?"

Chapter Thirty-Eight

It was three blocks to the Tiber's edge. Larson walked south parallel with the water, peering between beech trees and a high river wall and checking his tail at two-block intervals. Boats and barges languished atop murky water, permanently moored to the river's concrete bank. At least one had been converted into a floating restaurant.

As the time grew closer, he increased his pace. It was precisely eight when he pivoted without warning and boarded a bus that pulled to a halting stop on the tree-lined vista. Church bells tolled the hour when the bus pulled away.

Larson welcomed the crowded interior as he wedged into a seat toward the front; perfect position to scan the face of every passenger coming aboard. Traffic was heavy along the Via del Corso. Near the heart of the old Roman Forum, he exited the bus, standing for a moment under a row of sentinel umbrella pine before crossing the street and disappearing into an avenue of chiseled ruins.

An ominous door situated halfway along a narrow alley

opened as Larson approached. Bluish light and the unmistakable sound of pounding music spilled forth. So did a billowing cloud of fog. Reaching the entrance, Larson stepped into the fog and immediately began to shiver. Blue light was omnipresent as a pair of rough hands grabbed him and a hooded parka was draped over his shoulders.

When his eyes adjusted, he was taken aback. The place was a series of rooms with white fabric running across the ceiling. But the walls, everything save the floor and ceiling, were covered in a thick layer of ice.

That explained the cold. The ethereal light seemed to emanate from the ice itself, spliced here and there with flashes of pink and purple. Pillars lined the walls, interspersed throughout with towering ice sculptures. The rooms teemed with people.

Larson maneuvered himself further into the place, unsure where to go, pushing past others in identical overcoats. A bar along the wall caught his eye. Vodka arrived in a frozen glass. He downed it in one and left to delve further into the wintry chaos.

He was starting to lose hope when a tenor voice spoke at his back in Italian-accented English.

"Welcome to Rome's Ice Club, Mr. Larson. You seem to be enjoying yourself."

The crowd ignored the two of them as they worked further into the place, leaving the main chamber for a side compartment that was empty save a few stragglers and devoid of pulsing music. His companion led him behind a cluster of pillars into an icy grotto before turning to face him.

Their eyes met, but that was all. The face opposite was covered by a thick balaclava. Larson peered through the fabric's slit, trying to piece together the rest of the face by what little he could see. The eyes themselves were magnetic; piercing blue with golden flecks that gave them an unnatural allure.

"You're the hacker?"

"Call me Agent Orange," the hooded figure said. "I'm

the one that can solve all your problems."

Even under the thick jacket, Larson could tell he was solidly built, about medium height with a rigid posture. The response came without thinking.

"Because you're from Vietnam?"

The head shook under the balaclava.

"No, Mr. Larson. Because I destroy everything in my path."

The hacker slipped deeper between crystallized pillars and Larson followed. A club employee appeared and pressed glasses of vodka into their hands before a nod from Agent Orange sent him disappearing. The hacker seemed to have the run of the place.

"You know why I'm here?"

Agent Orange nodded. "You have powerful friends. All this was arranged by a middleman I know as Pluto, but I understand he works for a man named Samit Bathari."

"Pluto?"

"Just a code name. An alias. We use them often in this business, although Pluto couldn't be anything further from a hacker. He simply happens to know plenty of them—the best, I might add."

"And what did he tell you?"

"The truth. I demand as much from all my potential clients. Pluto informed me that Mr. Bathari would see his philosophies come into a more mainstream prominence. Much more. It is your aim to take down the American government and install something new. And he added that this will be impossible, even with all your powerful friends, without my help, or someone like me—someone very good."

Larson tilted his head, looking past the hacker and narrowing his eyes at a pair of hooded men who had entered the club. His brow creased as the smaller of the two cast a lingering glance in their direction. They disappeared into the frosty maze of neon lights and pillars.

He refocused his attention. "Did this Pluto mention any

specifics?"

Even if it were only the electric blue eyes he could see, Larson had the feeling that his counterpart was giving him a sly look.

"Your federal government's network is vast, but it may be vulnerable. Since the turn of the decade, modernization and system enhancement have been on the decline, making much of what keeps the cogs of democracy churning border on obsolete. At one precise moment all of it will need to come crashing down."

"When will that be?"

The hacker peered at him. "That's where the details end, I'm afraid. Save one. Pluto gave me a name but would tell me precious little about you. I take it you're American intelligence, but you don't much look like one of the stiffs from Langley. Tell me, Mr. Larson, who are you? How did you come to be knotted up in all this?"

Larson shifted his body weight as he raised the glass to his lips, edging ever so slightly backward. "Who I am has no bearing on our meeting. I came to put a deal in place."

The hacker seemed to sway before him. "That's a shame, because my end of your proposed deal happens to be laborious not to mention wildly dangerous." Blue eyes gleamed. "There are few others that could accomplish this task if I were to decline. And our illicit professional circles tend to run small. If I were to warn them—"

"You would be making a mistake."

"Would I?"

Music, less boisterous in this corner of the club but still resonant, seemed to melt away. The crowds had gone invisible. There would be no cocktail waitresses or club employees approaching. Even though the hacker was whispering, Larson caught every word.

"Was it a grave mistake that your attractive lady friend came to Rome? That she's in room 415 at the Grand Hotel de la Minerve, across from the Pantheon. Will she be there when you return? Maybe she'll get bored and stray out for a bite to eat, unaware that men are following her, unaware that your fellow agent, who should have been tailing her, is still making passes half a dozen blocks away because his *own* tail isn't clean. Ask yourself these questions before you threaten me, Mr. Larson."

Before he could respond, Larson caught movement out of the corner of his eye. He grabbed the hacker and pushed him behind the nearest pillar as the first burst of air flew past them. An ice sculpture across the room exploded.

Chapter Thirty-Nine

Larson forced himself and the hacker to the ground as the next shots tore past. In the brief reprieve that followed, he pulled Agent Orange to his feet.

"We have to get out of here."

Whether out of sheer dread or experience Agent Orange said nothing as Larson led the way through the dimly lit club, shoving past unnerved patrons also clamoring to escape and a few who still had no idea what was happening. He didn't need to glance over his shoulder to confirm that the hooded men were following. The next bullet that whizzed past his head and lodged in the club's heavy front door was all the proof he needed.

On the cobbled alley outside chaos from within the Ice Club spilled forth with screams and exclamations of terror. Larson fought through the crowd and dragged Agent Orange left, down the long Via Della Madonna Dei Monti and past various parked cars and motor scooters.

It wasn't beyond reason to hope that the men who had

shot at them had lost sight of their prey in the mass exodus. That hope was dashed by the appearance of another imposing duo outside a closed *taverna* further down the claustrophobic street, comically out of place among riotous potted foliage and miniature cars. His rapid glimpse at what they were holding told him it would make for a poor decision to attempt an escape past the two hulking figures.

Shouts rang out as he changed direction at the last instant and pulled the hacker through a perpendicular alley that crossed several busier streets as it ran south toward the Colosseum. At this time of night, the area was devoid of life. Larson cursed the nocturnal crowds that favored high-end shopping along the Via del Corso several blocks north or the nightclubs in Trastevere across the river. Without a way to blend in, he and the still-masked hacker pounding at his heels were sitting ducks.

A motor scooter's whine coming from one street over washed him in dread. He glanced over his shoulder. The second pair of men were sprinting after them. One had his gun leveled. Larson yanked Agent Orange out of the way as several more rounds ripped through the night.

The street dead-ended at a wall lined with wrought iron spikes and wrapped to the left along a terrace. The illuminated Colosseum, still impressive even given the circumstances, materialized ahead as the validity of Larson's worry became clear.

Two men with their faces concealed sat astride the small, motorized craft as it rocketed up the cobbled street straight at them. The assailant seated behind the driver glared over the nose of a compact submachine gun.

The first volatile spray of bullets flew harmlessly over their heads. He pulled his companion against a crumbling wall and said, "We're trapped. They've got us from both sides."

Agent Orange glanced around and pointed at the ancient Roman Forum. "We can lose them in there."

The motorbike's whine grew louder. Larson couldn't

think. "How do we make it over there?"

"Split up. It's our only shot."

The motorbike was on top of them. As the gunman sent another stream of rounds that blighted every other sound, the hacker yelled, "Now!"

They each took off in opposite directions. In his peripheral vision the motorbike jerked violently, caught off guard by the sudden maneuver. Unsure of who to follow, the driver swerved in either direction before losing his balance. Larson ducked as another barrage of gunfire narrowly missed his head. Crouching behind a line of parked cars, he sprinted past the assailants toward the Colosseum.

Agent Orange reappeared at a railed path leading to the thoroughfare below. They were deposited near a discrete entrance to the underground metro system and sprinted across the street without bothering to check if they were being followed. The motorbike's whine in the distance told Larson that their attackers' reprieve would be short-lived.

He envisioned following the road until they could hail a taxi or bus to take them toward a more congested section of the city. Anywhere they could lose the men who seemed desperate to kill the pair of them. He dialed Diego's cell phone as he ran. Maybe he could help. It rang six times before going to voicemail. *Damn it!*

That plan was dashed by the appearance of another pair of motorbikes hurtling toward them along the thoroughfare. Unwilling to risk another encounter, Larson waited until the bikes were too close to make a sharp turn. He dashed down a cobbled footpath running between the Colosseum and an expansive area of ruins with Agent Orange on his heels.

Before the ancient path reached the colossal Arch of Constantine they forked to the right, running between walls lined with high, spiked railings into the mass of ruins. Larson's heart sank as he glimpsed what lay ahead. They were blocked by a high gate padlocked shut. Hopelessly trapped. Scaling it was not an option. He urged himself to think, to engineer a way out of this. His thoughts were stalled by his companion motioning toward an unassuming ticket booth to the gate's right.

"This way."

He watched in amazement as Agent Orange ducked through a small door and beckoned for him to follow. The air inside the booth was stale and warm. The hacker crossed to the rear and unlatched a miniature door that blended with the mottled wall. Stooping, Larson squeezed through after him and had to fight a growth of dense foliage that had overtaken the small building's rear. Pushing tangled vines aside he realized where they were.

The ancient Roman Forum stretched out before them. Arches, pillars, and temple remains dotted the landscape here and there like the chipped and crumbling teeth of a giant sunk into the earth. They hurried into the ruins, Palatine Hill rising gracefully on their left.

"Welcome to the heart of ancient Rome."

Larson's response was drowned by a bullet exploding against a piece of protruding wall and raining rubble and dust everywhere. Several more followed, lodging all around them and sending dirt and shrapnel flying. The landscape turned hazy; he caught sight of the mystery assailants advancing as one. Each had his weapon drawn.

They ran, weaving through preserved wreckage and doing their best to dodge gunfire that pelted centuries-old columns and limestone walls alike. Sirens blared in the distance, a welcome addition although it seemed to have no effect on the men hunting them.

One shot found its mark, nicking Larson's shoulder as they dove behind a faded column in the shadow of Septimius Severus's massive triumphal arch. Ignoring the stinging pain, he let Agent Orange take the lead and direct them toward a flight of steep stairs that led back to trappings of modern civilization.

The armed men reached the stairs as they crested the top and sprinted toward the Piazza del Campidoglio, a square designed by Michelangelo atop one of Rome's original seven hills. As the piazza widened, Larson grabbed the hacker and pulled him along the edge and under a shadowy overpass. They disappeared as the assailants burst into the square framed with regal buildings on three sides.

Slipping deeper into a narrow alley, the two melted into the thick gloom of a recessed doorway and waited. Ten minutes passed before Larson dared to speak.

Agent Orange paid him little attention. The hacker stepped back, and with a swipe of one gloved hand, his hood fell away. Next came the balaclava, tugged upward until it was pulled free.

Larson was stunned. Bubblegum pink hair stood in rebellious spikes after having been mashed down by the balaclava. Olive skin was punctuated by a nose ring with a gleaming diamond and a raised tattoo design that swirled from either temple to the base of the hacker's neck.

But it was not the tattoos, or jewelry, or shocking hair that took him aback.

Agent Orange offered a gloved hand and one of his own took hold.

"We have a deal, Mr. Larson."

He was still in numb disbelief. Agent Orange was a woman.

Chapter Forty

Reggie Thompkins would be dead soon. He thought of the old KGB—knocking on doors and dragging off dissidents and loyal party members alike to be shot and dumped in mass graves. Cold steel against the nape and a quick bullet.

He refused to go out like that. There would be no waiting for a thundering knock on the door.

The men supplying his doom technically did not exist. The alt-right's objectives were strictly political; never mind who they consorted with beyond the media's watchful eye. But they would come all the same. And when they melted back into the shadows nothing would remain save the fact that one of their own, ensconced in the movement's folds, had fallen casualty to an unforeseeable accident.

He had abandoned his Tenleytown apartment and now caught sporadic snatches of sleep at the Hay-Adams Hotel across the street from Lafayette Square. Several nights had been passed staring out of curtained windows until either the sun rose, or he succumbed to exhaustion in a firm yet inviting armchair.

Thompkins leaned against the door and felt the slightest sensation of comfort as the deadbolt clicked and the chain rattled.

What he needed was to think. Not that it mattered. When he did, he would come to the same conclusion he had arrived at hours ago. Often those first gut instincts were the best.

What he'd overheard would be more valuable than diamonds if delivered to the right people. In this instance, Thompkins happened to know the right people. He had been working with them for months. It was for this reason that his life's expiration date rapidly approached.

Satisfied there was no sound of imminent footsteps echoing down the hall, he retreated from the door and canvassed the window. The street was lined with cars. He thought he could make out a figure bent low behind the steering wheel of a black Volvo. It was hard to tell. An unmarked van near the hotel's corner could be monitoring his room. Men might have broken in and bugged it hours ago, even days.

Dusk approached but Lafayette Park still teemed with visitors, crowding police-lined gates that abutted the White House's rear lawn. The president had flown north that morning to meet with the Canadian Prime Minister. His absence made Thompkins feel no safer. These days the president rarely contacted the men he had allied with prior to the election. It was as if the far right ceased to exist the moment he took office. Of course, that couldn't have been any further from the truth.

Thompkins collapsed on an upholstered couch. The information he had overheard had not slipped out unintentionally. It had been served as juicy bait. The alt-right understood he had betrayed them. Thompkins wasn't sure how they knew, but it didn't matter. They knew.

Now the alt-right had an ironclad reason to kill him. He could not be allowed to remain alive lest he passed on the information. And he had every intention of doing so. He had to. Finally bringing his mission to a close had a nice ring to it.

He had to find Michael Larson. Track him down and reveal everything. Thompkins unchained the door and slipped into the carpeted hall.

A minute later, he passed the hotel's impressive foyer and stepped into a frigid December evening. It was a week before Christmas and the entire city was festooned with twinkling lights. A massive evergreen in Lafayette Square was dwarfed only by its companion on the White House lawn. Tourists across the street were beginning to disperse, dejected by the lack of a presidential sighting the way a whaling expedition returned home morose after witnessing nothing but water and seagulls.

Thompkins ignored them. The entirety of his being was focused on this mission, his one final objective. He didn't have a car. He had abandoned it when he fled the apartment. So, he stepped onto the sidewalk and hailed a cab.

As one approached, he dialed a number from memory.

Chapter Forty-One

Two days after returning from Rome, Larson locked his office inside Echelon's clandestine headquarters and strode to the elevator. Before it could descend, a hand forced its way between the closing doors at the last second.

Diego entered, saying nothing but standing closer than was necessary as the steel box sank lower. Larson had given his colleague a wide berth since Rome. Something about that night wasn't right. Now he became wary of his continued silence as the metal grilles slid apart on the ground floor.

His instincts proved correct. He found the lobby blocked by two men in dark suits. Neither moved aside to let him pass. On the contrary, both stepped forward in unison. To his right Diego eased in closer, wafting his cologne's florid scent.

"Now, don't do anything rash."

In less than three seconds, it was over. The suited men hustled him toward the door with Diego leading the way. Instinct begged Larson to cry out. His bandaged shoulder, still tender from his mishap in Rome, stung with pain. The other agent must have been thinking along the same lines. He turned and flung something suffocating and dark over Larson's head.

Thrashing beneath the heavy fabric, he entered the biting cold before being lifted and thrust through an open door onto a leather seat. The purr of an idling engine explained his new surroundings. Firm sinew pressed against either side as his captors slid in next to him. Diego spoke rapidly, presumably to the vehicle's driver, as they eased forward and put the finishing salvoes on his abduction.

Larson had a suspicion as to where they were heading. It proved correct when the covering over his head was removed. Halfway across Theodore Roosevelt Bridge, the Lincoln Memorial's ethereal façade loomed large on their right.

Diego faced forward in the passenger seat.

"What the hell do you mean by this?" Larson asked.

The other man didn't turn. Staring straight ahead, he said, "Be quiet, Larson. You'll understand what we're doing soon enough."

"Is this your idea of a mutiny?"

Diego met his question with silence.

They continued into Washington. Bright lights dimmed as they sped past the Vietnam Memorial and onward toward the National Mall. At this time of evening, traffic was relatively light. Larson leaned forward and the men on either side of him tensed.

"Where are we going?"

"I promise the journey will be short."

"And when we arrive?"

Diego whipped his head around to face his captor. "We had no choice but to do it this way. What you and Bathari are asking many of us to undertake is highly dangerous. Treason."

His heart sank. Diego had turned. He was being brought in. Where were they taking him? And had they already apprehended Bathari?

It was Diego who broke the stunned silence. He reached back, dangling something small and black in front of him. "Here."

He reluctantly took the cellphone and pressed it to his ear.

A tenor voice on the other end was familiar. Larson forgot his building panic as he realized who was speaking.

"I've entered the United States, Mr. Larson," Agent Orange purred. "I'm not going to tell you where I am, but I can assure you I did it without setting off any alarm bells."

"How did you get in?"

"Don't concern yourself with my methods. Just know that I'll begin work right away. Pass that along to Mr. Bathari."

"And the prognosis?"

"It will take time," the hacker said, "but I'm cautiously optimistic. Keep your ear to the ground."

The line went dead.

Confused, he handed the phone back to Diego as they passed a manned guard station. The road narrowed, curving left and sinking into the ground. At the spot where it disappeared altogether, one of the capital's most iconic structures loomed over them.

Doors opened after the engine died and Larson was prodded out of the vehicle. The door swung shut and he was marched forward.

"Diego, talk to me. What the hell is going on?"

A gaping manmade tunnel swallowed them. Diego led the way. He didn't bother answering until they had descended a story into what amounted to a concrete and brick-crusted tube wide enough to fit a small jet.

"There are all kinds of rumors about what goes on here. Everything from Freemasons to Satanists. The man responsible for these tunnels studied bugs and bacteria. Is it that hard for the public to accept something as mundane as government officials needing a quicker way to get around?"

Ancient brick shifted to pristine concrete. Sterile lights along the ceiling made the walls glow white. The tunnel widened, and after rounding another curve, Larson observed a track bisecting its center with Plexiglas barriers on either side. Train tracks or a monorail.

So, they were directly underneath the Capitol.

Diego refused to offer further explanation. Not until Larson was being steered through a heavy door leading away from the white tube did he continue.

"Just because you're an Echelon agent doesn't mean you can be trusted. Wise people don't know who to trust these days, so they trust no one."

Larson tried to make sense of the riddle. They had reached a warren of beige hallways lined with identical doors and polished floor that reflected a pipe-laden ceiling. The doors reminded him of prison cells. Dread set in. Larson couldn't shake a feeling he was being led to his death, galvanized by the fact that Diego refused to look at him.

The suited men and their leader must have memorized their way through the maze of corridors. Larson couldn't help visualizing the man he had once trusted as executioner leading him to the gallows.

After half a dozen turns along identical corridors, he lost his sense of direction. Not once did they come across another soul. He feared Diego was done speaking when, after what felt like their hundredth turn, he looked over his shoulder.

"Your escorts belong to the United States Secret Service."

Larson glanced to his left and right. Neither man acknowledged him. Ahead, Diego continued, "I'm sorry for the secrecy, Michael. You'll understand everything momentarily."

They came to a stop at a heavy door identical to all the others. The Secret Service agents hustled him inside while Diego stood back to let them pass.

"There are all kinds of useful amenities down here," he

said, following them into the dark room and pulling the door closed. "Many bureaucrats keep their offices below the Capitol, along with meeting chambers, a cafeteria, and commissary. Of course, it was all dreamed up to provide easy transportation within the Capitol Complex. There's even a secret underground built alongside the D.C. metro that connects the Capitol to several important buildings."

Lights flicked on, throwing relief over the room's sparse fixtures. The walls had been converted into floor-to-ceiling dry erase boards on three sides. One lone desk headed a cluster of rolling chairs.

Larson lurched backward in shock. Standing across the room was a clone of Diego Rivera. Nearly a replica, save the close-cropped haircut hugging his scalp and a grim expression that reached from his pointed chin to a pair of narrowed eyebrows. Like his counterparts flanking Larson, he wore a dark suit.

"Michael," Diego said, "I believe it's time you met my twin brother, Armand."

Armand Rivera stepped forward and shook Larson's hand. It was easy to observe, even beneath the suit, that he had Diego beat in muscle mass. His handshake threatened to crush bone. As he retreated, Larson heard a foreign sound for the first time since he'd been brought beneath the Capitol, echoing outside their room.

The footsteps grew louder. Then they stopped.

"This meeting is confidential," Armand confided in monotone. "But we're about to be joined by one more."

The heavy door opened, and their grouping met eyes with another dark-suited agent. He led a second figure. A wave of shock passed as Larson took in the face.

The Secret Service agents dispersed to the background. Reggie Thompkins said nothing as he walked to the head of the room. Armand eyed Larson imploringly.

"I've summoned this man tonight to share information that could alter the course of United States history."

Chapter Forty-Two

"I don't understand what's going on."

Larson pivoted from Thompkins to the man that was the spitting image of his partner. "How do the two of you know one another?"

Before Armand or Thompkins could speak, Diego stepped forward. "They insisted on secrecy while I was bringing you here. Armand is my twin brother, and the Deputy Assistant Director of the United States Secret Service. Like us, he works for the Department of Homeland Security if we're getting technical. As for Thompkins—"

"Reggie Thompkins has been working as a paid informant," Armand interjected. "He was handed to me by Rahim Gilbert, via your man Katz. That's why I summoned him this evening. Your team has exposed corruption deep within our political system. Thompkins passed on another bit of alarming information. You need to hear it directly from his mouth."

Larson stepped forward. His brow furrowed. "What use

would the Secret Service have with an alt-right source?"

"The Secret Service is just as concerned with threats to this country as you are, Mr. Larson," Armand replied. "Even if the threats stem from some of the very men we are sworn to protect."

"The threat isn't the one under constant protection," Thompkins blurted out. In an instant, every eye in the room focused on him. "That's the point," he continued, "the president is nothing more than a pawn. Take him down and you won't get anywhere. There's another pawn waiting to fill his place, and another, and then half a dozen more."

Larson turned back to Armand. "Does this mean you're agreeing to help us?"

He remained stoic. "I said no such thing. I believe Diego warned you about the treasonous implications of tonight's events. To every soul not standing inside this room, this meeting never took place."

"But if it did—"

"If solid proof arises that high-placed members of the federal government have been funneling weapons to the alt-right who in turn use them to distract the public while government officials usurp power, it would be wholly within our means to take action. Protecting America comes before everything, even the president."

"But it's not the president you're after," Thompkins insisted. Urgency swelled in his voice.

"Who are we after?"

"Someone who wasn't elected. Someone who isn't part of the Cabinet but sits in on every meeting anyway. He insisted pawns be appointed around the president—a sea of them. That's his goal. No matter who resigns or gets impeached, the regime continues."

"Yes, but give us a damn name," Diego blurted.

Larson didn't need any more clarification. When he spoke, the room fell silent.

"Dillon Drollsworth. He's behind all of this."

Thompkins nodded. "There had always been

suspicions. A few days ago, I obtained concrete proof."

"How?"

The timid man, possibly remembering his interrogation in Las Vegas, shivered.

"It doesn't matter how we know," Armand argued. "This is a crucial bit of information."

"But Thompkins has been informing on the alt-right for months," Larson said. "Isn't it possible they got wind of his treachery and planted this story so he'd come running to us? They could have made it seem like he'd overheard something important and suddenly he's leading us in the wrong direction. We could end up fooled and hounding after a man who's no more than he appears—a presidential aide."

Armand took a powerful step forward. "How much do you know about Drollsworth?"

Larson made no reply.

"You don't find it the least bit odd that he's twice the age of the typical aide? Or that he never seems to leave the president's side? Or the fact that he's connected with the alt-right as well as several other white nationalist organizations? Drollsworth was the chief perpetrator in acquiring foreign weaponry for the alt-right."

Larson shook his head. "Hannah Harper was the one in contact with Volkov. She's working for us now."

"Drollsworth is her handler," Armand said.

Larson glared at him.

"Drollsworth is the puppeteer pulling the strings," Thompkins said. "Using the alt-right and acts of terror as the ultimate diversion is his masterpiece."

Larson appeared thoughtful for several moments. Then he pivoted toward the Deputy Assistant Director of the Secret Service.

"Are you agreeing to help us?"

Armand didn't flinch at the question. "This meeting never happened. But my men and I are willing to do whatever it takes to protect our country. If that means taking down certain figures who would do it harm, so be it. What happens after that is out of my control."

He turned to his partner. "We'll need a plan for when the federal government mainframes go dark."

Diego nodded in agreement. "We'll have one."

Larson set his gaze on Armand. "Let's say we put the puppeteer out of business. What do we do with the puppets?"

Chapter Forty-Three

Six square blocks in the nation's capital between Fifth and Eighth Street belong to Chinatown. Larson passed entwined red and blue dragons at the intersection of H Street and Seventh and slipped under the ornamental Friendship Arch amid a gaggle of teenagers waiting at a crosswalk.

Half a block from the arch, he checked his tail. The sidewalk swelled with people and the four-lane street was congested with afternoon traffic. With New Year's Day less than forty-eight hours in the rearview mirror, tourists and locals alike were still out in full force.

Muddying the waters, Larson thought. A throng of people might prove beneficial. If anyone was watching, it would be harder to spot him in a crowd.

Reassured that he was not being followed, Larson ducked once around the block and proceeded along H Street until he reached a building unlike the others around it.

It was much smaller; three stories and dwarfed by an adjacent concrete tower. A whitewashed façade with red trim and the traditional sloping tiled roof associated with all things Oriental. Larson glanced over his shoulder one last time and slipped inside.

Bathari sat alone at a table near the window.

"I saw you coming," he said.

He wore khaki trousers and a merino wool sweater that ended in a neat roll below his chin. A pair of reading glasses were perched halfway down his nose.

"The tea is delightful," Bathari exclaimed as he sat. "Ginseng. I ordered you a cup."

"Thank you. I hope we'll have much more to discuss then tea."

Bathari waved his impatience away. "In due time. I haven't had a chance to browse the menu. Cantonese is one of my favorites. Even if it's not quite as authentic as some might like."

Larson's tea was delivered in the shaking hands of a wizened Chinese man wearing a smudged black apron tied around his waist. They ordered lunch and watched the waiter disappear back to the kitchen. As he rounded a Formica counter piled with menus and an overflowing bowl of fortune cookies, Bathari murmured, "You weren't followed?"

"I don't think so."

"That is good news. Our new year is getting off to a positive start."

Larson's eye caught a small television screen—the only one in the restaurant—and he was reminded of something as he watched two reporters gesture in silent diatribe.

"Your following has grown considerably," he said to Bathari. "I'm impressed. You've succeeded in bringing yourself into the public spotlight."

"Don't be," the other man said. "Much of that has to do with our mutual friend, Mr. McInroe, pulling strings across the pond. It's a wonder what his influence has been able to accomplish."

It had become apparent over the past fortnight that Ian

McInroe was indeed a man of his word. A few transatlantic phone calls were seemingly all it had taken to turn Bathari into an overnight media sensation. Only one major network had run anything contesting his darling status.

The previous evening Larson viewed live footage of a rally starring Bathari on one network. Several others had aired snippets in the hours following. Cameras focused on a crowd at a park in Northern Virginia, teeming despite bitter winter evening cold. It had been an impromptu event, but by the time the news trucks convened, it had all the appearance of a legitimate political gathering.

"It's obvious much of the public adores you," Larson said as their food arrived.

Bathari waited until the waiter departed before he replied. "They have found someone they can relate to. Many Americans long for a leader with a varied background. A political outsider. Some people, and I do still have my share of detractors, see me as the refined version of this."

Larson spooned a mouthful of soup. "Your supporters… Why do they think these rallies are being held?"

Bathari hesitated.

"Many believe I'm campaigning for the next election. They assume I was born in America or have found some loophole around the law. Some have more far-fetched ideas that are closer to the truth. There are constant rumors swirling that the president will be removed. I daresay a faction of my supporters harbor pipe dreams that if that day ever does arrive, I will be appointed to take his place."

"But that's impossible. The presidency would pass to the vice president, and then the House Minority Leader—"

"And so on down the line past the Secretary of the Treasury and through the Cabinet," Bathari finished his sentence. "Except, if all these appointees were deemed corrupt and guilty, it would be reasonable to assume that one would have difficulty finding a suitable contender. That is a possibility heretofore never experienced or even pondered by the American public."

Larson let Bathari's words sink in while he studied a family bundled against the cold and pushing an infant stroller outside their window.

"You think the public would rather appoint an outsider than dip so low down the chain of command?"

"That possibility cannot be ruled out entirely," Bathari said. "The matter is unprecedented."

His gaze had moved to the television. Larson's followed and he started in surprise as his friend filled a space between the news anchors. Bathari continued.

"There arises the issue of how to deal with members of Congress who have proven equally corrupt. The president has many allies. They must be handled with care."

Larson wrapped a free-spirited noodle around his chopsticks and brought it to his mouth. "That will all be arranged in the coming days. An operation is underway, although it will need to be carried out with incredible precision. Timing is key."

"Am I allowed to know what will transpire?" Bathari asked.

He wiped his mouth and nodded. "Yes, but not while we're sitting in a Chinese restaurant on H Street. While you represent logic and hope to many people, you still have enemies. I'm told the alt-right have a bone to pick over some of your more non-traditional ideas."

Bathari smiled. "That's good news. Frankly, I'd be alarmed if they didn't."

Larson paid the bill and checked the sidewalk in either direction before guiding Bathari out of the restaurant.

"Is the coast clear?"

A man with a creased face in a long overcoat lingered nearby. He seemed to eye the pair of them with suspicion. Another woman in her mid-thirties was snapping photos of the Friendship Arch. Larson gave a curt nod.

Bathari was not frail by any means. Quite the opposite; Larson's trained eye spotted muscle tone under the unassuming sweater. Even so, he had ascertained that his counterpart was not a physically aggressive man. Bathari did battle with his ideas, leaving the physical realm to others. He seemed to be following Larson's line of thinking.

"If I have a personal security attachment one day," Bathari mused, "it would give me great comfort knowing you were on it, Michael."

"That day may be coming sooner than you think."

The academic ignored his remark. "Although, I think we may have bigger plans for you."

They passed a Cantonese market crowded with patrons that spilled onto the red brick sidewalk and turned down Sixth Street. Bathari kept his gaze on the ground, still specked with patches of graying snow.

Larson let his own gaze roam the sidewalk. Focusing on each pedestrian streaming past, he spoke to his counterpart.

"What we're doing, how can we be sure it's the right path? Many innocent lives could be lost. The country could plunge into another civil war."

"Am I detecting cold feet?" Bathari's serene demeanor remained unchanged. "There is always risk of innocents being lost, but it pales in comparison to the losses that will occur if we do nothing. The world will not thank us if we stand idle and allow it to collapse."

"How can we be sure that will happen? And how do you know what we're attempting will work?"

"I learned the power of faith a long time ago when I was still a boy in India. You must find your faith. Believe that we will succeed because, more than anything, the world needs us to."

They walked at a dirge-like pace. He led his charge left along I Street without any resistance. Bathari seemed content observing the eclectic collection of buildings—

traditional Chinese edifices sprinkled among modern towers and parking garages. But Larson could tell his mind was churning.

They paused in front of a synagogue with a magnificent stained-glass Star of David set aflame by afternoon light. Bathari took him in full view with a powerful, magnetic gaze.

"A leader cannot love his country if he does not love its people. This president is no leader. What he loves is himself—his own ever-expanding ego, his own power. Tyrants throughout history have been banded against and cast aside. And that is why it is so vital we must act now, Michael. The future is at stake."

Bathari began walking once more. Larson followed, scanning nearby faces and scrutinizing the windshield of each parked car they passed.

"If I fail, don't let them paint me as a rogue politician," Bathari muttered out of the corner of his mouth. "I was only trying to help."

"Don't think about failure. I've always found the best diversion before any kind of fieldwork is to lose oneself in preparation."

They looped around to the intersecting dragons and frenzied congregation assembled under the many-tiered pagodas of the Friendship Arch.

"The curvature of the roof was said to repel demons," Bathari said. "In reality, it was an invention by the Chinese to disperse rain while allowing smoke to exit from an opening beneath the roof."

"Maybe a touch of Chinese good luck is what we've been looking for." Without taking his gaze off the arch, Larson said, "I've been sent word that you should start preparing a speech. The best speech you have ever written."

"Where will I be delivering this speech?"

"There will be a rally. Far bigger than anything you've orchestrated thus far. A rally that will make the nation stop and take notice."

"When?"

The plan, devised by Katz and Gilbert, was genius. All that would remain afterward would be rounding up stragglers and cauterizing loose ends.

"January thirtieth," he said loud enough for Bathari to hear over the street's cacophony. "The same date as the president's State of the Union Address."

Chapter Forty-Four

Drollsworth watched the unlikely duo—tall Caucasian built like a soldier or athlete and diminutive Indian with flyaway hair—leave a restaurant and traverse the block from behind tinted windows. The ride was a loaner from POTUS himself but blended in quite nicely with the migraine-inducing Washington traffic.

He continued to follow as they made their way onto a less crowded cross thoroughfare; the Indian kept his eyes to the ground while his counterpart scanned the crowds. No one seemed to recognize them, Drollsworth noted.

Samit Bathari was becoming a nuisance. He had appeared on the news the previous evening. It wouldn't be long before the president's patience ebbed away. Drollsworth didn't mind playing the game for a while, but it was becoming apparent that Bathari needed to be dealt with. But not quite yet.

Less was known about Michael Larson. He was a member of United States intelligence, but so far,

Drollsworth had been unsuccessful in determining under which specific branch of the complex network of agencies he was employed. It was as if, upon commencing a search for the man's background, he vanished entirely. That wouldn't do.

It was obvious to him that the duo was planning something. If there was one drawback to armored motorcades that had carted him around for the past year, it was that they made eavesdropping next to impossible. Getting out and walking along the crowded street was out of the question.

He was interrupted by a firework lambasting the sky overhead. By the time Drollsworth refocused, both men rounded a corner onto a quieter avenue lined with barren oaks and a collection of shabby three-story apartment buildings.

The Samit Bathari conundrum had bothered Drollsworth ever since he had first learned of his existence. Digging for information on the man had not been that difficult, but it proved eye-opening.

The Bathari family had immigrated to the United Kingdom from India in the eighties. Drollsworth had uncovered proof of another son but had found no record of him in the emigration paperwork. Bathari studied at Oxford before obtaining a working visa and relocating to the United States in the early nineties. From there, things took an interesting turn.

The first five years adopted a semblance of normal. Bathari was hired by a medium-sized New York firm called Lincoln Faust that specialized in political consulting. As the economic boom of the nineties neared its peak the firm expanded, segueing into facets of economic planning while growing enough to offer their specialized services to much of the developing world.

That was where Bathari came in. He proved resourceful and creative. Naturally adept at the art of persuasion, clients found him both skilled and charming. By the time Lincoln

Faust reached its zenith, he was operating under the official title of Chief Southern Hemisphere Strategist, traveling to developing countries in South America and Africa and advising on various government and infrastructure matters.

It was not until a business trip to Nairobi that anyone discovered the first signs something was amiss. After the scheduled week, Bathari failed to return home.

Attempts to reach him proved futile. A private investigator was hired—one final pre-emptive measure before authorities were involved. After another week of searching, the detective reported that Bathari left Nairobi of his own accord. He had traveled south to Dar es Salaam where all trace of him vanished.

But not for long. The rogue Lincoln Faust employee resurfaced three days later on the semi-autonomous island of Zanzibar. The investigator could report nothing concrete, but rumors swirled that he was there at the behest of the second vice president of the island's Revolutionary Government.

Plans were drafted for Bathari's rescue. They involved a private plea forwarded to the president and both vice presidents of the island principality, as well as the Tanzanian president. After much fretful discourse, preparations were made to involve American authorities if initial overtures proved unsuccessful.

They needn't have bothered. Bathari showed up none the worse for wear in New York City a day later. He did not offer any explanation as to why he had been in the company of a notoriously corrupt man and frequent conspirator with Somali pirates. He remained mute on the topic of why he had broken off communications and overstayed his scheduled visit to Africa by a fortnight. Bathari's superiors were incensed.

Gossip grew to unheralded proportions days later when word spread throughout the offices of Lincoln Faust that an up-and-coming political strategist was vying for leadership of the company.

It never came to a vote. Bathari was terminated by the executive board of Lincoln Faust a week before the anticipated shareholder meetings.

After his ousting, leads on the man's life became tenuous. What could be gleaned painted the picture of work of a different kind. But at its core, Drollsworth was clever enough to realize, it remained much the same.

Early in the new millennium, Bathari went underground. His disappearance from the public eye was not permanent, and it served a purpose. He was building a following. Meager at first, Drollsworth and his skilled investigators were able to discover remnants of a website and an electronic newsletter. His ideas were disseminated via its pages and a subsequent message board where followers could convene and share them further.

Support was meager at first, but over subsequent months it took root and spread. It seemed a certain type of person was coming to support the message Bathari was selling. A fantasy pipe dream, as it were.

But that wasn't all. With his rise in the world of underground politics, Drollsworth discovered that Bathari had been befriended by many celebrities. Important people; some with powerful connections. And finally, those buying into his philosophies began to sour.

It started with a small gathering outside Los Angeles that went south. Another in Phoenix incited a minor riot that ended with the arrival of police brandishing shields and body armor. Each time a public show of support occurred, mayhem seemed to follow.

Bathari fled to Canada. There he bided his time, growing his influence and waiting for his next opportunity to strike. It came when a private Gulfstream jet took off from Washington and a man named Michael Larson arrived in Montreal on a blustery September afternoon.

Drollsworth stared intently at the duo from behind the SUV's mirrored glass. What were they doing together? And why had Larson, an agent of American intelligence, gotten involved with such a man?

He observed until the pairing rounded the corner onto Seventh Street. He motioned for his driver to speed up. A light had come on.

He headed west into the opus of the glaring afternoon sun, away from Chinatown in the direction of the White House. It occurred to him that he had heard once in passing of a small unit buried within the Department of Homeland Security. Eiran Katz, the team's director, was a prominent name in political circles. He'd had more pull during the last administration. The current president detested him, but also operated within the confines of a notoriously short attention span. It was quite probable the president wasn't aware of the unit's existence. That would change.

Drollsworth stopped himself. Maybe this could be used to their advantage.

Five more blocks passed before he remembered Pyotr Volkov's disappearance. Communication with the arms dealer had ceased, but he was rumored to have been spotted in Tirana. It all fell into place with a revelation that there existed a much more germane solution than siccing the hounds on Katz and his so-called radicalism unit.

His first call lasted less than five minutes and confirmed a critical piece of information. The second was dialed as they fought traffic past Georgia Brown's restaurant on Fifteenth Street and eased around the block to the back entrance, also known as the diplomat's entrance, of the St. Regis hotel.

He could have gone to pay her a visit at the White House, but Drollsworth didn't bother. Hannah Harper was just as easily interrogated over the phone. And he was confident that she would tell him everything.

Chapter Forty-Five

Faith in a sovereign nation. Faith in a government that by the day slipped further into chaos. Faith in one transformative leader.

For Larson, it came down to faith in an operation whose loose hold on success seemed more and more tenuous with each hour he spent conjecturing every possible outcome. Try as he might to remain optimistic, the odds were long.

Over the next fortnight, plans were put in place and specifics ironed out. A series of maps detailing the underground tunnels connecting various government buildings inside the capital were drawn and studied. Echelon agents began convening with Armand and his collection of loyal underlings. Dozens of different scenarios were practiced and planned for, each with its own exhaustive set of caveats.

Months later, hindsight prophets that proliferated mass media would say it all came apart on the thirtieth day in January. Chicago was the beginning of the end; they would espouse with vigor for dazed audiences across the nation. Chicago was where the United States as a nation finally broke and went careening off the tracks.

That was one take. Others, perhaps a majority, would counter that Chicago was the moment when America transformed into something reborn. On that frigid day before thousands of gathered onlookers, this group decried, America swiftly and decisively changed for the better.

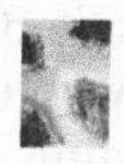

Elena shared in no such premonitions as the plane lifted high and trekked over rolling hills of cloud into the heart of middle America. For security reasons, she and Larson had boarded separate flights.

Upon landing, she disembarked and took a waiting car to a prominent hotel with a view overlooking the snaking Chicago River. A small placard with a place and time scribbled in shorthand was slid under her door sometime later by an attendant from the concierge's desk, a sign that Larson had arrived safely. Elena breathed a sigh of relief. She studied the placard while standing before a picture window that lent views of the frigid water a dozen stories below. Satisfied, she tore it to bits and dropped it in the trash.

She slid her laptop from a sleek Michael Kors briefcase and powered it on.

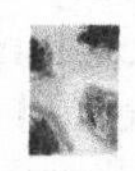

Larson stepped onto the busy street while reading a text on his iPhone. Word had arrived that Elena was safe in the city. Two plainclothes members of the Secret Service, unbeknownst to the public, had been stationed at the bottom floor of her hotel.

His heart lightened as he traversed the handful of blocks into Chicago's downtown district along the lakefront. There was no sign of a tail as he crossed Michigan Avenue and passed Water Tower Place. Adjacent limestone buildings housing a theater and public library paled in comparison to the behemoth mall. Larson passed both, following along Pearson Street as buildings gave way to a park that showed no signs of life in the depths of a Midwestern winter.

Bright yellow letters warned of his destination's imminence. Stairs leading to the square building's glass entrance were not crowded. Larson studied each face. Reaching the revolving front doors, he wasn't surprised when a figure perched halfway up the steps, not unlike the flock of pigeons he was feeding, rose and followed.

Larson purchased a ticket and entered Chicago's Contemporary Art Museum. A bold sign next to the ticket window stated that all attractions would be closing in two hours.

The interior was drafty and sparsely populated. As he crossed a tiled hallway, Larson glimpsed the man who had followed him inside stop at the window to buy a ticket of his own. Out of the corner of his eye, he caught another figure rising from a bench in the atrium. This second man tailed him down the hallway at a sluggish pace. Larson continued forward.

He climbed to the third floor and did a lap around the museum's right wing without incident. Slipping between patrons, he passed rows of paintings and rooms full of gathered onlookers with hardly a glimpse to their exhibits. A few irritable grunts were cast in his direction when Larson blew past a pair of vivid blue and red paintings accompanied by hypnotic music dilating from speakers set in the ceiling. He slowed to check his tail at another exhibit a floor below that seemed comprised of nothing more than several broomsticks suspended by fishing line.

The two figures still tailed him, following half a dozen yards apart and each paying no attention to the other.

When he reached the atrium twenty minutes later, Larson left without sampling the left wing or taking in the museum's lauded gift shop and restaurant. He had neither pondered nor appreciated any of the art. No one inside was sorry to see him go.

The next stop was for a glass of whiskey in a high-end pub several blocks south before venturing back into the crisp January weather. This time, his tail was clean.

The temperature had dipped during his foray indoors. Larson wore a fur-lined pea coat over khaki trousers and a wool sweater. He wrapped it tighter around his frame and tugged a scarf into place as he made his way down Grand Avenue in the direction of Lake Michigan. The chill became unbearable as he ducked under an overpass and emerged in the lap of a park, which abutted a sandy stretch that passed for beach in the minds of most Chicagoans.

This time, Katz was not surrounded by birds as he loitered in the shadow of a flashy condominium building near the lake's lapping blue edge. Larson and Katz met each other's eye, but they walked into the park without exchanging a word.

Gilbert waited near a series of stone arches supporting a trellis. Larson supposed in the summer the wooden planks would turn green with vegetation. Now, they were forlorn and barren.

Gilbert seemed not to notice as the pair walked past. But Larson sensed him turn and follow for the second time. When the other man had closed the gap and fallen into step, Katz spoke.

"It wouldn't have killed you to stop and admire a painting or two, Larson. A few of them were quite good."

Gilbert chuckled. Larson returned the favor with a seething look. "We aren't here to look at abstract art. How are things progressing?"

Echelon's chief lowered his tone. "It isn't safe to say much out here. Everything is in place."

The State of the Union and Bathari's subsequent address were to take place in one day's time. Larson glanced at the pair of them.

"And the hacker?"

"Agent Orange has been working around the clock. She's confident she'll have the system down by tomorrow night…Tuesday morning at the latest."

"The State of the Union Address is scheduled for nine that evening," Gilbert said. "Bathari will begin his speech at seven. We don't want to give the president time to prepare for what's coming. It will be important to lure him out into the open. If he thinks he's in trouble, he'll descend into the new command center under the West Wing. The old emergency operations center was six stories deep and able to survive a direct nuclear hit. The new bunker is impenetrable."

Katz said, "I don't think we'll have any problem luring him out. Running and hiding has never been his modus operandi—even when it should be. The president will be giddy to get in front of the cameras and respond when he hears Bathari's announcement to the world. I'm confident he'll insist on delivering his speech no matter what's being advised."

"And he doesn't know the Secret Service have turned against him," Larson said.

"Some of them. I would feel comfortable with the whole force on our side. But Armand assured us he can arrange the address's venue to be staffed entirely with men that are loyal to our cause. With any luck, we'll avoid bloodshed."

They delved deeper into the park, turning right where a bike path intersected their own. Ahead, Larson could make out the famed pier that stretched into Lake Michigan. The pier's mammoth Ferris wheel went out of focus as his head crowded with ideas.

"Are we sure our strategy is not misguided?" he asked.

Katz glanced at him. "What do you mean?"

"Thompkins made it quite clear that Drollsworth is the one calling the shots. The president is his puppet. Wouldn't it be more prudent to go after him rather than a figurehead that can be replaced at the drop of a hat?"

"It's crucial we take down the president." Katz's eyebrows narrowed.

"We'll exhaust all of our resources apprehending the wrong man!" Larson's voice rose.

"According to one informant."

"Yes, Thompkins," Larson said, "who happens to be our *only* source within the alt-right."

Like a noiseless ghost, Gilbert stepped between the two and laid a hand on each of their shoulders. His tone was calming. "Perhaps you're both right. But I can tell you with complete certainty that Drollsworth will be glued to the president's side. By felling one, it's inevitable we'll topple the other."

"Where is Drollsworth now?"

"He has been sighted at various locations in Washington over the past few days. Mostly coming and going from the White House."

"We have no one tailing him around the clock?" Larson asked.

Gilbert appeared unfazed. "If Drollsworth leaves the president's side, we'll know."

"And where is Bathari? I take it he's already arrived in the city."

The two exchanged a glance. Again, it was Gilbert again who answered. "Rest assured that your friend is safe and well-protected."

"You won't tell me where he is?"

Katz intervened. "It's important that we limit the number of people who know his whereabouts. For operational security. You, of all people, should understand."

Larson huffed and nodded. There was no use arguing. Either way, they were right. Each individual privy to the information equaled another potential weak point in Bathari's protection.

He walked between the two in silence. As they returned to the shadow of the condominium building across the street, Gilbert made a hurried explanation about needing to attend to a difficulty that had arisen and disappeared. Larson and Katz continued walking, bypassing the gated entrance to a water purification plant and bracing against the chill that swept landside in torrents off Lake Michigan.

They passed a luxurious yacht docked adjacent the Navy Pier boardwalk before Katz broke the silence. His question, while simple, caught Larson by surprise.

"Why Chicago?"

It dawned on Larson that he was closer to Bathari than any of the others. They had not blindly followed, but whereas men like Katz and Gilbert viewed him as a means to take down a dangerous and predatory regime, Larson saw something else.

"There was an age when Chicago stood for the American dream. Even in modern times, it persists as a beacon of industry. How many brave souls journeyed here with nothing and made their fortunes, created empires, along Lake Michigan? I think Bathari considers it vital to win America's heart. He wants to propel the world into the future."

Katz contemplated his response. Finally, he asked, "Do you think he's cut out for the job?"

"I believe he's the leader we need."

The sun was beginning to sink behind them as they reached the pier's end. The chief had chosen this place to reduce the chances of being overheard. What few brave souls lingered in their vicinity were not interested in two men wrapped in pea coats conversing on the boardwalk.

Larson proffered a question. It led to the real question that had nagged him over the past month while they'd undergone the tedious process of setting the operation into motion. "Do you think we can get to the First Lady?"

On Katz's part, there was no hesitation. "Not a chance. We've already conjectured on that point. Even if she would be open to an approach, which we have no way of knowing, she's too well protected."

He focused on Lake Michigan's endless horizon. The

green-tinged water was calm and splotched with vibrant hues of sunset. For a moment, he was overcome by a wave of peace.

"Do you believe the plan will succeed?"

This question, too, had been gnawing at him. Even so, he guessed Katz's answer before the other man spoke.

"Normally, this kind of operation would prove impossible. We happen to benefit from the perfect alignment of circumstances. Lucky for us, we have an ex-Chief of Staff and the third highest ranking officer in the Secret Service on our side. That gives us certain…advantages that wouldn't otherwise be possible. The intelligence factor alone offered by Gilbert and Armand Rivera is unheard of."

Katz gripped the railing with gloved hands and leaned over the harbor. "It all adds up to give us a slim chance, but that's a hell of a lot better than no chance at all."

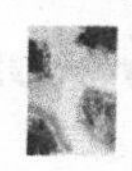

Later, as Larson returned to the penthouse flat lent to their cause by Ian McInroe, he relentlessly ran through the details of what would occur the next evening in his head. There would be one window of opportunity for success. Timing was critical. At the culmination of Bathari's speech, several separate components would move into simultaneous action.

Ultimately, the operation rested in Katz's and Gilbert's hands. Success or failure would be determined in a matter of minutes. And once the window closed, it would likely never open again.

While Larson ran through all the ways the operation could fail—sticking points, as he referred to them—there was a warm glimmer of optimism that refused to dampen. They were working in service of the greater good. Change was what the world needed, whether its citizenry chose to believe it or not.

Chapter Forty-Six

That optimism dissipated when Larson woke the following morning. Elena had disappeared by the time he tried to force down a breakfast of poached eggs on wheat toast while drinking coffee and reading the morning paper. She had been summoned to the control room, which was how all parties involved referred to Gilbert's bunker of a townhouse a dozen blocks away. A team of Echelon tech geniuses had arrived and swept the place before installing a computer bank with an array of video and communications software not available on the normal market.

The townhouse would serve as headquarters for the operation, although much of it would take place in the nation's capital. Gilbert would be connected to Armand via earpiece and live video feed. Likewise, he had commandeered Elena to serve as Diego's eyes and ears. The twins, both heading different legs of the operation, were to remain in loose contact throughout the day.

He returned to his newspaper. Headlines about the

president's impending address later that evening dominated the front page. He swallowed a final reluctant bite before pushing the plate aside. Coffee was all he desired.

It took several seconds of rifling through pages and miniscule newsprint before he found what he was looking for. The article was much smaller than the bold headlines, but the information it contained equally potent. Bathari was scheduled to address the people of Chicago, and subsequently the entire nation via live broadcast, at seven in Millennium Park. There would be thorough security, but all were welcome to attend.

He powered on a flat screen TV that slid into view from inside an unassuming bureau with the push of a button. Most news stations were speculating about which topics the president would address in his speech. The list was extensive.

Pausing on a local affiliate, Larson watched an enthusiastic reporter present her story with Millennium Park in the background. A small crowd milled about behind her. There was already a row of news vans with satellite dishes pointing skyward aligned in a bay to the left of the sweeping stage. The day was overcast, although a few rays of sun hinted at breaking the miserable cold front. He watched for another thirty seconds before pulling on his coat and a scarf and leaving the loft.

He stopped in a coffee shop on Lake Street before cutting west and continuing along the river. Two hours were whiled away walking the channel and admiring bridges and boats floating past.

It was warm enough by midday to unknot his scarf and let it dangle over his coat. By the time Larson crossed a bridge near the harbor mouth and doubled back, he was sweating.

The afternoon was spent perusing various tourist attractions along the Riverwalk and forcing down an early dinner alone at a popular local steakhouse chain. Afterward, Larson returned to the penthouse, showered, and changed.

On the street, he hailed a taxi and spoke his destination to the driver. His resolve strengthened as they pulled into traffic. The time for cold feet had passed.

Drollsworth sauntered past the metallic behemoth in blissful anonymity. He was dressed like a tourist in relaxed fit trousers and a nondescript jacket and didn't garner so much as a glance as he walked the park's length and then, satisfied, turned to take it all in one last time.

Arcs of waning light glanced off futuristic steel plates around the stage that had been seemingly warped by the hands of giants. A wire grid stretched beyond the platform over the park, suspended by monstrous pillars. The grassy expanse underneath was empty; in a few hours it would fill with people, witnesses to the abomination about to take place.

Drollsworth smirked as he vacated the park. It had been prudent to travel alone—not even the president was made aware. He walked back to where he had parked along a nearby street and slipped into the driver's seat. The gun pressing against his flesh was cold. He would have to use it later to preserve the health of the nation.

The president didn't need to know about such things. He was just as likely as not to go before the cameras and tell them everything, ruining the element of surprise.

It was becoming obvious to Drollsworth that the president's mental health was deteriorating. Of course, the other cronies he had surrounded himself with would never admit it, including the White House physician. Drollsworth was different. He could serve a man faithfully while still acknowledging the truth. The only truth that mattered right now was that he had a job to do a little under an hour before the president's speech. Bathari was a spreading disease. It was up to him to eliminate the threat.

The president would wonder why Drollsworth was not

at his side that evening in the House of Representatives chambers. He would have some explaining to do after the fact once everything was taken care of. The gun pressed harder into the flesh of his back as he drove into Chicago's bustling heart. Surely, the president would thank him when it was all over. He planned on being hailed as a hero after he eliminated the pretender.

And then he would deal with that lying bitch, Hannah Harper.

Larson eased past two Secret Service men with somber expressions and climbed a flight of stairs. He was dressed in a dark suit and wore a small earpiece that was hardly noticeable. It served one purpose—a direct line of communication with the chief. So far, Katz had remained silent on the other end. That didn't change as Larson traversed a path lined with bushes and pushed open a heavy door to the sloping backstage building flanked by another pair of rigid guards.

Bathari stood in a plain room. He was so calm Larson thought he was meditating. There were two leather chairs and a coffee table scattered with a few uninteresting magazines. The walls bore posters promoting acts that had taken place on the stage he would soon grace. A single door led to a claustrophobic corridor that gave way to the stage. Like the constricted belly of a serpent and its gaping jaws.

When Bathari exited the green room, Larson would not follow. Instead, he would watch from an elevated platform to the stage's right. From there, he would be granted a direct line of sight to Bathari as well as Katz, stationed in the park's sound booth with a contingent of Secret Service men. They would be surrounded by onlookers.

More plainclothes security would be scattered among the masses where amphitheater seats gave way to the lawn. Half a dozen of Echelon's agents were in attendance. Two had orders never to leave Katz's side. The others would stand poised on the catwalk beyond stage left. Larson tensed as his mind fixated on the events to come.

By contrast, Bathari's calmness was surreal. He wore his usual placid expression and stood with his hands clasped behind his back. A small smile appeared when he opened one eye and spotted Larson.

"It's good to see you, my friend." He pulled Larson close and embraced him.

"This is some show you've managed to arrange for yourself," Larson murmured in his ear.

"And you've only seen the beginning. All thanks to Ian McInroe."

"He couldn't make it tonight, I'm afraid. But he sends his best from Inveraray. He offered his private jet recently acquired from a sultan for our return trip to Washington. I told him perhaps flying in a 747 trimmed with solid gold wasn't quite the image we were trying to portray. But I thanked him for his generosity."

They would be flying east on a Gulfstream IV fueled and waiting at Chicago O'Hare after Bathari's speech concluded. Armand had pulled strings and arranged for Bathari, Katz, and Larson to skip security and be delivered to a private hangar for boarding and immediate takeoff. The rest of the Secret Service and Echelon contingent would fly commercial and leave several hours later.

Larson was struck again by Bathari's demeanor. As if reading his mind, the other man said, "I've been waiting my whole life for this. It's time."

"And if our plan fails? What then?"

"Belief is the first step on the path to success. I believe this operation can be successful. All we have left to do is share our news with the American people."

Larson had received word from Agent Orange via Katz earlier in the day that her part in the operation had been a success. When it came time later that evening to dismember the government's outdated computerized infrastructure, they would run into no hidden obstacles.

Energetic sounds of people issued through the walls backstage. A crowd was amassing, passing through security staged at intervals around Millennium Park's many entrances and flowing inward toward the stage. Fueled by curiosity along with bona fide support for Bathari, Katz and Gilbert expected a massive turnout. A live stream would beam the broadcast in real time to every corner of the globe. There was no going back. After tonight, Samit Bathari would forever live his life on the public stage.

"What is about to occur," Bathari uttered, "was cemented on a day in fall a little over one year ago. But the person I have become was created many years before that. I never finished telling you what happened to me all that time ago, still in the throes of childhood."

"When you were smuggled away from your home?"

Bathari's eyes seemed to glaze over. "After escaping the backbreaking work of a deckhand, I thought I might exist in Delhi as an anonymous speck among the masses. For three months I tried, resorting to thieving and performing odd jobs for scraps of food and a place to lay my head when the weather was not conducive to sleeping outdoors. Shop owners took pity on me—they could see I was educated, which lent me a pathos that others in similar position lacked."

"What changed?"

"Destiny has a funny way of intervening when one least expects it. Life came to an end the day I tried to steal from a man in long, brown robes whom I took to be sleeping under a tattered umbrella on a street corner in old Delhi. There was food in his hand. As I reached out, a firm grip locked around my wrist that I could not break.

"At first I thought it was another kidnapping. The man said very little. His head was shaved, and his mouth seemed to be sewed shut, although that was an illusion. He took me outside the old city, north along the Yamuda River to a place I had never been before. The next morning, the silent man put me aboard a truck heavy with goats and three others. We headed west. When the terrain got too mountainous and the roads ended, we continued on foot. When I complained about my bare feet in the snow, they gave me shoes and a tattered parka. Food and water were heavily rationed. It took two weeks to reach our destination."

"Where did they take you?"

For an instant Bathari's face assumed a childlike quality, guided along by men he didn't know. "High into the mountains of Nepal. Kathmandu sits in a bowl-shaped valley two miles high in the Himalayas. We came upon it one afternoon after I was certain my days would pass in a purgatory of snow-capped peaks and endless forest. I couldn't believe my eyes. A city that glittered like forgotten jewels. By nightfall we reached a monastery built on a hillock away from the western side of the city. It was the most beautiful thing I had ever seen. And it was full of life. In the days that followed, I learned the plight of the Tibetans."

"They were driven from their land when the Chinese invaded."

Bathari was solemn. "Many found refuge in Nepal, hidden by mountains and allowed to flourish once again. The monks turned out to be kind. They taught me English until I could speak it flawlessly. They allowed me to foray into the markets whenever I pleased. And they never pushed their beliefs on me, although I couldn't help being influenced by the predominant Buddhist culture. As I grew older, I would pray and meditate with them. But most importantly, the monks taught me how to think and how to love. They introduced the notion of balance—balance in all facets of life as well as cosmic balance. And they taught me that there was no greater path than devoting my life to the service of others."

"How long did you stay?"

"I was no longer a young boy when I left the monastery. No monk ever pushed me to go. Our collective simply knew it was time. I waited until the mild season and started my journey through the mountain passes. Returning to India was like re-entering a foreign land."

"And your family?"

"They still lived in the same village in the south of India where I left them. I returned six months after beginning my journey home. At first, my parents didn't believe it possible. My own mother didn't recognize me. Eventually, I was able to persuade them that I was their long-lost son. But things were never how they used to be. I had been gone eight years.

"By that time my father had saved enough money, and we moved to Great Britain where I attended university. After completing my studies, my parents stayed behind while I took a brief sojourn to a tropical African island and then sought a life in America. And I've never looked back."

Larson said nothing. He stood in stunned disbelief. Then, without restraint, he spoke the first question that came to mind. "Have you ever told this story to another human being?"

"My mother and father were uneasy around me for some time after my return, until I recounted for them my entire tale. More important, I tried to impress how this world is interconnected. They were skeptical. I assured them that everything has threads of commonality. Religion can be a vessel to impart good, to decipher right from wrong, to drive out the dark in each of us, and fill that void with light."

Bathari's gaze turned powerful and steadfast. Larson had a strange feeling that the other man was peering into his soul.

"This movement is not a radicalized one. It is founded upon pillars of reason and enlightenment. But the foremost pillar is necessity. Time is growing short for our species. Balance must be restored. Tonight, the first step along that path commences."

He faded, almost glided toward the open door. Then the other man was gone.

The echo of Bathari's footsteps had no sooner died

when they were replaced by another, more urgent sound. Without warning, Elena burst through the doorway, precisely where Bathari had stood. She was ashen faced.

"What's wrong?"

Her voice cracked with terror.

"We received word from Washington. Drollsworth isn't with the president."

Chapter Forty-Seven

There was no time to question how such an ill-fated turn of events was possible. Larson hurtled down the cramped hallway. As Bathari emerged to uproarious applause that sent tremors through the amphitheater's steel structure, he careened along a perilous catwalk that led to a platform overlooking both the stage and crowd below. Elena followed doggedly on his heels.

His lungs ached like he had run a race by the time he got into position. She slid to a halt at his side, doubled over. From the platform's edge, it was possible to view everything underneath a lattice of structural supports. Both sets of eyes focused on one thing.

They were not alone. The applause trailed off and then ceased altogether. Bathari held the focus of every spectator in Millennium Park. When he spoke, their collective gaze intensified like an ant under a magnifying glass.

It became clear at once that Bathari possessed a gift. His voice, magnified a thousand times beyond its normal volume, had a hypnotic effect on the swelling crowd. They stood, entranced, listening with avid expressions. Like the performance of a world class violinist, Larson thought.

He only half-listened. After witnessing Bathari mount the futuristic stage and begin to speak, his focus shifted out into the crowd. Now, he swept the rows of onlookers, scrutinizing each face. To his left, Elena did the same.

It was a hunch, but Larson had learned long ago to trust his instincts. Drollsworth was not with the president. Somehow, he had managed to vanish under the noses of the Secret Service agents keeping tabs on him. Larson had nothing to go on but his instincts. And what they whispered was not good.

"Are you armed?" Elena whispered.

He nodded.

She spoke again, but this time he couldn't make out the words. A slight buzzing emanated from the crowd. With every moment that passed, it grew, becoming more all-encompassing. Katz was out there, observing everything with hawk-like precision from the sound booth. Larson continued to scan the masses, searching for a face he had seen in photographs standing next to the president. A face he hoped he wouldn't find.

He was distracted by a roar that drowned out the buzzing. A cheer erupted, rippling outward from the crowd in a calamitous wave like a seismic shock. Elena tugged his arm urgently, and for the first time since Bathari had begun his speech Larson listened.

"—deceived the American people for far too long. It is time, tonight, in the heart of this great country, that we galvanize our ranks and stride forward into the future! But first we must expose the man that threatens to drag us into the forgotten abyss of the past."

The buzzing grew louder. Bathari's voice pulsed through speakers. News cameras and microphones set up in a row to one side glared at the stage and reflected a cache of powerful spotlights. And all around, the park swelled as if supporters crammed within its barriers were one pulsating organism. A wave of dread swept over him.

"I come to you now, citizens of this great country, with proof. Proof that the President of the United States has transpired to tear humanity apart. It begins with the alternative right—radicalized nationalists who helped put him in power. These heinous outliers made a pact with the president before he got elected. They would do his bidding if he promised in turn to propagate their terrible cause. Your president happily agreed."

A violent jeer issued from the crowd.

"Next came the Russians. The man in power could have never usurped office without their help. Through an arms dealer sanctioned by the Russian government, he transported illegal weaponry across our borders to the alt-right. All with the end goal of inducing chaos."

Another jeer. Larson wondered if a riot was seconds from erupting.

"You see, their aim was to distract the American public. A violent protest in Virginia, the deadliest mass murder on American soil—these incidences were nothing to the man sitting in the White House. He engineered them. All for the simple purpose of striking fear and distracting citizens while he signed orders and slipped more and more power into his own pocket."

The noise level in Millennium Park reached fever pitch. Larson spotted something, the first intimation of rapid movement that didn't make any sense.

"The president killed innocent Americans to further his own evil schemes. He sold his soul to Russia and the vilest outliers skulking within our borders."

A solitary figure extricated himself and pushed through the tumultuous crowd, rushing in the stage's direction.

"He has stolen from all of us, and he will take more."

Larson couldn't make out a face amid flailing limbs and bodies. Bathari's speech had worked them into a frenzy.

"Tonight, we end it! This is the moment we put a stop

to the madness and overthrow the monster. I've exposed him for what he is before all of you. Each one of us has a duty to take power into our own hands."

No more than a dozen paces away, the lone figure broke free of the writhing crowd. Instinct took over and Larson lunged over the platform barrier and fell until he collided with hard concrete ten feet below.

Pain didn't register. He was on his feet and sprinting, pulling the gun from the waist of his pants as he ran. His legs were numb and protesting, but still they carried him forward. Elena screamed behind him. She was running down the catwalk toward the stage. Larson didn't look back.

The only thing in the world that mattered now was reaching Bathari in time.

Chapter Forty-Eight

Not one soul in the crowd registered what was happening until the gun appeared. A glint of metal caught in the stage lights and reflected toward the first rows. Panic ensued. Swelling fear was palpable as Larson charged across the stage's apron and leapt onto the concrete floor.

Bathari stood like a beacon in the blinding lights, no longer speaking. The momentum from his speech had rushed out of Millennium Park like a deflating balloon. The first five rows of seats were roped off to provide a makeshift barrier between the crowd and stage. The lone figure who broke through stood stock-still, mere feet from the platform's metallic lip.

He wasn't going to make it. The gun had appeared from nowhere. Bathari held it steady, nose pointed at the heart of the man staring calmly up at him. Though Larson had never seen the face in person, it was immediately identifiable. He tensed as he ran, each momentous second dragging, praying that he wouldn't hear the gun's mechanism before he reached the unarmed man.

It erupted like three miniature explosions in quick succession. Larson was vaguely aware of Dillon Drollsworth teetering backward and falling to the ground as the front of his shirt stained crimson. He was also aware of the crowd dissolving into hysterics behind him, the sound triggering flight instincts of thousands into a mass exodus recognizant of a herd of terrified gazelles.

Amid the chaotic evacuation, several figures rushed forward. They surrounded the fallen Drollsworth as Larson changed course, no longer concerned whether the man was still alive. He had failed to stop gunshots from blighting the evening. Now, there was the matter of Bathari.

Larson turned and sprinted halfway to the stage before looking up. He dug his heels into the ground and stopped in his tracks.

Someone else had reached Bathari first. She was pinned to his left side, a mahogany hand pressed over her mouth. Larson found the gun right away, like a venomous snake rearing back to strike, its nose coiled inches from her neck. Point blank range.

Elena's eyes were the only thing emitting any sign of the fear coursing through her body. And then Larson understood. While he had instinctively ran in the direction of Drollsworth, she had made the mistake of trying to stop Bathari. Now, she was rendered quite helpless.

He tried to yell, to call the attention of the men in dark suits congregated around the fallen Drollsworth while the hysterical tides swept out of the park. His voice no longer worked. The gun held in his own hands was useless—Elena would be dead before he could fire a shot.

Larson watched helpless as Bathari dragged his quarry backward into the gaping mouth of the steel megalith. Their eyes never broke contact. His expression was unreadable. Larson detected a strange hint of sadness. Elena struggled to wriggle out of his grip. It did no good. Bathari whispered something in her ear. Larson couldn't make out the words.

Captor and hostage faded into the tunnel when bodies swarmed around him. Dazed by everything that was happening, he turned to meet them.

"He's getting away with Elena Stregor. You have to be careful—he has a gun to her head."

A wall of dark suits still blocked Drollsworth's prone form. Had the gunshots proven fatal? He had no time to think, no time to ask any of the million questions burning inside his brain, before two strong pairs of hands grabbed him.

"Let go of me. What are you doing?" Larson struggled. "He's getting away!"

The men restraining him remained steadfast and silent. The wall of flesh moved inward, closing ranks around him. Larson panicked. These men, all members of the Secret Service, didn't understand what was happening. They glared at him like he was guilty, oblivious to the fact that a man who had potentially committed murder and taken a hostage was escaping the scene unscathed.

"Leave me," he screamed. "Go after Bathari!"

With a sudden spurt of force, Larson broke free and with a running start leapt onto the stage. If he was fast enough, he could intercept Bathari and try to talk sense into him before he smuggled Elena off to God knows where…or worse.

He got no more than half a dozen paces before a thick set of arms roped around his waist and his body crashed to earth. The stage's surface was cold and hard. His face crunched against it painfully and he was dazed by the impact. Regaining focus, Larson kicked and struggled under the weight of several bodies all focusing their considerable might to subdue him.

The passageway to the building behind the amphitheater was miniscule from his vantage point pinioned to the ground. Much too far.

Doubtless, Bathari had planned all of this. An unmarked car would pull alongside the curb and he and

Elena would be gone.

Larson wondered why Katz had still not intervened when the piercing stab of a hypodermic needle breeched the flesh of his upper arm. A burning sensation filled him as the needle's contents were emptied into his circulatory system.

Katz would be along any second to rectify the situation. The crushing weight of the agents on top of him lessened. Throbbing pain from his collision with the stage faded away as the corners of his vision lost focus. There was a vague sensation of a needle being removed from his shoulder. Then blackness.

Chapter Forty-Nine

James Collins had witnessed much in the year since his ascension to the lofty role of Director of National Intelligence. On some evenings he would sit at his desk and wonder what forces had conspired to grant him such sheer luck; an unspectacular kid from Indiana who had become a senator and then, by unanimous selection, a member of the president's Cabinet and leader of the United States Intelligence Community. Other evenings he would find himself too engrossed in work to attempt to calculate the odds of success.

This evening fell to the latter. Indeed, it was perhaps the most unusual of any during his three quarters of a century's worth of life experience. Collins had watched the bank of flat screens hanging on a wall across from his desk with shock and bewilderment as a man outside the political realm graced a Chicago stage and attempted to usher the nation toward a realignment of power. His eyes were glued to various live broadcasts as the character many news outlets had dubbed 'the leader of the future' presented a gun to the crowd and shot a member of the audience. He had received word several tense minutes later that the victim was Dillon Drollsworth, one of the president's closest confidants. His mere presence at the rally unlocked a whole host of questions that would need answering.

The Director of National Intelligence sat behind his desk and pondered what he had seen. A digital clock next to a tidy stack of documents ticked past eleven. The bank of televisions had been powered off at the rally's conclusion three hours previous. Immediately, he had dialed the president and insisted he postpone his State of the Union Address. Something was brewing. The man launched into hysterics, but Collins remained firm. He put the final touches on the call by ordering him into the new West Wing bunker until all threats could be properly assessed.

His thoughts wandered back to Chicago. It wasn't lost on him the onus of the event. Before the spectacle of gun violence and bloodshed, Bathari had expounded on a plot unlike any other in American history. If true—he had a score of men digging and verifying while he sat and pondered—the holder of America's highest office was nothing more than a pawn for Drollsworth and the Russians. That the radicalized alt-right could be used to distract the public while the president's regime plundered more and more power was downright reprehensible.

And yet, the premise was not so far-fetched as it appeared on first glance. The president had a less than pristine background and a notoriously longstanding relationship with Russia. Many of his motives were questionable, as proven by the weighted accusations and investigations that had surrounded him since his election. The director had vowed to abstain on passing judgment until he had proof on the matter, but he couldn't quell the feeling that a serious criminal enterprise had been outed.

There was a knock at the door. Odd for this hour. Collins pulled himself from his reverie. "Come in."

Eiran Katz opened the door and strode into the office. He looked tired, his face drawn and pallid.

The two men had not stood in the same room in months. Still, the director was on his feet, coming around the desk to greet the head of Echelon like an old friend.

"Have a seat." He ushered Katz in with a sweep of his hand. "What can I do for you?"

"We have a problem, James," Katz said. "I'm sure you watched what took place tonight."

"I did. And judging by the timeline of events, your flight couldn't have landed more than thirty minutes ago."

Katz's tired face widened in shock. The director eyed him knowingly.

"Chicago is a little cold for my taste this time of year. You would have done better to take some time off, fly down to the Caribbean for a change."

"What do you know?"

He adopted a stern expression. "I'm head of the largest intelligence contingent on the planet. I know everything. Except, that is, why you did it. Explain that to me, please."

Thirty years the other's junior, Katz nonetheless eyed the man across the desk as his equal. "Something had to be done. You speak of vacations; now isn't the time to run away. The ideological balance of our nation, and the world, is at stake. I know with absolute certainty that what Bathari recounted tonight is the truth. Despite his other transgressions, he exposed quite possibly the most nefarious ploy this country has ever faced. I take full responsibility for my hand in that."

The director let the other man fall silent. He sighed. "Things were so much simpler twenty years ago."

Collins had met the other man while serving an appointment as ambassador to Germany after the turn of the century. Katz had arrived at the embassy in Berlin as a freshly recruited CIA agent with an unending work ethic and a thirst to prove himself in the field. Their friendship had strengthened once they returned home and continued to ascend the hierarchy of their respective careers. The director also happened to be one of precious few who was aware of Echelon's existence.

"No, they weren't. We faced many of the same challenges we do today. Except, back then, nobody wanted to admit they existed."

"Perhaps you're right," Collins said. "But that doesn't get us any nearer a solution."

"A solution can wait. I came to you to discuss something else. And I'm afraid time is of the essence."

"The public will expect me to throw you in jail when your hand in this becomes known."

"Just hear me out."

He waited. Katz's expression was resolute. "At the rally's abrupt conclusion Bathari managed to escape Millennium Park with a hostage. Elena Stregor is a renowned psychologist, not to mention an instrumental asset in helping us uncover the president's scheme involving the alt-right—"

"And in helping Bathari on his quest for power," Collins said.

"Certain misguided actions aside, we cannot allow her to die at his hands."

"You want to get her back."

"With the added windfall of capturing Bathari. He murdered a presidential aide on live television."

"Drollsworth is officially dead?"

Katz nodded. "Forcing his killer to face justice would top any rational agenda—"

"Don't attempt to sway me with politics," he said sharply. "We both know I can still best you despite my years beginning to take their toll. What is it that you want? And why should I do it?"

"We both want Bathari captured, and Elena Stregor to emerge from this ordeal unscathed. And there's something else," Katz said.

Collins arched a graying eyebrow.

"Echelon agent Michael Larson was taken into custody by Secret Service agents present at the rally before Bathari's escape. I need to procure his release."

"If he is equally guilty as Ms. Stregor, why should I not allow him to rot in a prison cell?"

Katz leaned forward. "Because Larson is without a doubt the most integral piece in all of this. If we are ever going to bring Samit Bathari to justice, we will need him."

James Collins was a pragmatic man. He was starting to see things the way the recalcitrant man on the other side of the desk wished him to. And Katz was right. The time for high morals and doling out punishments could wait. A momentous shift had occurred earlier that evening. What they needed now was swift action. Transgressors could be dealt with—they would be—in the aftermath.

"How do you ever hope to track our fugitive?" the director asked.

A shadow of a smile stirred for the first time on the other man's face. Behind the weary mask was a rejuvenated glimmer.

"I believe I know someone who can help."

Chapter Fifty

Armand Rivera was in the act of dialing a number at the moment the jet's wheels grazed tarmac. His instructions were explicit. Subordinates were to do nothing other than follow his exact orders. He was on his way.

He deplaned into the back of a waiting Town Car that wasted no time spiriting him east in the direction of Lake Michigan.

His destination was little over a mile from Millennium Park where Bathari had delivered his speech several hours previous. It was now two hours past midnight.

The Town Car pulled to a stop in front of a nondescript monolith of glass and steel a block from the river. Unlike the surrounding towers, the building was not lit up to accommodate spectacular views from the water. It did nothing to draw attention to itself in any way. The top right corner was emblazoned with the name of a Dutch multinational that wouldn't solicit a glance.

Given the hour, traffic entering the city had been light.

Armand exited and strode toward a revolving glass door while the car idled curbside. Despite the tower's ordinary appearance and seeming lack of security, it was one of the most heavily monitored in all of Chicago.

As the elevator rose past the eighth floor, the interior underwent a meaningful yet imperceptible change that stopped two levels above. While the remainder of the building's floors played host to various commercial entities, the ninth belonged to an agency that was the cause for such stringent surveillance.

Security had changed over the course of Armand's career. No longer was it deemed necessary to have a multitude of guards pacing about. Now, cameras and computers did all the work. That explained why Armand met nary a soul as he stepped off the elevator on the ninth floor.

He had never visited Chicago's Secret Service headquarters, but he strode past the unmanned visitor's desk as if he were quite familiar with the place. At the first carpeted fork, he turned left and was met with initial signs of life. Voices issued from a nearby cache of offices. Hearing footsteps, a slight man with tousled hair and a rumpled suit appeared.

"What can I help you wi—"

Armand said nothing, instead pulling official identification from his breast pocket and holding it aloft for the man to read. A lowly analyst, or someone in a support role no doubt. The man's jaw dropped when he realized whom he was standing face to face with.

"Take me to him."

The analyst opened his mouth to speak, then perhaps thought better of it. Running a hand through his tousled hair, he turned and led Armand down the hall.

Larson was not sure who he had been expecting when the door opened. But the man filling the frame had surely been farthest from his mind. He was trailed by several agents crowding the hall, casting anxious glances at one another and shifting their weight uncertainly. When Armand entered the holding room, they remained clustered in his wake, peering in like family members eavesdropping on an uncomfortable situation.

"We didn't receive authorization for his release," an agent who appeared to be the most senior ranking said.

Armand pivoted, drawing himself to his full height.

"Authorization comes straight from the Director of National Intelligence. It needs no further vetting. I did not fly out here in the middle of the night to get halted by nagging formalities of bureaucracy."

He rounded back on Larson.

He was handcuffed to a metal chair in the middle of the otherwise empty cell. The floor was carpeted and the walls, despite no trace of anything other than plaster and paint, were certainly bugged.

"Katz has brokered your release. I've been sent to collect you."

He freed Larson of his handcuffs in one swift motion. Before he had time to shake off the stiffness accumulated by four hours of captivity, Armand strode out of the cell.

"I had no idea what he was going to do," Larson said, hurrying to catch up. Armand quelled him with a stern glance.

"Not here. Too many ears. Wait until we're in the car."

Five minutes later the pair were seated in the Town Car's backseat speeding toward Midway International Airport. Larson shifted his attention to the Deputy Assistant Director, ignoring the panoramic tapestry of urban development flying past his window. "Tell me what the hell is going on."

"Everything has been unfolding rapidly. It was a small miracle that Katz was able to pull you out of there. Even I didn't truly have the authority."

"Why was I being detained? Bathari is who they should

have been after."

"Think about it," Armand spoke over him. "Men in their shoes are used to protecting the figure on stage from loose cannons in the audience, not vice versa. When Drollsworth collapsed, they rushed to his aid as they are trained to do. Next thing they know, Bathari is gone, and you're standing at the foot of the stage holding a gun."

"The whole world saw Bathari shoot him."

"I know, but these men are instructed to eliminate each threat in order of severity. Bathari was no longer an immediate threat. You were."

"Did they not understand what transpired?"

"No, the agents at the park didn't realize their mistake until it was too late. They brought you in to question you. And it wasn't without valid reason. Every agent in that building understood that you were instrumental in aiding Bathari throughout all of this. It goes to reason that you could have also helped him plan Drollsworth's assassination."

"That's ludicrous." His pulse rose. "I had no idea Drollsworth would be there. Nobody did. Why would I advise Bathari to squander all his momentum from outing the president's scheme to the world by committing public murder?"

Armand's forehead creased. "I don't know, but Bathari knew Drollsworth would be there. Clearly, the rally was bait to lure the latter away from Washington. To the Secret Service, you appeared guilty by association."

Larson paused and collected his thoughts. The Town Car headed west now along a canal on the Stevenson Expressway.

"How did you manage to avoid being implicated in all this?" he asked. For the first time, Armand turned uncomfortable.

"With great care. I witnessed Bathari's transgression on live television. Thanks to a few seconds of forewarning from Gilbert, I was able to abort my team's phase of the operation.

It was a close call, one that could have ended with me, and several others, thrown in jail on treason charges."

"Would you have gone through with it had Bathari not pulled the trigger?"

Armand sat silently for several long moments.

"I was committed to change. I still am. Those congressmen and Cabinet members we planned to apprehend need to be dealt justice." He looked hard at Larson. "Some good might still come of this. The world knows what Drollsworth and the president did. You helped spark something. Whether they believe is another matter, but the kindling may take despite our plans not coming to fruition."

"What does any of that have to do with securing my release?"

They exited onto a six-lane avenue that cut through a suburb stylized by squat brick buildings and fast-food chains. A sign for the airport loomed.

"It has everything to do with you. What comes next cannot be accomplished without your help."

"And what is that?"

"You have to take down the man who could have changed the world. You're going to help us catch Bathari."

Chapter Fifty-One

It became clear that Larson would be spending the two-hour flight back to Washington alone. Upon reaching cruising altitude, Armand disappeared behind a curtain into the rear of the private jet.

And for good reason. Before making his way down the aisle, he paused and handed Larson a sophisticated earpiece. "We think we might have a lead on Bathari and Elena Stregor."

"Where?"

Armand motioned for him to insert the earpiece. As the Gulfstream's turbines roared and the constellation of lights along the banks of Lake Michigan sank away, buzzing static was replaced by crisp voices.

"Somewhere closer to home than you might expect."

A team of six Secret Service agents had been tasked with the actual raid. More waited in unmarked vans—one out front and two more lingering on an adjacent street and around the block. Every precaution possible had been taken, although time was limited. Supercomputers at the NSA had provided the address. Minutes later, a drone had been launched skyward. It hovered over the target, maintaining enough altitude not to alert anyone on the ground to its presence.

Luckily, the night sky over their destination was clear. Initial infrared scans appeared promising. Thermal imaging showed two figures inside the dwelling. The drone snapped a constant barrage of photographs that transmitted in real time to both the Secret Service headquarters south of Washington and Armand's open laptop.

A dark SUV of a popular European make, not at all out of place on the vehicle-lined thoroughfare, glided up Twenty-fourth Street and turned right. It had been retrofitted; two rows of plush seats were replaced by a minimalist bench that ran around the interior. Six agents, eschewing their customary suits for nylon jackets, stared straight ahead. On Tracy Place, the engine quieted, returning a prevailing heavy silence to the neighborhood.

Kalorama Heights, Washington's equivalent of Beverly Hills, as it was infamously known, had for centuries housed a premier assortment of the capital's elite. A residential labyrinth dotted with foreign embassies and multi-million-dollar estates shaded from street view by a shroud of tree cover. Presidents had lived there; Woodrow Wilson's former house, nestled blocks away between the embassies of Myanmar and Cameroon, had been restored and converted into a museum.

It was three in the morning. Kalorama Heights was quiet. The team braced for a blast of wintry chill as they silently unloaded. Without a word, they fell into a loose formation and set off on foot.

The team had been assembled with excruciating care. The senior detective chosen as lead had been tasked with investigating Bathari for weeks. It had been thanks to a bit of exceptional intelligence he had uncovered prior to the

Chicago rally that the NSA had been able to mine Bathari's potential whereabouts in the first place.

The duo of first-class standard officers had received promotion to the top of their ranks and were considered among the best the service had to offer. The same could be said for the two security officers flanking them.

A field agent bringing up the rear was an anomaly all unto himself. He would be the first to enter the residence when they arrived. Serving two tours in Afghanistan, he had taken bullets to the shoulder and abdomen protecting his commanding officer when his unit was ambushed and pinned by enemy fire. Adding to the mystique, he had been stationed at the White House three years prior when an armed malcontent scaled the perimeter fence and entered the building. He was the first agent to encounter the crazed man upon bursting through the front door. The intrusion had not lasted long.

Skirting ivy-strewn mailboxes and keeping to the shadows, the team watched their destination swim into view. Six exhalations puffed white and visible like a train's exhaust as the temperature hovered around freezing. Stone edifices passed; all interior lights doused. Tracy Place, nestled in the slumbering heart of Kalorama Heights, was a gentle upward slope. Their target sat at its apex.

The three-story brick manor with a rose window on the first floor could have belonged to any wealthy senator or diplomat. Six weapons were drawn in unison and their pace quickened. Layouts of the house and grounds had been committed to memory during the rush to depart headquarters.

Units dispersed around the block would provide surveillance as well as relay information in real time from the drone overhead. Two clear heat signatures still shone inside the house as the senior detective overtook a flight of steps that cut through the small, manicured front lawn.

It became apparent the house belonged to neither a senator nor a diplomat as the officers dispersed and the field agent, turning square and aiming a powerful kick near bronze handles, blasted the immaculate double doors inward. The team moved forward into a spacious foyer as one.

The floor was constructed entirely of white marble. The senior detective followed the field agent, who had halted upon sight of an ornate statue erected between two glinting chandeliers. It was lifelike, as much so as the surreal visage that had been laid into the floor with an intricate black tile fresco. Examining the two, the senior detective noted the faces were identical.

With a nod and two simple hand motions, he instructed his men to sweep the first floor. He waited in the foyer while they worked.

It took three minutes to secure the ground floor. Splitting off, two officers made their way to the basement while the field agent and remaining officers scaled carpeted stairs to the upper floors.

The senior detective had a decision to make. After a moment's pause, he too padded cat-like up the stairs.

On the second-floor landing, he once again met the face that had graced the statue and hallway below. Samit Bathari's haunting visage stared from a framed black and white photograph that faced the stairs.

Now, the detective was beginning to understand. Bathari did not own this house. The person who did, judging by their unique choice in decorations, had contracted a case of hero worship that bordered on fanaticism.

He followed in the wake of his men as they combed the second floor. With each cleared room, the coils of their net wove tighter. A voice through his earpiece informed him that the foreign heat signatures had not changed their behavior in any discernible way since his team entered the house. That told him they were unaware the Secret Service team was present. A stroke of good fortune that made the job much easier. It was doubtful Bathari would have time to hold his hostage at gunpoint if he had no inkling a threat was imminent.

Finding nothing on the middle level, the field agent headed for the last flight of stairs leading to the top floor. The senior detective followed; gun held close to his chest. The house had four bedrooms—three had been cleared. A bathroom and study sporting a lavish entertainment center and fireplace were bypassed. The senior detective tried to ignore a pang of worry.

Radio silence downstairs informed him that nothing had been found in the basement. They would comb every inch of the back porch and yard, making sure the fugitive could not slip the bank of fir trees at the lot's edge or scale the fence into a neighbor's yard. The drone would alert them if he managed to get far.

He followed the field agent toward the third floor's lone remaining room. The door was shut. Going off what had become second nature long ago, he maneuvered to one side and waited for the field agent to back against the adjacent wall. Reaching out, he grabbed the doorknob and confidently twisted.

The field agent slipped into the room like a blur, his gun in firing position. The senior detective waited a beat and followed.

What he saw made them lower their weapons in shock.

"Heat signatures located," he murmured into his earpiece. In moments, the rest of the team assembled in the bedroom.

A terrified man and woman sat huddled on opposite ends of the king bed, having broken apart from their locked embrace when the senior detective and field agent barged in with drawn weapons. They turned out to be the housekeeper and a lover she had invited over for a romantic tryst.

Stammering in broken English, she explained that she had not seen the house's owner in weeks. She had flown somewhere in Europe, for business.

As for the persona whose likeness graced various pedestals and works of art.

"Oh, yes," the housekeeper said, "He used to come very often."

"When was the last time you saw him?"

She shrugged.

"Did he say when he would return?"

The housekeeper thought for a moment. Then she perked up. "Mr. Bathari says I will see him on television!"

The senior detective walked out of the bedroom in disgust. "Target still at large," he said, removing his earpiece and hurling it at a wall.

Chapter Fifty-Two

Armand looked capable of murder as he reappeared from the curtained rear of the Gulfstream's fuselage. Furious and crestfallen all rolled into one, cemented by a palpable fatigue etched into every line on his face. Larson watched him knead bloodshot eyes that wouldn't know sleep for the foreseeable future as he paced the aisle.

Larson knew it didn't make any sense for Bathari to return to Washington. Not when he had suddenly become the most wanted man in the nation. Hiding out in the capital with a hostage would make things difficult bordering unfeasible.

No, if he were going to hide it wouldn't be a mansion in Kalorama Heights. But where? He tried to pry the answer out of his head with no success.

As if sapped of all his fuming energy, Armand quit pacing and slumped in the seat across from him, fixing Larson with an expectant stare.

"Who did the house belong to?" Larson asked. One

thing was certain, the answer to uncovering Bathari's whereabouts wouldn't be found by slamming his head against a metaphorical brick wall and waiting for it to appear. It would have to be excavated, detail by detail. Larson had a hunch, the outcome of which would hopefully be determined in short order. Armand's expression indicated that the last of his patience was ebbing.

"The property is owned by a notorious venture capitalist."

"Does he have a name?"

"*She*. The venture capitalist is a woman. Her name isn't important. She invests heavily in the media and entertainment, providing high-dollar slate financing for every major studio in Hollywood. Recently, real estate has become a more significant part of her empire. But it's not her name, rather, the name of the man she's in business with that aroused suspicions enough for the NSA's all-seeing eye to loom over her head."

Larson didn't have to ask. "Ian McInroe." He tried to make sense of the string of information Armand fed him. "How did the NSA link her to Bathari?"

"They started with the already well-established connection between Bathari and the Scottish technology mogul," Armand said. "The next step involved digging into every person on the planet connected with McInroe in a personal or business sense. From there sheer force of numbers took over which has always been, as you're aware, the NSA's most potent advantage. Agency computers sifted through mountains of data until our venture capitalist was identified."

"Why did the NSA believe Bathari was hiding in that particular house?"

Armand closed his eyes and frowned. "It took little time from the initial lead for the NSA to home in on certain clues that pointed toward Kalorama Heights. One seat on a flight bound for Washington had been booked under one of Bathari's known aliases. Analysts confirmed that he had visited the residence and its owner a week prior. It's apparent now that the intention was laying a false trail to throw the NSA off the scent of his actual destination."

"Which brings me back to my initial question. How do I play into all of this?"

The incessant drone of the jet's engines faded away. Armand eyed him intently.

"It's quite possible, over the past three months, that you've spent more time with Bathari than any person on this planet. That's why you're sitting across from me. Katz and the Director of National Intelligence are convinced you can be valuable in tracking him."

Lurching to his feet, Armand pinched the bridge of his nose and resumed pacing. "Think, Larson. Did Bathari ever confide in you? Did you ever suspect he was deceiving you? Think hard. Is there anything he might have said that could prove relevant to where he went?"

Ignoring the urge to sleep, Larson rifled through his foggy memory, rehashing everything Samit Bathari had ever told him. The shutters on the jet's windows were all closed. He opened one and stared out, not seeing but instead focusing on a series of unconnected images and thoughts flashing through his mind. There had to be a link somewhere. Perhaps it didn't lie buried in what Bathari had told him, but in what he *hadn't* told him.

The man had been coy about much of his adult life before Larson's first introduction in Montreal. Except…

He returned his attention to his beleaguered counterpart. "This venture capitalist of yours, you said she has other real estate holdings?"

"Quite a few, yes."

"Where?"

Armand was befuddled, but only for an instant. "She maintains various global holdings. There are too many to list. However, there is a central theme among all of them; she has expensive taste."

"And if the property in question was once controlled by

royalty or a well-known government figure?"

"She would go to any lengths to acquire it."

Larson leaned forward on the edge of his seat. He felt a racing surge of energy as his pulse spiked. Feigning calmness, he closed his eyes. "Has she been successful in acquiring any such properties?"

He let them open a fraction to watch the other man wrack his brain.

"A handful of times. A chateau outside of Paris was traced to the royal family. There's a house in Venice, on the Grand Canal if I'm not mistaken, that was sold to her by the Duke of Parma. She acquired an island palace off the Eastern coast of Africa. Another—"

Larson motioned for him to pause. "How did she acquire the palace?"

"It was sold to her after the owner disappeared."

His heart thudded in his chest. "What is the island's name?"

When Armand told him, Larson slumped back in his seat. His throat had gone dry, making it difficult for him to utter the words that accompanied the charge of understanding that rocked his body.

"I know where he's taking Elena."

Armand already had his cellphone waiting as Larson spoke. When he finished his explanation, the Deputy Assistant Director said nothing for a long moment and then dialed a number.

"This is Rivera. I need to speak to James Collins immediately."

The night sky cleared and miniscule webs of interconnected glowing lights that represented cities and townships became visible as they descended over Washington.

The Gulfstream's reprieve would be short-lived. Larson was forbidden from exiting after they taxied off the runway and stopped near a small concrete terminal. With a parting nod, Armand descended stairs to the tarmac and hurried into a waiting car with his phone pressed to his ear.

Four men came aboard as the jet took on fuel. Compared to the outgoing passenger, the first three seemed relatively well rested. Diego, a less encumbered replica of his beleaguered twin brother, took a seat across from Larson and fixed him with a wan smile. Two other field agents—Marco and Gavin—were competent but had little excess attention to spare on trivial things like pleasantries. They nodded and continued down the fuselage.

Katz was the last to board. He looked, if possible, worse than Armand. With bags under his eyes to match deep creases in both his forehead and charcoal suit, he strode down the aisle and collapsed next to Diego.

"You're sure about this?" he uttered.

Larson nodded. The other man let his eyes droop shut while the cabin door was sealed, and the plane taxied to the runway. They sat in near darkness during takeoff, guiding beacons along either side the only source of illumination.

As the nose turned upward and they gained altitude, Larson leaned forward and asked, "Were the NSA findings able to corroborate my theory?"

Katz became more alert as he opened his bloodshot eyes and straightened in his seat. Work had always taken precedence over his health and wellbeing. And it was what now spurred a second wind in the chief as their plane banked over the Chesapeake Bay toward the Atlantic Ocean.

"It's amazing what forty thousand employees and a quantum supercomputer can dig up," he said. He snapped open the briefcase he'd brought onboard and pulled forth a bottle of gin. Reaching for a tumbler and a handful of ice from a chrome bucket on the lacquered tray between them, he poured a generous measure and stoppered the bottle.

"The palace Armand mentioned is now under surveillance, although we have no way of knowing if it's Bathari's destination."

Producing a stick drive from inside his jacket, he plugged it into a monitor that swung out from the jet's bulwark on a swiveling arm. After a moment, Larson watched a map of the earth projected in real time from a satellite zoom in on a speck of southern hemisphere thousands of miles away.

"It was bloody difficult to find, owing to the fact that your venture capitalist had gone to great lengths to keep its location secret." Katz pointed as the map continued to zoom. "That's the estate, in that small cove south of the city. Aside from the location, the NSA analysts were able to uncover quite a bit more."

The image stopped and revolved around a square plot of land surrounded by high walls. An impressive structure with minarets and several tiered levels stood within. A no man's land of dusty grounds separated the walls from the main building.

"The whole thing was owned by a powerful man in the principality's government who disappeared suddenly. After months of searching and no body turning up it was ruled an accidental death. Then his will was discovered. It stated that the palace and grounds were to be auctioned as quickly as possible. The man's family was irate. Counting extended relatives that lived in town there were dozens of them. None of his blood relations ever saw a cent."

"That's when our venture capitalist acquired the property?"

"A company called Diamond Holdings Ltd., to be precise. But they're one and the same. Diamond Holdings is a simple front company to make it more difficult to identify the buyer."

Larson frowned. "That still doesn't prove Zanzibar is Bathari's destination."

The satellite image paused mid-rotation and zoomed in on the compound's elaborate front. It appeared deserted.

"We have established a verifiable connection."

Next to the chief, Diego looked bored, trading sporadic

glances at the monitor for the opaque blackness of the Atlantic Ocean.

"The NSA is keeping watch. They will notify us the moment Bathari, or anyone else, arrives. There's nothing to do now but wait."

He removed the stick drive, and the monitor went dark. "You should try to get some rest," Katz said, polishing off his gin in one final swig and pouring another. "There won't be much time for recuperating once we arrive."

Larson leaned back in his seat and knew it would be useless. Despite the chaotic and stressful events of the previous twelve hours, excitement's hold was still firm over him.

"Assuming Bathari and Elena show, how will we reach the estate once we land?"

Katz swirled his gin and took another long sip. "The palace is situated on an island. You will go by boat."

Chapter Fifty-Three

Sleep proved hard to come by as the Gulfstream traversed the pitch-black Atlantic Ocean. Larson closed his eyes and dozed for intermittent snatches of time stolen from another man's life, only to jolt awake at the realization of what was to come.

Diego passed the hours in a snoring stupor. Next to him, Katz sat ramrod straight, his lids never slipping despite looking as if they threatened to sag and give way under their own weight at any moment.

Daylight came and eventually cascaded back into night. The plane landed once halfway through the trip to refuel somewhere in Spain. Larson spent the remaining hours restless—his mind refusing to cease an endless whir of activity and go blank. It was with great relief when the Gulfstream's nose tipped downward at long last.

They touched down at an airport that consisted of a single runway and a small cluster of red buildings and hangars. A wave of muggy heat smacked them as they disembarked onto the tarmac. Devoid of the usual bustle of taxiing planes and small vehicle traffic, the airport appeared deserted. Larson stood befuddled when a white Jeep screeched around the nearest edifice and gunned its engine in their direction. It stopped several yards short.

Despite two hours remaining until sunrise, beads of sweat formed along his exposed neck as the driver door opened and a grinning man in khaki military uniform stepped around to greet them. He could make out an armed passenger, similarly dressed, sitting rigid in the adjacent seat.

With a hurried greeting in broken English, the driver helped them aboard and wasted no time commencing a breakneck journey out of the deserted airport and along a wide and straight road that Larson surmised ran toward the coast. Megaliths of industry lined the highway, churning through the otherwise quiet night.

He watched with vague interest as Dar es Salaam unfolded. The largest city in Tanzania, it had served as the nation's capital until twenty years previous when the title was usurped by neighboring Dodoma.

They turned left, their driver alerting the Echelon contingent that they were entering a district called Upanga. His partner remained stoic. The buildings were becoming smaller; a few towers interspersed with whitewashed residences and a plethora of tropical foliage. The absence of manmade light and overwhelming darkness caught Larson by surprise.

Around him, the rest of the team appeared disinterested. Katz had lost the battle and let his heavy eyes fall shut. Marco and Gavin stared at their feet while Diego fiddled with his watch.

He caught Larson taking him in and mumbled under his breath, "You think this guy has any idea where he's going?"

"Let's hope so."

The road curved east and rounded north to hug the coast. Larson smelled salty sea air through the open windows. He tried not to imagine the devilish heat that would occupy the place by midday. On their right, the Indian Ocean was visible as a vast expanse of darkness. They crossed a bridge and a wide swath of swampland, and their driver took an unexpected left that sent everyone in the back groping for something to clutch onto.

"Almost there," he muttered.

They careened down a narrow street, kicking up clouds of choking red dust that seemed to hover over everything and coat every still surface. Estates fit for kings, all fast asleep, with high walls and vibrant palm trees flew past. Without warning, the driver turned the Jeep hard to the right and screeched into a driveway blocked by a tall gate.

They sat motionless. Larson caught sight of a camera's fisheye lens hovering on a wall above them. Satisfied, the gate gave a groaning lurch and slid inward.

The courtyard beyond could have been transplanted from the Garden of Eden. Looking wholly out of place, their driver let the filthy Jeep's engine die and hopped out to shepherd them around the circle drive past a pair of tinkling fountains.

It was a marvelous house in its own right. Larson got a quick view of dual minarets bathed in shadow framing the front door and an overhanging wrought iron terrace before he was ushered inside with the rest.

In the foyer the driver paused. He faded into the background when a dark-skinned man who introduced himself as Rex appeared. Dressed in fine trousers and a linen shirt rolled at the sleeves, he had a goatee and an expressive face that betrayed both wariness and excitement as he led them through the black marble foyer.

"Welcome to Tanzania. I'm sorry it isn't under better circumstances, although we are pleased to be working with you." Rex mounted a sweeping staircase and bade them follow. "Please, hurry. We have much to brief you on and very little time."

The second story was less elegant. Not understanding

for what purpose Tanzanian intelligence used the house, Larson assumed this floor revolved more around mundane bureaucratic tasks.

The room Rex instructed them to cram inside was small and sweltering with a low ceiling. There were no windows. A cluster of folding chairs sat facing a topographical map projected over the wall adjacent the plain door. He motioned for them to sit while he strode across the cramped room to stand before the hazy image. Two more men that had the telltale look of intelligence officers hovered near the projector.

"Zanzibar lies thirty miles off the coast of Tanzania," Rex said in accented English. "It has been a semi-autonomous region within the United Republic of Tanzania for sixty years."

"And it's harboring a murderer," Larson said in a low voice.

Rex smiled to show a row of white teeth. "I'm getting to that. To best understand how this operation will be carried out, you must comprehend the political climate. The relationship between greater Tanzania and Zanzibar remains peaceful, but that would change for the worse if the island's government thought the mainland was attempting to overstep its boundaries."

He tapped the map and the image changed, now a static frame showing the idyllic, walled compound overlooking crystalline sea. "Which is undoubtedly why Bathari chose Zanzibar as his refuge. Be it that the island is relatively unknown, he assumes the political situation will offer him protection."

Katz rose to stand on the other side of the bird's eye view. Rex motioned for him to speak.

"NSA sent an updated report a few minutes ago. Bathari and Elena have reached the palace."

The photograph changed again—a grainy shot of two individuals little more than dark pellets frozen between the estate's walls and main structure.

"They have not exited since that photograph was taken. The palace is guarded. We have to assume everyone inside is armed."

Rex cleared his throat. "Island turmoil and violence erupt on occasion, typically associated with the struggle for power between its two political parties. Tanzanian officials are reluctant to attempt any kind of operation on Zanzibar soil that could incite the Revolutionary Government's rage." His disposition turned dark as he eyed them. "This means your team will have no support once you land. We are sending three of our best men with you. But it is imperative that this remains an operation to capture—not kill."

Katz added, "Their leadership may not be sad to see Bathari gone, but whilst he is on the island, he is technically their guest. His death would be viewed as an act of outside aggression."

"One other thing," Rex interjected. "Nearly all Zanzibar's population is Muslim. According to our intelligence sources, when Bathari graced the island in the past he posed as a retired Sunni Imam. This has garnered him allies and the favor of his neighbors and all but the highest in government who are aware of his secret."

Katz adopted a brisk tone. "Your target is situated several miles south of Zanzibar City. With any luck you'll be gone before anyone notices."

"That's starting to sound like quite a long shot," Diego said with a smirk.

Katz did not share his humor. "The Gulfstream is already fueled and waiting to shuttle us home. It's time to make things right."

Rex leaned in as they stood in a forest of scraping aluminum chair legs.

"My men were ecstatic when they learned of this. Please forgive the one in the passenger seat who came to pick you up. Trying to impress the Americans is all."

Larson grimaced while Diego let out a weak laugh.

"How was your driver?"

"He could use a bit of work on his English," Larson said. "And his driving."

At that, the Tanzanian let out a full guffaw. "That's truly funny. He's one of my best agents."

Rex led them downstairs and back through the foyer into the driveway oasis and reigning darkness. Katz, who would be staying behind, did not accompany his men. Dawn was not far off. Before seeing them off, Rex ducked into a side room and returned holding a steel box with a handle.

"I hope these do the trick." He clicked open the box and handed Larson and the others sleek Beretta pistols. Larson checked the magazine and nodded as he slipped the gun into the waist of his trousers.

This time a different driver chauffeured them south along the slumbering coast in absolute silence until the thoroughfare ended at a crescent-shaped harbor. They passed a ferry terminal and disembarked near the harbor's lip, stepping through a swath of palm trees onto a narrow beach littered with debris and flotsam. Larson almost missed the craft in the meager light that had only brightened a few subtle shades during the drive.

The Tanzanians were already onboard. Each was dressed in full tactical gear and heavily armed. The rigid hull inflatable boat bobbed in the inky shallows. Larson and the others waded out until their knees were soaked and were hoisted aboard one by one. The Tanzanians gave curt nods but said little. Their leader, who stood at the wheel under a small canopy, reversed away from shore with two powerful propellers mounted at its aft and engaged the throttle.

He turned and caught one last glimpse of the Dar es Salaam skyline as they gained speed and raced into open water toward the first vestiges of sunlight.

Chapter Fifty-Four

The ride lasted one hour. Sunlight broke over the horizon as the island swam into view, rising out of the calm sea like a mirage. They passed a deserted archipelago and turned north, speeding into a bay surrounded by jungle on all sides. The water grew shallower and turned a stunning shade of topaz.

The engines whined as the Tanzanian at the helm depressed the throttle all the way, sending a wake of saltwater trailing behind them as they ripped through the surf. Land rapidly approached. Larson wondered what waited for them beyond the compound's high walls. Had Elena put up a struggle when Bathari took her hostage and transported her halfway across the world? Where was she being held now? And in what sort of state?

At that same moment, Katz sat between Rex and a nameless assistant in a plain room, observing a bank of monitors. One displayed a pixelated image transmitted by the drone hovering over Bathari's compound. Another, fixed to the prow of a small craft with seven armed men aboard, showed a peninsula carved like a dagger bisecting a stunning bay. It grew larger by the second.

There was no time to marvel at the island's aesthetic quality. Katz flashed his eyes to the next monitor projecting live feeds from miniscule cameras affixed to the Tanzanians' chests. They showed assorted views of waves and tropical jungle rushing past and the same strip of land coming into focus. Cacophonous sound emanated from microphones the size of erasers. Katz imagined rustling palm fronds and calls of waking birds eclipsed by the roar of the craft's engines.

"I hope this works," he muttered.

Rex patted his shoulder in a soothing gesture. "Don't worry, my friend. I have a strong feeling that fortune is on our side."

Katz scanned each monitor once again. He tried to ignore a tightening in his chest—a normal occurrence during operations. Rex had offered him a beer. One glance at Katz's expression had been all the answer.

The craft's rigid hull ground to a halt on an immaculate white beach and the engines died. Larson hardly had time to take in his surroundings before they piled over the rubbery bulwarks onto shore.

The Tanzanian manning the craft handed out machetes. Marco and Gavin took hold of leathery handles and flexed ominous blades as the group started toward the jungle's imposing cusp. Reversing, the rubber boat pushed back into navigable water. It would act as lookout and wait nearby in the bay for their return trip home.

Bringing up the rear, Larson and Diego removed their guns and held them ready at waist level.

Hacking through the jungle proved strenuous work. Larson and his counterpart swept the dense, forested area with keen eyes as Marco, Gavin, and the Tanzanians chopped vines and branches, forging a path where there should have been none.

"Surely there was a road we could have used," Diego muttered under his breath.

"Cannot enter by the road unless we want to risk being spotted," the larger Tanzanian said in a guttural voice between grunts. "This is the only way."

Darkness brought on by the jungle canopy increased to an impenetrable apex and then lightened in steady shades half an hour into their trek. By now, it was hot and muggy. Mosquitoes buzzed relentlessly and each man was drenched in sweat with nothing but a light breeze from the forgotten beach to sate them.

By degrees, Larson made out an area cleared of palm trees and mango groves ahead. Fifty yards beyond stood a wall constructed with what appeared to be felled timber. As their unit cut through the last of the underbrush, they emerged from the jungle in a line. They flattened along the edge of shadow put off by limbs bowing under the climbing sun.

An imposing gate fashioned from unfinished vertical beams sat dead center along the knobby stretch of wall. Larson checked his watch. It read half past seven local time.

"The gate should be opening."

Without another word, all six stole forward. The land around the perimeter wall had been cleared of everything except tall, coarse grass that reached their waists. Moving closer, Larson's vantage point shifted. A gap in the form of a dirt track led around to the wall's far side. It disappeared under the gate.

A road. The NSA had been helpful with the logistics of comings and goings on the property. A man like Bathari, hardly a survivalist, could not be expected to subsist without resupply from the outside.

The moment had arrived. Whether it was something he caught out of the corner of his eye or caused by a disturbance in the sweltering air, Larson noticed the gate tremble and open. As it spread outward, he understood—it was being pushed by hand.

Larson spotted Bathari's estate for the first time. If an island where European, Middle Eastern, and Asian societies had once convened could be considered a cultural amalgam, the palace was no different. Seeing from the eye of a drone and satellite images failed to do it proper justice.

Tiered coral edifices transplanted from Stone Town cultivated to the north by the Sultan of Oman two centuries previous gave way to a ballooning roof that could have hailed from Mumbai. Each balcony running the upper two floors was carved with intricate detail and cast shadow on various entrances and shuttered windows. An inner courtyard with a pool and lush greenery was all but certain.

"We have a visitor," Diego whispered.

An armed man in khaki fatigues strode toward them. Focused on the gate, he didn't notice six figures crouched in the tall grass like hungry lions, silently observing. The departing supply truck, bed concealed under a tarpaulin stretched over an aluminum frame, belched a puff of black smoke. The armed guard stood back to let it pass.

While sight of their position was blocked by cracked tires and rusted flanks, Diego edged closer to Larson.

"How are we going to get past that guard?"

"I'm thinking."

Surmising the conversation, the Tanzanians glanced at them. Marco and Gavin kept their focus on the open gate, machetes traded in favor of cocked Berettas.

"I suppose we could try running inside before he closes the gate and pray he doesn't shoot us."

"If he shoots you first, he may be doing all of us a favor," Larson retorted.

He shifted his gaze off the lone guard. Diego had a mischievous glint in his eye. Larson had seen it before. Its presence filled the pit of his stomach with worry. The cargo truck was nearly past. The moment its rear tires rolled away, Diego straightened above the tall grass's cover and darted forward.

"What the hell are you doing?"

Even while he formed the words, something in Larson's brained clicked and he understood what Diego intended. He rose and tore after him, the rest of the extraction team at his heels.

Luck was on their side. The guard pivoted, disturbing more red dust, and wandered lazily back inside the compound. From what Larson could make out the grounds were sparse—manicured grass and a cavalry of spotless Land Rovers and all-terrain vehicles arranged beside a grove of palms hanging swollen fruit over the wall. Next to no cover presented a challenge.

What compelled the lone guard to turn away from the beckoning palace Larson would never know. Perhaps it was fate tapping urgently on his shoulder. At any rate, he did, only to discover Diego closing the distance between them with a Beretta leveled at his chest. Two hollow rounds, fired in lightning quick succession, ended his life in an instant.

The tall grass waved its lazy approval.

Larson and the others slowed as they slipped past the felled guard and inside the walls. Turning back was no longer an option. It was no use reprimanding his partner. Diego understood with equal clarity what Larson did; there was no other way to gain access to the palace without putting their lives and the mission in jeopardy.

Luckily, the next obstacle presented himself unencumbered by anything save a large assault rifle as they passed Bathari's expensive safari fleet. He crumpled with two well-placed shots to the neck from Marco and another from Gavin that tore through his chest cavity.

A chill overtook Larson as he crossed the threshold. It was much cooler inside the palace. Tiled flooring did little to mask their footsteps. A fresco adorning the opposite wall had been shattered by rounds exiting the neck of the man who now lay lifeless in the entrance hall.

Crouching, he let the rest of the team hurry past. The Tanzanians split off around the perimeter in case their adversaries got the bright idea to flank them. Marco and Gavin darted forward, eager for more khaki-uniformed guards to appear. Owing to the expanse of the estate, clearing it would take some time.

Larson straightened as Diego swept by him into a dining room with a long table arranged as though the host was expecting a large dinner party. Together, they inspected each empty room.

Elena was here, and Larson was determined to find her. So was her captor, the man who had nearly stolen the sovereignty of the United States. He would be discovered too, although his fate was much more tenuous. Larson chambered a round and hoped no innocents were caught in the crossfire.

Elena tried to move and met stiff resistance. The world around her was dark. A speck of infrared light, in the distance several feet above her sight line, announced that her eyes were functioning fine.

Memory was a different story. She worked to clear the mental fog that seemed to convalesce over everything much like the pervading darkness. Where was she? And how had she gotten there?

The last twenty-four hours—maybe it was longer—had passed in a blur of unconsciousness and scattered flashes of image that made little sense. But what came previous? An invisible barrier had descended, blocking all recollection prior to being transported into this new dark, foggy world.

Her feet were bare and immersed in warm liquid. Another attempt to struggle left her panting, and she didn't try again. That's when she felt it. Something heavy draped around her like a corpse. It weighed her down, squeezing her slender frame too compact with a pressure that became uncomfortable and triggered the urge to begin squirming again.

But that wasn't what filled her with dread. It came, much like the revelation that her hands were bound behind her back, washing over her like the warm liquid she stood in, when she silenced her thoughts long enough to hear the ticking.

In that same instant, the name Samit Bathari popped to the forefront of her convoluted mind. Elena tried to scream.

No sound was emitted save a soft exhalation like a dying flame. She breathed in and tried again.

Another stab of panic. Why wasn't it working? Had the air always been so thin? Her cell was damp and musty like a cavern hidden deep underground. But now each shallow breath came with increased difficulty. Like something, or someone, was sucking the oxygen out of the room.

For the first time, her body broke free of her mind's restraint, and she thrashed and churned as much as the weighty apparatus that held her hostage allowed. Dark walls were closing in.

Don't give in to panic, she urged herself. Just think.

It took a surge of mental composure to force the blackness to stop its steady inward march. There had to be a reason. She took deeper breaths, forcing herself to believe the dank air would deliver oxygen her brain desperately needed, and her thudding pulse dropped. Shortness of breath could have been caused by any number of intravenous drugs.

She was interrupted by a muffled blast overhead. She could discern, like the distant tap of pickaxes inside a stone quarry, the dull percussion of footsteps. Elena tried to shift her weight and the smooth ground under her bare feet rocked side to side. Liquid lapped against her calves.

Another burst of gunfire. When it went quiet her first instinct, even though she didn't understand why, was fear. It was compounded by a solitary pair of footsteps growing louder. Whether friend or foe, someone was coming.

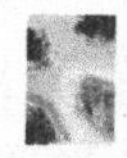

The Echelon operatives cleared the bottom floor and mounted a grand staircase when the Tanzanians roared past, headed toward the top floor. Larson held Diego back with a hand on his shoulder.

"They won't be up there."

"Where?"

"Do you trust me?"

"Do I have a choice?"

Diego allowed Larson to lead the way back to the ground floor. Sure enough, there was a courtyard

"We should wait for the others."

He shook his head. "By now he knows we're here. There isn't time."

The courtyard, just as he had imagined, was picturesque with a fountain flowing into a pool lined with azure tiles. Larson pictured Bathari basking in the shallows, ruminating on plans to take over the world.

But the pool had little connection with why he had dragged Diego out here. Amid potted plants and greenery wrapping around several divans was something else. A discrete door set in the opposite wall. Larson's spine tingled with excitement that had nothing to do with coursing adrenaline brought on by the high stakes of the raid. He pointed at the door.

"Where do you think it goes?"

"Call it a gut feeling, but I'd wager it leads to more than a supply closet."

"Then you better stand back and keep your head down."

The distant blast set the surface under Elena's feet trembling. Her soles had become creased and painful by

their extended time submerged underwater. How long it had been, she still couldn't say.

The lone pair of footsteps produced a man in a drab, khaki uniform with a large weapon slung across his back who materialized in the gloom like a wraith. He proceeded past her without a word and no more than a quick leering glance. Where he went was a mystery, although Elena could still sense his presence nearby.

Was that shallow breathing or the echoing noises of her dark prison? Bound as she was, with the weighted vest pressing down, it was impossible to turn and see what lay behind her. Elena expected any moment to hear his whispered voice and feel the cold nose of a gun press against the back of her head.

It never came. After the blast she held her breath, waiting for the staccato of more footsteps. Everything above still sounded very far off. The sporadic bursts of gunfire had gone quiet.

There was a screeching jolt and the slick ground beneath her feet shuddered and began to vibrate. A low voice whispering against her neck made Elena start violently. She listened against her will, struggling against her bonds, trying to forget the ticking that was blanketed by a whine that grew constant and much louder.

Despite all this, the words floated around the nape of her neck and into her ears. Tidings of a fate Elena could do nothing to amend. The whispered words of death.

Chapter Fifty-Five

Larson led the way down the damp stairs with his Beretta drawn. Thick smoke had cleared to reveal a gaping hole in the courtyard where a door had once stood. There was no time for congratulations. By now, Bathari certainly understood what was happening. Elena's fate hung in the balance. He appreciated that with each precious second that ticked by, if she was still alive, her odds of survival plummeted.

The Tanzanians were still busy clearing the compound, but Gavin and Marco had appeared in the courtyard and joined them for their descent into the abyss. The first steps were accompanied by the strong scent of iron hanging on the damp air. Larson ran his left hand against the wall to steady himself. Red clay that gave little to the touch. Wherever they were headed had been carved deep into the earth.

The darkness wasn't complete. Further, somewhere beyond their meager line of sight, a dim light emanated. It cast the faintest glow on the precarious stairs. By the time they reached the bottom it grew brighter. Larson led the others along a rounded corridor that could have been tunneled into the earth by a giant serpent.

Gavin and Marco kept to the wall like Marines clearing a war-torn Baghdad road. Diego, weapon raised, drew alongside Larson.

"Suppose we're walking directly into a trap."

"We might be. What do you suggest we do about it?"

For the first time, Diego looked worried. "I'm not sure. But I don't like how things are progressing."

"Elena doesn't have much time," Larson said. "This is our only option."

The corridor grew wider. Around a shallow bend it ended in a circular room with a domed ceiling. Pieces of chipped and cracking tile clung to the red clay here and there. Four more tunnels, gaping and ominous, connected like spokes joining at a central axis.

Larson and the others ground to a halt. A curious sight met them. The dim light's source was revealed. Clusters of incense candles mixing with the permeating iron odor flickered at intervals. But candles were not what made the knot in Larson's chest tighten.

The four of them stared, trying to make sense of what they were seeing. In the center of the chamber, still shrouded half in gloom, a man's form seated atop a prayer rug with his back to them was visible. His legs were crossed, and his hands appeared to be folded in his lap. Larson took a tentative step forward, gun leveled on the seated figure.

The other three edged into the chamber behind him and spread out along the walls, eyes trained on the seated man. Larson took another step, ears peeled for sounds of an ambush.

"Stand up," he called across the chamber. The seated figure must have heard them coming. As his eyes continued to adjust, Larson recognized the back of the man's head—dark hair and a diminutive frame he had stood near so often.

Bathari rose and turned to face them. Larson was

relieved to see that his clasped hands were empty. He wore a patterned robe that descended near his ankles, though not so low that Larson couldn't make out a pair of Italian loafers underneath. He moved forward faster now with his weapon trained on the man who he once believed would change the world.

At each draw of ragged breath, he expected Bathari to take a stance of aggression, or else lunge for an exit as the dark tunnels leading off the chamber flooded with enemies. Neither happened. The only move their adversary made was to unclasp his hands and spread them wide in a welcoming gesture. It was cooler under the palace, but that had nothing to do with what caused Larson to shiver.

"Welcome to my home," Bathari said, ignoring the four Berettas trained on various parts of his anatomy. "You have journeyed a long way to come here."

"Where is she?" Larson demanded.

Bathari's expression filled with understanding. "Elena is nearby. I would be happy to point the way. Of course, we have a few topics to discuss, first."

The others closed in. Marco and Gavin pivoted in unison, sweeping the tunnel entrances for sign of newcomers.

"Like what?" Diego asked.

Bathari's neutral inflection remained unchanged. "If you want Ms. Stregor returned unharmed you will need to cooperate. You have no chance of locating her without my assistance."

"And if we decide we don't want to play along?" Larson asked.

"What alternative do you have?"

Bathari had called his bluff. It was Diego who responded. "We could kill you."

Marco and Gavin spun at the suggestion, leering at the man standing barefoot like a cornered deer. But unlike a normal deer, he did not appear remotely afraid.

Bathari shook his head. "I wouldn't do that if I were

you. I'm revered in this part of the world. My death would spring numerous problems on your end, not the least of which would be getting off the island alive."

Diego puffed his chest. "We'd be gone before anyone noticed."

Bathari shrugged. "If that's the risk you wish to take. Of course, you will never find Elena. I'm also aware that you've already killed several of my men. I assume that went directly against orders you received before arriving. Am I also right in conjecturing that you have explicit additional orders to bring me in alive? A few dead guards can be forgiven. My death, however…"

As he trailed off, Diego opened his mouth to retort, but Larson cut him off. More argument was counterproductive. Elena was running out of time.

"What are your demands?"

The other man's exhaustion surfaced in the meager candlelight. "I will point out the correct tunnel and give my instructions. All four of you will go to retrieve her. No one will make any move against me, not if you want your captive to live."

"Absolutely not," Diego said.

Larson's mind churned.

"How can we be assured there aren't men waiting to ambush us?"

Bathari made to place his palms on Larson's shoulders as he once might have done. The Echelon agent shook them off with a grunt of disgust.

"I'm a man of nonviolence," Bathari said. "Except for when it can't be avoided. I don't believe now is one of those times."

Diego shot him a look. He understood; they were leaving themselves exposed to any number of threats that could deteriorate the situation. But Larson's expression was clear. This was their only option.

He turned back to the captive. "Point the way."

"I am not to be harmed." He raised his open palms.

"These tunnels connect to form a kind of labyrinth. Without my instructions your mission is hopeless."

Larson lowered his Beretta a fraction. The others did the same. "Then we better hurry."

Bathari pivoted and pointed a steady finger at the gaping hole across from them. "Start through the east tunnel."

They moved in a tight formation. Every few steps he glanced back to see Bathari following like a wan specter floating through darkness. Here and there he called out directions, guiding them deeper into the beast's lair. Larson noted that while Bathari followed, he made sure to leave a sizable distance between them.

It took him several minutes to realize that the iron-tinged air was becoming saltier and more humid. After another mind-numbing series of turns, Bathari paused as if he could go no further.

"Follow that corridor to the end and you will find her," he said, gesturing to a passage slightly brighter than the rest. He stood rooted to the spot. Bathari met Larson's eyes, his own wide and full of meaning. "She doesn't have much time."

He beckoned the others forward and hurried along the tunnel. It continued to lighten as they ran. There was an unmistakable dull roar.

"Are there lions on Zanzibar?" Diego asked through tight lips.

"Just run faster."

The sound grew louder. They came around another bend and all four skidded to a halt, their boots losing traction atop damp earth.

Diego and the others rounded on him. "Now what do we do?"

Larson tried not to panic. He spun back as a metallic clanking eroded all other noise and a steel gate descended from the tunnel's ceiling, cutting them off from the way they'd come.

Marco and Gavin approached the metal bars and yanked them hard. They remained resolutely in place.

"Don't waste your energy." Diego stood between him and the others, the expression fixed on his tan face caught between bemused and annoyed. Larson ignored him, turning away from the gate that resembled prison bars and walking toward the source of the dull roar.

Bathari had fooled him, that much was clear. The passage did not lead to Elena. He strode forward until his boots were darkened by a spray of muddy water.

The tunnel culminated in a rocky outcropping brightened by daylight pouring through a slit the width and height of an average-sized human. The opening was concealed, however, by a gushing torrent of water.

Careful not to lose his footing, Larson edged closer and peered around the waterfall. It stood to reason the murky water originated at the palace itself. From wherever it left the compound, it tumbled over a ridge on the backside of the peninsula into the bay below. He made out pristine water twenty feet beneath them. And then something else caught his eye.

The boat rocked as someone else boarded. Then Elena was jerked backward without warning. Not just her, the slick surface under her feet moved as well. The deafening noise was disorienting. Her heavy harness, all that kept her standing, swayed back and forth.

She understood as brightness seeped in all around her, stinging her eyes. Daylight engulfed her. They were speeding up. Carrying her to the desolate spot the man in khaki had assured would be her final resting place.

Larson watched the speedboat cut a wake through the peaceful bay without blinking. Marco and Gavin abandoned the steel grating and joined him at the cave's mouth. Even from a distance, no one needed any assistance recognizing who was aboard the boat. It streamed out of the bay, traveling fast enough that the whining groan of its powerful engines threatened to drown out all else.

A man with dark skin and a beard piloted the nimble craft. Bathari stood several feet behind him, one hand gripping the chrome gunwale. And tethered to the bobbing stern, strung by taut cords like a pig headed for slaughter, was the unmistakable raven-haired form of a woman.

"What do you propose we do, boss?"

Diego and the others stood ready at his side. Nothing could have prepared them for this. But to Larson, it was clear that one avenue of action remained available.

He ignored the question and produced his iPhone from an inner pocket. It may have appeared ordinary, but the device had many useful tricks not privy to the general public. Powering on the screen, he opened an innocent looking app while the speedboat and Elena shrank in the distance. The app coaxed a display of numeral buttons arranged like a telephone receiver.

He dialed a five-digit combination and slid the iPhone back inside his vest. He didn't bother powering it off. It wouldn't survive what was about to happen.

"What are your orders?"

Realization fell into place on the others' faces before he spoke. He didn't mince words. Stowing his Beretta against the small of his back, he said, "We jump."

Chapter Fifty-Six

A blast of muggy air that might have lasted a brief eternity ended with the force of impact and the rushing wetness of saltwater. They didn't have to squirm long. Larson had hardly breached the white capped surface when more reverberations disrupted the surf. The friendly boat that had been standing by on the peninsula's far side screamed toward them. In seconds it rounded the cape and swung its prow in their direction.

Bobbing atop the waves, he and the others treaded water as the boat came to a stop and they were scooped aboard one by one. Wasting no time, Larson hurried to the Tanzanian standing at the wheel.

"Did you get a visual of a speedboat with three people aboard?"

The driver nodded. "About five minutes ago."

"Where was it headed?"

"South. Out of the bay. I lost contact before I could gather anything more."

Larson gave the order without hesitation. "Follow it."

Their rigid-hulled craft possessed one sizable advantage—it was top of the line in military technology. As the driver eased the throttle forward and they shot out of the shallow cove, kicking up a wall of churning seawater from either side of the sleek stern, Larson felt a glimmer of hope.

There was a problem. Jungle on either distant shore receded and an archipelago of sandy landmasses dotted the bay's mouth. But there was no sign of another vessel. The sea ahead was turquoise and undisturbed.

He tried to clear his head. Where would they have gone? He'd made little progress when the Tanzanian driver tapped him on the shoulder.

"I think that's your target."

He motioned to a radar screen nestled among the boat's controls. A lone dot weaved its way north. The opposite direction. "It's headed up the coastline toward Zanzibar City."

Without warning, they banked right with such force that Larson and the others were nearly thrown overboard. Staggering into a row of seats that had been doused with wake, they watched a narrow island and strips of white sand beach flash past as they rounded the cape.

Straightening along a northward trajectory, their pilot opened the throttle, hitting them with a bout of acceleration that made Larson lurch for the nearest handhold.

But none of that mattered. They were in luck. Looking through the cockpit beyond the dripping windshield, he could make out a dark shape and a long white trail that could only be another boat cutting through the crystalline water. The engines groaned as they urged the rubber craft forward.

Forty miles away, Katz thrummed his fingers restlessly in a dark room next to his Tanzanian counterpart and stared at a backlit computer monitor. Two blips on a grid flashed their way up the Zanzibar coast. He said nothing. In contrast, Rex fumbled for words.

"I-I don't understand how this is possible. The men I sent along are some of my best. This can't be happening."

Katz refused to take his eyes off the screen.

"Understand that, unless your equipment is lying, and since it is all state of the art, I very much doubt it, Bathari found a way to escape. Don't be too surprised. He's clever."

"But my men would never have allowed this to occur!"

"Well, they did. They also failed to prevent half a dozen of Bathari's guards from being gunned down. I thought you impressed on them that this was to be a diplomatic mission."

The Tanzanian looked distraught. "Perhaps there was no other way! They couldn't talk their way through the palace doors."

"And I don't think Bathari's men would have been fooled by a peace offering." Katz's tone was edged with sarcasm. He ignored the screen for a moment to lock eyes with Rex. "Operations turn messy once they are released into the world. And hostage extractions rarely go as planned. But that doesn't mean all is lost."

He turned back to the monitor. "Plans change."

The blips on the screen continued moving toward the hooked landmass representing Zanzibar City. What was more, the trailing blip was closing the distance. Images sent from the powerful satellite overhead, refreshed every thirty seconds, corroborated this.

A little closer. He surmised that Larson and the others had given Bathari chase. Whether the latter was leading them toward something, or running, he remained unsure. One thing was all but certain, however. With his fate so close to being decided, Bathari was bound to adopt the mentality of a wounded animal. Survival at all costs, no matter the destruction that was dealt to others.

A refreshed image showed the two boats less than half a kilometer apart. He could wait no longer. Finding his cellphone on a nearby desk, Katz dialed a secure line belonging to a man halfway around the world. It was the middle of the night his time, but there was no question he was wide-awake and waiting beside the phone.

He was proved correct by a grunted answer on the first ring. Katz skipped the greeting.

"Make the call," he said.

Larson's premonition proved correct. Bathari's vessel, fast in its own right, could not outrun them. Resorts and outcroppings of civilization dotted the shore amid tethered swaths of jungle as they flashed past. He wagered that no one on land had any idea what was happening. Not even the wildest imagination could fathom a murderer and his hostage being pursued by men from a secret team headquartered thousands of miles away before first cups of coffee were poured.

He put the thought from his mind and held the Beretta in his lap. The shark's tooth cape of Zanzibar City swam into view on their right. They sailed along the coast through a channel formed by sandbars and miniscule clustered islands on their portside.

"We're gaining." the driver called from his position at the helm. He needn't have said anything—it was obvious to all they were minutes from overtaking the vessel ahead. Larson could make out Bathari, facing forward but glancing over his shoulder every few seconds, his eyes wide and feral.

At that precise moment, the boat ahead swerved. Following its lead, their vessel did the same. Pirouetting around a tear shaped island that proved little more than a sandy speck protruding from the calm sea, they regained speed.

Morning sun cast a nasty glare across the windshield that hindered Larson's view. They headed toward a sliver of island surrounded by shallower turquoise water, away from the mainland. He leaned forward, trying to get a clearer sight line on Bathari. Why did it look like he was stepping toward the boat's stern? Toward Elena.

"Why the hell are they slowing down?"

It was Diego who spoke. Larson staggered to his feet and approached the driver.

"We can ram them," he said in a thick Swahili accent.

Larson didn't respond. Their adversary's vessel was now barely crawling toward a mound of sand rising from the water.

"Take us as close as you can," Diego said.

The driver moved his hand forward to depress the throttle. Larson's own shot into frame, yanking the darker man's palm away.

"Keep our distance."

His eyes focused on what Bathari was holding. Whether or not it was the same gun he had used to kill Drollsworth, he couldn't be sure. But one thing was certain—Bathari was now aiming at Elena's temple.

Chapter Fifty-Seven

The first fired round skimmed the brilliant water. A warning shot. Larson understood—they weren't to come any closer.

Bathari wasted no movement as he prowled around his captive. Behind him, the man in khaki reappeared. He unsheathed a large, serrated knife from a scabbard hanging on the outside of his thigh. Larson watched horrified and helpless as he raised the blade even with Elena's exposed neck.

"We have to do something."

The driver's hands fidgeted over the throttle. Diego eyed them.

"Make any move toward them and they'll kill her."

"They're going to kill her anyway."

"I can make the shot," Gavin said. A look from Larson quelled him. His pistol was raised, but from a distance of at least one hundred yards there was no way he could drop two targets in time.

He watched frozen as the jagged knife continued rising

past Elena's throat and head. It hovered near one of the taut bindings holding her body erect. He made sense of what he was seeing a second too late as Bathari nodded and her captor cut the cord in one powerful, sweeping movement.

Elena lurched violently to her right. Bathari lowered his gun and reached out to keep her from dangling. It appeared her legs had given way.

The large man sawed at the other binding. When it neatly severed, Elena crumpled into Bathari's arms. Her hands were still bound behind her back.

"What are they going to do?" Diego muttered.

Larson noted the bulky vest obscuring Elena's torso. From this distance it was impossible to tell but judging by the way she had collapsed he suspected that it was quite heavy.

Diego leaned on the prow, staring across the sparkling water. "Is she wearing a suicide vest?"

The words alone made Larson's heart lurch. He begged himself to trust what he was seeing.

"There are no protruding wires, and none of them are holding a detonator. It looks like—"

The answer hit him. Elena's borrowed accessory reminded him of the heavy smock dentists draped over their patients before x-rays. The kind filled with…

"It's full of lead."

Just as he put it all together, Bathari gave an unceremonious shove and Elena stumbled backward, one bare foot catching on the stern's lip while she tried to regain her balance.

She toppled past the point of no return, the elegant arc of her form descending into the sea. In the moment it took to buckle and produce a reactionary splash she was gone, plunging to the depths like a net tangled with stones.

Their rubber craft went silent. Larson stood frozen, looking on in disbelief as the man in khaki sheathed his knife and plodded back to the helm. Bathari met his gaze for the briefest of moments before straightening and turning away.

One hundred yards away, the other boat ground into motion, sending a torrent of white froth spewing from its propellers.

"What are you waiting for?" Larson yelled to the driver.

He eased the throttle forward as Bathari arced left toward the western edge of the thin island. Larson leaned over the starboard gunwale as they gained speed. A steadying hand clutched the back of his vest. It was Diego.

"What are you going to do?"

He lifted his right leg, positioning himself on the craft's rubber bulwark. "I have to go after her. We can't let her die."

The boat slowed as they reached the precise spot where Elena had sunk. Larson hoisted his other leg onto the gunwale and tried to balance. He broke free of Diego's grip.

Several things happened at once. Out of the corner of his eye, Larson witnessed a cache of fast-moving boats loom around the distant island. It coincided with the unmistakable dull screeching thud of another vessel running aground. He could make out Bathari's slender form jolt forward as his own balance gave way and he launched himself headfirst into the blue water.

He kicked furiously, pushing himself deeper and cursing the heavy boots and thick vest that bogged him down and made it hard to swim. Twenty feet below the surf, a shadowy mass squirmed on the sandy ocean floor. A cloud of debris swirled from the spot.

He propelled himself downward. A mild pain was already developing in his lungs, letting him know oxygen was rapidly diminishing. Seawater pressed on his eardrums. At ten feet, the first bubbles escaped. By the time Elena was within arm's reach, the last of his air slipped out. She had gone still.

His left hand connected with Elena's shoulder. Her long hair swayed in the current, standing and dancing about in the sandy cloud her collision with the ocean floor had created. Elena's hands were bound behind her back. Her eyes, glassy and opened, stared at him but registered nothing as Larson planted his feet on the sea floor and grappled with the folds of the heavy vest that pinned her to the precipice of her demise.

Time was running out. He found it difficult to get a handhold on the slick material. Larson's burning lungs urged him to hurry. Finally, he caught hold of the latching buckles and heaved, pulling the vest away a little at a time. As she came free, Elena's limp form levitated a few inches off the sandy floor.

Larson's entire body screamed at him, a raging fire that he'd never experienced and wasn't sure he could overcome. He scooped Elena with both arms and pushed hard off the ocean floor.

All buoyancy had given way. His sodden clothes were acting as a counterweight, as was the lifeless form he clutched around the torso. His other arm clawed toward the shimmering surface. Each foot was a monumental struggle. Larson kept his eyes fixed on the morning sunlight glinting off the top of the water that could have been a mile away, aware that he couldn't carry on much longer. With each passing second, both of their deaths became more assured.

The urge to open his mouth and gulp huge lungsful of saltwater was overwhelming. He couldn't stand it any longer. The edges of his vision were succumbing to a blackness that intensified as it crept inward. Elena's body dragged… They were sinking.

Larson was on the cusp of letting go when his head broke through the surface and hot air caressed his face. He dragged Elena out of the water, elevating her lifeless head above the waves.

They were greeted by a scene of chaos. Half a dozen boats sporting blazing lights cut a swath through the choppy shallows surrounding the nearby island. Larson noted Tanzanian Navy markings as he spotted Bathari's craft still grounded and the small glimmer of a man in the distance doing his best to stumble ashore. Several Tanzanians disembarked a launch and gave chase.

None of that mattered. Elena still wasn't breathing. He pulled her dead weight close and pummeled her chest as they bobbed in the warm water, for the first time losing his composure and pleading in her ear.

"Don't die on me, Elena. Please, I need you to wake up. Don't die on me!"

PART FOUR

Chapter Fifty-Eight

The chill of winter had begun to thaw by early March, but not so much that the man donning a long coat outside a bus station in Mostar looked out of place. On this crisp morning, a lone carriage waited. When the rusted doors creaked open, he was one of the first aboard.

Larson placed an overnight bag under his seat and settled in for the three-hour journey. The space next to him was soon occupied by a graying Bosnian in a threadbare coat that smelled like stale soup. Luckily, he did not seem in the mood for conversation. As the aging bus—sounding like it hadn't seen more than a fresh coat of paint since the Cold War—rumbled away from the station and across the rushing Neretva River, he lolled his head against the seat and began snoring.

In between snores, Larson allowed his thoughts to wander. Snatches of conversation in Bosnian and Serbian mixed with the grumbling engine and filled the cabin. He glanced out a fogged window at the narrow pass between clumsy peaks that signaled they were leaving Mostar behind and recalled the previous evening.

He had traveled to the ancient Bosnian town with the intention of meeting someone. As he'd stood on the Old Bridge, a picturesque landmark dating back half a millennium, the realization sank in that his efforts had been fruitless.

Larson remained unperturbed. He'd returned to his charming hotel to make a brief call. Within a matter of minutes after hanging up his phone rang, a new destination blossomed. Another few seconds secured a seat aboard the first bus departing the following morning. International train travel in this part of the world was inconvenient. Where he was headed, a bus was much more sensible.

Bosnian countryside slipped past, and a familiar chain of events replayed. After dropping the Tanzanians in Dar es Salaam, his team had returned home—before authorities in Zanzibar City had time to realize what had happened. Bathari's premonition proved correct; uproar over his capture had been exhibited by certain of the island's elite government circles. Already spirited across the channel onto Tanzanian soil, there wasn't a thing any of them could do about it.

As more information shrouding the operation came to light, the next round of perfunctory outcries was directed at the Americans. It fell on deaf ears, owing to the fact that at that moment the world's greatest superpower was in a state of unforetold flux.

The president had fled. Larson learned this upon returning to Washington. He, along with most of his large family, had snuck out of the capital in the dead of night and boarded his personal Cessna Citation X, eschewing the much larger and more renowned jet bearing his infamous last name. Wheels left the tarmac while Larson and the others soared across the Atlantic, and from there they had vanished.

With their disgraced leader gone, the former president's Cabinet had promptly resigned. Several slunk back into anonymity under a barrage of unrelenting questioning and bad press. As soon as official impeachment and conviction proceedings could be held, the vice president, much to his own chagrin, took over his former counterpart's vacated post.

He had spent the first week in his new position neither appointing a replacement Cabinet nor working to sort out the prolonged crisis gripping the nation but hiding in a locked Oval Office and refusing to make any appearance whatsoever to the outside world.

All this explained why several furious calls from the Zanzibar ambassador and the president of Zanzibar himself had been fielded by none other than a young aide still wet behind the ears from law school who had been attached to the White House little over a year. Over the muffled sounds of shouting, he explained in a shaky voice that the Secretary of State was not available because currently the all-important post stood vacant.

Finally, moments before the aide exhibited inaugural symptoms of a panic attack, a senior staffer decided it was time to take charge and relinquished him of diplomatic phone duties.

Little was done to keep the American public in the dark. Quite the opposite. In the days following the presidential regime's fall from grace, the mainstream media did everything they could to provide a play by play of the carnage. A select few networks still seemed intent on attempting to spin the hysteria as it unfolded. However, little could be done to mitigate the situation. The effect of Bathari's revelation in Chicago was damning.

Larson settled back in his moth-eaten seat and couldn't help smiling. The former president's whereabouts had been a major subject of interest in the weeks following the fiasco. Irony reared its head when a simple contraband camera phone, and not the mighty media, unearthed the answer in late February. Based on grainy video taken inside the dour halls of a government building, rumors soon abounded the Western world that the former Commander in Chief had resurfaced in Russia.

The collective gasp reached neither Langley nor the black cube behemoth at Fort Meade belonging to the NSA. The United States Intelligence Community relied on much more than rumors. The man who once led their nation had indeed defected to Moscow. Owing to his outstanding debts to the Russian autocrat and several high-profile oligarchs, this was no great surprise.

What was more, multiple informants corroborated a singular piece of intelligence—construction on a downtown Moscow tower bearing the man's trademark name was underway. However, it wouldn't be an addition to his global holdings. Each informant agreed that the Moscow tower would serve as little more than a shiny prison for the former president and his family. Apparently, even in Russia, the fall from grace had been complete.

Larson reached over his snoring neighbor and presented his passport to a heavyset conductor in a double-breasted uniform as they neared the border. In the man's clouded blue eyes, a sliver of sand in the Indian Ocean thousands of miles away glinted.

The arrival of Tanzanian naval forces had been a coup Larson could have never foreseen. Fortunately, James Collins had. While Katz oversaw the operation from Dar es Salaam, the Director of National Intelligence monitored things from his office across the Potomac. It was he alone who insisted on the necessity of a backup plan. The director had only needed to place one call. In hindsight, it was genius.

In Upanga, a mile from where Larson and his team boarded their patrol boat, Rear Admiral Francis Kamala of the Tanzanian Naval Forces had answered the phone. The Director of National Intelligence was no stranger to the admiral. The latter had come to Washington as part of a diplomatic envoy years ago when the director had been a junior senator from Indiana.

All of this had been explained to Larson after he

returned to the eighteenth floor of a nondescript tower on Clarendon Boulevard in Rosslyn, Virginia. It had not been Katz doing the explaining. Echelon was in a state of flux to match the nation. No one knew what was going to happen. Bathari's exposure of the president's misdeeds caused the economy to correct harshly as fear and rumors spread in a torrent across the nation.

So, it was a bit of a shock when the Director of National Intelligence had presented himself within the hushed confines of Echelon's headquarters and requested a private audience. Drawing Larson into a soundproof conference room, he proceeded to debrief him on everything that had taken place following the now infamous Chicago rally. Before leaving, he had recited a downtown Washington address.

Larson pulled up to a brownstone on Kingman Place as the sun settled behind momentarily gilded masonry crowning a row of townhouses. Hannah Harper waited inside.

She was dressed as if she had just returned from exercising. Sipping green tea from a thermos, she greeted Larson with cool indifference.

The interior had a decidedly modernist feel. Hannah perched on a polka dotted chair and crossed one leg. Larson lowered himself onto a firm couch across from her.

"I'm sorry you lost your job," he said.

The sacking of the White House Communications Director had not been lost amid the churning tides of political embarrassment. Though lacking the clout of an entire Cabinet resigning in disgrace, the story carried enough weight to become a national byline.

She shrugged. "It would have happened sooner or later. I was not foolish enough to overlook the fact that I was being set up for when this whole thing came to light. At least I wasn't the only one thrown under the bus."

"Why do it?" Larson asked, leaning forward. "Why help Drollsworth establish an arms trade with the Russians when you knew it would be your undoing?"

She gave him a stern look and then seemed to soften. "I didn't have a choice. Not unless I wanted to resign. Plenty of others did. But I never felt obligated to take that moral high road. Trust me; I understood perfectly well that I wasn't the most qualified candidate for the position. In this day and age, looks are currency. Sometimes, so is knowing how to keep your pretty mouth shut and follow orders."

"You must know more about Drollsworth than most."

Hannah grimaced. "I hated Drollsworth. When he wasn't ordering me to contact that vile arms dealer, he was either trying to coax me into bed or ignoring me."

"How did he get close to the president in the first place?"

"Drollsworth understood what it takes to win much more than his former boss. He was trying to do something unprecedented. Voters were becoming frustrated with the ineffectiveness of career politicians. It was perfect timing."

"Which put Drollsworth in perfect position to manipulate the president after he was elected."

She rolled her eyes. "I always thought, deep down, he wanted someone to tell him what to do. Drollsworth whispering in his ear made decisions that much easier, and the man was notorious for his unwillingness to put himself under mental strain. In hindsight, I'm not sure why he ever wanted the job in the first place."

Larson shook his head. "There's more to it. The whole time they distracted the public with minor issues while they wrested away more and more power."

"That was Drollsworth's brilliant scheme. He never mentioned it outright, but everyone in inner White House circles understood what was happening. It was also pointless to try and stand against it. The few congressmen who became aware were afraid to do anything. Either they backed the president's initiative, or they feared him."

Larson understood. The president's ability to start a witch hunt on national television and his zeal for retribution were legendary. "But why?"

Hannah didn't answer. She reached into a tote bag at her feet and pulled out a careworn manila folder, holding it out in front of her. Larson rose and accepted the offering.

"I had a time escaping with that, but I was able to manage."

He flipped open the tattered cover. The bulky file's top page was printed with a location—Fort Belvoir, Virginia—and the three-letter acronym for an agency Larson recognized at once but knew a vast majority of the public remained unaware. The fact that they had the capability to bring the America to its knees, not with guns or wiretaps but a much more potent and indefensible weapon, turned his insides cold. He closed the file and gave his counterpart a questioning look.

"Read it. You'll understand how much damage has already been done. And it's only going to get worse."

He nodded, directing the conversation back to the former president and Drollsworth. "What was their goal?"

For the first time, a look of true disgust crossed Hannah Harper's face. Her hands clenched into fists.

"It was simple; usurp enough power to transform the republic into something resembling an authoritarian state. Borders would close, permanently. Citizens would possess the illusion of freedom, but everything would be controlled. Those who understood what was happening would lack power to do anything about it."

"What could a man want with that much power?"

"Don't be naïve. It wasn't entirely about power. Much of their efforts stemmed from the idea of the glorious golden days of America. They dreamed of turning the nation into their vision of an alt-right idealist state. Expel the immigrants. Cow the women and return them to their place. Reintroduce white men to the forefront where they belong. Oligarchs and big corporations would rule and all else would wither away and die."

Sincere hatred filled her voice. "And it almost worked.

Bathari had his own shortcomings, but in a way, he saved the world by outing the plot and shooting the mastermind behind it all."

The scenery outside the bus's grimy window was changing. Wooded countryside dissolved to craggy cliffs and endless shades of blue caught between cypress trees. Islands dotted the horizon, and snatches of beach were visible far below their hillside route. Larson found himself drawn to the scene while Hannah's words rooted around in his head.

The alt-right had remained silent. That changed two weeks after the country's upheaval when a statement crafted by the National Policy Institute's leader, Robert Spencer, made waves. It stated what the nation knew to be false; the alt-right was an unofficial collection of like-minded people with the purist intentions for America and its citizenry. They had been unfairly implicated, and it was a shame the country could be torn apart by the divisive tactics of a criminal spurred by fear mongers and the evil media. Nobody paid it much mind.

Larson had picked her brain to near satisfaction. One question still hung over the awkward pair convened in her living room.

"Why was Igor Stregor killed?"

She had given him a curious look. "You already know the answer."

"Tell me anyway."

"He was a critic of the regime." She sighed. "One that had the ability to threaten everything they were trying to accomplish. Stregor stood for the precise opposite of Drollsworth—a man of science who spoke with truth and integrity. He tried to warn the public that time was running out. There was no room for that in the society of mass fear and paranoia the former regime was trying to induce. In their eyes, Stregor needed to be deleted from the picture."

"And Elena?"

"You undoubtedly saved her life."

Chapter Fifty-Nine

Larson disembarked outside an inconspicuous bus station. Despite the time of year, the weather was mild and afternoon sun shone over a clear day. He judged the distance with a map he had downloaded before leaving Mostar and decided to walk.

Dubrovnik was much like any Mediterranean town. The third largest along the Dalmatian Coast, it had gained notoriety in recent years for inclusion as location on a prominent television show. Larson ambled past the familiar amalgamation of quaint stone buildings that had aged beautifully through the centuries alongside concrete monstrosities wafting the distinct architectural tinge of failed communism. He skirted a flagstone retaining wall lined with palms and cypress trees.

As the Old City neared, cobblestone streets became thick with pedestrians ogling a forest of red brick buildings. Larson wended through an open gate in the Old City's six-century-old walls—harkening back to a time when

Dubrovnik was known as the Republic of Ragusa—and slipped inside.

The rise in the city's popularity was understandable. Larson passed an ancient monastery and entered the Stradun. Here much of the tourist force congregated among shops and cafes lining the iconic limestone paved street. Larson passed unnoticed.

The church of St. Blaise and Sponza Palace lay at the Stradun's far end. He ignored remarks of wonderment expressed in Croatian and a medley of other languages and cut through a passageway in the impressive stone bulwarks adjacent the Rector's Palace.

A spectacular view of the glassy Adriatic heralded the Old Port—pristine backdrop for a walled city transplanted from the depths of history. He walked along the causeway and turned right. The port was full; a dozen sailboats sat moored to the jetty while countless others floated in a harbor created where the town's ancient walls stretched into the sea.

The boat he sought bobbed halfway down the aisle. Larson might have passed over it a dozen times if it weren't for the craft's name scrawled on either side. As the angle shifted, a man lounging on the forward deck came into view. An empty chair sat next to him. Larson didn't ask permission to come aboard. The boat's owner hardly batted an eye as he edged around the cabin and eased into the vacant seat.

"*The Magdalene*? Quite an interesting name for a sailboat."

Rahim Gilbert declined to answer and instead handed him a short-stemmed glass. He poured Larson a generous amount of amber liquid from a bottle stamped with blocky Croatian print. He took a cautious sip. The spirit burned and tasted of anise.

"*Rakija*. I abhor the stuff, but when in Rome. As for the boat, I didn't choose the name; I simply paid for it. Although, it seems fitting. Just as Mary Magdalene devoted her life to Jesus Christ, I devoted mine to my country. Look what good it brought me."

"You aren't supposed to be in Rome," Larson said sardonically. He took another sip and shuddered. "I missed you in Mostar."

"Mostar is a charming town. Full of history. But Herzegovina is a little dreary this time of year. If it's all the same to everyone else, I prefer somewhere I can smell the sea and enjoy my exile in peace. You seemed to have no trouble finding me."

The premeditated roles played by Gilbert and Echelon's chief in Bathari's attempted rise to power had not gone unpunished. In the fallout, the pairing had been singled out as the plan's masterminds. Such branding was usually followed by swift sentencing that included a life term in prison, or worse.

But Gilbert and Katz had also been instrumental in Bathari's subsequent capture and extradition to the United States. James Collins and his intelligence apparatus understood that. So, under the circumstances, each was presented a choice—flee to a nonextradition country with the federal government's full knowledge and blessing or remain in America and face criminal charges beginning with treason. It had been an easy decision.

Larson's own situation had stood on equally perilous footing. His collaboration with Bathari would have put an end to his career and made his prospects for remaining in America difficult. James Collins had intervened. In his eyes, Larson had done enough. Leading the team that captured Bathari and brought him to justice mitigated all previous damage. He would face no indictment, on the condition that he remain in Washington and serve in whatever role the Director of National Intelligence and the new presidential administration saw fit.

Larson frowned. "That's my point. If I can find you, imagine who else can. You aren't exactly in hiding. They'll realize you left the country—"

Gilbert cut him off with a booming laugh. "Do you

think Collins and the rest aren't aware? The enormous breadth and scope of the United States information machine isn't lost on me. It tracks everyone and everything at every moment. I can't take a step without their knowing. So, if it's obvious no one cares to stop me, why shouldn't I slip into Croatia every now and then?"

Larson was stymied. They sat in silence, listening to the chatter of tourists mixed with the gentle lapping of waves and watching boats drift in and out of the harbor. The sun perched high overhead; the day having turned just warm enough to be comfortable.

The bottle of *Rakija* was empty by the time Gilbert rose to his feet. He led Larson to a black Citroen parked outside the Old Town and drove him to a cottage nestled among a residential area on the nearby hillside. It held the distinct air of a bachelor's hideout. There was a dusty patio, barely large enough for two chairs, with a phenomenal view of the crumbling walls and peaceful sea beyond. Larson was transported to a century long buried in the past. The enchantment was broken by the distant sound of cars trundling along a narrow road cut through the steep hillside.

Gilbert appeared and squeezed into the chair next to him. Larson accepted a glass of red wine. Neither spoke for a long time.

"This part of the world is a lot different than Washington," Gilbert said in contented tones.

"Do you miss it all?"

The other man took his time answering. "Yes, but the world of politics has its disadvantages. I won't miss the stress. The gnawing feeling of responsibility every time something unfortunate happens. I never got to have a family… Maybe I'll find one here."

"An attainable goal, I would imagine."

He shrugged. "I do love that boat. Maybe I'll leave

everything behind and set sail for open ocean. I doubt my handlers would mind much."

"They might mind more than you think."

"You're probably right. The thought arose that they might have sent you, of all people, to keep tabs on me."

Larson smiled and placed his empty glass on the ground. "Nobody sent me."

"Are you staying the night?"

"Yes. I'm leaving early tomorrow morning. I'm expected somewhere."

"That's good."

The other man spared a quick glance at the darkening alley below their perch. It wound across the hillside until it was blocked from view by a cockeyed row of dwellings sharing the vista. Aside from an elderly woman hobbling with a quilted bag on her arm, it stood vacant. "I'm leaving as well. I suppose it's time I headed back to Mostar."

Larson recalled the picturesque hamlet. "You could do worse."

Gilbert set his own glass down and stood. Understanding that it was time, Larson rose and followed him inside.

The air smelled of a hot meal simmering in the miniscule kitchen. They stood in a sparse living room. Gilbert placed a small, black recording device on an antique wooden table. Worried about anyone outside overhearing, Larson closed the patio door and praised the steady rumble of automobiles for at least providing some cover. He waited on the other man to begin the show.

"It's no secret that this was why you came. Sooner or later, you would want to hear it."

"I could have listened to the copy in Washington—"

"But you would need it from me. Want to hear it from the one living soul who was there to experience it firsthand."

It took Samit Bathari an entire month to return to the United States. The Tanzanians insisted on having a turn before they extradited him. It wasn't pleasant. By then, it had come to light that Bathari had a hand in the death of the previous holder of his lavish Zanzibari estate. Autonomous state or not, the Tanzanians were not happy.

Tasked with one final objective before his own exile, Gilbert had been allowed, under heavily armed supervision, to question Bathari while he festered in a dank prison cell in Dar es Salaam. A transcript of the conversation was forwarded west to the intelligence analysts and experts in Washington. They had pilfered whatever they could to devise an interrogation strategy for when the prisoner returned. Word traveled through the grapevine that the interrogators at Langley were even more motivated than their African counterparts.

"In hindsight, the Tanzanians were willing to overlook you cutting down a few guards to get their hands on Bathari. Although, I hear he wasn't nearly as forthcoming with them."

"Play the tape, Rahim."

Gilbert hit a small button on the device's sleek casing. After a pause, Bathari's calm, earnest voice filled the room. If Larson hadn't known better, he would have sworn the man was standing next to him.

Chapter Sixty

It came as no surprise that Larson still mulled over the recording of a marked man's confession as he stepped onto a palm-lined street in the Ville Nouvelle. He handed his driver a few wrinkled notes before the white cab pulled away. The pedestrian area around Algiers' Grande Poste was crowded with chanting revelers, many wearing red and green jerseys. Sensing the excited energy of a sporting event, Larson didn't linger and let himself get swept west toward the city's ancient Casbah.

Promenades overlooking the bay were lined with the same impressive white buildings that surrounded the thrumming square. Many were completed by the French before they relinquished control of Algeria in the sixties. The rest came after, a show of strength and homage to the country's imperialistic roots.

Algiers was likened to tea whose contents came steeped in many cultures. He continued away from the Ville Nouvelle, along an elegant walkway bordered by arcades that spoke to a multi-layered past. The Algerian capital had been passed from the hands of Phoenicians and Carthaginians to Roman and subsequent Berber rule before existing as a boisterous, piracy-fueled outpost of the Ottoman Empire for three centuries. The avenue under Larson's feet that led to the fortified citadel had once been a Roman *viam* many iterations previous.

Muslim and Berber had mixed with a lasting French culture that still purveyed great influence. Deemed the 'Paris of Africa', Algiers was not wholly unlike its namesake despite a backdrop of palm trees and riotous foliage that spilled over its bounds.

Before long, Larson entered the Casbah's well-preserved labyrinth. It was quieter here. Formidable mosques stood on corners in the same spots they had graced for centuries. Everything was crammed together, and no line seemed straight. He followed a winding alley, understanding that the quiet was caused in part by the fact that not even the trimmest vehicle could squeeze between these limestone walls. Uneven stairs led deeper into the maze.

There was no need to consult a map. If anyone had been watching, they would have been disconcerted to see him round a corner and slip under a cerulean-tiled portico marked with a bold sign exhorting all to refrain from entering.

A frescoed courtyard lay beyond the entrance. Ornate pillars supported a balcony spanning the entire second level. The tinkle of running water emanated somewhere nearby.

She sat at a wrought iron table with a drink in her right hand and a tome sporting a spartan cover that made Larson's mind jump to academia in her left. Hearing his soft footsteps, she turned and stood.

He was caught off guard by Elena dropping her book and flying toward him. She wrapped her arms around his torso and clutched him tight.

"I thought I'd lost you," he managed to say as she squeezed him tighter. She made no reply but hummed a lilting tune.

Elena had survived her plunge to the sea's bottom off Pange Island by the slimmest of margins. Upon breaking the surface, Larson tried to restart her breathing to no avail. Heaving her aboard the boat, when all seemed lost, Gavin had managed to pummel the trapped seawater from her chest cavity.

"You can't lose me," Elena murmured, breaking away and staring at him with glistening eyes. "I'm afraid you're stuck with me whether you like it or not."

"This is quite a nice place," Larson said, glancing around. Elena nodded.

"It pays to know people."

"I wasn't aware we knew anyone in this city."

"We do now. He hasn't been here a month and yet he's already become influential. You might have heard of him. He used to head a little-known intelligence outfit back in the states. They took down a corrupt president and captured a madman."

Larson nodded knowingly. "A powerful friend, indeed."

They walked the Casbah's narrow streets until they passed beyond its ancient outer walls. At the coastal promenade, Larson hailed a taxi that ferried them beyond freight liners and cruise ships tethered at the port and into El Hamma. The Martyr's Memorial loomed like a modernist Eiffel Tower from an overlooking ridge as they disembarked and continued down a less crowded street on foot. An eternal flame burned under the shelter of the monument's three fins, each constructed to resemble palm leaves.

He let Elena lead the way. "Where are you taking us?"

"You don't always have to know everything," she said. "Trust me."

He did. They bisected another avenue and without

warning Larson stood on a sweeping terrace that overlooked a garden unlike anything he had ever seen. It was as if Algiers had melted away, replaced by a forest of soaring palms and shrubbery along a magnificent esplanade interlaced with pools that ran out to the sea. Elena stood by his side.

"What do you think?"

"After this, I'll have no choice but to never doubt you again."

Satisfied, she led him down the terrace steps into the midst of an Eden jungle. The esplanade was crowded with sightseers and locals alike taking advantage of the mild weather and strolling between tracts of lush grass or lounging on benches dotting the path.

"What is this place?" he asked, mesmerized and impressed.

"It's called Jardin d'Essai du Hamma. It has been here nearly two centuries. Horticultural scientists come off and on to study various imported species."

"You brought me here to show me plants?"

She gave him a teasing smile. "Follow me."

The trees were a mere backdrop, albeit a magnificent one. Elena led him deeper by the hand until she steered them both down a much smaller path that crossed the esplanade. Bordered by rows of tall pine trees beginning to flourish in the Mediterranean spring, the trail concluded in a circular clearing littered with several people who paid them no mind and a small café.

They passed through an adjacent grove, and Elena dragged him along another shadowy walkway hidden from sight by knitted cypress boughs. They gave the illusion of traveling through a claustrophobic tunnel.

Larson tensed in the tight space. He needn't have bothered. Sunlight was already peeking through the far end. They emerged alongside a lagoon dotted with a small island covered in subtropical species and dense underbrush. A marble statue of a woman sunbathing on a plinth rose out of the murky water. Elena approached the wire fence surrounding the lagoon and stopped.

She had gone still. Advancing with soft footsteps, he laid a gentle hand on her shoulder. "You know this place well?"

"I don't. Igor did."

She stared at the lagoon and tears rimmed the corners of her eyes.

"He had been planning a trip here for months. I found the itinerary details one night in his study before he cut off communication. He hadn't told a soul as far as I'm aware. If he had sought my advice, I would have urged him to find a nice beach resort where he could put his feet up and relax. But it wouldn't have mattered. Igor never listened."

"Why here?"

Elena responded by gesturing to something above them. No less than a dozen butterflies fluttered to and fro in the light breeze playing off the coast. Elena watched them before continuing to speak.

"Algeria has well over one hundred native species of butterfly. Igor found what they represent fascinating. All life is sustained by other life. Society is dangerously close to forgetting that. Butterflies are recognized as an indicator of an ecosystem's health. As the fate of the invertebrates goes, so does life for the rest of us."

They trekked around the lagoon. There was hardly a soul in this area of the gardens. Larson and Elena passed a small girl pointing at a school of orange fish and speaking in excited Arabic to her bemused father. A mallard trailed along the opposite end. Larson said nothing, waiting for Elena.

"The most vital species on this planet are often the smallest and the easiest overlooked. Igor worked tirelessly in a field that often confronted him with morbid evidence of what seems certain to come if we don't act. To escape it all he came to places like this and tried to lose himself in nature."

"Could he truly detach?" Larson asked. "Is it possible for a man in that position to ever let go of reality?"

"I think he was sometimes able to trick himself into believing for a second or a minute or maybe even an hour that there's still hope."

She leaned close so that Larson could smell the intoxicating scent of her perfume.

"Is there still hope?"

A butterfly rested on the wire fence as Elena pondered. When she spoke, it lifted off again.

"I'm not sure. Common wisdom would answer, no, but humanity has surprised in the past. What you did could have sparked something, a true time of change and reckoning for our actions. Time will tell."

Neither one of them had any idea what would happen next. A new president would be elected. Talking heads had already begun to call for widespread reform. Inertia seemed to be building toward a critical mass. Staunch supporters of the former president had crumpled back in on themselves and closed ranks. They vowed to be back, but the less dedicated legions surrounding their nucleus shrank by the day.

"Igor would have loved it here," Larson whispered.

Deep within the garden, as if it on another planet, nothing else seemed to matter. The turmoil and uncertainty gripping the outside world could wait. For now, they had each other, and that was enough.

"You did a great thing," Elena said, turning to face him.

"I didn't do much of anything."

She ignored his modesty. "Without you, Michael, none of this could have happened. America would still be ruled by a tyrant."

"But I helped create an even greater monster who almost took his place."

"Do you believe that?"

"Bathari committed murder while the world watched."

"He wouldn't be the first to go too far while striving for

a cause. I doubt he'll be the last."

Larson wasn't listening. His thoughts were once again filled by a string of echoing words recorded from within a dank prison cell. All of history's greatest causes had martyrs. He wondered if it was possible for a fallen angel to ever rise anew.

Chapter Sixty-One

Exile had treated Eiran Katz well. Another taxi carted Larson and Elena through town and up sloping terrain that led to the many suburban districts surrounding Algiers. Past Atlas Forest, the road leveled off as they reached the western plateau.

There was no mistaking Hydra for anything but one of the wealthiest areas adjoining the North African nation's capital. Elaborate walled compounds and embassies dotted the landscape. Some had the look of palaces set so far back from the road they were hardly visible. There was much more foliage here, and the modern glass and steel buildings were further apart than along the waterfront. Larson noted an air of elitist seclusion that reminded him of Washington. The areas where diplomats flocked were always filled with similar amenities.

The chief's new abode could have passed for an embassy in its own right, or at least a respectable consulate. Down a quiet street, they turned into a gated drive surrounded by high white walls. After being buzzed in, the taxi deposited them in front of a three-story stucco manse with ornate pillars and a driveway that swept around the property. At the moment, it was lined with expensive cars, many sporting diplomatic tags.

"Is he entertaining tonight?" Larson eyed the nearest car—belonging to the ambassador of Egypt judging by the plates—and followed Elena to the door.

She surveyed him before they had a chance to be ushered inside. "It appears so."

Katz *did* have reason to celebrate. An elaborate silk banner wishing him the happiest of birthdays hung inside the door. His second wife, Linda, whom Larson had met a handful of times, played the role of host. Throwing dinner parties had become quite the hobby of theirs, she explained as she directed Larson and Elena inside and commenced an endless stream of introductions.

Apparently, Katz had taken it upon himself to become Hydra's chief entertainer and deal broker. No relationship flourished that he didn't have a hand in. Being American, it naturally fell on his shoulders to lead and bring together the diverse group of expatriates stocking the neighborhood's many embassies and consulates.

To hear it from his wife, the pair had already met and advised several influential figures from around the world. What was more, though their son remained at his New Hampshire boarding school, they had adopted a young Libyan refugee named Assad.

Larson caught sight of Diego and Armand Rivera in the rustic dining room talking to a group of turbaned men caught in uproarious laughter. The party was coming into full swing. Linda led Elena off to meet a group of activist women. Larson helped himself to a glass of Regent and continued to wander.

Half an hour passed before he caught sight of the man of the hour. The sun had set behind palm trees shielding the house from street view. A terrace at the back of the property doused in torchlight and overlooking a manicured garden was alive with cigar smoke and the babbling sound of many languages being spoken in unison. Larson caught Katz as he stepped inside, slipping an unlit cigar inside his jacket pocket.

"Congratulations are in order," he said. The two embraced like old friends.

"I would have sent a car to come get you."

"I've never minded public transportation."

"It would have put my mind at ease." Katz glanced around. "See what I've been reduced to? Hosting soirees to keep myself busy. Toasting and rubbing elbows with the same breed of men our kind have always looked down on."

Despite his words, the chief seemed to be thoroughly enjoying himself.

"I suppose diplomats are necessary to keep the global political machine moving forward."

Katz raised an eyebrow. "The machine creeps along too slowly for my liking." He leaned in. "The new president isn't long for office if you ask me. Word has traveled through back channels that resignation is already being discussed."

"Who will replace him?"

He shrugged. "For now, I'm not sure. It hasn't been as easy to keep my ear to the ground over here."

"I'm sorry. If it weren't for me, you would have never—"

The chief cut him off. "Save it. I knew what I was getting into. So did Rahim. Neither one of us blames you in the slightest. And, besides, this is a whole hell of a lot better than prison."

The two men toasted Katz's good fortune. The former chief offered a cigar, which Larson declined. He could feel himself begin to long for peace and quiet.

"You're taking her back with you?" Katz asked, nodding at Elena who had reappeared across the room.

She had gone upstairs and slipped into a tight black

dress that showed just enough to turn the eye of every man present. Larson was no more immune than the rest.

"If she'll go."

"You won't have any trouble there. She cares about you, Michael. You could pass your days comfortably enough in a place like this. But America needs the two of you if we ever hope to steer ourselves out of this mess. The fight is far from finished."

Larson nodded. A place like this, far from the action, would be nice one day. But he wasn't ready to throw in the towel. Not yet.

By the time midnight neared, the party had started to exhaust itself. Elena found him standing alone to one side of the terrace, enjoying the cool evening and a glass of wine that tasted better with each sip.

He didn't hear her approach until she slipped a thin arm around him.

"Did I ever thank you for saving my life?"

Larson stared off into the Algerian night. Hydra was quiet, but in the distance, he heard the faint sounds of a coastal metropolis coming alive. He draped his right arm over her bare shoulders.

"Undoubtedly you'll find a way to repay me."

"We could always stay here, you know. Linda offered us a suite of rooms on the top floor. They looked lovely."

Larson smiled at the thought. It would be the easy way to go about things. But he had never been one for choosing a path because it was easy.

"Washington needs us. I'm not sure what's going to happen, but I'm not ready to give up hope yet. Your brother wouldn't have wanted that."

Elena said nothing. She simply nodded.

It was the right choice. The world was in a state of flux. It needed someone, something, to guide the way. But that could wait, at least another day.

Right now, all there was left to do was look out over a calm Algerian night and hope.